Glass Asylum

Glass Asylum

JoAnn Bren Guernsey

North Star Press of St. Cloud, Inc.
St. Cloud, Minnesota

For Andy—my friend, my muse, my strength.
Together we're still writing this love story.

author photo: Meghan Gordon
cover art: Rita Bernstein, www.RitaBernstein.com

ISBN: 978-0-87839-427-2

Printed in the United States of America

Published by North Star Press of St. Cloud, Inc.
PO Box 451
St. Cloud, MN 56302
www.northstarpress.com

*T*hree a.m., still a swampy eighty-seven degrees. A bayou night in Minnesota. I can't possibly sleep—my body in meltdown, my mind at its monkeyest. So I return to one of the windows yawning open in my sunroom, a place for watching and writing, for suspicion and salvation. A resumed window-vigil. My gaze prowls the street of my not-so-big city. In the muffled moonlight, the sidewalk appears smudged in shadows, and lampposts too standoffish to join together in the job of illumination. I don't spot any children out there—not at this hour—but I cannot ignore the scattered strollers, bikes, and trikes; neighboring yards wear them like body piercings.

My fixation on children and their wheeled toys is nothing new. Tonight, however, my view of light and dark can be blamed on the movie I just watched on TV. One of those old black-and-white films where it's never daylight, murder is too commonplace to rattle anyone, and romance is nothing more than a whispery strap slipping off the shoulder of the real story: The Mystery, The Crime. On the case is a jaded detective who looks like he's as much a stranger to sleep as I am (and could use an introduction to personal hygiene as well), and yet he is somehow irresistible to anything in a skirt.

Sprawled on my living room couch in the wee small hours someone actually used to croon about, it seemed possible that film noir might lead me into my own writing style. Novel Noir? Memoir Noir? Each choice a mouthful. And a bite into the question of truth.

But at my window now—released by THE END in gritty lettering across my TV screen—I can see that the other houses appear unthreatened. A single light in one upstairs window turns on, then off, like a lazy lightning bolt. Across the street, Mona's house is completely dark. She's asleep, of course. Her baby's asleep. My belly endures a familiar nudge; Mona lost one child—Tracy—and she already has another one, the way a starfish effortlessly grows a replacement arm. Another child at risk? Maybe.

Shaking my head to dislodge the notion of rescue (at least for now), I force myself back to the task of writing. Not the stories that occupied my mind for a while. Instead, an account of what happened starting last July—could it really be only twelve months ago? Another brutal heat wave, three-year-old Tracy crushed under a car, and my friendship with Mona about to expire. I mind-travel back to that summer night not unlike this one, except my house still had a sleeping man in it, a second heart with a sturdier beat, the promise of touch and dumb jokes. Jake.

1

In my noirish revisiting of the scene, the bloodstain left by Tracy's death on the street would appear black, only suggesting the florid color I've avoided for as long as I can remember. Since the police did not draw any ghoulish outline of her little body, I'd have to invent that. For the melancholy soundtrack I can hear either a tenor sax or muted trumpet, and I can easily picture—in a kind of lurking slow-dance—my handsome hero. He's ludicrously overdressed in a trench coat and fedora, but nonetheless cool. Of course, I'd give this detective Jake's face— features I never forget. And he was, after all, my own "private dick" for years.

He'd appear abruptly at my door, knock sharply until I open it.

"You caught me in bed," I'd say. Or rather, these words are drawled by the sexy mystery woman I am not. Stanwyck-thin, her nightgown clings but not damply—she doesn't sweat. Despite the late hour, she's wearing a thick pout of lipstick. "Let me get a robe."

"Never mind that," the detective says, making fleeting eye contact. . . with her chest.

Poking through the silky fabric, her nipples have awakened more than the rest of her. She takes a drag from his cigarette, imprinting the filter with dark lipstick.

"You awake enough to answer some questions?"

"Why not? Come in and make yourself comfortable." Exhaling a sinuous ribbon of smoke, she leans in close, aroused beyond reason by his stubble and ungargled mouth.

"Listen, dollface," he says with a sneer (which I'd have to train Jake's face to do). "Park those lips on the other side of the room. I'll get around to kissing you when I'm good and ready, but first you'll have to tell me where you were the night the kid was knocked off."

But wait . . . there's no way I'd refer to Tracy as "the kid" or discuss her death so casually .

No. This style is a clumsy attempt at emotional distance and strictly off-camera copulation, and I've been marginal long enough. Erasing the fake sneer and all the clothing, I put Jake and me into bed instead, enduring a bad night last year. That's my beginning. And I'll forge ahead from there, through all the botched relationships and losses. I need something besides my stories, something more factual, to leave behind. For whom, I'm not sure. Mona? Jake? The police? Still, it was on that summer night last year—a few hours before Tracy's funeral and ten years after my own little girl's death—that the stories began coming to me like lost children, taking my hand.

Vigil

July, last year, another middle of the night. It was the beginning not only of the creative surge but the insomnia, if only the first toss-and-turn hints of it. Easy to blame on the weather. Beyond hot, it was like Minnesota had somehow reached down to pull the equator up around its tapered waist. I was lying naked on my side, the sheet beneath me damp. The aging window shades were fringed by yellowish light from the street. And Jake was fidgeting next to me, trying to figure out if I was awake without saying anything that might disturb me, in case. He was like that.

When I whispered his name, he wrapped himself around my back and ventured inside me—a slick move some women might have resisted. But in those days I was rarely an *unwilling* partner in lovemaking, one of the things Jake and I did right. Smiling as I made the necessary limb adjustments, I said, "Who is that? Is that you, Guido? Or, no—Trixie! With your strap-on, but why not use the bigger dildo?"

"Very funny," Jake said. "Shut up."

Moments later we were face-to-face and kissing. Slippery-skinned. It was hard to ignore the fact that we both pretty much reeked. That kind of heat wave can turn beds into morass and good intentions into mirage.

His sweat dripped into my eyes like tears in reverse. "Ow," I complained and blinked.

"Sorry," he said, grabbing a T-shirt to wipe his face. The moment seemed to be passing us by, but he lingered above me. Grinned big enough for me to hear. "Hey," he said, "did I tell you the one about when Ole and Lena got a pet monkey?"

"Oh God, here we go . . . ."

"And Ole told his neighbor Sven how the monkey slept with them every night, so Sven asked, 'In your bed?' and Ole said, 'Yah, between me and Lena.' 'But Ole,' Sven said, 'vat about de smell?' and Ole said, 'Vell, *he'll* have to get used to it yust like I did.' "

3

"Boy, Jake, you really know how to sweet talk a girl, don't you?"

He nuzzled my neck, burrowing deeper into me.

"Wait," I said. "We have to get the . . . " his next determined thrust cut me off, but he knew that I was about to call for protection.

"Don't make me leave," he whispered.

"It's not like I'm asking you to run to the store, Jake. We have some condoms right over *there*. Besides . . . you know what? I have to pee anyway. I'll get my diaphragm."

"Let's not get anything just now."

"What?" I tried giggling, but that fizzled. Something serious was happening. "Jake, let go. Come on. I'm ovulating,"

"I know that." He paused for a moment. "You told me this afternoon. That ache you get in your belly—like your ovary is giving you a kick, reminding you there are only a few good eggs left in there. Must've been a reason you told me."

"The reason is that it hurt and when have I *ever* endured pain in silence?"

I felt his considerable weight on my belly now, compressing the ovary that had been raising a ruckus earlier. The phrase "I've got you covered" leaped into my mind, and it felt surprisingly right. *Oh God . . . maybe . . . .*

But he blew it. "This would be the perfect night for making a baby." *Making a baby*. Like it was something akin to making a loaf of bread from scratch, or a golf shot.

Clamping myself shut, I managed to push away.

He sighed and flopped onto his back. His disappointment made me wish I could, just for that night, be someone else. "A baby would be nice," he said.

"Nice," I said. "Not a word usually applied to babies."

"And *your* word, 'applied to babies' would be…?"

The options formed a word chain that yanked at my throat. I may even have made a choking sound.

Jake rolled over onto his side, facing away from me, slapped down. Maybe I silenced him at times like this, but he did the same to me and didn't even recognize it. I thought of silencers, screwed onto gun muzzles to diminish the bang. More and more it seemed that he and I were diminishing each other's bang.

4

I left the bed and tried not to notice how good that felt. Lighter, almost out from under the whole overdone summer. Slipping on a nightie (the barely-there type meant to be seductive if it weren't so frayed and stained), I went downstairs to pace and inhale deeply, to savor the wide-open wilderness that is solitude. Perfect time to crave a cigarette even though I'd quit years ago, in sync with Jake. But caffeine, now that was one of the good-guy drugs. As I made myself some iced coffee, I listened for sounds of my lover upstairs. Hoping he'd gone back to sleep.

That's when I ventured into my sunroom to stare at the street where little Tracy had died a few days earlier, with me an unwilling witness. I scanned the other windows for a glimpse of even one other sleepless person, but the nighttime windows seemed blank as paper. And I found myself aching (even in my ovary) to write in my journal. Or maybe something more. Stories, and not necessarily about me. How freeing that would be. Other people's lives seemed to be blending with mine a lot lately, to blur the very meaning of I and *she* and *they*.

"Madelyn?"

And especially *he*.

Jake's worried, searching voice was coming downstairs.

My sunroom already felt like a refuge—walls of windows, outward, and inward. Exhale, inhale. Each window just large enough for me most of the time. But if I turned, moved to one side and held my breath, Jake could squeeze in too. He was still, that day and for many weeks to follow, trying to help.

"There you are," he said from behind me.

I nodded. Several slow minutes had passed since I'd left him in the bed. Gazing out the window at nothing and everything, I composed myself, or some version of myself.

"Maddie, what is it?" He handed me the small pointy word *it* and a question mark large enough to curl up in.

"What is what?" I asked.

Jake paused, then asked if I was okay.

I nodded *yes, I'm fine*. But I was lying. Standing and lying. So many contradictions, idioms, words to ponder. The cool shuffle of letters.

"Hot, huh?" Jake's fondness for verbalizing the obvious alternately soothed and rankled me. "I'm sorry," he said next, "about that baby thing."

5

"That 'baby thing'?" I echoed. "What, I wonder, might be the word for a baby *thing*. Maybe a thingling—you know, like duck and duckling?"

"I can't talk to you lately." He heaved a sigh that felt thick in my hair.

I waited a few beats. Then—better late than never—I said I was sorry too.

"Why don't we go back to bed," he said. "We need each other. We need to make love. Don't worry—we'll use protection."

Now it was the word *protection* rattling around in the hollow of my head. Synonyms: defense, safeguard, preservation. In this context, another word came to mind: Barrier, as in Barrier Method. But that could be spelled Burier, which could be further altered into Bury Her. I took a shaky sip of coffee to ease open my throat.

"I worry about us, that's all," Jake continued. "About whether or not we'll ever . . . ." He couldn't quite resist asking it, point blank. "Do you think we'll ever have children? I mean, Jesus, I'm over forty, and . . . and never had one."

"So am I, Jake," I shot back. "Over forty, as of last year. And I *have* had one." Another choking sensation when I referred to my dead child in this offhand way. *I had one, almost two. One two buckle my shoe.* I shook these invasions out of my head and focused instead on my lover, on *his* demons. "Our histories, Jake . . . they just keep colliding with each other. I hate that. And I hate your ex-wife, but I can't help what all happened with her."

"I realize that," he said. "Yes, you've got the right to have no more children, but I have the right to want them. Our rights clash. You win, I lose, fine."

"Fine," I answered, but had a sudden, horrible urge to hand over to him—instead of a baby—a freshly written short story about a forty-one-year-old woman, unexpectedly pregnant, who must scale a wall of protesting pro-lifers to enter a women's clinic. To free herself. But the story was conceived and aborted in almost the same instant. He would not understand. How could he? An image popped into my mind, of Jake as a bull trying to mate but, instead, scattering his seed on a field. Watched by me—a calmly chewing cow. A writer.

"I think this is one night, that's all." I said. "Just one bad night." I wanted to explain again that I was not, to put it mildly, myself. I wanted

6

to remind him that, later today, we'd be burying a friend's only child. It was not my child's funeral, but it may as well have been.

He sighed again. So much expended breath and energy.

I shifted my weight, one leg to another, felt the stickiness between my inner thighs and worried about pre-ejaculate. Had he "won" after all?

"Can I get you anything?" he asked in his softest voice.

"I don't suppose we have any old cigarettes squirreled away, do we?"

"You're kidding, right?"

When I failed to answer him, he disappeared. I was surprised to feel his absence like a rebuff. Empty space. Damn him. Then he was back, with a wet washcloth which he used on my neck and shoulders. It felt heavenly and I told him so. Yes, Jake certainly could be faulted for his pushiness and his dreadful timing. But the fact remained that he was very dear to me. And very known. Without turning to look, I knew he was wearing his old blue boxers, so threadbare, soft and transparent, they were more like a suggestion than a garment. This pair was the worst of his collection and his favorite. Jake always waited until his belongings virtually evaporated with use. He had new underwear still in its packages in one of my drawers and in his own at home. They were lying in wait.

"Iced coffee," he said to the mug in my hand as though the dark liquid needed to be labeled.

I offered him some. What was left of the pebbly cubes in my coffee mug clinked as though tapping out an important message. He shook his head, either declining a sip or missing the message.

"Aren't you coming back to bed?" Carefully, he added, "to sleep, I mean."

"No, thanks. I'm fine out here, really. I'm sort of meditating."

"Well, okay then. I'll keep you company."

"Meditation," I pointed out, "is generally a solitary pursuit."

"Hmmm. Maybe I'll head into work early since I'm taking the afternoon off for . . . uh, you know, for the funeral." He paused but I didn't jump in. Some words, I noticed, carried their scents with them—*coffee* could float in and out of a room like its own pleasant aroma. But *funeral?* Fumes, overdone flowers, and dusty candle wax.

"Is that actually a breeze I'm feeling?" Jake wondered aloud. "That's why you like it in this sunroom so much."

"It's an interesting view from in here," I admitted to him. "The people in these houses, they all have so much . . . life." I resisted giving him more, for now, about the peculiar habits within the walls of that neighborhood I'd begun collecting, especially the female ones. Mona vomiting for no reason other than to feel fashion model empty, a clean collapsed shell fighting bloat. Suzanne clinging to an extra-large leather jacket as though her longing could slip the disappeared man back into it. Lovers and other strangers. Mothers, daughters, past, present. And me, in the middle of the storm—the eye.

"But watchers can be watched, too," Jake told me as though I hadn't thought of that. "Don't you feel kind of exposed? If I do this—" he reached around to fondle my breasts—"can the neighbors see and wish they were us right now?"

His hands felt right, rearranging me that way, and his face fit in the crook of my neck perfectly. But I couldn't imagine anyone wishing to be me. "Jake, I'm not . . . ."

His hands froze. "You're not what?"

To him I said, "Myself." Internally, my response was quite different— *I'm not worthy.* I eased away, managed to gently detach him. "Here," I said. "Could you put a few more ice cubes in this cup? The clink is gone."

He nodded and took my cup into the kitchen. When he returned, he pointed toward the curb across the street, where somebody had left a bouquet of flowers. I could just make out the petaled, gathered shape of them near Tracy's bloodstain, or what was left of it. I stared at the flowers, astonished. How had I missed seeing them? I wondered which neighbor or passerby might have left them. Or . . . and this notion prickled the back of my neck . . . the flowers may have been from Mr. Jankow. The old man who'd been driving the car.

I remembered watching him, after the accident, barely looking at the little body on the street, rushing up to Mona's house, pounding on the door to call 911, not even certain it was the house Tracy had come from, but it was the closest. And Mona at the door, letting him in, running out to Tracy on the street, her left hand covering her mouth. At some point catching sight of me at my window.

Jake cleared his throat, startling me back to his side. "Someone else with little ones," he said.

"Huh?"

8

"Someone else with kids probably left the flowers."

"Oh. Probably." I lowered my face to the rim of my coffee mug, closing my eyes, wondering how long I could keep the tears tucked inside.

"Hey, Maddie . . . honey." Jake forced his voice into the hale-and-heartiness that was always meant as a boost for me. "Listen. Did I tell you the one about when Ole brought Lena the flowers?"

"Not now, Jake," I said. "Please." He had an endless supply of Ole and Lena jokes, but he didn't always recognize when a chuckle was needed. . . or possible.

"So Ole comes home," he continued, "carrying this big bouquet of roses, and Lena says 'oh my, tank you,' takes off all her clothes and spreads her legs. And Ole says, 'But Lena, honey, don't ve have a vase?'"

I'd heard this one before, but this time I didn't laugh. Jake heard how loudly I did not laugh. And he cleared his throat again, trying to dislodge and swallow the crumbs of a mistake. "Sorry," he said.

I was still staring at the flowers on the street and he stared along with me for several beats. "We're still going to the . . . uh, funeral today, aren't we?"

I nodded, grateful that Jake wasn't assuming anything in this matter.

"Have you talked to Mona yet?" he asked.

This question was probably not meant as an accusation. "No. Not yet." Mona, little Tracy's mother, was a friend of mine. How was it possible I hadn't talked to her yet or tried to console her? "They haven't been home since it happened." This was, to the best of my knowledge, true. "Maybe staying with relatives," I added.

"Hard to believe it's been only four days," he said. "Seems like much longer."

"Years," I agreed, thinking *almost ten years* since it had happened to me. For a moment I could see my own little girl's face, seconds before it hit the windshield. Always fidgety, she had worked her way out of her car seat and was clearly testing me. I had been irritable, pregnant again and feeling like shit in so many ways. When she had somersaulted into the front seat and accidentally kicked me in the neck, I had called her a *fucking brat*, maybe to myself, maybe under my breath but audible, I couldn't be sure. Had she heard? Had these been my last words to her? I closed my eyes now, clenched against flying glass and obscenities.

"Wouldn't you know," Jake continued, "the one morning you needed me here most, I was at my own house instead. Was it this early?"

"No. Later." I didn't add that the cops' 9:00 a.m. appearance at my door, once they found out I'd been a witness, gave me the only time reference I had. They had "reconstructed" the scene, taken their photos, examined the car, the skid marks, questioned the old man, all before knocking on my door.

"It must've been tough on you," Jake said, "seeing the accident . . . so helpless . . . thinking back to your—"

"Jake, I'm . . . fine. Please try not to worry so much about me. And stop trying so hard to crawl into my head, okay? It's not such a great place to be."

He had no idea the territory he'd ventured into. Instead, he was simply hurt, always hurt by my tone when I couldn't handle his kindness. I could feel his scowl crease the air.

"You should go back to bed," I told Jake. "One of us should sleep."

"Okay, sure. I'll see you later then." He scratched his bare chest, hard, as though to reach a persistent itch deep inside. But still he didn't leave. The sunrise held him. "Beautiful," he said and stopped scratching.

A layer of rainless clouds fluffed the horizon and, as we watched, a pink streak appeared like a woman's arm, stretching out of her blankets. I wrote it that way in my head, filing it away for later. Then, almost too quickly, most of the sky turned lavender. Silhouetted trees seemed about to applaud.

"So beautiful," he said again. "Just . . . " he searched and didn't find. "Beautiful."

Such a failure of language, I couldn't keep my irritation to myself. "Would you say it was beautiful, Jake?" I instantly regretted being such a bitch and started to apologize again but it was too late. He was gone. Ponderous footfalls, up the stairs. A few muttered words.

An urge welled up in me to follow him, not only to apologize but to . . . well, *change*. To be what he needed and deserved. But instead I turned back to my neighborhood for the fix it offered. A block of modest two-story houses, like mine (inherited from my parents) and yet each one so distinctive. Touched and retouched by generations. The ordinariness of these houses appeared to keep the people in them safe. But I wondered about the word *safe* and knew nobody was, not really. And a safe was also a kind of locked box. As dawn and jobs began to beckon and jab, the windows around me, one after another, began to leak illumination and secrets even as their covers were yanked into place.

In the house immediately to my right, lights began to blaze, figures rushed around and voices scolded. It was the chaos of a family trying to shower and eat and get to work and daycare on time after hitting the snooze button too often. The marching minutes would ordinarily concern me as well, but I had taken a vacation day, so no work awaited me. Only a funeral. Jake was going to work and then taking off mid-day for the service.

I glanced at the house across the street. *The* house, Mona and Jim's. Nothing happening. Where were they? More to the point, where had they been when Tracy had slipped outside? Jim had probably been traveling, as usual, but Mona? Merely asleep, I supposed, and yet that seemed too bizarre—to lose your child while you slept, perhaps snagged in a dream, somehow blissfully ignorant of Tracy's dexterity with locked doors. I imagined my friend and her husband immobilized in bed now, wishing it were all a nightmare and that the familiar little voice would soon banish the gnawing silence.

I wondered where Mr. Jankow lived; that dwelling I couldn't observe. But I had seen him walking by the night before. He had paused, slumped over, at the exact spot where the bloodstain had been, still was. I noticed how old he looked—too old to have been driving? And then, before departing, he had glanced toward my window, but I had pulled back into the shadows just in time—I knew he'd look my way. He knew I'd been a witness. A witness who . . . what? Claimed to have been temporarily blind and mute? If only I'd had a history of sleepwalking. If only I could, for that matter, rewrite history.

After awhile I heard Jake coming back downstairs, clearing his throat. Maybe he was brooding, or rehearsing what to say and do next. He wasn't quite ready to give up on me. When we first met, Jake had been in a joyless, barren marriage full of lies, and I'd been mired in grief and guilt over losing my family. We brought each other back to life. For the past seven years, although periodically making a lot of melodramatic noise about breaking up, we never quite managed to let go. But it was possible, I knew, that this time would be different.

A radio blared in the house to my left and I heard scolding in that house too. *You can't be serious . . . in the laundry . . . I'm not cooking eggs if . . . .* During any summer, neighbors share all kinds of sounds. The musical ones are the easiest to absorb. On my block, there was at least one other house (besides mine) with a piano. A sign on the door said "Piano Tuning and Instrument Repair." I used to play. Sometimes, on good days with my mother, lively duets. Now an old piano tuner from my childhood seemed to be vying for attention, but my memory of him was both fleeting and overwrought, like a *glissando*. I tried to follow along but, when I heard Jake call my name from the kitchen, the memory skittered away.

It was fully morning now, and I sat down to breakfast. In between my oversized buttery bites of toast, I didn't even try to engage in small talk with Jake. He was still sulking, and who could blame him? Another ending seemed to have invited itself into our midst. It was understood that this breaking-up habit of ours was why he retained his home and I retained mine, so that *he* had someplace to go.

But the last time he came back, he was armed with a Leonard Cohen CD. The track he played over and over—Cohen's voice rasping and rumbling like a bass fiddle in labor—contained these lyrics: *Oh baby, let's get married. We've been alone too long. Let's be alone together, let's see if we're that strong.* Jake watched me listen to the song until I commented that *alone together* was a nifty oxymoron, but I doubted Leonard knew any better than we did how to turn a love song into everyday life.

That day in the kitchen, the ending seemed to be because we had to go to Tracy's funeral later and could not respond as a couple to grief. But that was only part of our trouble together, the front part. The ending was actually because I was in transition; my voice was still mine and yet would soon absorb all of the others, grounded in the reality of that block of houses with the heat and the music and the grieving, and yet fashioned by me into something else. Thus, I had removed myself from my lover. I was attending to other sounds by then (a branch tapping on a nearby window, for instance), and other tugging hands—hey, write about *me*. I could no longer ignore who that first set of hands belonged to: Mona.

I'm at the window now and . . .

I'm looking at her house again, realizing that before I can proceed with that July day last year, I must reach back to the previous fall, when Mona and I first met. Did it really start with a rainbow? Was it little Tracy who called it rainglow or was it . . . ? No, my own baby girl was not an early talker. She was . . . never mind. I'm not writing about her now. This is about Mona. A kind of flashback, I guess. With no flash.

As though on cue, my neighbor emerges from her house, without Tracy, of course. Carrying her new baby, who is not so new. The child has begun to sit unsteadily by herself, making sounds that are pre-words but meaningful, and will soon start to crawl and wander fearlessly. As usual, I have to swallow the tears and, yes, the rage. I imagine the baby glancing my way (Mona no longer does) and catching my maternal gaze, residing in it, extending one hand in my direction. Mona tucks the baby under her arm for a moment, sideways, wriggling, to pick up a toy from the middle of the sidewalk and toss it onto the lawn—I hear it rattle, see the vacantly smiling face on it. And then they hurry off in the direction of the park. No stroller today for them, but the worn handles, the fabric scoop, the comparisons to other past strollers are always in my mind.

I hope Mona knows better than to plop the child into the sand—babies put everything in their mouths. I feel the grit between my own teeth and wash it down with yesterday's warm wine. Everything tastes so sour now. Things go bad quickly in the heat of memory.

Sand

W hen their moving van pulled up to the house across the street, I watched from my sunroom window and took inventory of the parade of belongings, many of them clearly indicating at least one small child. Eventually I saw a tall, thin woman with nervous hands and straight pale hair that reached to the middle of her back; I would soon observe (in the typical female obsession with hair and its shade at the roots) that her white-blond color was natural, almost freakishly so. The child was a girl who appeared to be just shy of three, also a towhead, slender, animated, and painfully familiar.

I watched as my new neighbor flitted from box to box, in control, everywhere at once, occasionally glancing at her child but never keeping her out of the way of the movers. The little girl seemed to be cheerfully at play—her toys and dolls were also busily moving. At the time, I assumed the woman was a single mom, otherwise her husband would surely have been involved. But he appeared later, handsome in that weary, careless way some men have, like it's almost too much work to look so tantalizingly good. I noticed right away that this very young wife and mother seemed to have a bold and outgoing nature, even though she also seemed to use her hair and untrimmed bangs as a kind of curtain.

Since winter would soon begin its siege, I didn't expect to see much of our new neighbors, but that was before I discovered Mona's apparent aversion to being inside. She and little Tracy, or she alone, always seemed to be venturing out, no matter how cold or gray or snowy it happened to be. She was one of those snowman-building, Christmas-tree-light- hanging, shrub-tidying types. Her husband Jim was virtually invisible, but Mona became a familiar sight to me. And my window watch began to get her attention too. She often waved to me, and motioned for Tracy to do the same. I began to imagine that she waved even if she couldn't quite see me, just in case. I figured we would be talking regularly by spring—if not my doing, then hers.

She was always in motion, the kind of electrified person you can't envision ever just sitting and reading a book or watching a movie. On her jaunts outdoors, she usually had a camera attached to her hand and lifted to her face like an oxygen mask. Her child, of course, was her most frequent subject. But she frequently snapped whatever came along. I was intrigued and found myself longing to see the world through her viewfinder every now and then. I imagined her photo albums swelling now with my neighborhood and wondered how my house, maybe even the outermost layer of my life, looked when it was framed by her.

One afternoon the following April, a rainy day that began to brighten, I came out to my sunroom to read a new short story collection. But instead I got my first close-up view of Mona and Tracy. They were on my front lawn, staring eastward with their necks stretched, hopping up and down to make themselves taller. I thought they might be trying to catch a glimpse of the Mississippi River which ran wide, muddy, and stunning only a couple of blocks away. But then I saw that Mona was taking pictures of something in the sky.

Naturally, I joined them. "Hi," I said. "What's up?" I was trying to sound neighborly but also a tiny bit trespassed upon, just in case Mona was a nutcase. I still couldn't see what they were looking at. You had to be in the right spot with a view between two trees, and when I saw the rainbow I understood why they'd come to my side of the street which was higher than theirs.

Mona didn't answer. She looked to Tracy who said, "Raingo." Her voice was unexpectedly husky. "Rainglow," she tried again. "Rainblow."

While she let her daughter work on the word, Mona grinned and motioned for me to stand next to them. The arc smeared vivid colors on the entire segment of sky visible between the two trees, and I was grateful to my neighbor for not letting me miss it. We introduced ourselves, but that was all for that particular day. They quickly left my yard to head for the nearby park. "There's a bigger hill there," Mona informed me as they hurried away. "And the jungle gym. With Tracy up on that, maybe I can get a shot of her and the rainbow at the same time. Like she's climbing *it*."

From that meeting until the awful day in July when Tracy was killed, Mona and I had several conversations, but perhaps it was the first extended one that ranks as the oddest. And it certainly set the tone for our relationship. Not only could Mona not stay inside her house, she also couldn't keep much inside herself. Stray information, ideas, opinions, even secrets oozed from her; silence and restraint were as unwelcome as the pollen that made her a heavy-duty sneezer.

The day of this first talk was only a week or so after the rainbow. I was heading for the convenience store at the corner, three blocks from our houses. I needed milk but also thought a treat of some kind was in my future. It was Saturday and I was more alone than usual, with Jake out of town. As soon as I emerged from my front door, out sprang Mona, her hands uncharacteristically free of her camera and also her child who must have been with Jim. "Headed for the SA?" she called out to me.

I nodded and ambled over to her side. Staying on our respective sides of the street would have been much more awkward than simply falling into step together as though we'd planned it all along.

"I thought I detected that quick-food-errand look on your face," she said. "One of those single necessities that going to the supermarket is too much trouble for. Let me guess—bread?"

"Milk," I told her. "And whatever else might leap into my hands." I squinted up into the lusciously warm sun and smiled. "Good day for a treat. Something big and chocolate."

That was all it took. Without meaning to, I'd unleashed something in Mona. "Food junkie, huh?" she said. "Me too."

"Well . . . uh, I guess." My smile slipped from my face and I felt a twist in my stomach. The fact that I was almost always hungry, for something, anything, was one of my most closely guarded secrets. Jake was perhaps the only person who knew this about me.

"Relax," Mona said. "We're women."

I laughed nervously. "What does *that* mean."

"Well, we have all these empty places to fill, right? Not to be gross, but isn't that one of the things that make us women? There's not a whole lot of difference between craving a nice big Snickers bar and craving a man's penis. I mean, I know I can say that to you, because I've seen you with your husband—"

"We're not married."

"Whatever. Boyfriend, lover . . . so, the point is, I know you're not a lesbian or anything."

16

I was quickly learning that, with Mona, nothing was gradual. Not conversation, not friendship, not intimacy. She never tested the water with one toe, but rather plunged in and only then looked around. I felt the uneasiness of being exposed to someone devoid of tact and caution, and I wondered if she simply spent too much time with her child and not enough with adults. My response was a noncommittal *hmmmm*.

"Listen. You seem nice, and I'm *supposed* to tell people this whenever possible, according to the shrink who runs my support group. The thing is . . . I'm bulimic. Have been since I was sixteen. Talking about it freely is supposed to help me recognize that I have a problem."

We were walking very slowly, and I looked up to a leafless, scratchy maple branch as though the next thing to say was perched on it. "Well, that's a common problem," I finally said.

"Yeah, it really is. You'd be amazed at the numbers. I'm supposed to stop being ashamed."

I thought she'd chosen an interesting moment to blurt this out to me. We were, after all, headed for those beckoning shelves of food. Perhaps I was supposed to provide some sort of brake system on her eating disorder.

"I've been there," I lied to her without knowing why.

"Really?" She looked at my body, up and down. "You've binged and purged too?" There was surprise in her tone that could only be taken as an insult. Jesus, did I look too fat to be bulimic? She seemed to look at my bosomy shape with both envy and disdain. Walking next to her I suddenly felt very heavy and full, like every ounce of fat, muscle and liquid began to slosh as I walked, while she slipped through air in silence, like a mere sliver of her rainbow.

"I suppose there are degrees of anything, including eating disorders," she said. "If I'm a ten, you may be a one, or whatever."

I wanted to say something startling in return, something that made me at least a five. But I felt I understood Mona. Almost too much—I had to pull myself back from the seduction of what *she* did in private, as opposed to what *I* did. Private acts were supposed to be . . . well, private.

I stopped to tie my shoe and then examined the bark on a young locust tree, stalling. She waited for me. I felt my toes wriggle and curl inside my sneaker. "When I was much younger," I told her, inspired by my foot, "I wanted to be a ballerina. That's when food became . . . well, kind of an enemy."

Mona widened her eyes and nodded. Her birdlike fingers flew into her hair, raking through the fine strands.

I felt only mildly guilty for having exaggerated. It was true I'd experienced the young dancer's obsession with being skinnier. But when I got curves and my instructor began to pick on me mercilessly, I quit ballet forever, without regret. I decided not to admit this to Mona just yet. Instead I elaborated as freely as she had confessed. "One of the older ballet students taught us younger ones how to throw up," I said, already semi-aware that I was writing a story. "I remember we were standing in the bathroom, still in our leotards—mine was light pink and showed *everything*. It was—"

"How old were you?"

"Oh...about eleven."

"Were you an early bloomer? Little titties already?"

I nodded, trying not to get irritated. *Titties?*

Mona lobbed an awkward laugh into the conversation. "I used to lie on my back in bed," she said, "with a huge dictionary on my chest, to flatten myself. Weird, huh?"

"Yes," I answered. "Weird." The weight of all the words in that dictionary, squashing femininity. The image stuck like an aspirin in my throat. I swallowed. "Anyway, it was right after the dance studio's piano player had brought in a birthday cake for herself and we'd all pigged out on it. So there we were, one by one shoving fingers down our throats. I'll never forget how that older girl—one of the rising stars there—just threw up cake as easily and naturally as exhaling." I was disappointed in my story, which came to a quick halt, and had the mess and stink of vomit about it, but no real drama.

Mona didn't seem to mind. "Oh, God. I know," she said. "There are these ballet dancers in my support group . . . a whole gaggle of them"

I laughed. The word *gaggle* was so utterly appropriate for ballerinas. Mona's way of speaking and experiencing things may have been why I'd started right off re-creating myself for her (nicer way of saying I was lying). Whatever the reason, it just happened.

"What about now, though?" she asked.

I shrugged. "I love to eat, and maybe food is still complicated. But I'm learning to accept the changes in my body since I hit forty. Trying not to obsess about every pinch of extra flesh."

She started to say something and then sneezed instead. Even her sneezes were interesting—abrupt and explosive, almost violent. Her folk-singer hair jerked into flight, with a few silky strands getting tangled in her eyelashes and sticking to the moisture under her nose. I offered her a Kleenex that was only slightly used, and she took it gratefully. "Fucking allergies," she managed to blurt out just ahead of the next sneeze.

Her attack, combined with our finally reaching the store, ended our conversation. But her sudden confession and the lanky, wired look of her gave me an urge to experience some of her angst. It would be part of what I'd desired since first watching her with that camera—to see the world through her eyes now and then. I bought three cartons of Ben & Jerry's ice cream, with plans to eat them all at once and then purge (couldn't manage to throw up, as it turned out). But having me as a kind of involuntary sponsor and escort to the SA (in this case, not so much Super America as an impromptu meeting of Snackaholics Anonymous), Mona left with only celery and yogurt. *Who the hell did she think she was fooling?*

A few days later, I was returning from a long walk when I spotted Mona and Tracy at the park. It had rained the night before but now the sun baked. I was sweating heavily for the first time in the season. Tracy was digging in the damp sand, and Mona was lying on the bench, her thin legs steepled. One hand shaded her eyes from the sun and the other held the camera; she appeared to be taking a picture of an empty blue sky. I figured I'd slip by them, but Mona was more alert than she appeared. She abruptly sat up and motioned me over to join her. As I approached, she snapped a quick picture of me, and I groaned. Stringy hair, armpit stains, mouth-breathing from my walk. I wished I'd at least sucked in my stomach.

"Here, allow me." I took the camera from her and backed up to get a shot of Mona on her bench, watching Tracy play. Behind them, several naked branches trimmed the extravagantly blue sky with black rickrack. I liked the picture, but saw that Mona looked almost as bedraggled as I did. Her hair, I could see now, was something she rarely attended to, and it was a waste, with that startling color. Most of all, she looked very lonely.

"Hey, thanks." She took the camera back into her lap and I sat down beside her, leaving several careful inches between us. I wondered what I'd gotten into. Would I never be able to leave my house again, unless I went out the back and headed in the opposite direction from the park?

19

"Jim's out of town again," she said, as though I were already well acquainted with her husband and his habit of disappearing. I must have looked puzzled, because she added, "He's in sales. I don't even know exactly what he sells—some tiny part of some *thing* people apparently can't live without. I ask him what it is and he tells me and then I just forget again. Anyway, he's on the road pretty much our whole fuckin' married life. Except of course we're not together enough to fuck much, so I guess . . . ." Her voice trailed off. She scrunched up her face and sniffed juicily. I couldn't tell if she was stifling a sneeze or tears. Maybe both.

"But it's Sunday," I pointed out to her.

"Well, I know that, but he likes to travel on Sunday and begin working early on Monday. And usually he drags his sorry ass home on Saturday, so you do the math. Yesterday Tracy ran out to this strange guy walking by our house and called him Daddy."

I managed to pick up Mona's conversational style again pretty effortlessly. "Jake's gone today too. Visiting his brother in Brainerd who hates me and, behind my back, calls me Jake's Bimbo."

"How do you know that?"

"Jake told me. He thinks it's funny, so I started calling his brother Elmer Fudd behind his back because he wears one of those earflap hats when he goes out to shoot anything that moves and happens to be in season."

"Our initials are the same."

"Huh?"

"Maddie and Jake, Mona and Jim."

"Amazing," I agreed amiably enough, but then I figured Tracy into the mix. Oh God. My daughter's name had been Teresa. I'd never believed much in premonitions before, but one filled me at that moment, wave after wave of sickening dread. In some dark internal place, for just a moment, I envisioned Tracy as bloodied and lifeless, like my darling girl had been.

"Are you all right?" Mona asked me. "You're so pale all of a sudden. Kinda green. Gonna be sick? You're not preggers are you?"

For some reason, that made me laugh and feel better and want to cry all at once. "Good Lord, what a word . . . and what a thought."

Her right foot was tapping constantly, I noticed, as though to some erratic rhythm in her head, or as though revving up for a run. If we'd been in a car, this foot would be pushing, letting up, pushing on the accelerator. "I envy your freedom sometimes, you know," she said.

I knew she meant because I was childless, and I decided not to begin that conversation. Not yet. "Well," I said with the best smile I could muster, "you know what the old song says about freedom—just another word for nothing left to lose."

Mona showed no signs of recognizing "Me and Bobby McGee" and, like a prospective lover, I considered rejecting her as too young for me.

Next she launched into another story about Jim. Conversation with her was like channel-surfing. " . . . and he hides his razors from me now, I mean actually *hides* them so I can't use them on my legs. To me, it's like sharing toothbrushes, really intimate . . . but he doesn't like when I use his toothbrush either. I tried to get him to shave my legs *for* me, once, as foreplay, but he said that was about as erotic as wiping my nose."

All I could do was nod as she rambled on. The sun was picking up the white-gold highlights in her hair, virtually the same color as her daughter's. I noticed that even the fine hairs on Mona's forearms and thighs were blonde, and that the stubble on her calves where she shaved was only a shade or so darker.

For a few moments, she watched Tracy play in the sand and cheered on her artistic efforts. "What's the deal with sand?" she asked me. "I mean, why can kids, even hyper ones like her, sit for hours playing in it like that?" Tracy was constructing mostly nondescript sand bumps. "Jeez," Mona continued, "I hope she doesn't make two big ones and stick nipples on them. She's been totally obsessed with my chest since I weaned her. Talk about embarrassing, if that guy over there happened to see what she was making," she motioned to the man reading a book on a nearby bench. "He's cute, isn't he? I'll bet *he* doesn't spend more time in motels than in his own house." He may have heard, because he slapped his book shut and left the park.

I wondered if she had *just* weaned Tracy, this gangly three-year-old. The thought was a bit unsettling to me. My daughter had nursed for only a few months, and then I'd run out of milk for some reason. I recalled how sore my nipples had become, and that had been *without* teeth. An older child, big and ravenous and toothy . . . how was it possible? For once, she seemed to be waiting for a response from me and I decided to return to the safe topic of sand. "When I was little," I said, "my dad and I used to go to the beach and build these incredible sand castles, big enough for me to fit in*side*. I've got pictures. Never my mom, always Dad, I guess because he was an architect. And she just hated the cleanup—grit everywhere. So when my parents split up, that was the end of the sand for me."

I thought Mona would pick up on the topic of my parents' divorce, but she got a strangely pensive look on her face and said, "I heard something really amazing about sand once that I wanted to make sure to remember and tell someone...or, no, it was about lightning, *and* sand...maybe I read it or saw it in a movie...let me think..." She frowned and gazed into the distance, trying to pluck this sand-lightning-thing out of the muddle of memory, and I got the feeling it was important, because she rarely gave her words so much thought before springing them on me. I remained silent and waited.

"Oh yeah, I know," she said at last. "Apparently, sometimes lightning hits sandy earth—I suppose like certain deserts that get electrical storms—and the lightning can melt the sand underground in streaks, spreading kinda like tree roots, which then cool and harden into glass. Glass roots. Honest. I mean, people go searching for them and dig them up, like digging for fossils or bones or buried treasure or shit like that. And the idea is to get them out of the ground in long, unbroken pieces. Cool, huh?"

Glass roots. I became enthralled at the idea of digging for them, pulling them out whole, and made a mental note to tell Jake. Maybe if such things existed we could go dig for them together. I wanted to find out more and started to ask Mona before she could move on to something else.

But I was too late. "Hey, Trace—good job. That's the best sand-titty yet." She nudged me and pointed but I couldn't quite get myself to watch the child very closely.

My childlessness didn't come up again that first day. But I began to prepare a lie—a story—just in case, about having endured the whole fertility work-up, having unsuccessful in-vitro fertilization, and whatever else sprang into my crazed mind. I'd borrow shamelessly from Jake's experiences with his ex-wife. Maybe that was really what I should tell Mona about, sometime when she was in the mood to listen—all about that poor, barren, witch of an ex-wife, and how one of the most unlikely and unseemly facts of Jake and me was the way we met. His wife had been my gynecologist. She'd had her fingers inside my vagina and, more subtly, inside my skull, fucking with my brain. I didn't need to make that up, or even exaggerate.

It had been three years after the accident that left me childless and several months after my husband moved out. Divorce crept out of our unspeakable grief, a bogeyman who may have been there all the time, just waiting for the shadows to deepen enough. And it was Christmastime. I'd been noticing—no, obsessing about—all the Santas, all the red (never a jolly man or color for me, even as a child). And all the cars with trees tied to their roofs and rosy-cheeked children bouncing around inside like lottery balls (*watch out,* I wanted to scream . . . *strap them in for Christ's sake . . . hold them close*), and these visions and muted screams were making me too ill to work. I'd been experiencing sharp abdominal pains but couldn't quite face the doctor who had delivered my daughter and who had performed a D&C post-accident to eliminate the dead tissue that would've been my second child. So a friend of mine recommended Dr. Crandall and I went because I seemed to have no choice.

This doctor, young and pretty but with an iciness about her, started by asking how I knew Constance, referring to our mutual friend. But before I had a chance to answer, Dr. Crandall was all business. "Number of pregnancies?" Her face was blank. We could've been discussing any old uterus anywhere—pick one, what's been in there?

"Two," I managed to say.

"Children?"

"None." With this I started to sob, grasping myself around the middle as I'd been doing off and on for three years. I managed to tell an abbreviated version of the accident. Her response? She tapped a pencil and averted her eyes until I was able to stop crying. Then she donned her gloves, instructed me to lie back and hook my feet into the stirrups, and she proceeded to poke around, a *lot,* until the pain was almost unbearable. She might have been stuffing a goddamn turkey for all the care she was taking with my insides. *Get your hands out of me,* I wanted to yell but didn't (you simply don't yell at your doctor, even when she's not really yours and you'll never, ever be in an examining room with her again).

After tests and what, for her, passed for a consultation, she said I was physically fine, pronounced my pain trauma-induced, i.e. not real or very interesting to her as a medical professional. But strangely, she did not

23

prescribe drugs, not even an anti-depressant. Her recommendation? A vegan diet, herbal tea, yoga, and musical theatre. I laughed a little maniacally, but she was serious. As though regretting her innate coldness just a bit, she then did something astonishing, utterly unprofessional, and downright warm-spirited—she invited me to her house for a party. She and her husband (Jake, of course) were bringing in the New Year with a group of friends and colleagues. "Constance will be there," she told me, but I must still have looked puzzled by her invitation, so she continued, "You need to get out of your house, out of your pain. You need to be with people. I can't promise anything immediate about that abdominal discomfort, but this party could give you some . . . I don't know. Maybe some joy."

Little did she know, when she said this in her office, that what the party would give me was her husband. Our first touch—a simple handshake—caused an instantaneous, flinty spark. I'm not sure what all I saw in Jake beyond his sexy good looks and kind heart. But I think what he saw in me was salvation. As it turned out, the lovely Dr. Crandall was not only cold and witchy, she was an ob-gyn who had no viable eggs inside her and that cruel irony made her even more bitter and indifferent toward Jake. Worst of all, she was also a pathological liar. For years (Jake told me much later) she had blamed his sperm count for their inability to conceive, and she had described his supply of testosterone as diminishing the way oil leaks from an aging car. Once, she even claimed she *had* gotten pregnant (implying with someone else) and then had an abortion because Jake had been hinting at divorce. All bullshit.

Some of her lies nearly, but not quite, destroyed the love Jake and I fell into right away; I became fair game, of course, and was said to be a sociopath, a nymphomaniac, fat, floppy-titted, and a lousy cook (well, some of that's true). Long after the dust had settled, as the ex-wife finally receded into history, I still thought about the lunatic part of her and pictured her with patients, claiming their perfectly functioning organs could implode at any moment, or that their healthy baby boys could be born without testicles. Where does a pathological liar draw the line? Maybe I would find out, if I spent enough time with Mona, because she brought out the liar— make that fictionalizer—in me.

We began to spend time together in that park at least twice a week as spring promenaded into summer. Sundays were the most firmly set, but there were other times too. My solitary walks were important to me but,

24

with the days extending at both ends, I could walk very early in the morning before work and also engage in shorter, after-work strolls to better accommodate Mona and Tracy's park time. We always treated these get-togethers as though they were spontaneous.

Occasionally we were joined on our bench by Suzanne, who lived next door to Mona. They had become fast friends, it seemed, right after Mona's family had moved in, partly because Suzanne's daughter Cheryl was a handy babysitter for Tracy. I'd observed Cheryl for years, a girl transformed from chubby toddler to chatty grade-schooler and now, presto change-o, a sullen teen-ager, volatile in her walk and glare.

"Never again," Mona told me as we watched Suzanne approach the park one day.

"Excuse me?" I said.

"I won't be having Suzanne's kid baby-sit Tracy any more," Mona whispered. "She's kind of a freak. Tracy had a tattoo—a skull and crossbones—on her little tummy by the time I got home last night . . . I mean, it washed off, of course, but shit!"

"Hi, guys," Suzanne said as she sat down.

"Hi, yourself," Mona answered.

I over-greeted, over-grinned at Suzanne. Even if she was saddled with a juvenile delinquent, she was an appealing woman about my age, a fellow female who, unlike Mona, might know a bit about cellulite and old song lyrics. The urge for a true pal sneaked into me, an embarrassing desire for my life to resemble a TV sitcom. We could even be a jocular little threesome. But Suzanne also seemed, at times, as immature and vulnerable as Mona. When she smiled back at me, I noticed the tiny line of SOS dots-and-dashes on her lower lip, from her habit of biting it. She had a red-headed, freckled, thin-skinned kind of beauty and peeling nose that made the latent mother in me want to slap a hat on her head against the pounding sun. Mona's hair glowed, Suzanne's was fiery—sitting between them, I felt like a burnt-out candle.

"How's Cheryl?" Mona asked. Without waiting for an answer, she nudged me with her elbow. "Suzanne's a single mom."

Suzanne nodded distractedly. "She's okay, I guess. Beautiful day, isn't it?"

"It *is* beautiful today," I small-talked back. "Sunny and high of eighty." I wondered what people, especially in the Midwest, would chat about if forbidden to mention the weather.

But our companion wasn't about to be deflected. "Cheryl," Mona informed me, "is going through a rebellious phase. They have a family therapist, but she's is now refusing to go. How *do* you force a kid that age to do *anything?*"

I wanted to strangle Mona. It was one thing to reveal all about herself, another to drag someone else, blinking and naked into the unflattering glare. "My parents divorced when I was twelve," I said directly to Suzanne, "and I was an only child too. But it was no big deal. I survived . . . thrived, even. Had lots of loving attention." The first statement was perfectly true, the rest was a tidy bundle of lies, meant to soothe. "My mom was all I needed," I said, completing the sunny scenario. "She had me kind of late— in her forties, so I never mistook her for a friend. She was always motherly." I glanced at Mona, wondering if I'd stepped on her toes, but not worrying about it. Toe-stepping was habitual for her, after all.

"Did you see your father much?" Suzanne asked.

"Well, he died a few years later. I was still in high school." I didn't add that my mother also died, when I was barely out of my twenties. Both, freakishly, had the same rare kind of cancer, as though to highlight all of the things they *didn't* share in their later years.

This brought about an awkward silence. I wanted to steer things away from marriage and from men in general, but Mona jumped in with a compliment that surprised and pleased me and yet, oddly, also sent a jolt of jealousy through me. "Madelyn here has a winner," she told Suzanne. "Have you seen him? God, I'd love to find someone like him."

"Haven't seen him. Does he live with you?" Suzanne asked me.

I wanted to say yes, in a way, to keep him more securely mine, but I resisted that particular lie. "No, he doesn't."

"Too bad," Mona said.

"Not really," I said. "He's not perfect. Tries too hard to please and—"

"Oh, like *that's* a bad thing," Mona said.

"And there's his habit of spouting lame Ole and Lena jokes . . . ."

Suzanne chuckled. "I like those. Norwegians . . . well, Minnesotans in general really do seem to love a good joke at their own expense."

"Yup," I said. "What else would explain *Governor* Jesse Ventura?"

Suzanne nodded gleefully and started to say something. But Mona was apparently apolitical and relentless on the subject of my boyfriend, "Does Jake have any other brothers besides Elmer Fudd?"

I laughed. "Why? Honestly, Mona, Jim's one of the handsomest men I've ever seen. You aren't thinking about dumping him, are you?"

"Don't need to," Mona said. "I could have a dozen affairs and he'd never know."

"Ah, affairs . . . " I adopted the tone of world-weary older woman. "They aren't worth all the extra hair-removal and dieting and perfuming and endless soul-searching."

Suzanne bit her lower lip harder. Mona didn't seem to have heard me. She continued about Jim, "Just think about it—someone *that* good looking, out of town so much, staying in cheap motels. Do you suppose *he's* faithful to *me*? When he comes home, he treats me like his sister (except in those rare romps in the hay, of course), and he treats Tracy like a niece."

In her nearby pile of sand, Tracy perked up at the mention of her name, then starting singing to herself, "Niece and meese and please to meetchoo. This my kishen and my bakefast."

"It occurs to me," I said with more of an edge in my voice than I'd intended, "that the way we talk about men . . . my man, your man . . . oh, why doesn't he love me . . . oh God, does he find that other woman more attractive . . . am I good enough for him, and all that shit . . . it goes way beyond obsession. I mean, it's nuts. It borders on—"

"Necrophilia," Suzanne blurted out.

"Huh?" I laughed uncomfortably.

She was deeply flushed now and staring into the distance, maybe pretending somebody far away had tossed that appalling word like an errant frisbee into our laps.

"Necker-what?" Mona asked innocently.

"Nothing." Suzanne stood up, looking at her watch as though she'd just remembered an engagement. "Gotta go." As she drifted off, she said, "Cheryl's coming home in a minute, or she's supposed to, and we have to . . . uh, talk about something."

Mona watched Suzanne's departure with a mournful look on her face. "Poor thing. Her boyfriend died last year. His heart I think. She hasn't gotten over him yet."

"Apparently not."

Tracy approached her mom with a sand-pancake which Mona pretended to eat with relish. "Oh honey, that's a delicious bakefast." I wondered if it was such a good thing, the way Mona studiously avoided correcting her daughter's speech. Nursing her for years, encouraging babytalk . . . I wondered if she was letting this child grow up, but what did I know about such things? There was another larger sand-pancake on Tracy's rump; as I brushed it away, I felt a diaper inside. When the child returned to her "kishen" a few feet away, Mona said, "He was still married to someone else."

"Suzanne's boyfriend was married?"

"Uh huh."

I recalled one day the winter before when I'd happened to see Suzanne flying out of her house to grab Cheryl, rip off the man's leather jacket the girl was wearing, and storm back into the house. I wondered at the time about the importance of that particular garment, and now I asked Mona if Suzanne had maybe hung on to her boyfriend's leather jacket.

"Yes. I've seen it. Suzanne told me she didn't feel like she could go to his funeral, with the wife and kids there and all. But—get this—she snuck into his house and took back the jacket she'd given him for Christmas. That's all she has left of him."

A momentary heart-attackish pain seized my own chest. "I had a nightmare once," I told Mona, "about Jake being rushed to the emergency room with chest pains and me being shut out of his hospital room by . . . well everyone else *officially* belonging in his life. That can happen with relationships that start later, after failed first marriages. Jake's got an ex-wife out there somewhere, too." I scrapped my plans to launch into the whole sordid tale.

"Does he have any kids?" Mona asked.

I didn't feel like any more talk, truthful or otherwise. I shook my head, stood up, said good-bye and headed home. Behind me, I heard Tracy's sweet little voice. "Maddie mad?"

"No," Mona answered. "Maddie sad."

In that same husky, persistent singing voice, I heard Tracy carry on with the new word game. "Maddie saddle, Maddle gladdle, fiddle faddle, liddle laddle . . . ." And at that moment I wanted so much to run back, gather them both into my arms, and let them gather me into theirs. But I didn't.

I'm at the window now and . . .

I realize that this is a little like being a puppet master. Just as I finish writing the scene in the park, I see Mona and the baby returning from it. They have been there for hours, it seems. The baby has no bonnet on and she could've easily suffered a major sunburn in all that time. She is crying, limp in Mona's arms. Before continuing with the scene that I know must be written next, I flee into the kitchen.

When did I last eat? As though Mona pushed some weird food-button in me, I have swung between gluttony and near-starvation in the past year. Food feels unreliable, maybe worse. Like the steak in some old horror flick that was suddenly alive with wriggling maggots . . . after the heedless first bite. My kitchen lacks food now but is full of foreboding anyway. When will I stop expecting to see Jake at my counter? I envision him making one of his special sandwiches—outrageously multi-layered and tall—and then offering me half. I'm reminded of my daughter, her habit of stacking puzzle pieces into "sandwiches" instead of laying them in place, and invariably offering me the best one to chomp on. Yum, Mommy, yum. I gulp down these words hungrily and wait until I'm sure Mona's baby is inside her house, fed, asleep, safe.

I'm tempted now to write about Mona's and my last conversation before Tracy's death, our light-hearted chat during my garage sale. But no, I need to get to the funeral and back to Jake. No more evasion. Once we're settled into that church—Jake and me, Mona and Jim, and Suzanne—I'll find a moment to inject that last, unfortunate conversation.

Words

The church music they chose was all at the level of "Jesus Loves Me." This was, after all, the burial of a three-year-old child. A photo enlarged to poster size stood nearby, no doubt one that Mona had taken. It showed Tracy sitting on a step somewhere, elbows propped on her knees, chin resting on her fists. She seemed to be talking or, more likely, singing. I swallowed, hard. My throat had felt engorged so much of the time in the past few days, it felt sore, like I needed a throat culture. But can you see this kind of pain under a microscope?

A brand new blond teddy bear sat on the closed white coffin, staring out at us as we sang. *Jesus loves me, this I know. For the Bible tells me so. Little ones to him belong. They are weak but He is strong. Yes, Jesus loves me . . . .* Loftier hymns would have seemed wrong. And yet, when we all rose to sing together, "Children of the Heavenly Father," the simplicity of these messages—how heaven is the perfect place for the innocent and pure, and God wants the children for Himself, in a way—I began to choke on the very words that were meant to console. Were we supposed to be *glad* somehow? Didn't this make God sound selfish and cruel?

I stopped singing and looked around, the message now lost on me. Mona and Jim were not singing either, at least not out loud; they remained seated, leaning into each other's slumped shoulders. The rest of the congregation stood and sang out with gusto, almost as if the hymn were "Joy to the World." I spotted Suzanne nearby. We glanced at each other and then glanced away. She had not, apparently, managed to talk Cheryl into accompanying her. The last time I'd seen Suzanne's teenager, she had shaved her head. Poor Suzanne. It occurred to me, as if for the first time, that my daughter would now be thirteen years old, officially a teenager. I wondered what kind of kid she would've been. A skinhead? A cheerleader? A joy, or a burden, or both?

After the service, I made my way to Mona and hugged her for several humid seconds. "Oh, honey." I didn't say anything else, and neither did she. This was so odd for the two of us, the lack of language said it all. She was not crying. She appeared to have used up her supply of tears. Jim was at her side, looking handsomer than ever in his grief. And more distant. I wondered if he might have been partially blaming Mona, thinking she had not been vigilant enough with their child. And, as if that weren't enough, Tracy may have died because of her restless nature, the compulsion to leave the house, venture out, a trait she so obviously inherited from her mother.

"Aren't all these people coming to the cemetery?" she asked Jim, who patiently told her no, he'd already explained to her that the burial was going to be private. "But isn't that what's *done*? Isn't it?" She glanced at me as though for support.

"Mona," Jim said, pointedly *not* glancing my way. "Please."

Jake had gone to get me some punch and now joined us. He shook Jim's hand and said he was sorry for their loss. Jim nodded stoically and thanked us for coming. The two men had only spoken a few times over lawnmowers. Mona appeared headed into a hug with Jake and then sidestepped it. "Good to finally meet you, Jake," she said.

"Maddie's spoken of you so often," Jake responded.

Mona nodded. "Likewise."

Their formality struck me as peculiar and I glanced from one to the other. Hadn't they ever met, at least briefly out in our street? Mona being Mona, was that possible? They almost seemed to be *pretending* not to know each other, but why? Jealousy and paranoia elbowed in like referees. I recalled my comely young neighbor's casual threats to cheat on her husband and her remarks about Jake's attractiveness. Also, once when I'd been talking about Mona, Jake had commented that she sounded "charming in an offbeat whitebread way" (what was I, *on*beat and pumpernickel?). Was it my imagination or had he, in the last few days, seemed to be expressing sympathy for and concern only about *Mona*, not *Mona and Jim?*

"I'm just so terribly sorry about your little girl," Jake said to Mona, who launched into her frantic questions about Tracy's burial with *him* now, until Jim gently led her away.

"This is just too painful." It was Suzanne, coming up behind me, who said the words out loud for me. She looked as though she hadn't slept in days. Her face was a frenzy of freckles and jangled nerves. "Such a sweet child," she whimpered.

31

I nodded, my throat too full to say anything.

But Suzanne appeared to need to talk. "You know, I looked at Cheryl over the breakfast table this morning, knowing I was coming here later, knowing I'd be seeing Mona without that child attached as she almost always was, and do you know what I did?"

I gazed at Suzanne and, at the same time, checked around us to see if there was someone else to help, in case I needed them. Because this was a woman clearly on her way over some edge. "What did you do?" I asked.

"I slapped Cheryl, as hard as I could." Suzanne's face was blotchy now and her eyes wild. "I mean, she was sitting there, looking so . . . I don't know, dreadful and smug in her new skinheaded way, just sort of grinning at me and saying things like, 'Shit ma, why don't you ever get the right kind of cereal?' And then a minute later she launched into this tirade about some girl at school who got all A's and loved making everyone else feel dumb and 'unmotivated' and then Cheryl actually said to me, 'But of course she's a Jew, so that's what they're all like. So fucking motivated, aren't they?'" Suzanne paused for a breath. "Well, I just lost it. Slapped that hateful grin right off her face. I don't even know her anymore. She's someone else entirely." Without giving me a moment to respond, Suzanne hurried away.

Jake had overheard most of this and he put his arm around my shoulder. "Let's get out of this place."

We threaded our way through the crowd, toward the door, but got stopped by another one of my neighbors who apparently had become buddies with Jake. They began to settle into a conversation, so I made my way to a corner and sat down, scanning the room.

What the hell did these people know about burying a child?

I knew plenty about that. Jake knew that I knew, and he'd been checking on me all during the service. But my reaction, at least visibly, was not to renew my grief. I felt awful for Mona, and now also for Suzanne. But this little dead girl was not *my* little girl. So I was able to return each of Jake's glances with one of relative sanity. Until my stoicism backfired . . . badly.

Sitting in that corner by myself, watching everyone *but* Mona, I had to stifle what was unmistakably laughter. Yes, *laughter*. Like I was a misbehaving child. Next I'd be spurting punch out of my nose. Or farting.

I fled to the church ladies room where I was, thankfully, alone. Sitting in the stall, I emitted a terrible, lonely guffaw. Oh God. How could I *not* be reminded of my garage sale, only a week earlier? I could still hear us—Mona and me—giggling inappropriately like eight-year-olds. And I recalled our last conversation.

I had been sitting out by my garage alone most of the morning. Handfuls of customers came and went, some dropping coins and dollar bills into my cigar box, others just sniffing at all that I'd once wanted or been given and now wanted to dump on someone else. Jake was in the house dismantling a rusty old metal shelving unit with some difficulty—he and hand tools seldom got together without a squabble. I'd eaten my third donut—greasy, possibly rancid—and, after checking out the alley to make sure nobody was coming, I emitted a big released-balloon of a fart, followed by a few musical little pips. Mona appeared from behind me and chuckled. "Don't bother," she said. "Nobody expects entertainment at garage sales."

I felt myself blush but joined in her laughter. "It never fails," I said, "when you want to sneak one."

"You're telling me." Mona refolded some of the sweaters I'd displayed and, at the same time, surreptitiously checked them out. One in particular, she seemed to be considering, and I decided to give it to her. "You know that old urban legend," she said, "about the girl going to her prom and farting in the car after her date closes her door?"

"And there's a couple in the backseat . . . yeah, I've heard that one."

"It was me," she said matter-of-factly.

"Come on, Mona. I heard that one before you were born, practically."

"I swear."

We laughed again and, with the next few clusters of customers, whispered to each other our bets about what items each person would explore.

"That lady over there is looking for exercise equipment and at the same time eyeing what remains of my donuts," I said, momentarily forgetting about Mona's eating disorder.

But she was cool about it. "Maybe also a vibrator—got any to spare?"

"All of mine are essential. I'm high maintenance."

Mona nodded. "That kid there," she said, "the one looking through all the copies of *Penthouse*—is he actually salivating? You should have a sign—'you drool on it, you buy.'"

A bedraggled-looking woman with two young children in tow chose a crockpot, two sweaters, and several paperbacks. "Don't you have any kids' stuff?" she asked.

I was struck dumb by the question. Wasn't it *clear* that I had no kids' stuff? Did she really have to ask?

Mona glanced at me and then said, "Sorry. Adults only here. X-rated."

When the woman started writing a check, Mona told her, "No checks. Cash only."

"What?" I asked.

Mona shook her head. "Everyone knows that about garage sales these days. No checks. They can bounce like titties on a trampoline."

I laughed, of course—thank God for Monaisms. But my customer was not amused. She ended up leaving in a huff, counting out several quarters for the books only.

Mona looked apologetic. "I'll buy the crockpot," she offered. "I need one. Really."

A few minutes later, I asked Mona where Tracy was.

"Bonding with her dad. They do this about once a month, conveniently timed to coincide with my worst PMS day." To illustrate, she growled at a child rummaging through my "FREE" box. "I wonder how old she'll have to be to notice," Mona added.

"Tracy? Notice what?"

"What a truly lousy mother I am."

I started to protest that she was, in fact, a perfectly good mother, but Mona wouldn't have heard me. She was staring boldly at a good-looking man who sauntered over to examine the hiking boots Jake had contributed. "Where's that hunky boyfriend of yours?" she asked.

With one thumb, I motioned toward my house. "Jake says garage sales are 'women's things' and wouldn't be caught dead out here."

"Jim won't buy tampons or panty liners for me when he's at the store. Like the cashier's going to snicker or something? But hey, put a Victoria Secret catalogue within his reach, no squeamishness about 'women's things' then, huh? Jake too?"

I nodded. "Do women really look like that, do you think?"

"Hell, no. I saw one of those so-called supermodels at the airport once and she looked like a complete skank, I swear. Hair like straw sticking out every which way, blotchy skin. Jim stared at her anyway, of course. He used to claim that *I* should . . . oh, never mind. Uh, Maddie, do you think Jake's coming out to check on things, though?"

"I doubt it."

"Too bad." She shrugged. Her restless right foot accelerated its tapping. "Hey, listen, I've gotta go."

I nodded, disappointed—she had such a way of making time pass more pleasantly. Had she come over mostly to see and flirt with Jake? I swatted the suspicion away. "Take the crock pot," I told her. "And that sweater, the blue one. Both free."

She grinned at me. "I'll take them as a bribe to keep my mouth shut about how you farted up your alley."

"And I promise not to tell anyone you're a lousy mother."

Mona had taken the teasing in stride. But . . . Jesus. That was the last thing I'd said to Mona before Tracy's death. My bathroom stall no longer seemed like much of a hideout. I could hear the funeral crowd chatting away and, even louder, echoes of my own voice calling Mona a bad mother. How could I have blurted out such an unfunny joke? Maybe it had been mean-spirited, in part, because I'd felt that stab of jealousy. But jokes could be so treacherous if followed by the wrong tragic events, as though God said, "You think that was funny? I *dare* you to laugh at *this*."

I finally dragged myself out of the stall. Glancing into the mirror, I couldn't ignore what seemed to be evil lurking there, like a foggy little graveyard was gathering to take over my face. My hair was as lank as my spirits, and my eyes were raw and red but startlingly dead-looking. A stranger's face. I looked down and washed my hands over and over, until another woman came in.

The moment I left the church bathroom, Jake grabbed me. "I've been looking all over for you. Let's go already."

"Sorry. I thought you were talking to what's-his-name." I stared at Jake as we left the church. "Or maybe consoling Mona some more."

"You've got a strange look on your face," Jake told me.

"Sorry again. My face seems to be getting stranger every day."

The moment Jake opened the car door for me and I got in, I remembered Mona's fabled prom date and felt the laughter re-threaten. I knew this would be misinterpreted, of course, even by Jake. But there was a reasonable explanation beyond funny bodily functions.

First of all, I'd spotted Mr. Jankow, the man who'd been driving the car when Tracy had darted into the street. He was outside the church, by himself, standing in a shadow. I'm certainly not proud of my reaction to seeing him—it was cold-hearted. But I needed to feel better. The whole thing seemed right out of a movie to me, a funeral scene, with a guilt-ridden perpetrator and maybe an astute undercover cop judging his every move. This generic movie scene was the first one that popped into my head, but then, God help me, the next one was from a black comedy. I thought of Michael Palin in A *Fish Called Wanda*, sneaking into each doggy-funeral he, an animal-worshipper, had inadvertently caused, his face a glorious mess of pain. Such a sick, yet playful, unreality floated me away from the actual funeral and made me smile. How, after that, could I avoid fast forwarding to a more acceptably funny scene in the same movie? It was proper Brit barrister John Cleese, spouting love and Russian nonsense as he performed his gangly strip tease.

And then, as Jake rounded the front of the car, I envisioned him totally naked. It had started with his shoulders and, then gradually, all of him popped out of his careful church clothes. His penis, shrunken by the cold splash of funeral, was bobbing listlessly. It was all I could do to hold off the laughter until we were driving the hell out of that parking lot. But by the time we got home, I was holding my stomach and wiping away tears in a combination of mirth and horror that struck me, even at the time, as bordering on madness. In my case, laughter was worse than untimely. It was like comedy made *so* black that it becomes a tomb. It was no accident that I'd tried to take Jake, my dearest friend, in there with me. I'd learned what the inside of that tomb was like long ago.

Many people, it seems to me, lead a themed kind of life, filled with recurrences. Like a road that appears to go straight ahead toward the promise of horizon but, in reality, circles and passes all the same scenery, over and over. My theme involves children who die. When Tracy had been killed in front of my house, in front of my *eyes*, she was added to a list, the kind that is words on paper, black on white, not unlike a harmless shopping list. It included not only my own three-year-old daughter and four-months-along fetus, but also my cousin's toddler who drowned. And as though that weren't enough, the list sometimes felt incomplete, partially erased. The next logical phrase seemed to begin "And then there was . . . ." Or perhaps "And then there *will* be . . . ."

Anyway, I was doomed, it seems, to forever witness the unthinkable, and to explain the inexplicable, to cry and, yes, to laugh because sometimes life just has to be turned into a horrible joke. And laughter can wash away shards of irony and terror from our throats, hopefully without ripping any flesh.

Jake knew about my theme. He thought he knew everything there was to know about me. And yet, my laughter in the car seemed to shake him more than the funeral itself.

He began pacing in my living room as soon as we got home. I could see what he was thinking: No sane person laughs when a child has just died.

"Jake, sit down. Stop looking at me like that." I laughed again, couldn't help it.

But as he paced and raked his fingers through his hair, he was looking at me like I'd sprung from a snakepit he thought he'd managed to fill up and plant a garden on. He was sweating and saw that I was too. So he turned on the old table fan I stole from his parents, and it began to hum grumpily, looked at us side to side through its cage—blank-eyed, much like his parents used to do. When Jake finally spoke, his voice was grave (so appropriate, for where we'd just been). "You'd think," he said, "having lost a child of your own—"

"A child and a half," I automatically corrected him. "I miscarried after the crash."

Jake stared at me and then shook his head. "You'd think having lost *children* of your own, you'd find nothing *funny* about this little girl's death."

"Having lost all that, I'm glad I still have a chuckle or two left in me. Aren't you?" The fan slowly shook its head.

"But Maddie, what were you laughing at?" Jake paused, cleared his throat and added questions he'd probably meant to keep to himself. "What's going on with you? *In* you?" When I didn't answer, he continued. "That driver—"

"Mr. Jankow," I said.

Jake nodded uncertainly. "Yes, whatever. He said, afterwards, that he thought he saw you in the window before the kid ran in front of his car. So you saw the whole thing, right? You haven't told me yet. You won't answer my questions. If you did actually see it all happen, I can understand why you're behaving so oddly."

I glared at him. Had he said *oddly* or *badly*? How was my behavior ever going to hold up to scrutiny? Why did it have to? How? Why? Question marks appeared then like ferns sprouting from my wood floor, slowly unfurling. I stared at them; I swear they were real. Punctuation solid enough to trip over. I would not address that window question. But there it was, his first verbalized accusation, that I could have, *should* have saved that poor little girl.

"What, exactly, did you tell the police that morning?" Jake asked.

"They asked what happened, I told them I didn't really know, it all happened too fast. Why are *you* interrogating me, Jake?" I could feel my face getting hotter and hotter.

"I'm not. I'm just curious. And I'm worried because, honest to God, you haven't been the same since. Did you just tell them you were looking the other way when the car came along and hit her? If it all happened *that fast*, the guy must have been speeding, right?"

I nodded, then shook my head. No, this topic would have to wait.

"Was he—?"

"Mr. Jankow."

"Yes, *yes*. I know his name, Maddie. Was he speeding? Were there any other witnesses? What did the police say to you?"

"That Tracy had been killed instantly. That Mr. Jankow had been out getting a newspaper, because his hadn't been delivered. And he was also out of milk." Actually, when this came out of my mouth, I realized that these were details not supplied by the police at all, but by me. Jake seemed to sense this. He'd seen as many cop movies as I had and knew that the officers in this case would hardly be chatting with me—the only eyewitness—about newspapers and milk.

"I heard," Jake said, still pacing, "that they're trying to take the guy's drivers license and he's fighting it, saying the accident was totally unavoidable. He's got a lawyer by now, so you'll probably get deposed."

"What do you mean, deposed?" I asked. "You mean like *dethroned*?"

Jake took me too seriously. "No. Depose, as in take a deposition from you. They'll want to determine whether or not the guy was driving too fast, or that his reflexes were shot because . . . well—"

"Because he's so old," I supplied, all too eager to come to the right conclusions, there in my living room. As if that could actually be the end of it. The word *deposed* trembled in a corner. De-posed . . . forced out of a pose.

"I feel terrible for him," Jake said, "but he probably shouldn't be driving."

"And the newspaper should have been delivered as promised." I knew this was a reach even as I said it, but I was achieving that distance I needed. From a distance, you reach, and you also, if you're lucky, disappear.

"What newspaper?" He raised his voice in exasperation.

"Please stop yelling at me, Jake. This is getting us nowhere." Where, I wondered, were all his stupid Ole and Lena jokes when I needed them? "Hey," I said. "Do you want to go swimming or something? Maybe catch a movie?"

I didn't actually want to go anywhere and was relieved when Jake said no. But I was still desperate to divert him, so I considered confessing that what I'd been laughing at on the way home from the church was a scene from a movie, but also it had been at *him*, although that would hardly soften his anger or curiosity. I thought about trying to explain to him the symbolism of what happened in that parking lot—the fact that he had become too relentlessly naked to me. But he would have simply pointed out that of *course* we were naked to each other, known, open . . . of course. Because we loved each other.

Another of my themes: I apparently don't love people enough. A better, more attentive love could certainly have kept my babies alive, right? That's how my husband—as he was becoming my ex—saw the situation. I eventually agreed. Then, all of my arguments with Jake started ending this way, with his accusation that I didn't love him enough. Enough to live together, get married, and have babies.

Jake halted his inquiries at last, removed his damp shirt and left the room to get a beer from the fridge. By the time he came back, he was his old self—amiable, generous, too good for me. He knelt in front of my chair, too close, his breath laden with dark ale and grief. "Honey," he said. When I lowered my chin, he pushed aside my hair and kissed my forehead. I felt the chap of his lips and tried to ease away, but he stayed where he was, still kneeling in front of me, wedged between my knees. Oh God, were we going to make love, of all things? Talk about dancing on a grave. He smiled and said, "What's up?"

Such a sprightly thing to yell into someone's snakepit, I wanted to laugh again, but swallowed it. I tried to answer, to find the explanation. That was when I became aware that the room had filled not only with punctuation, but with words as well. At first, they seemed to be spilling like red wine on a tablecloth—*quick wipe it up, get the club soda.* But I recognized that the spillage was neither accidental nor messy, because the embryonic words took readable shape upon hitting the floor. Most of them began to float and shimmer before me, but Jake was unintentionally squishing some with his oversized body. I glanced away from him and saw all the c's and s's in the words, real enough to hook around my wrist and into my earlobes. A swarm of q's and g's looped their tails across my cheek and got tangled in my hair.

"What's the matter?" Jake asked me as he glanced around.

I had no idea what may have been visible to him, either in the room or on my face. I felt a momentary, irrational urge to tell him that he *should* be able to see the growing garden of words too . . . therefore, he didn't love me enough. Ha! I opened my mouth, but nothing came out. The words were so miraculous in this new, unspoken, visible form. I recognized a phrase of my mother's in them from far back in my childhood, a question my ex-husband and I used to ask each other in bed, and the first real sentence uttered by my daughter (*Mommy's here*). Oh—I'd forgotten all about that! *Mommy's here mommy's here mommy's here,* came her adoring choo choo train of words. And seeing them like that didn't make her loss sear into me as usual—it brought her back instead. She was practically in my arms.

"Honey, are you all right?" Jake asked.

Better than all right, I wanted to tell him. *I'd been lost,* as the hymn says, *but now I was found.* Saved by the words themselves. The word *found* even looked like a sanctuary with its cupping, circling, pointing symmetry. And, yes, that amazing word—*grace.*

"Talk to me," Jake said. He was a very kind man. And loving. I let myself gaze directly at him for the first time since we'd gotten home. The reluctance of a moment before shifted abruptly and inappropriately to lust, strong enough to taste and pass to his tongue like a lozenge. Wildly contradictory images flashed—his naked body moving in its powerfully angled, athletic way through a church parking lot, but this time with an erection spearing the air, a divining rod with me the hidden water. I wanted him inside of me. Immediately. But I wasn't actually sure of the words to ask for that. Too many of them presented themselves and, just then, none of them were conveying the right kind of meaning for Jake. One word in particular, the word *Come,* wavered before me in all its nuances, tender and obscene, and it was hand-in-hand with its inevitable partner, *Go.*

My mind was becoming gridlocked, so I tried pulling from it just a few easy words, as sane and plain as *hello* and *now* and *help.* I imagined writing him an explanatory note. It could solve everything, I told myself, if only I could get it just right. Just write.

"What's happening?" Jake persisted. "Tell me. Nothing else matters to me right now except you. Nothing."

"I'm mute," I said and then laughed again. For a moment it was unbearably funny that someone would *say* she's *mute.* That's when the words started piling up between us like snow on a window, but visible only from the inside. *Mute. Moot. Loot.* How interesting. Jake had, for years, been looting my home, hauling away my solitude, my self-reliance, digging my silence out by the roots, glass and otherwise. *Root. Toot. Tooth* (one shot pain into my jaw like I'd bitten into tin foil). *Truth.*

That last word I said out loud, and Jake gave me one of his knowing nods. An *ah yes* reaction when, of course, he didn't have a clue. "So," he said, "you don't believe me."

Believe him about what, exactly? Exact, Extract, Distract. The word-garden had become a thicket, until *distract* got me out. Because there it was—a tree branch was tapping on a nearby window, demanding my attention as it had early that morning at breakfast. Now the branch tapped like fingers on glass. And I was suddenly twelve years old, standing at the school bus stop, feeling ugly and chunky, and then enthralled by the tapping fingers from inside the bus. Lovely, skinny, glorious Viv Jordan was actually motioning to me, beckoning for me to sit by her on the bus. Except in the next moment I felt the presence behind me of the girlfriend Viv's fingers really *were* tapping for. Of course, I'd be on the bus alone as usual. On top of everything else, I suddenly got my period and felt it soaking my new beige pants, right there on the bus, before school even started.

41

And as Jake droned on about something I couldn't decipher, I felt it again at age twelve, the tug of uterine lining, the gush, rush, hush, and then also the crush—the boy I adored, just inside the school doors, ready to lend me a sweater to wrap around my hips. The man, Jake, also there, also adored, also ready to help me hide stains of all kinds. A past and present love. A recreated dilemma of blood soaking fabric, the humiliation and panic of unpreparedness. This should not, *could* not be ignored.

Time to write.

I stood up, awkwardly since Jake was still wedged in. His words broke through. "What are you doing?" he asked. He looked so innocent and pure, even holy. Jesus loved *him*, this I knew.

Through the jungle of words, my voice cut like it was wielding a machete. It could hack away at Jake, too, if he got in the way. "I'm writing," I said simply.

"Right at this moment?" he asked.

"Yes," I confessed. "At this moment I'm turning you into a fourteen-year-old boy I had a crush on, in junior high. Who helped me one particularly humiliating day. Except he didn't really. Only in my story."

Jake stood and backed away from me a few steps as though to get out of range. "You're turning me into someone else? But . . . why?"

The only answer that occurred to me was a shameless cliché but I grabbed onto it. That's what clichés are for, after all. "Why turn you into someone else? Because I can." And then I removed myself from the room, shaking off some of the words, scooping up others and carrying them with me to soak up sounds, wounds, even imaginary blood. I was also, of course, removing myself from Jake. But he was not responsible for any of my demons, so I turned at the bathroom door, just long enough to try to explain further. "Maybe, I'm not meant to participate."

Then, I was gone.

Jake's voice was far away. "But . . . ."

Hush.

I'm at the window now and . . .

It's another warm morning. I've been wearing the same raggedy sundress every day and it's beginning to smell, but I tell myself that creativity is not sweet-smelling or pretty. It is, in fact, like labor. Not the construction kind, the baby-delivering kind. I can feel myself cramp up. And now I need to settle into a more simple, straightforward narrative, what my former writing teacher and temporary good friend, Eugenia, used to call "finding the Heming-way into the story." Eugenia will make her grand entrance here later, sweeping in, part duchess, part drag queen. But for now, my characters are in place and moving, interacting, talking, fighting, making up and avoiding. Where I left off, I have begun to write stories and, not so coincidentally, to lose Jake.

I glance across the street before continuing. Baby has been plopped out in the front yard like a bag for Goodwill pickup. Hot sun, no bonnet, no water, no visible Mona. Still, the child seems eerily content, plays and gazes around, chirps back at the birds, and watches something (I hope it's a harmless ant) on its journey up her leg. Then she pinches it between her fingers and puts it in her mouth. I imagine it tastes a bit like cinnamon if it's a red ant, pepper if it's black. I know that kind of perverse hunger . . . I feel it now, watching.

Edge

My first story ended in minor triumph for my shy and chubby pubescent character as she navigated through the rest of that day with a sweater wrapped around and hugging her hips to hide the blood stain. The sweater had been lent to her by a boy whom she'd loved all year. When I finally forced myself to read it through, beginning to end, I promptly deleted it from my computer, the whole raw, self-indulgent, and utterly predictable story. Nothing more than another spurt of blood, terrible writing, unworthiness. Work in name only. But it had started something. Oh my.

The next day, I called the office and said I was sick, and then a day after that I quit my administrative assistant job altogether, using my remaining two days of vacation as a pathetic substitute for two weeks notice. I went in only to clear out my cubicle and get called flighty and ungrateful by my boss (who had just given me a raise), after which I was marched into Human Resources to sign forms and get scolded some more, this time about benefits. The HR woman—*girl* really, she looked about twelve—warned me about bad timing. (Actually, what she said, of course, was that my timing "sucked," a word so unpleasantly ubiquitous now . . . whatever happened to its reference to lollipops?) I was informed that the company's benefits would soon include a great dental plan. "You can do the whole COBRA thing, if you can afford it," the girl told me, "but dental won't be part of it for you. Sorry. And after eighteen months, you're on your own for medical, too."

I could see how much she enjoyed delivering this news, but I calmly replied, "Fine. Paying my own premiums is not a problem, and my teeth are perfect." This was a double lie, but it gave me the illusion of strength. Quitting like that was undoubtedly crazy, but I could justify it—I hated the job, owned my house, and had managed to save a few thousand dollars. Plus, I'd recently been offered freelance work writing catalogue copy that promised to pay extremely well, and that freed me to write other things. It was not only possible to quit my job but also necessary. I felt that I was

44

running out of time, running out of steam. More writing income would surely kick in by the time I'd gone through my savings.

But my new job—writing copy for a mail order company offering artwork, glassware, pottery, collectibles, and furniture—was already giving me trouble. I'd seen the "Writer Wanted" ad in the newspaper, applied in a rather larkish way with sample copy I wrote in no time at all, and was shocked to be hired. That had been a month before I quit my real job and it had seemed I had plenty of time to whip off more crisp cataloguey words in the same vein as my application sample. Nothing to it. Except that I was simply not doing the work, and I had an impossible deadline pressing in on me slowly, minute after minute, day after day.

It was about that same time—a few days after Tracy's funeral—that Mr. Jankow paid me an official visit. I'd seen him near my house a few times, but this time he rang my doorbell. After introducing himself, he shook his head about the horror of the accident and the key role he'd played in it. I shook my head too, said "I know, I know," and then noticed that there were now *several* bouquets of flowers on the curb near Tracy's house.

Jankow asked me what I'd seen that awful day. He peered at me with watery dark blue eyes, the startling color of a north woods lake at which I'd vacationed once with Jake. I fished for the perfect description of that color and found *indigo*. The word imbedded itself in my mind, no longer conjuring up Jankow's eyes at all. Jake's eyes were light blue, mine muddy brown to match my hair. Tracy's? I didn't remember. I was stalling, Jankow still waiting. He seemed to be wondering if I was dim-witted, and measuring me for my witness suit. But it wasn't a good fit. "You saw her dart out between those cars, right in front of me, right?" he prompted. "There was nothing I could do, nothing anyone could have done."

I shook my head, clasped trembling hands behind my back.

"Can you tell me exactly what you saw?"

I said what I had to say. "Sorry. I was looking the other way." It was what I'd told the police, what I'd told Jake, what I'd been telling myself until I believed it was the whole truth. "I'm sure you were driving responsibly—I would've noticed you more if you weren't," I told him, trying in vain for a soothing, sane voice. "But I didn't actually see much of anything."

He didn't seem to quite believe me. For a few nerve-jangling moments I looked over Jankow's bony shoulder, to the darkened house, the flowers and now invisible bloodstain, and I found myself watching a scene unfold— real or imagined, I wasn't sure: Tracy in pj's, unattended and drifting out her front door, Tracy crouching to jabber at a stray cat who heads for the street, Tracy on the curb calling *kitty kitty* long after the cat has scooted between parked cars and vanished, Tracy reduced to carnage. Why the sudden slow-motion? Where had that cat come from? Was I writing about it now, embellishing, or simply remembering it that way? Nothing was simple or clear.

Jankow stared at me and I stared back, until he calmly informed me that he was a widower, seventy-five years old but in excellent health, self-reliant, active, and dependent on his car to get him wherever he needed to be. He would not give up his right to drive without a fight. He finished with, "My attorney will be in touch with you." Then, with a pronounced straightening of his shoulders, he left, no longer looking nearly so old or feeble as I'd been thinking the last few days. He looked, in fact, ageless, wiry and tough in that way of certain men (Clint Eastwood, Henry Fonda, my own father even though he never got that old), especially when they're facing a worthy foe. Apparently, that was me.

Meanwhile, Jake (who was at work when Jankow visited) was doing his best to continue standing by, kneeling by, and sitting by, ever patient, kind, and giving. He had the most tempting lap. We made love in lieu of harshly reviewing my finances or discussing legal procedures. He kissed and held me in spite of the sheer stupidity of my blithely giving up a good job with benefits to commit to work I probably couldn't do, not to mention the prospect of my getting *deposed*. But we could ignore the obvious only so long.

One Saturday morning, after making love, I sensed company in my bedroom. A clutch of intruders huddled in the corner—my former boss, the HR girl, Jankow together with his so-far faceless attorney, and now also a catalogue editor who would be crushing me with demands, deadlines, and dread lines. They were all shaking their heads. I didn't know if they were disapproving of me in general, my methods of escape, my lovemaking techniques, Jake as a suitable partner, or just that particular orgasm I'd had which, truth to tell, had been selfish and melodramatic.

Immediately after coming, I'd started crying . . . no, *sobbing* into Jake's neck, and then felt him recede inside me, even his penis wondering *what the hell?* No climax for him, of course, not during my breakdown. He continued to hold me close until I'd stopped crying. After that, once again, I found myself chuckling (my laugh reflex still recurring like a stubborn case of hiccups). Then I withdrew into momentary silence, hoping, wordlessly *begging* Jake to do the same.

But he didn't. And it was his turn to chuckle. "Well. That was something. Feel better?" He made sure I nodded. "Good. So, Maddie . . . "

I squirmed.

" . . . you want to be a writer." He said it like a brand new proclamation. A validation I didn't need. "That's great. It's what you're meant to do. Writing stories. Of course, first you've got that catalogue . . . ."

"Don't remind me," I said. "Please. Kiss me instead. Can you do that?"

He did, but he was distracted. When he started surveying my bedroom (for what I had no idea), I launched into a tour guide's explanation of the clutter. The buildup of dust and books, the scatter of dirty clothes I'd shed each day like hasty decisions, a few smudgy glasses, and a plate with smile-shaped sandwich crusts waiting for ants to find them. That was when I realized that this sobbing-after-sex thing had flung me into a mysteriously manic mode. "I know it's a mess in here," I told Jake, "but I'm going to clean today, I swear. And do the laundry. Want to help? We can put on the B.B. King CD—the thrill *isn't* gone, right? Or Bonnie Raitt. I love dusting to Bonnie. Her voice sometimes *sounds* dusty, but in a good way, like that tiny old shop we found on Lake Street. Let's go there too, today. But first, let's fuck again. Wanna? Jake?"

He wasn't actually listening to my jabbering. He found what he was looking for in my room. "Over there—" He pointed at last to the old white vanity I'd salvaged from my childhood bedroom. "Describe that for me, like you would if it were going to be in that artsy fartsy catalogue. She hired you because your writing samples were . . . what did she call them? Witty? Erudite?"

"Edgy."

"Right. Edgy. So tell me about that vanity. What's the selling point?"

"Good Lord," I said. "That piece of junk. It still has fingernail polish on it from when I was eight years old."

47

"Well, that doesn't detract from the style of the piece. And the fact that you saved it shows you have an eye for such things. It'll just take a little research. You're a natural, with great taste in . . . well, nice stuff."

I snorted. "Yup, too bad that's not the catalogue's name—'Nice Stuff.' I could use words like *cool* and *wow* and *awesome*."

He ignored me. "That editor hired you for a reason. Relax. You can do it."

"I know."

"Freelance is tricky," he continued. "You hate deadlines, but the truth is you need them. Deadlines are good for—"

"Jake, you know what? I'm really thirsty."

But my boyfriend was on a mission. "Listen. That catalogue's a godsend and, eventually you'll have fun with it. Still, money's going to be tight for a while."

I knew what was coming and tried to head it off at the pass. "Jake, will you please get me some juice? My saliva is absolutely gone—you know how I get. On second thought, refill my wine glass from the sunroom. I just opened a new bottle of Riesling. Help yourself too."

He headed for the refrigerator. "So, about your financial situation," he said across the distance of two rooms. I heard him shaking and pouring juice while broaching The Topic and, under my breath, I repeated that wine was what I really wanted. Not a lecture about money or how we're in this together.

"I'll be fine, Jake," I practically shouted. "Maybe give me a fresh wine glass."

Jake returned to the bedroom, orange juice and nothing else in hand. "It's still early," he said. "Here's breakfast." But when he saw my face, he also went back for wine.

I thanked him, reclined in bed as though never more comfortable in my life, but held on to both of the glasses to steady my hands. "Jake, about the money thing . . . the catalogue pays sixty-five bucks an hour, and they estimated it should take me at least a hundred hours, per season. That's a healthy piece of change, four times a year." I slurped from each glass and gave him a smug grin, but something about what I'd just said made me more anxiety-ridden than reassured. I hadn't yet written a word for those people, after all. And this would be four catalogues a year? Yikes. I polished off the wine and shuddered.

That was when my bout of minor mania took a strange turn. For some reason, my thoughts and feelings started to rhyme, and I studied this strange new phenomenon as though the words could now be pinned on a board—rhyming bugs. My heartbeat quickened, my brain thickened, my smile sickened. But I quickly rejected the *ick* at the center of these. And took a closer look. Responsibility loomed, panic bloomed, the room gloomed and doomed . . . . Cool. I was lying in bed, trying on a whole wardrobe of double O's. I could poke my feet into them and pull them all the way up my legs. Or ease them seductively onto my chest as a see-through bra.

This wordplay quickly lost its allure once I noticed that Jake was also zeroing in on my tits, which were serving as flattened fleshy coasters for my beverages. I followed his gaze and saw how my left nipple was magnified by the empty wineglass and the right one was obscured by orange juice; my chest was winking at him. It was hard to ignore the fact that he was springing back to life and, as was often the case, our clever, tenacious bodies started reaching for each other across whatever distance our unwieldy minds seemed to create. I sipped my orange juice before putting the glass on the floor, sprinkled wine drops onto my belly, licked my lips, and stared at Jake's nakedness.

I knew every angle, color and texture of him. Every hard and soft, hollow and jut of him, everything that was beautiful and also each place where age was being less than kind. And because of all that, I wanted him again. Not only to make love, but also to dance with me. In an earlier, happier phase of our relationship we'd taken ballroom lessons together, and our steamy tango was the hit at his niece's wedding reception. So, at that moment in my bedroom, I wanted everything Jake could offer.

Except, apparently, his words. Because later, after we'd made love again (better, more like the old days), he couldn't resist relaunching the discussion. Still winded and flushed, still holding me, he said, "God*damn*, we're good together, Maddie. Aren't we? Why not look at this as a time for even more change. Good change."

Just as suddenly as it had appeared, my mania was gone. I was utterly drained and couldn't respond to what Jake was saying or even to what corner he was easing me back into—not dancing me in, but dragging my uncooperative flaccid body.

49

He continued, "I mean, why not sell your house, or I'll sell mine? We'll move in together, pool our resources."

One of the words he said leaped into bed with us, painfully sharp and clear. It was staring at me with what were now *dangerous* double O's. Something terrible floated between the walls formed by P and L. *Pool. Oh God.* "I can't . . . ."

"What exactly is wrong with my suggestion?" Jake demanded an answer.

But my mind had taken a terrible journey away from him, even though it was only for a few moments. *Pool.* A pool in which someone could drown if you're not careful, and not drown in love either. I saw not just the word but the hellish image—the swimming pool with a pale little body bobbing in it. My cousin yelling as he jumped into the water, his wife screaming. Me? Mute. Moot. *Here we go again.*

"What the hell's the matter with you?" Jake said, standing beside the bed now, tall and dark but not handsome, not now. "I wish you could see yourself," he said and I silently wished the same for him. He grabbed his clothes and began ramming his body into them as though innocent fabric could be, *should* be punished. But he was also staring at me. "You've gone all white and blank on me again. Jesus, Maddie. How can you make love to me like you just did and still seem to distrust . . . maybe even dislike me? Where do you go when you pull away like that?"

I shook myself clear of pool water and rhymes and terror, back to the bedroom, back to us, or what was left of us. What I said to Jake was as clear as I could make it. "I'm here with you. I am . . . here. But, Jake, I need to live alone. Forgive me. We've been over this ground before, and now it's even more of a problem, the idea of our living together."

"Why?"

"It's hard to explain," I continued, tears gathering for an unwelcome encore. "I love you. But it is so crowded inside my head lately that having this house to myself is becoming more and more necessary. I'll only hurt you, trying to make the room I need." At the sight of his face, I repeated the best part. "I do love you, though."

His response was utterly predictable: "You don't love me *enough*."

I ventured into my kitchen for more wine as soon as Jake left. He said he needed to take a walk. I said nothing, tired of words—where were they getting me anyway? When I opened the refrigerator door, it breathed cool but smelly air into my face so I threw away the leftover Hamburger Helper, a jagged chunk of cheese, and a shriveled zucchini. Then I searched for other things in the house that needed disposal, including a few white socks with holes in the heels, a mud-stained tank top, and a moldy old backpack . . . all Jake's. Fastening the bulging garbage bag and holding it against my torso as I headed for the alley, I marveled at how simple some tasks could be. The bag felt solid, silent, self-contained, and I wanted to lead it into a tango through my backyard. *Slow, slow, quick quick, slow.*

Dance dance dance. I seemed to be stuck in this groove and didn't know why, until a few hours later, when Jake returned. He was flushed from his walk, and from his idea. "We need to go out," he said. "To the Riverside. We need to go out dancing. Tonight. Now, after my shower. After you stop gaping at me like I've lost my mind."

I closed my mouth and gave him the warmest smile I had in me. It was clear how much we needed to do some dancing, even if it also seemed a bit desperate. All that fighting or almost fighting or avoidance of fighting until we were practically bruised—dancing may have been an unlikely remedy, but I couldn't say no because, after all, he'd read the idea from my own mind. I loved it when my thoughts became his, when my words toppled out of his mouth.

As we got ready, he kept pulling my body into the sway of his. Music wasn't even necessary. He was holding me, not grabby or greedy, not even sexually, just *close*, until there was nothing I could do but follow. Our ballroom dance lessons had taught me to enjoy something previously alien to me—relinquishing control. Of all the myriad instructions we sorted through, the simplest and perhaps most important one seemed to be this: the man leads, the woman follows. Naturally, at first, I balked. I wanted dance to be about freedom and expression and art. I wanted to be Isadora Duncan, except with a partner, as if that were possible. But there I was, trying to let Jake make every single decision about which step we would do, what size and direction, which flourish. And I was instructed to simply submit to his will.

Jake was not a natural dancer—his feel for rhythm was somewhat inconsistent, even whimsical. A metronome with a stutter. But his enthusiasm carried us both, and he led with powerful certainty that he was

51

on the beat and doing swell, even when he wasn't. Although I happened to be too rhythmically correct for my own good, I adjusted to him, usually, and eventually felt taken, in the most pleasurable way, each time we stepped on a dance floor. We were clearly right, in our current effort to reach out to each other, to retrieve something from our dancing history. Why had we ever stopped?

The answer to that became obvious as our time together at the Riverside slipped by us, along with our opportunity for reconciliation. The evening got off to a shaky start. We hadn't bothered with reservations, so we had to wait over an hour, then got set up at a makeshift little table right at the edge of the dance floor. The air conditioning at the Riverside was no match for the heat outside combined with a kitchen and too many bodies. Our dinner (which we should've just skipped, but it seemed necessary) was slow in coming and seemed tossed together from scraps. And our conversation was no better. "Do you think this heat wave will ever stop?" "How's work?" "Fine." "How's the writing going?" "Fine." "So, this English professor asked Ole if he liked Kipling and Ole said, 'Don't know, never kippled.'" Etc., etc. Until, finally, we cleared the way to dance instead.

But something had already infected our ability to dance that night. We had been forced to watch others dance while we ate and while I drank (too much), and that particular night several members of a dance club dominated the floor. These six couples, all in their forties and fifties, had clearly been dancing together forever. They were so in synch with each other, so intimate in their approach to music, movement and mutuality, it was almost embarrassing to watch them, as though we were peeking into their bedrooms. That was probably why Jake and I lingered over our meal, and why I ordered a second bottle of wine. We hadn't danced together in over a year, and we'd been fighting a lot, so getting onto that dance floor with those others seemed risky at best.

We might have salvaged the evening, except at one point, while watching this talented older couple, I burst into tears. Again. Their dancing seemed the perfect expression of love that not only endures but blossoms with age: the way his hand looked at home on her back, the way her hand strayed from his shoulder to tease his neck and loosen his collar for him, the way they fit together and focused only on each other and forgot about everyone else . . . damn, I really wanted to be them. Instead of us. Jake read this in my face and he began to join me in drinking too much. By the time we got out there to dance, we were doomed. We might as well have been strangers, and it didn't take us long to call it a night and go home. I went to mine, he to his. Something had been irreparably broken.

It was soon clear that Jake wasn't about to return to my house or into my arms. "Time out," he called it, like what you prescribe for a bratty child. I marked the day by pigging out on cheap wine, peanuts, and music—all of Bach's suites for unaccompanied cello. This is said to be the instrument that most closely approximates a human voice, and the recording I had was of an inspired performance by Yo-Yo Ma. But it was music that annoyed the hell out of Jake. That defiantly moody solo instrument "scratching away," he said, caused an itch inside of his head. He was gone, so I could wallow in Bach along with my other vices all I wanted.

I pondered a word I'd learned in music classes years ago: *rubato*. It's an instruction from composers regarding tempo, allowing musicians to play with freedom, faster or slower as needed to express changes in mood. I felt perhaps I could listen that way too, varying the tempo I heard according to my wildly swinging moods that day, from feeling ecstatic about being alone and drinking and listening, all the way down to despondent.

By day's end, everything around me smelled and tasted stale. I imagined my Bach-buddy Yo-Yo eager to defect, racing (although certainly not in a cheerful way) through the sixth and final suite, and when the music stopped, silence descended like mustard gas. But I couldn't get up to restart a CD. I couldn't even get up to pee until some indeterminate time later, when I toppled off the toilet and settled on my side like a big boozy comma, one cheek against ceramic tile that pressed a tic-tac-toe grid into my skin. That's where and how I fell asleep, but not before I saw with one eye as though fitted with its own magnifying lens that my bathroom floor was littered with hair, both female and male, straight and curly, dark and light. A floor that mapped the daily, hygienic journeys of a couple. Except now I was only half of one.

The next morning, the phone woke me up but I couldn't answer it until at least a hundred rings later. "What!" was the way I answered. I rubbed my cheek and aching shoulder.

It was the catalogue editor, Nicole. She had given up on reaching me by e-mail. How much copy had I written? When could she see it? I said I'd been sick, that I'd been in a car accident and that there'd been a death in my family. This absurd overload of excuses, combined with my shaky voice, must have given her serious doubts about me, but she wished me a speedy recovery and let me off the hook . . . for now.

Why had she been so damn nice? Now I truly couldn't let her down any longer. Hung over or not, I was left to stare at the pile of paper that I was supposed to transform into a witty, erudite . . . no, edgy catalogue—something actually mailed to thousands of sophisticated home-shoppers. The pile at hand included photos, brochures, sample copy from other catalogues, and my scrawled notes from the day I'd spent in the warehouse viewing the merchandise. Many items came unadorned with helpful explanation from their makers, but the buyers at the catalogue publishing company had offered descriptive tidbits from which I was supposed to spin copy.

Eighty-some items in all, to be described in approximately one hundred words each. It was actually an impressive collection, I had to admit. My enthusiasm for beautiful things, no matter how seemingly useless, should translate well into my writing, if I just gave in to it. Eventually, I would understand and be able to explain why every American home should have its very own Buddha or glass egg, right?

Wrong. I was woefully ill-equipped to describe *faux* antiques and clever whatnots and, more importantly, to place them in some artistic and/or historical context. I was out of my element and had figured this out, too late, during that endless day strolling through the merchandise with the catalogue's buyers and Nicole—a petite and savvy French woman with sleek dark boy-hair. Art and interior design were not my *forte*. During those endless hours looking at things and reviewing how they came to be so aesthetically pleasing, the allusions made by my companions kept leaving me behind, starting with the first two items: a blue and yellow ceramic hen and a wrought iron hook rack. Everyone agreed that these were so very typical of a kitchen in 18th Century Provence. I nodded like an idiot . . . *bien sûr*.

I immediately became a tourist, an Ugly American with a camera hanging around my neck, looking for a McDonalds. Language barriers sprung up right and left. I heard the word *glaze* and thought doughnuts not pottery, and then someone said *impasto* which likewise made me hungry, until I figured out I was hearing the word wrong and that it actually related to a painting technique. A reference to *Chippendale* made me grin foolishly at the mental image of naked men dancing. *Mon dieu.* I was hopeless. How could I not know (without looking it up) what Art Nouveau was, or not understand why I should hate something they described as *kitsch*? How could I become so dented and bruised by words, enchanting words at that? The problem was, I'd been dropped unprepared into the land of neo-this and post-that and all the various ism's, as well as words I thought I knew, like chasing, kinetic, relief, until I heard them in this new and baffling context . . . and I'm not sure I *cared* enough to make the effort to learn the language. I wanted simply to "write what I know."

By the end of this time in the warehouse, I was all bluff. With a nod and toss of my head, I packed up the papers and photos, appeared downright eager to begin writing, ready to play my role in this grand offering to our wealthy, knowledgeable, and kitsch-sensitive customers. We parted company after I had nodded again, most amiably, at the ridiculous deadline they'd imposed, five weeks from that day. *Mais oui. Absolument.* But I had a feeling that Nicole was onto me. Maybe I gave it away when she saw me scribble in my notes her reference to *Rococo* and she whispered to me that there was no *a* at the end of the word. Any association with hot chocolate was clearly another of my hunger-induced blunders.

At that point I was tempted to draw her aside and confess that my love for antiques and collectibles was *tres faux* indeed, and that I, on the sly, shopped at a place called The Furniture Barn. But I resisted such a burst of honesty because what I began to see in her face was a healthy slice of fear. She had, after all, been the one solely responsible for hiring me. Burdened with her own deadlines and formidable pressures from above (those who'd spent a small fortune ordering this merchandise in hopes it would all sell), Nicole would be the one taking my copy and doing whatever was necessary to make it exactly right, within days of *my* deadline. My facility with language had gotten us both into this quagmire. The sample writing I'd sent? Edgy, maybe. Informed? *Non.*

That had been a week before Jake's departure, and the catalogue job-pile remained untouched for several more days afterwards. My phone was ringing every few hours and I didn't answer. Nicole left increasingly urgent messages about needing to see whatever copy I had so she could make suggestions. When could I drop it off? Some of the items had been replaced; when could I come "visit" the new ones? Shit.

My car was in the shop; it had developed a nasty habit of stalling whenever it was asked merely to idle, and sometimes it wouldn't start at all (I tried not to identify too closely with it). Jake was making himself—and his car—unavailable in order to get me interested in him again. I was homebound and treading water in a bog of bills, doubt, guilt, shame, and, yes, stories. Following the girl on the bus with her period, I had one false start after another. I was less a writer than a deleter, but it was the only thing I was doing that felt somewhat right.

Whenever the phone rang, I knew it wouldn't be Jake calling, or any other welcome voice. It would be Nicole, my mechanic, or Jankow's lawyer who'd left a message about scheduling my deposition. I wanted to retrieve whatever had been good and solid in my old life. I wanted to stop lying. I wanted to disappear. I wanted to find a Rumpelstiltskin to spin my catalogue copy for me, magically, while I danced or slept. And I wanted Jake.

As though all of this wasn't enough, my house was invaded.

I was awakened, one morning, by a loud thump on the ceiling, right above my bed. Then another, and another. I scooted lower in my bed and covered my head with a blanket as I tried to identify the scribbling and scrabbling sounds from my attic. When all of this noise culminated in a kind of mewling, like a large cat was hurt and dying up there, I whipped off the covers and ran out of my bedroom, slamming the door behind me.

I didn't (couldn't) do the obvious—venture up there, into the attic. It wasn't the type of room that contains dusty old trunks filled with stored treasures from yesteryear or anything like that. My attic was just an empty crawl space between my ceiling and my roof. I started to dial Jake's phone number, but stopped. How predictably female of me, to call a boyfriend, insisting he's the man, let *him* poke his head up into a dark, inhabited space. Let *him* get attacked by vermin. No. I decided to call a professional instead.

The phone book offered several exterminators, but the one I chose emphasized that it was *humane*, implying that they didn't poison any critters or beat them over the head. That cry I'd heard up there had given me a surprising compassion for these animals, whatever they were.

"I've got some kind of beasts up in my attic and I think one of them is hurt," I told the guy who answered my call. "Maybe raccoons? Aren't they usually rabid?"

"Morning or night?" the guy asked.

"Excuse me?"

"What time of day did you hear the noise?" His calm, this-happens-every-day voice was reassuring.

"Just now," I replied. "Morning."

"So, the animals are diurnal."

"They're what? Is that what's ailing them?" In my panicked state, this word sounded ominously like it had to do with urine.

The guy laughed. "No. I mean they're not nocturnal. Describe the sounds."

When I did, in great detail and with what I recognized as a creative flair, the guy chuckled appreciatively. "Squirrels," he said.

"No way. They sound way too big to be squirrels." I tried to picture them—wasn't it the gray ones that were bigger, bolder?

"They're heavier than you'd expect, and incredibly frisky. The sounds they make seem pretty darn loud when separated by only a thin layer of ceiling."

The "thin layer" part destroyed the reassurance he'd been offering me.

"What about the crying?" I asked.

"Squirrels make that sound quite frequently. Even outside—haven't you ever heard them?"

"Never." I hadn't paid much attention to squirrels before. But now, with them in my house, I shuddered. They were rodents, after all. Nothing but big rats, except with better posture and fashion sense.

"They're nesting up there," the guy said. "Enjoying the warmth, storing food, anticipating the winter."

"Nesting? You mean they're having babies up there? Oh my God."

"Not yet they aren't. No. Here's what we do." Then he explained how he'd find the opening to my attic from the outside and set traps by it. As each squirrel (he called them "visitors") exited my house for food, the trap would catch it. He'd empty the traps daily, and soon there would be no more noise. Then he would seal up the hole in my house.

"What do you do with the squirrels?" I asked.

"We are humane in our treatment of all animals."

"I know. Your ad said that, but what does that mean? Do you take them somewhere nice and set them free. Maybe Florida for the winter? The squirrel version of Disneyland?"

In response, the guy only laughed again. He was very jolly, this exterminator. And an appreciative audience for my hysteria.

But he was also efficient. Several days (and a couple hundred dollars) later, my attic was empty again. I still brooded, however, about the possibility of babies up there, abandoned and slowly starving to death. It took a week of absolute silence above my bed before I could begin to forget about these uninvited guests. For days after the trap was set, I told anyone who might listen (at the grocery store, the coffee shop, the video store) that I had squirrels in my attic. I began to like the sound of that. It was so wonderfully, and horribly, metaphorical.

Release

Enough home décor, booze, and squirrels for now. No more convenient (albeit pesky) detours around my themes. One in particular.

When a child dies, the fallout is everywhere, both obvious and subtle, and keeps on spreading. In addition to my divorce, the casualties of my daughter's death ten years earlier included my female friendships—all of which had revolved around our husbands and kids. How could I continue to chitchat and laugh with women whose three-year-olds were somehow managing to turn four, then five, then go off to school, ballet classes, gymnastics, and soccer. How? I looked at the other children I'd known so well and could not avoid seeing the black hole next to them where my daughter should have been.

Other friendships later developed at work, but they were the weekday eight-to-five variety and never flourished. And when I quit my job, I stopped seeing those women too. My relationship with Mona had held promise, but it withered when Tracy died even though that should've given us *more* in common. And I hadn't quite connected yet with my other neighbor, Suzanne. She always seemed distracted and overwhelmed, plus her confession about slapping Cheryl, the day of Tracy's funeral, seemed to have sprouted some kind of hedge between us.

It appeared that not only had Jake been my best friend but my *only* friend. When my isolation grew more and more complete, I began to wonder if agoraphobia was next. I had never before had to force myself outside, especially on a bright sunny day. I had always been the kind of person who inhales fresh air deeply and tips my face upward to drink in the sun. But now I had to order myself out of the house. With Jake absent, it meant going out alone. No problem, I told myself. Writers are invariably loners, aren't they? Reminding myself to adopt as many writerly habits as possible, I took a notebook with me. And surrounded myself with a safe, cushioning distance from the rest of the planet. At least I *thought* it was safe.

I started walking without a destination in mind, but eventually found myself at Minnehaha Falls. I could hear the water roar long before I got to the overlook. It had been a rainy spring and summer, so the volume of water was impressive; more often by summer's end it was a trickle. At the center of this popular old park is a pavilion (where the bathroom floors are always damp), and picnic tables are scattered throughout the grounds. I avoided the inevitable playground, but wandered through rows of benches semi-circling the stage for summer concerts. Adding fiddles and voices to the water music, I could almost hear a familiar cadence—something love-glittered—even though I hadn't been to Minnehaha Falls in years. Not since . . . oh. How on earth had I arrived here so unaware? Was it my writer-mind attempting to be fearless? Because my husband and daughter and I used to come to this place all the time.

My heart tumbled like a trapped squirrel. Light-headed, I settled into a heap on the nearest bench and tried to regain control of the situation. A woman ambled by, pushing a stroller. I didn't look at the child. Tears blurred my vision. Another woman with stroller . . . and another. I was surrounded, or so it seemed. They were nearly identical, weird, aimed at me like mommy-missiles. If I couldn't get up and walk, much less run, how could I escape?

I felt my empty notebook in my pocket, pulled it out. Clicked my pen into action and wrote down three words without thinking: *Bluegrass* and *Pregnant* and *Nap*.

Closing my eyes, I saw us. My husband with our daughter on his shoulders, and me, starting to bulge at the tummy. It was Labor Day, the annual Bluegrass Festival at the park. A perfect late-summer day. It was . . . The only word that seemed to describe it was one I've never actually used—*bliss*. On a blanket some distance from the bandstand and the hot dog vendor, we all three took a cat nap together, even though the music and crowd were noisy, and there was always the contingent of wasps and ants. We shut everything else out. And slept. Blissfully.

But wait. No. Only I slept, and only for a minute. I heard the two of them talking, giggling, sharing intimate daddy-daughter jokes and rituals. I shook myself awake and tried to join in but felt rebuffed, as usual. I rubbed my belly, caressing the little one in there, promising *this* one would be all mine in the same way Teresa now seemed to be all *his*. And it was so unfair, because he hadn't really wanted her at first, especially since she was a girl.

He had run from her as a newborn, complained about how "boring" little babies are. "They don't *do* anything." How could he not see her beauty and complexity? How could he resist cuddling with her, nibbling on her perfect fingers and toes, telling her all the things there were to tell her? "Baby talk," he called it. "Spare me."

But when she turned two, oh how the familial landscape changed. Bulldozers couldn't have done more damage, and I kept falling into the sudden holes. Feeling left out at the park was nothing new; it had been going on for over a year by that time. But my anger starting building that Labor Day. If they were going to pull further and further away, so could I.

It was exactly one week after the Bluegrass Festival—September 13— a date I learned to habitually skip over much like some buildings that go from the twelfth to the fourteenth floors. My husband and I had a terrible fight. I accused him of stealing my daughter and shutting me out. He accused me of being a selfish, chronically unhappy bitch. "You wanted me involved," he said in his steeliest tone. "You begged me to love her. I do. What the fuck is your problem?"

"You can't have *this* one," I yelled at him, clutching my belly. My hormones were rioting, carrying little picket signs full of hate and defiance. Because that day I had felt hate for him. And, oh God help me . . . for *her*. The little traitor. She had been my sweet cuddly girl. Now she only let *him* give her baths, only wanted *him* to tuck her in. All the books we'd shared had been tossed aside. *Their* play was all about balls and roughhousing and climbing. She loved tromping through dirt and being upside-down, tossed around, somersaulting off beds, leaping from couches and chairs with squeals and thumps that made me run and hide. Could she survive this kind of play? I'd have to keep her safe. I'd have to make her mine again, at least for that one day.

I cut our fight short by grabbing her and putting her in the car. She and I, alone. We would do something girly. Go shopping, go to the bookstore like we used to. Or maybe see a Disney movie. I didn't know where we were going, I was just *going*. She fussed and wasn't properly strapped in. Neither was I. A car pulled into an intersection right in front of us, glass shattered, darkness grabbed all of us and wouldn't let go. Ever.

Somebody said something, touched my back. *Are you all right?* The words filtered through now. I was bent over on my lonely park bench where

I'd sought refuge from all the strollers, my tears streaming out to plop on the dusty ground next to old popcorn and trampled grass. I heard thunder—no it was water. The Falls. "Are you all right?" A passerby was worried about me. I nodded and gestured. He went on his way. My memory also went on its way, back where I'd stuck it years ago.

In my notebook, I wrote one more word. *No.*

On my way home, it started to sprinkle, and by the time I ran into my house, the downpour had begun. I shut all the windows and grabbed a beach towel to wrap around myself, head to hips. Something else was grasping at me, insisting on being remembered, examined, dealt with in some perversely maternal way. I told myself that nothing could be as bad as reliving the accident, and the pre-accident mishmash of love and hate and guilt and blame. And yet, there was something else, someone else... Wet and shivering, I sat in my sunroom and watched rain pummel the windows, tiny fists, *let me in.*

No .

And yet, I was aware that I would continue to stand vigil at those windows as much as possible. It was about "the work," where it started, where it would continue, and possibly even end. It was my glass asylum, offering both relative safety and confinement . . . all with a view.

The next day the sun returned. And so did my energy and courage. Images from the park were already evaporating, along with the moisture on the sidewalks. I flung all of my windows open again and breathed in the clean air. I was determined not to become a shut-in, one of those loony ladies that neighborhood children point at and talk about. A writer, though? An "artistic" type? Creativity was being crazy in a legitimate, even admirable way.

I tried to write all day, got beginnings, no middles, no ends. I messed with words, banished my old grammar lessons forever. I even pulled out a box of tiny magnetized words meant to help someone "write" poetry, threw them all onto my refrigerator and, as I munched on my Cheerios, I rearranged the magnet-words into phrases. Maybe they'd ignite something besides the grasping need for another, and yet another bowl of cereal, with a snowcap of sugar added to it for good measure. My stomach bulged, but my mind felt hollow.

That evening I went to a pizzeria. This, I told myself, was truly brave. Not just because eating alone can expose a person to the pity of couples and families at other tables. But also because this particular restaurant was special, with its black and white linoleum, red padded booths, and vintage jukebox. It was a place that lent itself to celebration. My ex-husband and I had discovered it years ago, *decades* ago, had gone often as a couple. And when Teresa was old enough to eat pizza, we'd brought her there.

Some days are made for such foolhardy courage. The sunshine, the concerted efforts to write, some deep breathing, all helped. As did the fact that I'd freaked out the day before, extra incentive to be okay now. I was armed with my notebook and my resolve, just brave enough for some very dangerous nostalgia.

The place was not yet mobbed as it would be later. I sat down, ordered a small Alfredo pizza with spinach and mushrooms, and forced myself to look around. A young couple sat in one booth, touching each other's fingers and talking earnestly. I could see the girl's face and the back of her boyfriend's tousled head. Her mouth and chin looked chafed, pleasantly roughed up by a man who could've shaved closer but didn't, and who couldn't stop kissing and kissing her. In another booth was an elderly couple, also engaged in easy conversation, while nearby was a couple who appeared to be slightly younger than I, grimly silent, staring in opposite directions.

The booth directly opposite the silent couple held half-a-dozen young girls, about ten or eleven, engaged in a giggly birthday party. The jukebox was playing Sinatra, of all things, and one of the girls—clearly the birthday girl and the couple's daughter—scurried over to her parents for more quarters. She did not seem disconcerted by the lack of current music; in fact she seemed delighted by Ol' Blue Eyes, as well as Peggy Lee, the Temptations, Jerry Lee Lewis, and the Beatles. Whenever one of the parents looked over at the girls, I could see a glowing smile. But then, back to each other, back to stone-faced waiting, nothing to say. Or maybe they were holding back a fierce argument—I couldn't quite tell. I was reminded of the day my ex and I acknowledged that our marriage had dissolved, also in this restaurant, but, of course, with no little girl's birthday nearby.

Before I could dig into my pizza, I began to write in my notebook. A story began, a female character/narrator who clearly was not me, and yet...

I admit my timing was bad. But is there a good time to end a marriage? The setting was unlikely too—a small neighborhood pizzeria. The place was filled with spice and music and promise. Plush red booths, candles on the table, and a vintage jukebox. A setting for celebration and romance, winter hunger and warmth. When my husband and I arrived that bleak November afternoon, we added a birthday party of giggly ten-year-old girls to the mix, but also an undercurrent of misery.

As chaperones for our daughter's party, we settled into our booth some distance from theirs, letting them order their own pizzas and giving them quarters for the jukebox. "Hungry?" Rick asked. I nodded. He had no idea. A hundred pizzas wouldn't have been able to fill the empty spaces in me. Earlier that day, I'd brought his shirts to the cleaners, sorted and grabbed each by the starched-collars-gone-limp, and the smell of them, of my husband, his cologne and body chemistry, made me gag. That can't be a good sign.

I put down my pen and chewed on an already cooled slice of pizza. Those two paragraphs felt like a strange kind of breakthrough. It reminded me of an ad I'd seen for invisible fences, how dogs could somehow be stopped from running free, but nobody could *see* the barrier surrounding the yard. I knew how the dog felt. Confinement can be such a subtle phenomenon. Like a bad marriage. It's the invisibility part that makes the confinement especially grim . . . and lonely. Writing about my failed marriage combined with this fictional marriage felt like that goddamned invisible fence had been dismantled at last. I could roam where I wished without the risk of punishment.

Writing the words "our daughter" for instance—that should have stopped me cold, but it pushed me on instead. And getting sickened by the smell of the husband's shirts—as true as anything I'd ever written or even tried to write about. It had happened just that way to me, but I hadn't really remembered it until the words tumbled onto the paper. What an awful thing to realize about someone you supposedly loved. I wondered almost casually what kinds of similar moments my ex-husband had endured about *me*. Was it the sound of my voice? The feel of my skin? What had it been that he'd once loved but gradually found revolting?

I finished my pizza, watched the birthday party progress and the parents struggling to enjoy it. Rereading the two paragraphs I'd written, I crossed out the first two sentences, and relocated the husband's single-word question to the top. "Hungry?" That was where the story should begin. Then, right after that, I could establish the setting.

But I was already stuck. I knew I needed somehow to convey the conflict between this husband and wife, but what should they argue about, or *avoid* arguing about? In my case, Teresa's death had colored everything, and I wanted my fictional couple to have that child with her friends, reaching the magical double-digit age. I wanted their conflict to be much more ordinary, about something trivial, because that's the kind of thing that can sneak up on a couple. Like with Jake and me. Maybe that's what was stopping me, the worry that Jake would read this story and see himself in it, see the woman's bitterness and emptiness as mine.

Before I could push it away, an image caught me in its grip: the couple dancing at the Riverside, Jake and I watching them, my tears ruining our evening together. Could I find a way to write about that in this story? Would it be . . . well, *okay* to do that?

I paid for my meal and then stood by the jukebox for a minute, writing down some of the titles. Music needed to play an important role in my pizzeria story. As though to confirm this notion, on the wall by the door was a big musical staff, with a treble clef sign and several eighth notes dancing along it, a black metal sculpture playing me out the door, into the night and ultimately into my created world. There would be more comfort there, I decided, than danger.

The pizzeria story may have been an important start for me, but it also became a quandary; I found myself trying several husband-wife arguments on for size and deleting them all. I eventually wrote about an older couple putting quarters in the jukebox and sneaking a loving, painful-to-watch slow dance, right there in front of the unhappy younger wife's eyes. But the parts in between eluded me. Just when I seemed ready to savor the kind of freedom and joy writing might be able to give me, Mona came back into view for the first time since the funeral, and up went the invisible fence again, that stubborn barrier between the old repressed me and the new creative me.

It was about two weeks after Jake's post-Riverside departure. I was alone in my sunroom, sorting through pieces of mail shuffled together with some of the random paragraphs I'd written and printed up optimistically. And there she was. It was Mona all right, but different. She was tending some terminal-looking shrubs in front of her house. More than neglect and drought were in play here. Their whole house seemed altered, painted by death, stuck in a bad horror movie. Was it my warped imagination, or had a family of huge, scavenging crows taken over that narrow airspace across the street, forcing all the songbirds and other sweet things to vacate?

As I backed away from the windows, aware of hiding from her view in the deep shadows of my house, I counted all the ways Mona looked altered. Her white-blonde hair had been chopped off to about an inch, the same sprouting length all over her head, as though growing out from chemotherapy. The startling thing was that it looked good on her, more stylish and tended somehow than her old long stringy locks. She appeared very withdrawn, however, and empty-handed. No child, of course. No camera. But her hands weren't fidgety. She didn't touch her shorn hair, she didn't sneeze or rub her eyes and nose as I'd seen her do so often. Medication, I decided. She appeared to be on something that dried her up and made her logy. I waited for her to glance over to my house, but she didn't.

The most dramatic difference was with her body. I emitted a small gasp when I realized—she was clearly pregnant. Close to six months, I guessed. Which meant that she had been about four months along at Tracy's funeral. Four months pregnant when we'd laughed together at my garage sale. It was unfair, I knew, but I was furious at her for not telling me. When so much gossip and so many stray thoughts and revelations leaked from her constantly, how is it that she didn't give me this, the juiciest of tidbits? Maybe she hadn't known or taken a test yet, but it seemed more likely that she simply didn't want to tell *me*. Why? And then I remembered something she'd said—that Jim hadn't made love to her in a long time. "Months and months," was the way she'd put it. Either she'd been exaggerating, or had forgotten one encounter . . . or the baby was someone else's.

I automatically calculated backwards (although I couldn't be sure how pregnant she really was—she had one of those lithe bodies that barely show until the last few weeks, when they suddenly burst forth like a Rodgers and Hammerstein song). But *if* September was her sixth month, she'd conceived some time in March, which was unsettling news for me. March had been a bad one, another brief but cantankerous break-up with Jake. We'd fought while trying to plan a trip, couldn't agree on a destination, and then I'd unwisely suggested that we could take separate vacations. Had he sought comfort, even love, elsewhere? Across my own street, in fact? Is that why they had *pretended* to have never met at the funeral? Well, Jake really wanted a baby. Maybe now . . . .

No way. I was losing my mind. Jake wouldn't do that to me. I didn't think Mona would either. The baby was Jim's. But where the hell was he? From what I observed that day and the next few after Mona had returned, something told me that Jim was gone for good. It was like I could see his ravaged closet, the hangers yanked empty, bent and scattered, the shaving gear and toothbrush confiscated. I itched to go out there, to talk to her, but I didn't trust myself. Too many inappropriate questions. Too much shit between us now. Like what was up with this unrevealed pregnancy? And where was she, where was *I*, where was God herself, when Tracy wandered out of that house one hot July morning?

Mr. Jankow's lawyer had finally gotten me into his office for a deposition, and it turned out to be anti-climactic. All that dread and those unanswered messages and images of me in prison garb . . . all for nothing. I had been looking the other way, to the south, downward, inward, whatever, but I hadn't really seen the accident. Only the aftermath. I was sure, I added, that Mr. Jankow had not been speeding or weaving around— *that* I would've noticed. The lawyer seemed satisfied, although he peered at me as if he knew I was hiding something. I banished thoughts (in case he could read them) of that stray cat, of Tracy's following it calling *kitty kitty*, of my monumental and fatal lack of foresight about where the cat, and consequently the child, might be headed. By that time, I was even more uncertain about what was real and what I imagined. The cat might have prowled only in a dream, one that had awakened me and sent me down to the sunroom. Or it could've been a trick of light and shadow, with the *kitty kitty* in some other child's voice, some other time.

Details

Early October. It was still in the sixties and seventies most days now but cool at night, sinking steadily toward the freezing point, hinting of the winter air waiting in the wings. To accommodate my daily vigil, my writing, and my flower-like need of sunlight, I'd moved my desk and computer into the sunroom, ignoring the prospect of future cold drafts (another interesting word—how did it end up meaning both a gust of wind and something written roughly, unfinished?). My computer waited for me each morning as I drank up my view of the sky and the gradual stirrings of neighbors along with my coffee. Thus I was led toward that day's output of words.

On a promising Monday morning, I watched as Suzanne came out of her house in shorts and faded plaid, sleeveless blouse. I recalled the jacket incident with her daughter I'd witnessed, her tearful anger, and what Mona had told me about Suzanne's grief, the married boyfriend who had died. As I watched, she sat down on a front step, curled her arms around her knees and tilted her face upward with what could have been a grimace, but I decided was a squinty smile. She appeared to be basking in her own private sunbeam and I knew exactly how that felt. I wanted to join her and strike up a conversation, but what good would that do? Did I want to be drawn further into her life and maybe even start sharing responsibilities, including that scowling, bald, anti-semitic daughter of hers? Besides, I was working. I was pretending to have punched a time clock.

Most of the time (when I wasn't trying to avoid writing catalogue copy), my eyes traveled only so far—computer screen to window, back and forth, my gaze always longer by far on the words and the pulsating cursor. But my window-glances were as necessary as punctuation. Suzanne was in my line of vision now, but soon she wouldn't be. Someone else would take her place. Perhaps the woman (either an older mother or a youngish grandma) with the double stroller—a toddler and a baby each in her own compartment, always accompanied by their strange, spunky three-legged dog. They walked by my house nearly every day. Or maybe I'd see the two girls who had, mid-summer, set up a Kool-Aid stand a few houses down from me, yelling for hours, in unison and with amazing stamina, "ICE COLD KOOL-AID! TWENTY-FIVE CENTS!" On and on they yelled until my only recourse was to go down there, finally, and buy from them. When I paid a whole dollar for a Dixie cup of warm undrinkable liquid and told them to keep the change, they didn't even bother to thank me.

I automatically watched for these girls to reappear as the summer progressed. One of them was deeply tanned and had black wavy hair trailing all the way down her slender back. The other one . . . well, I couldn't remember her, so I molded her into a larger, older and wiser version of Tracy. Silken eyelashes, bristly ponytail, defiant pout and fists, sandled feet, singsong voice . . . so many details to notice and later describe. So many colors.

I became acutely aware, however, that the color red (except for the auburn of Suzanne's hair) stayed on the periphery. This may have been the case all my life, but it had never been as clear as it was now. I didn't wear red and rarely ate it (avoiding cherries, eating only Granny Smith apples). I've never gravitated toward it the way some people do, as though red represents boldness. To me, it has always represented . . . what? Something as obvious as blood? Not likely, but finding no clear alternative I made a note to explore later. *Scribble Scribble.* Even on the computer, that's what I seemed to be doing. Scrib-bull.

It occurred to me that October morning how Monday meant that most everyone else in the world was beginning their week fresh. They didn't have choices to make, as I did, about what chores they should tackle. They simply had a job to do and did it, then came home to loved ones, watched TV, went to bed, and woke up to a Tuesday. And Wednesday, on and on. I had stepped off that particular overcrowded bus, happily, with a superior flourish, until I'd realized that the Grand Canyon gaped beneath the exit.

Okay, I told myself. Be a writer. Being a starter and a deleter is fine, too, but finish something, make something stick. Stories kept coming and going, great fun while I felt the rush of words, descent into hopelessness as I disposed of them. In addition to the stalled pizzeria story, I'd tried a children's tale—that must be easier, right? But I found myself writing about a black dog of unrecognizable mixed breed named Rufus who saved its little girl-owner's life by running in front of a car at just the right moment. Did the poor mutt die for his efforts? Would the little girl have cornsilk hair and be running after a kitty? Time to delete. These were all exercises, really, like scales for a pianist, *pliés* for a ballet dancer. My real work would come— if I survived, that is.

My safety seemed in question because working in this way sometimes interfered when I was trying to complete a simple errand in the outside world. My driving seemed increasingly impaired, for example. I was distracted, dazed, almost tunnel-visioned much of the time, and I'd punished my ailing car a few times with dents and scrapes—all entirely my fault. But I was truly alarmed one day when I nearly walked across the street in front of a racing, screaming ambulance. It registered not as reality but only as something from the recent past (Tracy's ambulance) or possibly from the story I was working on at the time.

I was saved by a stranger who grabbed my arm and yanked me back to the corner. I thanked him without truly acknowledging to myself that I'd had a close call. *Be careful*, the stranger had told me as he hurried away. But I stepped blithely off the curb without looking again, wishing I could sit down somewhere and talk to my rescuer, ask him for *his* story, turn him into a romantic interest or a hero. I needed to write something romantic or heroic, didn't I? Otherwise, what was the point?

Meanwhile, I kept forcing myself to get to the only paying work I had at the moment. The catalogue. I'd been given a temporary reprieve since they had decided to delay publication until January. I had the feeling the company was in serious trouble; Nicole had mentioned regretting that holiday shoppers would have to rely on the Fall issue instead of getting the usual December catalogue. The holiday season, she said, had always been such a boon (she'd pronounced it *bon*, which I imagined at first to be *bone* as in something that was being thrown to me). Even with the extra time, however, I was still floundering.

Nothing much happened until that particularly promising Monday morning. That's when I stared at the photo of a tea set, each piece cutely designed to look like a flying saucer, all sleek and shiny and about to pour out a stream of tiny aliens along with the tea. Telling myself this would be just another kind of rush, finally I wrote:

Close Encounters of the Oolong kind. Whether you wish to steep yourself in science fiction or borrow a simple Asian serenity, this tea set will serve you well. All pieces are made of stainless steel and brass, formed and polished by hand. The tray is roomy enough for any kind of landing or lift-off.

Okay. Not bad. I added the dimensions, price and other particulars supplied by the manufacturer. One down. Still eighty-some to go.

I checked out my window. Suzanne was gone, and no sign of Mona. Nobody stirring now. A clean slate of a street, and I wished it could somehow stay that way, at least until I got a chunk of catalogue done.

I stared at the next item in my work pile. Oh goodie. A big leather chair and ottoman. Brown, fat. Nondescript. What "edgy" thing could I say about such furniture that would inspire people to spend almost two thousand dollars? I scanned my notes and the manufacturer's detailed information and, after several meandering minutes, finally wrote:

Don't let the husky masculinity of this chair fool you—it is strictly EOE (Equal Opportunity Ecstasy). Soft as a sigh and becoming softer with age (don't we all?), this chocolate brown chair and ottoman are completely upholstered in full top grain, pure aniline leather. Slight scars and imperfections add to the chair's character (and our own) as well as the ease of living with it, worry-free.

Too many parentheses—they looked on the page like the laugh-lines on either side of my mouth that I pretended to cherish (hey, she's old but at least she's done her share of laughing). After reading the thing over and over, I decided my paragraph was just cheeky enough, and I felt on a roll. Until I glanced at the next item, which was a small bedside table, about as inspiring as a TV tray. Four long knobby legs, horizontal top barely big enough for a clock radio, collects dust beautifully, topples over when you sneeze in its direction . . . . Shit.

I decided to tackle instead a strange little item called a Tussie-Mussie. Staring at the picture of a small, cone-shaped silver vase nestled in a stand of twisting vines also made of silver, I wondered about its name. No clue emerged from the info provided, and I had been too embarrassed to ask the buyer what it was other than a vase. That had probably been another dead give-away to Nicole—very, very few people would know the term Tussie-Mussie. It would've been fine to ask. Not asking and probing for specifics revealed my incompetence.

I almost proceeded to the next item, but that was when Jake dropped in to get one of his CDs that he had to have (a flimsy excuse I graciously accepted). It was as if he'd heard me summon help. He smiled when he saw me hard at work on the catalogue, and heartily approved the copy I'd written so far (of which I implied these two were only a small sample). Then he kissed me brusquely and seemed about to leave.

I nearly grabbed hold of him, but instead I blurted out, "I had squirrels in my attic."

Jake gave me a bemused look. "I believe the expression is bats in your belfry."

"No. I mean it. Actual squirrels in the space above my bedroom. I had to call an exterminator. They took the damn things to Squirrel Disneyland." When Jake didn't respond to this, I added, "Oh, and Mona's back. She's pregnant."

His eyes widened and he glanced out the window, then at me. This news clearly took him by surprise, and he looked so innocent, I was flooded with relief. If Mona was pregnant with his baby, I'd be able to read it in his face.

"Have you seen Jim too?" he asked.

"Nope. I think he's MIA. Or would that be AWOL? Anyway, it's probably not his baby anyway, so . . . ."

Jake crouched down to level his sad blue gaze at me. "Maddie, I hope that having a vivid imagination doesn't necessarily mean being so unkind."

His comment was a pointed finger jabbing my solar plexus, and I wrapped my arms tightly around my middle.

Then in the awkward silence between us he began to stare at me. I felt his gaze scanning upward and downward, taking in the fact that I'd put on a few pounds. More than a few. His eyes asked the question he was afraid to give voice to.

"No, Jake. I'm not pregnant too. I've just been eating and drinking too much. Sorry."

He stood up and, again, seemed about to leave, first asking, "Have you talked to her yet?"

"Mona? No." I wanted to add, *Have you?* But instead I veered off this path onto one less thorny. "Do you have any idea what a Tussie-Mussie is?"

"Afraid not."

"I should've just asked Nicole," I admitted to him. "But by that time I was so intimidated by those people."

"Well," Jake said, leaning over me in a protective yet pouncy way, "We'll just Google it. Give me the exact spelling."

Within a few minutes, we had our answer. The Tussie-Mussie originated during the Victorian age when affluent young ladies were known to carry around small bouquets of flowers to make their walks around town more aromatic but didn't want to dirty their gloves. Then, upon arriving home, they could simply slip the small vase of flowers into a holder for display, or to await their next lady-like stroll.

With Jake chugging a Coke nearby, I wrote with my whole demeanor altered—more refined and Old World. "The embrace of silvery rose vines here is intended to take over for the elegant hands of a pampered, unsoiled woman," I began, and after deleting *unsoiled* and succinctly defining the term, kept writing furiously about capturing the romance of a bygone era for weddings, proms, or just to dazzle a loved one. Such serious effort on my part deserved a little recreation. I grinned at Jake, who was looking incredibly sexy at the moment, and added to the copy that, when used for a bridal bouquet, after the flowers had wilted and after the honeymoon— the unfettered conjugality—even in those mustn't-mussy times, the groom could add epsom salts to the thing and soak his . . . hmmmm, fetter.

Of course, I deleted this last part, but not before Jake read it. We laughed together (something we hadn't done for a while). And I couldn't ignore the arousal wafting into the room, entwining us like that silver vine I'd just written about, only softer, warmer.

Jake ended up staying the rest of that day, that night. And the next days—he took some long overdue vacation, for *me*. He was back, and I was glad. I was hard at work, and *he* was glad. We were Harry and Sally long after they'd met, when they finally passed through all the fussing and resistance and misunderstandings and emerged into an admission of their love, settled in to the notion that they belong together, for better or worse.

But I knew it was temporary. It always was. In fact, whenever I saw the movie *When Harry Met Sally* my laughter was marbled with stubborn streaks of melancholy, especially at the end, with its implication—no, its certainty—that Billy Crystal and Meg Ryan were destined to be another one of those old couples interviewed in the movie for their love stories, sitting side by side forever. I didn't believe in that particular fairy tale any more than I believed Harry could be that consistently funny or Sally that adorable, day after day. I figured that, with the onslaught of age, his jokes and funny voices would become stale, he'd shrink even shorter, and develop high blood pressure for which he'd have to take drugs that left him impotent, while she was socked with hormones from hell, chin whiskers, osteoporosis, and an expired sense of humor.

Worst of all, maybe they ran out of things to talk about, passions to share, common ground. One of them would want to go kayaking and mountain climbing while the other started knitting afghans and collecting ancient uncuddled Beanie Babies. If they had children . . . ? Well, I didn't want to go there. But what about sex—wasn't that always a casualty of marriage? The heat has a nasty habit of cooling, especially if verbal communication has scampered away, taking true intimacy with it. Maybe Harry and Sally each secretly harbored fantasies they were too ashamed to share with the other. Foot fetish? Whipped cream? Costumes? Threesomes? S&M? Their intimacy would end up tainted by creeping conventionality.

To combat this, I imagined the opposite—that Harry and Sally had, in fact, become quite the out-there kinky lovers, even opening gifts of leather outfits and whips for their silver anniversary. A story stirred inside me, but I knew it was not something I could write without research. "Let's go on a field trip," I told Jake a few days after he'd returned. And he didn't look at all surprised when I added, "to a sex store." We both knew where the nearest one was and didn't ask each other *how* we knew.

Hanging out in the black leather section, I was delighted by the variety of shoppers there—my favorite being the woman who had to be at least sixty and who, honest to God, gave Jake's rump a playful swat before departing. We stayed undercover by groping each other shamelessly as we

74

pretended to debate which dildo, wrist/ankle cuffs, edible thongs, or vibrating eggs suited us best (in my mind I wrote catalogue copy for *these* tasty items). But I ended up buying only a raunchy sex trivia game called "Lewd and Clear." I planned to study the cards for language, then send the game anonymously to my former boss, for her birthday.

The man who rung up my purchase had both arms and a neck vividly crawling with tattoos and a large silver stud pierced into the tip of his tongue that gave him an extremely pronounced lisp. "That'll be twenty-thixth theventy-five, pleathe," he said. I paid without comment or exchanging glances with Jake for fear of getting the giggles.

We were quiet on the way home, until Jake started darting the tip of his tongue at me, then said, "Leth go to your plathe and have thome hot thexth, whaddya thay?" And when we got home, we made out like teenagers. Then, we got out a box of watercolors and covered each other with tickly curlicues and smile-faces (neither of us gifted tattoo artists) which we'd planned to let dry but ended up smearing liberally into skin, mouths, and sheets.

In an adjacent room, the phone rang intermittently. We both pretended not to notice, and neither of us answered it. After our lovemaking, Jake managed not to talk about anything important, and I managed not to pull away and run to the computer or my windows. The next few days blurred together, resisting time-imposed boundaries, and the clocks covered their faces. Early morning stretched lazily into afternoon which eased itself into evening and finally night, but we noticed only the play of light and shadow on each other's skin and the varying energy in our voices.

Meals were irregular as well. We might have spaghetti for breakfast and Cheerios for supper. We could make a single orange last several juicy minutes, each segment suspended between our mouths and slowly mashed into the cool pulp flavoring our kisses. Once again, after all the distance and bitterness of recent months, we began to taste alike.

6:15 a.m. Saturday, still the week of Jake's return. Days getting startlingly shorter. I pushed aside thoughts of the catalogue deadline, mentally paid off all my new debts, ignored the sounds of my sweetheart/best friend/nemesis upstairs. And I let myself bask in the freedom I had that allowed me to keep the writing going all day if I wanted, to write anything I wanted to, even sex. I let my mind roam all over town like a stray dog looking for scraps, eating whatever didn't move, and depositing little piles of prose all over for people to step in.

No, that was not the way I wished to think of my work. I wanted to feel touched in strange new ways by my characters. I wanted to feel stirred. Strummed. I'd seen my piano-tuning neighbor carry in an armload of violins one day from his car, and then go back to retrieve a cello. Apparently he fixed all kinds of stringed instruments, not just pianos. He was kind of interesting, this neighbor, and I'd ventured over to his back door that day.

"Hi," I'd said with a bright, hopefully musical and in-tune smile. "I live just two houses down and I have an old piano that badly needs tuning." He seemed to have trouble focusing on my words, so naturally I rattled off another string of them. "My house—it belonged to my parents . . . I was born in that house, actually. And the piano used to be my mother's. I haven't played in years, but I'm getting this urge now . . . ."

"My schedule is a little tight at the moment," he finally answered, his voice a rather flat-sounding baritone.

"Okay. There's no hurry." I expected him to grab a calendar and "pencil me in" somewhere, but he seemed to be willing to lose me as a customer without regret. Frankly, he seemed not to like me, and I wondered if there was something—food, dried saliva, or worse—stuck to my face. With a shrug, I'd turned away, but he said he'd be "in touch."

With my computer now, I wiped clean the indifferent, even hostile look of this man. I replayed our encounter, this time with pleasantries, flirtation, innuendo. And music, which always did things to both my mind and body. Maybe that's where I should go to feel stirred, strummed— straight to the music. Accompanied by Yo-Yo Ma again, I became a cellist in my mind. No, the cello itself, luxuriating between my neighbor's knees.

The story began when the voices began. My own voice grew younger, more innocent, while the piano tuner aged as magnificently as Sean Connery. From the beginning, the guy's voice inexplicably adopted a Russian accent. He sprouted a beard and opened a shop that I could simply enter, holding an ailing, dusty guitar that had belonged to my dead grandfather. I listened to the man playing something for a minute before he saw me. I began, tried not to censor myself. The mere act of writing was enough for now. Composing. A perfection not possible with reality. My fingertips made their muted little clacking sounds with an urgency I'd never before experienced. Or if I had, I'd forgotten. Maybe I'd felt it playing the piano years ago. Or on the playground that was Jake's body. Or tickling my daughter. No, no, back to the music. Safer there.

I waited in his shop until the proprietor emerged from the back room. My first glimpse of his hands reminded me of a drawing on an old piano book—an artist's rendering of Chopin's hands. I nodded at Misha and handed over my grandfather's battered guitar. He examined it with polite respect, then held it against his body, his long sensitive fingers roaming across musty wood, frets, and strings. He nodded to me, put the guitar on a shelf and then seemed to be indicating I could go now. But I didn't. Instead, I watched him restring and tune a cello, then sit down to play. Bach. I closed my eyes and listened, and it wasn't long before I felt myself *become* that female-shaped instrument leaning expectantly between his thighs. The bow in his hand stroked rhythmically across *my* belly and produced the low, resonant notes from hollow places inside *me*. And a flutter began in my abdomen that spread lower and deeper with an urgency I'd almost forgotten I could feel.

Was *that* the urgency I'd been feeling when I sat down to write? No, but it's related.

I paused in my typing and lip-chewing to look away from my computer screen, out my window, and there he was in the flesh, so to speak. The real-life inspiration for Misha. His name, unfortunately, was Biff. He'd ventured out in baggy shorts and pajama top to get the newspaper that the delivery person had left at the curb instead of on his steps. He looked up and then toward my house, caught me staring. Or at least I *thought* he could see me in my window, at my desk. I waved like a beauty queen on a float.

He appeared to want to wave back but tucked the newspaper into his armpit instead and trudged back up his sidewalk.

I tried to force myself out of that musty music shop and back to the catalogue. But Jake started singing upstairs. "If I were a rich man, yaba diba diba diba diba diba diba dum . . . " My own private Fiddler on the Roof, way better company than the squirrels had been. And a boyfriend who, although periodically running off, always came back, smiling and joking and singing, knowing I'd want him again. Which I invariably did. I let myself be enfolded because it felt so good. Until it didn't.

Maybe it was my effort to resist Jake that sent me into thinking and writing more erotically about other men. But I could have simply pulled a man whole and desirable out of my imagination. How had I settled instead on Biff the piano tuner? Just because of the musical element? Or because he was conveniently two houses away?

Not much potential for an affair, really. So I tried to be good and *write* an affair instead. Making Misha struggle with English and throwing that thick beard on his face helped me along. But Jake was still hovering, and he might want to see if I was writing about *him*. Could a writer be considered unfaithful just for creating a sexual adventure with someone else? Was Jake my muse or was he forcing me to find another one to take his place because, as muses go, he wasn't enough?

I considered writing a scene that Jake would love to read. About dancing, of course. *Let's face the muse . . . and dance.* But then I remembered our disastrous night at the Riverside that almost ended us for good, and the scene got stalled in the second paragraph, as though the music had abruptly been interrupted by a power failure the minute he took me in his arms. Talk about dancing in the dark . . . and in oppressive silence.

My next attempt involved meatloaf. There were times, several years ago, when Jake and I would get wildly passionate in the kitchen, of all places, and I considered writing such a scene. When I tried writing one as a memory (the time I was making meatloaf), it turned out stale as the bread crumbs I'd used. I decided to try it from Jake's viewpoint instead. Any good writer should be able to take a scene and switch it around, write it from the opposite point-of-view. Maybe good ol' Jake could clarify some things about *both* of us.

I didn't just try to walk in Jake's shoes or read his mind. I tried to crawl inside his skin, a layer I thought I'd penetrated before but hadn't, not really. I imagined testosterone flowing in minuscule channels throughout my body, felt myself sprout calluses and body hair, and finally the interesting weighty bundle between my legs. My ovaries shriveled and dried into raisins, my tearducts got blocked, and I had a sudden urge to watch a football game from beginning to end. Then I looked at *me* through his man-eyes and noticed that my nipples were poking into the tanktop I was wearing in a most alluring way. The words fell into place.

It was shortly after we'd started sleeping together, and Madelyn was teaching herself to cook. I came over one evening to find her not just making meatloaf—experiencing it.

"Jake, come here. Quick. Feel this."

"What?"

"This." In a large glass bowl in front of her, I saw the glob of hamburger, breadcrumbs, chopped onion, spices, milk and raw egg. Her hands were coated with the stuff. She was flushed and the strands of her hair that had escaped her ponytail were moist, sticking to her cheeks and neck. She had no makeup on and she smelled of onion, but I kissed her on the mouth. I was salivating already and not over ground round.

She hardly noticed. "Put your hands in here," she instructed. "I'll get another egg. You gotta do an egg."

Once I'd plunged my hands into the cold slimy mixture, she added the egg, its yolk and whites sliding under my fingers, escaping my grip. Then she was in there along with me, breaking the yolk and marbling it with white against my knuckles. For a long time we squished the softening, warming meat mixture between our fingers and clasped it between our hands. "What is the word for that sensation?" she asked.

"Primal?" I managed to say even though my throat felt tight. "Primordial?" My groin was swelling against the table.

"No, something else. Like how your fingers could slide right through my skin and up my arm and into my chest and down into the deepest part of me and curl up there."

"Maybe there is no word for that," I said, and without washing our hands, we made love on the kitchen floor. It occurred to me, but only briefly, that what covered our busy, groping fingers—especially the raw meat and spices—should not be going inside Maddie the way it was. What must it feel like, I wondered (not for the first time), to be entered and plunged into that way? Even if there were adequate words for such sensations, I would never be able to understand.

Afterwards, I caught my breath and rested on the floor, only gradually becoming aware that I was naked against cold grimy tile. But Maddie was up and cooking again, energized by sex (another baffling difference between us). Her still-restless fingers divided our meat mixture into two parts—one small, one large—on a cookie sheet. She sculpted detailed, life-size models of male and female genitalia, almost unrecognizable once the meatloaf had baked, but we had never enjoyed food more. Even after Madelyn had added a glop of catsup to the meat-vagina and proclaimed it "that time of the month."

This scene was making me sad. It brought happier times back to me but the effect was to make me feel *past* something important, like our relationship would never be that passionate again. So I deleted it before Jake could see it. It might make him sad too.

As I wrote, deleted and gazed out the window, I sensed Jake's movement throughout my house . . . and heart. Maybe we should give the Riverside Café another try, or at least I should try to *write* it (minus the in-love older couple, or making *us* that couple). Dancing was so erotic but in a much more subtle and dignified way than raw-hamburger sex. Why didn't he come out to the sunroom now so I could say "Let's dance tonight?" Maybe later. Meanwhile . . . back to work.

Because it was the only thing I seemed to be able to sustain interest in, and not delete as though it never existed, I returned to Misha's shop. My female character quickly acquired an insider's view, habitually coming to watch him at work.

One day I was watching from across the room as he fixed a harpsichord and something began to happen. How can I explain it? A harpsichord has always looked to me like an underfed, spindly-legged piano, so maybe I was affected by the contrast of his strong, bulky form bent over the delicate workings inside that instrument. I stared at him and imagined my hand exploring his bent shoulders and spine, journeying south . . . then blushed when he looked up at me but, of course, he misunderstood.

"Is interesting, yes," he said. "Come watch." When I got to his side at the harpsichord, he showed me a small mechanical part from inside, one of the pieces that moves up and down to pluck strings when the keys are pressed. "This . . . " he said, pointing to the tiny plectrum in the center of the piece, " . . . must be strong, sharp. Like so . . . ." He took one of my hands and ran the pointed baby-tooth-like plectrum across my palm, sending a wave of shivers up my arm. "This one," he demonstrated with a piece he'd just removed, "not good. Broken. Cannot pluck now."

I suppose I was giddy from the close contact with his hands, the way they were opening and tickling mine, and that's why his words made me giggle. *Cannot pluck now.* With someone else, I might have said, "Well then, can we pluck later?" But there was simply no way to joke in this way with Misha.

He gazed at me, apparently enjoying my unexpected mirth. "Very very pretty girl," he said. "Should not be here . . . all tied up with ugly old man."

This time I managed *not* to giggle even though the image of being tied up with him, or *by* him, was irresistible. "I'm honored to be here with you, and you're not ugly or old."

We puttered some more together, bent over the harpsichord, and I suppose I can blame what happened next on the fact that I was wearing a low-cut blouse. Because, the next thing I knew, I was guiding his hand my way, to draw the next shivery plectrum-line between my breasts, up and down. And . . . .

Of course, this is when Jake chose to join me, to *sneak* up behind me. Shit. I wished now that I were back with the meatloaf scene instead. He'd see *us*, recognize the deliciously slimy, grimy copulation as ours. But Jake didn't know a harpsichord from a harmonica. I clicked to close the window on my screen so he couldn't read what I'd just written about Misha-Biff. *Save changes to document? Yes.*

Jake's chin settled sharply on top of my head. His hands rested heavy as expectations on my shoulders. My hair was dirty but he didn't seem to mind. "How's it going?" he asked.

"Fine," I answered compliantly.

Jake smelled wonderful. I didn't. Why did he like me at all? I wondered. He deserved someone who had already bathed and washed her hair, who had made enough coffee for two, and who was not thinking about being strummed by someone else's hairy fingers. He deserved the woman I used to be.

I lifted one of his hands from my shoulder so I could kiss the palm and then cup it around my left breast. "I'm going to take a shower and brush my teeth," I told him meaningfully, still comfortable now and then with this way of getting the old me back for a pleasant visit.

He understood my meaning, although new-me/old-me, he seemed to care about both equally. After he kissed me sweetly and strummed (yes, *there* was that sensation I'd been writing about) my nipples lightly, we climbed the stairs, and I could see the little ovation already beginning in his shorts.

An hour later, I was back at the window. I could feel that wonderful throbbing between my legs, the resonance. I'd just put on an oversized T-shirt of Jake's, but now I took it off again, felt sunlight drape across my bare skin. Words stretched lazily into phrases and then into sentences, curling around themselves like a sleek cat, sleepy but ready for anything. The sound of strings being plucked resumed inside my head. And that brought me back to my story. I leapt ahead, positioned my character deeper inside the shop, disrobing, hiding . . . .

In the corner, presiding over the party of instruments was an ancient harp with all but its lowest octave of strings missing. When Misha left to greet a customer out front I did the unthinkable. Undressed. Approaching the harp in the corner, I felt the spread of goosebumps. The harp was taller than I, and sturdier. It looked sadly incomplete but the remaining strings felt taut and fat against my fingers when I tested them. I slid in behind the harp and didn't have long to wait. Misha returned but I was afraid he'd leave again without seeing me, so I plucked two of the strings in front of me and let them vibrate with a deep and surprising resonance that ended only when my left breast got in the way.

He was startled by the sound, but far more shocked by the sight of me, naked, in the corner behind the harp. I heard him gasp and utter something in Russian. Flustered, I plucked the same two strings, but then gained some resolve and swept my fingers vigorously across the whole octave. When I leaned in with my body to dampen the sound again, I felt the wiry tension as my own. In the hazy orange light I saw him approach. His face was

unreadable, but his hands were already in motion
before they got to me. His fingertips reached for
the small, soft ridges my skin formed between the
harp strings and stroked across them, then along
their length from my collarbone all the way down to
my belly, then below.

Jake started banging around in the kitchen. The pots and pans
sounded angry, as though he'd managed to read telepathically what I'd just
written . . . not more than ten minutes after having made love to *him*. This
was not a healthy activity, writing. It was not something a *nice* person
engaged in. But instead of repenting, I saved the file and closed the window
again on my creation. Since my Misha story was too inhibited by Jake's
presence, it would have to wait until he ran off again, or at least was leaving
me alone.

Hunger

Jake finished his kitchen clamor, declared my cupboards nearly bare, and went out for groceries. I nodded a combination thanks and goodbye and returned my attention to the open-to-anything computer monitor. My fingers rested on my keyboard, waiting for inspiration. A car backfired as it drove by, startling me and my right index finger into a fleeting line of jjjjjjjjj's. A dog barked, and I wondered if it was the three-legged one, the one always accompanying that overloaded double stroller. I dared to look up and out my window, just in time to see a dark, handsome man step out of a nearby car. He automatically got me thinking about Jim, Mona's husband, recalling how I used to watch him come and go, mostly go, always looking a bit movie-starrish. I'd admired the way he moved when he mowed his lawn.

It was after one of Jake's over-the-lawnmower chats with Jim that I heard something interesting. Someone had left a note to Jim on his windshield, Jake told me. It had been an anonymous love note. This stranger apparently wanted Jim, who was more or less bragging about it, and he felt both appalled and just a bit aroused. For one wild moment, I worried that it had been me and somehow blocked it out. But a few days later I learned who it really had been.

Mona and I were in the park, with Tracy playing contentedly, as usual, in the sand. Suddenly, Mona burst into tears. She admitted to me that she'd done something incredibly stupid. "I left Jim a note, stuck it under the windshield wiper of his precious car that he won't ever let me drive. It was a love note, telling him how sexy I thought he was, and how much I wanted him."

I stared at Mona. "You didn't sign it?"

She shook her head and her pale hair looked softer and more staticky than usual. "Well, I figured he'd recognize my handwriting. And I also figured that he'd just know it was me. I mean, who else? But he didn't say anything to me about it, like he was hiding it, like he was kind of getting off on the idea that someone *out there* had this crush on him, and maybe he'd be getting some action soon. How stupid am I?"

"You were just trying to get his attention, that's all. I don't blame you. He *should* have known it was you. He *should* have written one back to you, and one thing would lead to another."

She wiped away the tears and curled her hands around one of mine.

"You know, Mona," I said without letting myself think about it, "I left a note like that for someone once—a stranger who lived across the hall from me. Years ago when I lived in an apartment. I was lonely and he said hello to me a few times. I've never been so humiliated."

"Why? What did the guy do?"

"Reported me to the landlord. I guess I scared him. Maybe he'd just seen *Fatal Attraction* or something. I moved out shortly after that."

Mona smiled. I had helped soothe her that day, and I never heard anything more from her about the note to Jim.

I typed in the words *love note* and *humiliation* and *stalker*, hoping they'd lead me to a story. But from whose viewpoint? The guy's? Had Jim simply been caught up in the prospect of a secret admirer. Most men (aside from my long ago neighbor who had overreacted to my note and gone running to the landlord) would not respond to an anonymous love note as a threat. But what, really, did I know about "most men?" If I was to be a writer, didn't I have to be almost genderless? I jotted down a note to myself: *What makes men tick?* Then I had to immediately disconnect *men* from *tick* as in blood–sucking parasitic insect.

Back to Jake. I certainly knew him better than any man ever, but somehow I didn't think of him as being typically male; he never had fit neatly into any pockets of predictability. What about my husband? We'd started drifting apart virtually on our honeymoon. My father? Well, we weren't close once I went "out into the world" of school, and then my pubescence (together with my mother's melancholy) sent him running, only to die a few years later. I've often fantasized that he would've been a great pal for me in my own middle age. A wise curmudgeon, a Grandpa Walton. When I was a child and we watched *The Waltons* together, my dad would impersonate Will Geer, and baggy overalls would practically materialize on Dad's slim, straight, architect's body.

I thought maybe I should explore this idea later for a character—my father in his eighties. Idealized, of course. Everything could be, so why not? Then I closed my eyes, massaged my neck and shoulders. I'd produced very little that day at my computer, and yet my neck and back were going into spasm. It was time to get up and stretch. Writing felt like a sport. The muscles would whine and stiffen and you could injure yourself in so many ways. I climbed the stairs for a bath, one that would allow me to soak and to think.

Okay. My father. He was a very quiet man. Kind of sad, I thought. But not as sad as my mother. If we laughed as a family, it always had to be induced artificially, watching Mary Tyler Moore reruns on TV, for instance. Or old black-and-white comedies they remembered loving as kids. Spontaneous laughter didn't happen. If I'd ever tried to amuse them, that must have stopped before I entered Kindergarten. They were fond of referring to me as an only child "by choice." *How could they improve upon me*, they said to each other but for my benefit. And yet, somehow I knew they had been trying for years to have a big family. My mother had numerous miscarriages. I was the only survivor.

With the benefit of hindsight I could guess about my mother's condition—hormonally out of whack, perhaps. Or even clinically depressed. But about my father, who knew? Just beaten down by life somehow. He worked hard designing beautiful yet functional buildings, but he couldn't manage to install joy or emotional stability into our household. He was always so proud that we never moved out of our modest home even though he could've afforded more opulence. He put the money away, building an estate, and it's a good thing he did. My mother and I had plenty to live on after he died in his fifties. He left behind no debts, but also a diminished chance to reclaim joy.

A household of sadness and . . . what? Regret? Guilt? Once, only once, I told my mother I'd always wanted a little sister. And she closed down completely, didn't get out of bed for a week. I was more careful after that.

Well, this waterlogged rumination was getting me nowhere except in a funk. I emerged from the tub and the bathroom nearly in tears, went down the stairs, and there was Jake, sitting at my computer, reading.

"Who's the hairy foreigner?" he asked. "And wouldn't those harp strings hurt on bare flesh?"

I lurched forward to turn off my screen, poking Jake's chest sharply and meaningfully in the chest.

"Ouch. Hey, I'm sorry," he said. "It was just lying around. I didn't think you'd mind my reading it."

"Nothing on a computer screen is 'just lying around'. It's physically impossible." But then after a moment when my breathing returned to normal, I asked Jake what he thought of the story.

"Good," he said vaguely. "Erotic, I guess. But kind of Penthouse Forumish."

I felt my face flush with irrational anger. After all, I *had* asked for his opinion. "Who died and made you resident literary critic?"

Jake looked surprised by my defensiveness. How could he not instinctively *know* to be careful in his criticism of my work? He smiled. I wanted to punch him in the face. "Well, I'm sorry," he said, not sounding sorry at all. "I'm just offering an honest opinion."

"An honest opinion," I shot back, "from someone who barely cracks open a book. So why should I listen to you?"

But I ended up listening to him after all. It was Jake who, a few minutes later, reminded me of something about Mona. And his reminder started me on the road to my first full story, the first piece of writing that felt authentically mine.

It was during lunch shortly after our blowup about my Misha story that Jake brought Mona into the conversation. "Why don't you go over there and talk to her."

This suggestion put my wild-eyed suspicions about the two of them to rest. For now. "I will," I said. "She just seems kinda unapproachable at the moment. Why?"

"Well, you could try writing about *her*."

My sandwich, chips, cole slaw, and a second sandwich had all but disappeared by that time. I'd scarfed down lunch as though someone were about to snatch the plate away from me. Jake often commented on how my eating style got greedier, depending upon how angry or frustrated I was. Or happy, bored, renewed, tired, scared, or celebrating anything. "Why are you staring at me?" I asked him.

He grinned, still picking at his food. "No reason," he said, and then grinned some more.

"What?"

"Oh, nothing. It's just that . . . if you write about Mona, you might plug into something that relates directly to *you* as well."

My insides vibrated like piano wire. "Such as . . . ?"

Jake shrugged.

"You mean because we both lost little girls, right?"

He must've known he was treading onto dangerous ground now. "Who am I to tell you what to write?"

"Look, Jake, I don't *want* to write about my sister. I don't—"

"Your what?"

"My daughter."

"You said sister."

My stomach roiled and I feared I might get sick, just about the only thing I'd never done in front of Jake. "What is this—a scene from *Chinatown*?" I managed to joke. "Anyway, you know who I meant."

He nodded.

I took some deep breaths and swallowed, forcing myself to feel better.

"Just a suggestion," Jake said. "Since your neighbors seem to be such an obsession."

It occurred to me that, for once, I didn't know what he was thinking or talking about. "Jake," I asked as nonchalantly as I could. "Did you ever see that note?"

"What note?"

"The love note someone left Jim."

"Oh, that. No. Why? Worried I'd recognize the handwriting?" Jake laughed but he was also scowling.

That was the reaction I'd been after. Suspicion of *me* for a change. As little sense as that made, I wanted him to wonder just for a moment if the note-writer had been me. "No," I said calmly. "I happen to know that it was Mona herself who left that note. That's how pathetic and neglected she was. Is that what you were thinking about, though, when you suggested I write something that more directly involved me?"

"Being pathetic and neglected?"

"No, Ole. The *note*."

"How does that involve you?" he asked.

"Because of that note I wrote to a neighbor a long time ago and practically got evicted for—I told you about that."

"You did? I don't think so." He looked troubled, but then seemed to shrug it off. "No. Actually . . . uh, I was just remembering something else about Mona."

"What?"

"Something you told me about that first conversation you had, on the way to the store. Remember? About her eating disorder?"

My food lurched inside me again. Why *had* I eaten so much? I glared at Jake almost as though he'd force-fed me. "Go ahead, Jake, don't be coy. Are you suggesting that I have an eating disorder or am simply a glutton?"

"Neither one, not at all. Are you?"

"Am I what? A glutton, or *suggesting* that I'm a glutton? Make yourself clear, Jake. I need to get back to work. That catalogue bitch has been—"

"Listen, honey. I happen to know that most women struggle with their body image—even you. You're always complaining that you should lose ten pounds, and yet you eat . . . ." Here he finally recognized the need to shut up.

"Like a pig. I know." I finished his sentence for him and left him to finish his lunch alone. He thought I was mad at him again. But I wasn't. He'd been right, that's all. He'd coaxed my work into another direction, and I was anxious to get to it. Juxtaposing a misguided and humiliating love note with a bulimic woman who had left it. Poor Mona. Poor me. Poor all of us delusional, hungry women.

Mona had not only admitted to me she was bulimic. Another time, she had also told me that eating disorders often spring from sexual abuse during childhood, but that her dad had never touched her, not even to hug, once she hit puberty. Like her body had become not only off-limits, but maybe disgusting. This had sounded alarmingly familiar to me and I'd started to ask her something, but then she'd abruptly changed the subject, and that had been the end of it. Until the story started to write itself, thanks to Jake, my misplaced guilt about secret admirers, and my unladylike eating habits.

I returned to the computer, feeling a character being born. I actually felt like she was growing as much inside my body as in my mind. Gradually she squeezed into the chair beside me, this fat woman, or more accurately this new alter-ego of mine who *thought* she was fat. I recognized her as an old companion, someone who'd often been lying next to me in bed, nudging me, breathing her heavy, sugary breath on me. Someone I'd tried over the years to ignore or banish.

My mind began to binge on imagined details of Mona's life, possibilities metabolizing into facts. And I felt the need to purge—words,

90

food, whatever. Feelings of despair and wintry loneliness. Emptiness both sought and disparaged. The explosion of words felt wonderful. Addictive. After writing the first draft of "Indigo" I ended up exquisitely hollowed-out.

The next day I woke up refilled. And the following week continued this way—emptying and refilling. Creating and recreating. After finishing revisions of "Indigo" I kept going. Even though I was fearful of Jake's reading it and taking it wrong, I finally completed the story about the couple breaking up in the pizzeria, calling it "Slow Dance." These were both very small manuscripts, and yet they seemed monumental to me at the time.

Sleep and food both became something necessary for survival that I only grabbed in small quantities. My eyes ached and became susceptible to unexpected tears. I ignored the phone and Jake, so he left me alone. He didn't seem to mind, though. He made me eat, got me into the bathtub now and then, kissed and touched me to keep me grounded, but he saw something happening that he knew better than to question or to halt. Neither of us knew enough at that point to be afraid of what was happening.

Indigo

Late at night, she is thin. Afloat in the darkness warming her bed. So dark she can keep her eyes open and still not see. It's good to keep your eyes open underwater—that's what daddy told her before their long ago swim in the indigo lake. One time, only, they'd gone to that lake cabin. She'd been eleven and wouldn't start for a whole year gaining all the ugly flesh that pushed daddy away. No, she was still his baby girl.

They were both thin, and smiling even as they swam underwater. Deep purply blue at the surface but clear as air underneath. The fish kept blindly bumping their noses against her skin. Don't they keep *their* eyes open underwater, Daddy? Why do the fish keep bumping me? Maybe because they love you, he'd said.

Now in bed, alone, she pulls the lake water over her once again, feels her daddy's arms skimming slick across her back. Dive, baby. Stretch yourself into an arrow. Come up just long enough to gulp some sunshine and then go under to let it out oh-so slow and blue. He shows her how to make the bubbles, popping them against her ear, her back, her leg. Each time he exhales underwater, she feels the murmur against her stretched tight skin. And the fish noses bump... bump.

Except that now she's not eleven, not twenty-one, not thirty-one. And if there are fish, they swim with such urgent hunger. Not blind anymore. She opens her legs and feels one insistent nudge to swim into her, way into her, through the other-mouth that leads into such vast emptiness she is sure one day she'll die from it. The aching, unfillable void in her.

But already the night is washing away, lets go of her. She has to close her eyes for darkness until the alarm pierces it. Up and blinking into the unkind light of her bathroom. Puffed face, lumpy body that doesn't belong in any indigo lake. Barely deserves a shower. She submits to the nakedness and prickly water briefly, can wash her hair tomorrow. Or the tomorrow after that. It doesn't matter.

Before leaving for work, she checks the peephole on her door, the round, wide angle view of the hall and the door across the way. His door. Waits to make sure he's not about to leave too, with his little girl bundled up and ready for daycare. Adorable blond toddler, long-lashed and bashful. Motherless. What would she say to them...to him?

It's not like before when she *tried* to run into them, figured out their schedule, fitted herself around it. Listened to the cello music coming from his apartment and knew they were home. Bach on the cello. A young girl's singsongy voice. Her heart knocks. Come in. Please. But she knows better now.

Her escape is clean. No one sees her leave for work. Oh God—another lunch today, another party for another bride, or is it another expectant mother? Poking at food, knowing she can't eat. Feeling them stare at her fork. Her mouth. Smile wide now, pretend . . . practically explode with happiness for the new bride/ mother/grandma-to-be.

But she is a nothing-to-be. If only she hadn't sent that note across the hall. If she hadn't done that, at least she could still talk to him in the laundry room or lobby now and then. Catch them coming in with groceries, bend to say *hello* to the child, always discerning that there seemed to be no woman in the picture at all. He is tall and sturdy, with a wilderness smile, indigo eyes. The little girl once stared up at her, vaguely familiar gaze, aching, it seemed, for femaleness. But the note had been such a mistake—she just hadn't been able to wait and see anymore. Had to push it. *If you ever want a babysitter, or company . . .* God, the humiliation of that note, of his not calling or writing back. She envisions them moving, even, to get away from her.

Her stomach clenches whenever she remembers what happened last week, the day before the note. She'd fumbled with her keys and accidentally dumped her groceries outside her door just as he'd emerged through his. The little girl elsewhere, his hands, his arms empty. *Let me help you.* He'd crouched down to pick up her things. His hair smelled like apples and it was thinning at the top in a circle the size of a vanilla wafer. She'd longed to bend and kiss that spot of scalp. But the damn pint of Ben & Jerry's had rolled away on the carpet. She stared at it, mortified. The drunk whose concealed bottle has shattered on the sidewalk. She wanted to leave it there as though some other fat woman had dropped it.

He probably prefers the sparrow women who fill up each day on a few green leaves and stalks, whose bodies barely displace the air as they move. That's probably why he never responded to the note she'd stuck under his door the next morning.

Or was it even worse? Maybe, crouched there in the hall, watching the ice cream roll out of reach, he guessed . . . *knew* the disgusting sight it would be later, after the finger jab, the finger job.

94

Maybe the sounds of her devouring retching flushing, devouring retching flushing carry to him through the walls. These are not sounds or compulsions he could accept, or that a beautiful little girl should be exposed to. Whatever his reasons, her note lay in the garbage somewhere and she has to try to forget about it.

Lunchtime comes. Relentless. She can't back out of the party, has worked with the new bride for years. In the restaurant, she laughs and the hollow sound of it echoes in her stomach. *Your turn next, huh?* Right. Feels them all staring at her fork. Her mouth. *Aren't you eating?* No. You know...diet. They protest. Polite. Kindness makes them blind and stupid. *But you can't weigh more than 120 pounds!* Their words are as temporary as food. Seem to mean something, then nothing. In and out, come and go. They don't know her. They know nothing of the hungry fish, the bubbles, the shame of being her.

To the bathroom. Good—nobody in there. Too much of the salad has made its way inside while she carelessly laughed. The finger hardly has to even touch the back of her throat anymore. Reflex. Sour painful lurch, eyes streaming, then . . . so hungry.

She has to stop at the store on the way home. Her grocery bags bulge, make their usual extravagant, fragrant promises. She hugs them from the car to her building—watch out—hurries into her apartment. Then lines up their contents on her kitchen counter, in formation. First this, then this. Forward MARCH. In and out. Come and go. Her heart pounds.

But the knock is on the door this time. It is soft but insistent. A nudge. Tiptoe to the door, not easy for someone her size, must pretend to be gone, out, wanted out there. But through the peephole, she sees him. He is waiting, not turning away, must have heard her come home. Knocks again. He's holding something, can't tell what. She can almost hear his words already: *Leave me, leave my little girl alone.*

She opens the door an inch at a time. Ventures into the wilderness of his smile, sees the shy shadows she'd missed before. The little girl stands behind her dad, clinging to his legs. In his large uncertain hand is a pint of ice cream that he thrusts forward like a rose.

Slow Dance

"Hungry?" Rick asked.

I nodded. He had no idea. A hundred pizzas wouldn't have been able to fill the empty spaces in me.

We were in a small neighborhood pizzeria—a place special to us, filled with spice and music and promise. Plush red booths, candles on the table, a vintage jukebox, big lilting eighth notes fashioned out of black metal and scattered on the walls as though from a musical explosion. It was a setting for celebration and romance, winter longing and warmth.

When my husband and I arrived that bleak November afternoon, we added a birthday party of giggly ten-year-old girls to the mix, but also an undercurrent of misery. Earlier that day, I'd brought Rick's shirts to the cleaners, had sorted and grabbed each by the starched-collars-gone-limp. And the smell of them, of my husband, his cologne and body chemistry, made me gag. That can't be a good sign.

As chaperones for our daughter's party, we settled into our booth some distance from theirs, letting them order their own pizzas and giving them quarters for the jukebox. When the waitress got to us, Rick grinned handsomely, called her by name, then asked how she was doing and commented on her Mona Lisa smile—a flirtation I used to think was cute. When he ordered us some Chablis, I chose not to correct him until the waitress had left. "I wanted Chianti," I said.

"Gives me a headache," he said.

"I know, but you ordered two glasses. What *I* drink doesn't matter to your head—my glass could be filled with Draino if that's what I want."

"Sorry. Why the hell didn't you speak up?"

"What, and spoil the gooey little moment you two were sharing?"

"Good God," he muttered.

Truth is, I didn't have a good answer for why I hadn't spoken up, beyond the fact that I seemed to be feeding my anger, not only toward him, but also toward *us*.

He started to reorder but the waitress was already heading our way with the two glasses of white. "Could we also get a glass of Chianti?" he asked.

"Forget it," I said. "This is fine." To prove it (or something), I chug-a-lugged half the glass. He sipped and looked smug. I wanted to smack him.

From the jukebox, McCartney crooned *Yesterday*, and each repetition of the word dripped into me, alternately sugar water and morphine. I glared at Rick when he rolled his eyes—he claimed to despise the Beatles, always had. Defiantly, I mouthed the word *yesterday* after the song had ended. Then, oddly, when the waitress returned, he again proceeded to order for us: "a large thin crust with pepperoni, green pepper, onion—" the pause was meaningful "—and toss on some mushrooms, too." He knew I'd spend long seething moments picking off every single slimy little gray splat of mushroom before taking a bite of pizza. He knew.

I decided not to say anything. Anger can be such a delicate construction.

Meanwhile, the birthday party had quickly swung into action. Six ten-year-olds (our daughter the last of her friends to reach double digits) play-acting near pubescent cool and making fun of one oldie after another from the jukebox. No reason to update the machine, I figured. Most of the usual patrons dwelt in the past and demanded music that was so good it stuck around forever. Not a Black-eyed Pea or Goo Goo Doll or Lady Gaga in sight. Our daughter had stood surveying the selections for a long time before choosing the Beatles song, then Louis Armstrong singing *It's a Wonderful World*, and Van Morrison's *Moondance*. Good girl. Each of my glances at her and her pals gave me a full body smile; each glance *across* the table, however, erased it.

"She seems to be having fun," he said.

"She's always loved this place," I replied.

Our eyes met, then ricocheted. *We* had always loved this place, from long before she was born. We had often come in to hold hands across this very table, our bodies still jangling from having just made love. We used to sip glass after glass of Chianti, simultaneously burning our greedy tongues on cheese, then lingering, talking away the night and the cold.

Rick cleared his throat. "So . . . ." But our foray into conversation had already dead-ended. How had we become like this?

I tapped my foot and bobbed my head in that absurd way music sometimes makes us do. *Oh it's a marvelous night for a moondance . . . .*

"You okay?" Rick asked. He'd noticed my mood, and the way I was not arguing. Maybe his ordering the wine and the mushrooms had been a deliberate provocation, some kind of misguided test.

"I'm fine," I answered, head-bopping in perfect time with the music. Straining for levity, I added, "Groovy."

How could I give him a real answer, here, now? I wanted out of the marriage, and had known that for months, maybe years. But I swallowed the words along with the shitty wine, and waited to feel some affection for my husband again. After all, he was not a bad person. Certainly not a batterer, gambler, drunk, workaholic, cheater, nor any of those things that would give me a handy excuse to break free, with whole support groups cheering me on. I knew leaving him would invite blame and scorn and unanswerable questions if all I could come up with was loss of love, laughter, and meaningful conversation. Who would understand about my numbness and emptiness, about stale cologne and mushrooms?

An older couple entered the restaurant and chose a nearby booth, smiling at us, at the party-girls and at each other. They appeared to be in their fifties, maybe fifteen to twenty years down the line from Rick and me. The man was balding, she was getting plump—both quite ordinary-looking, and yet I found myself following their every move like they were movie stars. He guided her into the seat by cupping her elbow. She moved the candle to the middle of the table and her face glowed. He handed her a menu and then inexplicably stroked her hand. They immediately launched into easy conversation. He said something, she laughed. She said something, he chortled. The rigidity in the area of my mouth felt like dried face paint, about to crack.

The moment the jukebox went silent, the man stood and dug quarters from his pocket. It took him only a few seconds to choose three songs; it became clear that the first one was what he was after anyway. He returned to their booth but did not sit down as the raspy voice began its love song, each word unrushed,

tender. "You. Are. So. Beautiful . . . to *me* . . . ."
The man offered his hand, and his wife floated into his arms, right there, next to their booth, no dance floor in sight. It was November gray outside, an afternoon in a mostly empty pizzeria, and they were slow-dancing. As they swayed to the beat, his left hand clasped her right one, his right hand caressed the small of her back, her cheek fit snug against his neck. It was clear that they had danced like this countless times before, and yet it was as electric as first love. I started to cry.

The girls were oblivious to my tears, thank God, but I could see in my husband's face the alarm intermingling with resentment. I blew my nose, composed myself quickly. He tried to shrug the situation off. "Cocker," is what he said, rather harshly, and for a moment I thought it was an obscenity aimed at me or the dancing man. But he'd meant Joe Cocker, the singer. He gazed in the opposite direction from the couple whose dance had now drawn the attention of my daughter and her friends. No giggling, no poking each other. They simply watched, mesmerized. Maybe none of them had witnessed that kind of love before except in movies.

Rick and I looked at each other, resisted glancing away, held the moment between us. I opened, then closed my mouth. He nodded, looking terribly sad and not as angry as I'd expected. "Tomorrow," he said at last. "It can wait, can't it?" He gestured to the party. "Let her have her fun. It's her day."

So . . . . He knew. For a moment, I loved him again, just for knowing and making things a little easier for me. It had happened at least once before, most dramatically the moment I'd gone into labor. But this time the love-moment passed.

We finished our meal accompanied by Sinatra singing *That's Life* and I grinned idiotically, tamping down hysteria. The music and the party simultaneously came to a kind of sleepy, natural end, and as my husband paid the check, and the other girls trickled out. I gave my daughter a hug and wished her a happy birthday. And then I pulled her briefly into my own moody slow dance. In my head the sweetly deep, raspy voice was singing again, insisting *You're everything I hoped for, you're everything I need . . . ."* And I made a wish—no cake, no candles to blow out, no reason for it to come true—that our daughter would eventually forgive us.

Dream

There was a price to be paid.

I woke up trembling and sweating the morning after completing these stories. They were so new, I'd barely read over them and I hadn't shown them to anyone yet. Maybe they still felt vaguely embarrassing, or dangerous. But what woke me up in such a state was the dream, so similar, I realized, to a recurring nightmare I'd had all throughout my childhood, but had tucked away years ago, as invisible and crumbling as a forgotten box of toys. This dream had not resurfaced even when I lost my little girl. It's no wonder that, whenever contemplating all the children lost, my list always felt incomplete. As though there was yet another child, distant and growing ever more distant with time. Apparently, unleashing my imagination like I was finally beginning to do with some authority brought this nightmare back as well.

The dream revolved around my earliest memory, from when I was about three years old. My mother and I were going to a mall to see Santa—this I remember vividly. I was wearing a yellow hat with fuzzy pompoms dangling from the strings, and red rubber boots with elastic loops that gave me fits whenever I tried to fasten them over the buttons on my own. It was the two of us, plus a small baby sleeping in a stroller that was bright red in color. I remember lots of long rapidly scissoring legs, rustling Christmas packages, multi-colored lights and tinsel. And my poor mother, in one of her darkest moods—the holidays always deepened her depression.

I rushed toward Santa who was down a floor from me, and I wanted to crawl onto his ample lap before I got too scared. But the stairs were moving, fast. And all those legs . . . . My mom raced after me, down the treacherous escalator with its teeth that I could now see at the end, aiming to munch my toes. Then up in her arms, just in time. People smiling and nodding, my mom clutching me. But then . . . what happened? No more stroller. Lost, stolen, dissolved by magic spell, whatever. Screams, more adult legs, police officers, my mother covering her face, me shrinking to

103

nothing. End of dream. But what really happened, the way my earliest memory continued, my mother began immediately (and continued for years) to assure me that the occupant of that stroller was only my favorite baby doll Betty, and it was apparently stolen, maybe by some poor penniless soul whose child was begging for a doll. And, of course, I believed her. I have old photos of tiny me with tinier Betty in her little red stroller.

And yet . . . my recurring nightmare always brought that doll to terrifying life—a baby sister. Her loss? My fault. My rushing to Santa, leaving my mom's grasp to descend an escalator (another thing I tend to avoid when possible), forced her to leave the stroller at the top to rescue me from a fall or crowd-trampling. And then *poof*. No more stroller. Bye bye baby. The lesson became all too clear: be ever vigilant, babies can vanish, we can all cause death, however innocently, or at least witness it. Over and over.

The nightmare varied somewhat in its details and its sophistication as I grew older, but two images persisted: my small hand holding tightly onto an even smaller hand which ultimately, no matter what I do, gets yanked away; and a red stroller, the same fake-cheery color as Santa's suit. Haunted by an innocuous piece of baby equipment, I'm tempted to call the damn thing "Rosebud" and predict that, like Citizen Kane, I'll utter this word as I die . . . alone and misunderstood. But it's difficult to play around with this particular ghostly item, because it did not stay buried in my youth. And its resurgence coincided meaningfully with my first completed stories. This new adult version of my nightmare also had a crib in it, and was distinctly more realistic in the sense of all those TV movies and crime shows I'd seen about kidnapped and/or mysteriously dead babies.

Still, I had plenty of proof that I'd lost a toy, period. My vivid imagination in this case was my enemy. The dream-story ached to be told to my mother, even now, long after she was gone. So that she could, as always, gently revise it with her beautiful, sad smile and a kiss goodnight. All's well. You are a good girl. An angel. Go back to sleep.

I am at the window now for . . .

Another brief appearance by Mona and child. She still does not glance my way. The baby, I swear, continues to do so. Mona is now whisper-thin. I look down at myself and realize I, too, have lost weight. I was gaining during the time I'm writing about, eating like crazy as though, along with my squirrels, I was storing up for the long winter ahead. But now Mona and I are both becoming diaphanous. And I've lost sight of her somehow in this account. Like the conjurer I've become, here she is, but only for a moment. And I circle back to that troublesome word, friend. I have become as much a serial friend as serial monogamist. Love 'em and leave 'em. Try to be a good friend, but end up causing pain instead. Then move on to the next. As the old Kander & Ebb song goes, "Maybe this time . . . ."

Suzanne will reappear in this account, and both Eugenia and Arthur will take the stage soon. But for now Jake's the only constant; at least he was a constant. But why didn't I reach out to Mona right after she reappeared, to help her heal? I knew what she was going through better than anyone. Residual guilt about not saving Tracy, perhaps, kept me away. And then her pregnancy. As her belly pushed out, it was as though it filled and blocked the street between us. Now, the baby? It both keeps me at bay and draws me in. The first child since I lost mine that I don't avoid looking at. I watch her for as long as I can, drink her in. This baby is life, a second chance, hope, love personified. If it can survive.

Longing

I tried just once, after the blaze of words and images had resulted in my stories, to explain it all to Jake.

"This is unlike anything I've ever experienced," I told him. We were in my kitchen—why did our conflicts so frequently occur there? I'd been back to work on my catalogue for a few days, but the experience of fiction was still reverberating. "It's making me high," I told him, "on language, on control, on my own mind. I had no idea such feelings and ideas existed in me. I'm, like, reborn, or something." I winced hearing myself trying to beef up a statement by inserting an adolescent-sounding "like" into it. What a strange time for words to be failing me.

"That's great, hon."

I hated him calling me "hon"—the way it always seemed a reference to "Attila the . . . "

"Really great." He was looking idly through my cupboards at the time.

"It's scary too, though." I persisted. "You know how everyone has nightmares about . . . " Here I hesitated, shuddered, then swept aside my recent lost-doll-nightmare. "You know how everyone has goofy bad dreams about being caught in public half-naked? Or in my case, it's accidentally leaving the house half-dressed. That actually happened to me. When I was in this kind of zone after writing. I got into my car and drove all the way to the store parking lot before I realized I'd forgotten to put on my pants. There I was in only shirt and panties—if I hadn't noticed in time, I could've gotten arrested or something.

Jake nodded. "Yeah. I've had dreams like that. Do we have any of that tuna left?"

I let the *we* pass good-naturedly, and I didn't bother to correct his perception about my bottomless wanderings being only a bad dream. "No, I used up the tuna a few days ago. But, Jake, most of the time it's not scary. It's this amazing sense of all the possibilities writing gives me, like . . . like, oh shit, like looking through that cupboard for a boring little can of tuna and finding a sizzling steak platter in there instead, or maybe the *cow*, not even slaughtered yet, or having a *calf* or whatever . . . it's . . . ."

Jake nodded distractedly, still searching for something to stuff in his face. I stared at this nodding, rummaging man who, it seemed to me, used to be such a good listener. Maybe I'd been a bit incoherent lately, but shouldn't that make him listen more closely? He had suddenly become about as interesting and as interested as those empty slices of bread he was holding up for me to fill. "I'm sorry, Jake. *We* haven't been to the store lately because *we* have been doing other things. Use *your* imagination for a change." I grabbed a box of pasta shells and threw it in his direction. Unfortunately, the box had been opened. Crispy little shells scattered like the forgotten words to a love song.

His gaze alternated between the floor and my face. "What's the matter with you?"

"You weren't listening to me. I was trying to share—"

"I know, I know. But that's all you're about lately. I know you're writing. That's great. I can't wait to read these stories. But—"

"But . . . what?"

"Well, when was the last time *you* listened to *me*? I have work too, in case you've forgotten. I have things on *my* mind too."

"Jake, you're an electrician."

"I know!" He grabbed another box of pasta shells, opened it and tossed those around too. My whole floor turned into a beach of boringly perfect white shells. "Does that mean I don't think?" he asked. "Does that mean I'm not creative? What do you imagine me doing all day, wandering around sticking electrical plugs into sockets?"

"No, of course not. I'm sorry. You're right. I know your work is interesting too, and I know I've been difficult lately." I started sweeping up the pasta shells. When I stepped on a few with my bare feet, they seemed almost alive, tiny mouths chomping on my skin. "Let's go out to eat, okay?"

We ended up ordering Chinese food and eating it in my living room, in silence except for the comforting blare of the TV. I don't know about him, but I pretended for quite a while that this disillusioning exchange with my "soulmate" had never happened. Deleting had become so easy.

A few days later, in a strange attempt at apology and support, Jake handed me a gift-wrapped book. One of those ubiquitous yellow and black

"Dummies" books. Cliff Notes for life. This one was *Creative Writing for Dummies*. I vacillated between gushing a *thank you for your interest* and throwing the book at his head. "Let me get this straight," I said, forcing girlish pleasure into my voice. "Is this book aimed at dumb wannabe writers like me, or will it teach me to write for an audience of dummies?"

"Listen," he said. "I initially picked this up as a kind of joke. But then I skimmed through the thing, and it gave me a lot of insight into what you're going through. I think you'll find some good, solid info in there. And it's even funny at times. Very tongue-in-cheek."

"Okay, okay. I'll keep my mind open."

"Actually, I almost bought another one—*Relationships for Dummies*. For us *both*, you know? There was some interesting advice in there too—much cheaper than couples therapy. But I didn't think you'd appreciate that at all."

I avoided giving him a direct response by donning my cynic's hat, something at which I was getting quite good. "Is there anything out there," I asked him, "that *doesn't* have a Dummies book written for it?"

He smiled uncertainly, not yet all that familiar with me in this hat. Slow learner, Jake was, at times.

"I mean, where do publishers draw the line?" I asked. "How about *Adultery for Dummies?* Or *Child Molestation for Dummies?* Did you see any of those titles at Barnes & Noble? *Armed Robbery for Dummies? Manslaughter?* Just think about all those criminals out there who could be writing them and raking in the money, enough to pay off their lawyers. And then the lawyers' ex-wives will get their alimony and their children can all have their $200 sneakers. It'd have a really interesting ripple effect if you think about it."

Jake sighed and started to take the book back. "Jesus. I'm sorry. I just—"

"No." I hugged the book tighter, clueless about the source of that outburst. "Hey, I'm the one who's sorry. I'll look through this. Honest. Thanks."

He left the room and inside my head I began to consider titles of my own. *Relationship Sabotage for Dummies. Breaking Up for Dummies. Fucking Up for Dummies.*

*   *   *

ONE THING JAKE HAD BEEN RIGHT ABOUT all along: deadlines *were* good for me. Out of sheer necessity, I managed to plod through the catalogue copy, item by item, writing and researching and rewriting as best I could. And it was finally done! My energy level soared during those weeks and, looking back to the agony I'd put myself through with that catalogue, I was also playfully jotting down some ideas for the book that would be most natural for me: *Procrastination for Dummies*.

~ Avoidance can be a true art form. Use your body to postpone what you dread—take at least ten minutes to brush your teeth, two hours to bathe, one hour each to pluck your eyebrows, shave legs and underarms, cut and paint your toenails. If you happen to have a new lover, double those times; if you've been married a long time, find things about *his* body to fix instead of yours.

~ When you're out for a walk (take lots of those), find an ant carrying something twice his size and follow him to his anthill, hum and strain to remember all the words to "High Hopes" (*Everyone knows an ant . . . can't . . . move a rubber tree plant.)* Then sit cross-legged and watch the ant-city at work. Feel exhausted vicariously. Resist the urge to step on the damn thing.

My pretend *Dummies* book was just another work-in-progress, something I needn't take seriously or share with anyone.

When Jake and I talked about my work (in between amiably talking about *his* as well), we now divided it into writing for *me* and writing for *them* (the catalogue). He came and went from my house, stayed away more than he would have liked, but he knew how consumed by work I had become. And that, he reassured us both, was good. Probably.

Nicole had deluged me with requested revisions, mostly cuts—the catalogue publisher didn't have room for as many words or pages as they had thought. Money was looking tighter and tighter for my new employer. The internet was chomping away an alarming amount of business from old-fashioned mail-order catalogues. And, since there was so much essential product information to convey in my copy, what had to be cut was most of what seemed like *my* voice, my so-called edginess.

The copy ended up looking almost computer generated. For a few days, I grumbled and even shed a tear or two over some deletions, losing nearly everything I'd liked. *Why, I wondered, had I bothered to spend so much time and creativity, and how could I do this again and again as required?* But, at the same time, I was beginning to catch on, to believe that each time, each new issue, the copy would be easier to write than the last, until it became second nature. Besides, the money made everything else possible— it supported my fiction habit.

Jake read my first two stories—"Indigo" and "Slow Dance"—with acute interest, both in one sitting. As he made his too-careful way through each page, I tried to do other things but kept glancing at him, listening, wishing I'd withheld "Slow Dance" from him. He often sighed or cleared his throat, and once he grunted. I didn't like the sounds he was making *or* the look on his face, and I got myself ready to accept, more gracefully this time, some stiff criticism, maybe even something like, "Are you sure this is what you really want to do with your life?" But, when he finished, he smiled, his eyes glistened and he simply said, "Good work, Madelyn."

I could tell I'd made him afraid of saying too much, so if he had any criticisms, I'd effectively censored them—no freedom of speech between lovers sometimes. He hardly ever called me Madelyn. Still, I felt myself beam at him. He was my first, possibly exclusive audience. I'd never loved him more deeply, even though I knew it was a self-absorbed kind of love that had more to do with the pages he held in his hands than the person he was. I told him *thanks* and tried to leave it at that. But . . . he still had an odd look on his face, and seemed to be brooding about something.

"What's the matter, Jake? If you have suggestions, honestly, I'll try to listen and not get violent."

Jake smiled again and shook his head. "It's nothing." But he wasn't fooling me. He looked confused, possibly stricken. And then out of nowhere, he asked, "Why don't we make love any more?"

"Huh?"

"Making love? Remember that?"

"Jake, I honestly don't understand what that has—"

"These stories, Maddie—they're *filled* with longing. You wrote them, you must feel this kind of longing. Why isn't it for me?"

Dodging the issue slightly, I said, "We do make love. Just not so often." It was true, and I hadn't given it much thought until he brought it up. Our several-times-a-week pattern had diminished to a mere once or twice a month. "I've been a bit preoccupied," I offered, and then I threw in my trump card, something I had often resorted to in the past. "And it's the holidays, Jake. Thanksgiving is next week and I know you're not going to be here and that your family hates me and—"

"They don't hate you. Come with me this year. It's just a turkey dinner. Nobody has said you can't come."

"Then why do they always invite your ex-wife? Why is she always there?"

"She won't be this year. I've asked them not—"

"The point is that they want her to be there. They have made it clear I'm not a part of your family, and Thanksgiving is pretty much the ultimate family holiday. No thanks, no pun intended. And then, don't forget, there's Christmas next, and you know how I get . . . ." I finally gave up, because it was clear from Jake's face that my rambling was getting me nowhere this time.

He shuffled through the pages of my stories as though to emphasize their importance, then focused on lining up all their edges neatly, finally setting them aside in a perfect stack. We avoided each other's eyes, trapped in an overload situation; too many buttons had been pushed at once.

In spite of my growing uneasiness with Jake (or maybe because of it), I started recalling some of his Ole and Lena jokes. I didn't say them out loud. It was Jake who always came up with them seemingly tailor-made for whatever was happening at the time, but why couldn't I defuse this situation just like he so often had?

Lena: Whatever happened to our sex relations? Ole: Yah, ve didn't even get a Christmas card from dem.

Doctor (after giving Lena a physical): There's nothing seriously wrong with your wife, Ole, that having sex seven or eight times a week wouldn't cure. Ole: Vell, dat sounds fine—put me down for two.

I smiled to myself and, unfortunately, Jake saw me.

He got up and ventured into the sunroom (now my office) to stare out the windows. Was he mimicking me now? I decided he wasn't. "So,

Maddie," he said with exaggerated cheer, "what's next? Who are you going to write about?"

I nearly shot back, *You, buddy-boy, so don't fuck with me.* But then I realized what was bothering him. He *did* expect me to write about him, about us, more directly. And in ways that would make him feel good and loved. He didn't know I'd tried to write the meatloaf scene, and I decided not to tell him because he'd feel bad about being dismissed and deleted that way. Jesus, this was becoming too hard already, and I'd only begun writing.

"These are fictional stories, Jake," I reminded him. "There's a little of me and you and everyone I know and everyone I imagine in each character."

He was staring now, it seemed to me, at Mona's house.

"But hey," I decided to tease, "I'm working on this big stud-muffin of a guy. You know the type, with the tough exterior hiding a marshmallow center. Great in the sack, does a mean tango, tells dumb jokes with bad accents to cover up pain . . . ."

Jake was nodding emphatically now. "Yeah, I know the type. Listen. Do the poor schmuck a favor and give him someone in your story to love who loves him back, okay?"

The bitterness in this remark took my breath away. I wondered what, exactly, he'd read that had made him feel this way. Was it just the longing he'd detected (don't we all feel longing)? Maybe it was hurtful that I was imagining other men, other love, other everything. But more likely it was that I'd managed to write something he recognized in the couple who were getting a divorce. On top of that, they'd had a child. At least they'd had that much together. At a loss for how to make things better between us, I watched him depart . . . again.

Naturally, I turned to my new best friend—the computer. An old-fashioned desktop, a so-called tower (I liked that, since towers provide distant views), and a bulky squarish monitor. Its face was blank for now, but very open to anything. Optimistic. It seemed to approve of me and what I had to say. I wanted to write about Jake. I wanted to make love more. I even wanted to share the holidays with him and his cold-shoulder of a family. But none of that seemed within reach. Nothing was, except that wide-open, blank, welcoming computer screen, ready and waiting for me to dump the contents of my mind and heart into it.

But what to write? I almost wished it was time already to describe another trinket, some fussy little dust-magnet that I could pull magic out of and turn into a collectible. My first two stories had drained me for a while. And I didn't know who my muse should be next. That damn piano tuner was still striking some chords inside me, but they were becoming more dissonant. He'd turned back into plain old Biff who wears ugly pajamas around the house and probably has breath that could kill a cat. Misha had gone back to Russia, muttering about spoiled American cock-teasers who have tin ears and no notion of privacy. As for illicit sex, even the fictional variety, it seemed like more work than it was worth.

In desperation I returned to the *Dummies* domain. I was beginning, inadvertently, to rack up quite a few ideas for my pseudo-book on relationship sabotage.

~ Make a list of all your past lovers and reminisce about the ways they were better than your current one. Accidentally leave this list lying around where he can read it.

~ When he lumbers into bed next to you, naked and already erect, and you're not in the mood, avoid arguments by using nonverbal means to escape. Try pointing to one of these: the clock and/or the calendar, a large band-aid you've put on your stomach or inner thighs just in case, a tampon string, the TV, a self-help book you're pretending to study.

~ Eat, drink and smoke everything in sight for several days and then stagger around in your ugliest, oldest, baggiest sweats (unwashed), rummaging for Cheetos and cheap beer, muttering things like "Atkins, schmatkins" and "Oprah is wacko."

Enough. This isn't helping . I wondered about the people who write the real *Dummies* books—all experts. Do they ever turn the exercise against themselves the way I was doing?

I tried summoning a new story, something to cleanse my creative palate, by looking outside. But my windows offered nothing. Empty sidewalks, parked cars, and if the houses had anyone inside, I couldn't see or hear them. One of my windows was wide open and I heard some distant traffic and I thought I heard children's voices from the park. Maybe my neighborhood had managed to move away from me, or to hurl me into a parallel universe, punishment for being a spy, for failing to save Tracy, and for treating my boyfriend like shit.

It was turning into the warmest November on record. Highs in the sixties nearly every day. The usual chill and snow seemed a continent away as everyone kept wearing shirtsleeves and sometimes even shorts. When I went out for my walks I couldn't avoid the fact, of course, that the leaves had been shorn from the trees, the color was gone, dryness tickled my throat and eyes, but otherwise it felt like late summer. I tried to detest global warming like I was supposed to even though this weather felt like a gift. But as the holidays approached, I didn't have a clue who to give my *Thanks* to.

Jake didn't return that day, or the next. He didn't call, and neither did I. Loneliness and regret gathered in the corners of me like dust bunnies with teeth. In the car one morning, I had to switch off the radio, pull off the freeway to grab my belly and cry. The MPR announcer had just played one of Edvard Grieg's gloomier compositions and apparently wanted to stay in the Norwegian mood, but brighten it. He told an Ole and Lena joke, one that gave Lena a fatal disease, no less. In her final hours, she sympathetically wished Ole a happy life after she was gone. "In fact," she said, "I tink you should get yourself annuder vife, and you can even give her my dresses." "Von't vork," Ole replied. "You're a size eighteen, and she's a nine."

When I got home, I called Jake to tell him the joke. He laughed, I cried. He came over. We made love. He tried to talk me into going "home" with him for Thanksgiving. I was tempted. But now he'd decided to be there almost a week—too much. "That way," he said, "I've put in my time and can stay here for Christmas." I told him that was a grand idea and to have a good time. I promised to use the solitude and the holiday blues in a productive way, and lied to him about how I had a great new story cooking. He drove off. I dug out my stash of wine and self-pity. It was all so much like a story I'd read, or maybe written, with the ending forever getting pushed ahead . . . but inevitable as winter.

Confessions

On the day before Thanksgiving, I went for a walk and spotted a sign that said HUGE MOVING SALE. Following the arrows, I found an unbelievable array of furniture, electronics, artwork, winter clothing, and, most seductive of all, stacks of DVDs marked $1.50 each/5 for $5. The titles gave me my first smile in days—non-blockbuster movies like *Smoke* and *Fearless* and *Men Don't Leave* that had been favorites of mine for years, and now I could own them for less than the rate I paid to rent them. I had stuck a twenty-dollar bill in my pocket, having planned to end my walk with a trip to the convenience store, so I easily found twenty movies that I wanted, ignoring the popular titles like *Titanic*.

I wished I'd had my car—I'd never seen such a generous sale. Even the TV and DVD player were for sale and I wondered how anyone could survive without movies. Sitting alone by the garage was a woman who I figured to be the one who shared my offbeat taste in movies, and I had an urge to sit down and talk about them with her. But she was glowering, avoiding eye contact with people as she collected their money and watched her belongings disappear. A few times, she looked about to snatch something back, or maybe take a bite out of her chain link fence. She was fortyish, tough-looking, yet seemingly on the verge of tears.

A steady trickle of customers joined me, but if she'd had her sale during the summer, a mob of people would've shown up and she could have priced things higher, so I figured this move had come up suddenly, inconveniently. Maybe she was about to go on the lam (strange expression, I thought, determined to look it up when I got home). As I happily grabbed the woman's copy of *Thelma and Louise*, I flirted with the idea of writing a story about the garage sale woman and her younger girlfriend running away from their redneck husbands, Buck and Nacho, who didn't have a clue how to do their own laundry or give their wives proper orgasms.

While I was still searching through movie titles, I watched a young, hugely pregnant woman and her little girl turn into the alley on foot. For

115

one heart-thumping moment I thought it might be Mona, that Tracy was alive, and that I'd imagined the whole accident. But, of course, I soon saw that this was a stranger. She actually had her child on a leash and I couldn't imagine why, since this sliver of a girl seemed subdued and apathetic the whole time they were there. The young mother sorted through kitchenware and began to negotiate rather rudely with the owner over prices, pointing out all the flaws in each item. She seemed to be offering to take the junk off the other woman's hands, but the garage-owner argued over every nickel. Then the young mother asked, just as someone had asked me at my sale, "Don't you have any kids' stuff?"

"No kids," was the response. "No kids' *stuff*."

But the young woman kept scanning the garage and alley. "I just thought maybe you might have—"

"Look, lady, it's not like I have anything hidden. It's obvious I'm leaving everything behind but my undies. So go ahead and browse and pick. My life's an open book out here."

I tried to catch the garage-owner's eye, to smile at her encouragingly, wishing I had been that blunt to my customer a few months earlier.

"Jesus Christ," the young mother said as she rammed a potato masher back into the pile. "Pardon me for asking. I'm having this baby any day and when my ex-husband hears the word *support* he thinks jockstrap, and this one—" she yanked on the leash "—keeps outgrowing everything. So I just thought I'd ask. Your life's of no interest to me whatsoever." Then she and the child were gone.

This situation forced me back to the day I'd sat with Mona during my own sale, a recollection accompanied by renewed guilt pangs, sharp as a film critic's tongue. How we'd laughed together so oblivious to what was coming, and how I'd joked about her being a bad mother, and all the while, she'd been keeping her pregnancy a secret from me.

"Where are you moving to?" I asked the woman as she took my money.

"Florida," she said.

"Really? Lucky you." I was trying for a cheerful tone because the woman seemed about to drop her tough-guy mask altogether. "I mean, it's nice now, but winter has to hit here sooner or later." I stacked my DVDs into a grocery bag she handed me, and then felt reluctant to leave. I examined a key chain she was selling for a dollar (it had a polished purple agate attached and I was tempted to buy it instead of one of the videos).

"I'll throw that in, if you like," she said.

"No, I couldn't . . . if I had another dollar on me, I'd buy it."

"I insist. It seems to belong to you, a person who likes all the great movies other people ignore."

"Thanks." I put the key chain in my pocket and vowed to come back later with more money. "Well, I suppose I should be going." Peering into her distraught face, I asked if she was all right.

She cleared her throat. "My husband's been arrested for embezzlement, so now he's going to jail. And me? I'm going to live with my parents." She said this as though relating the details of her *own* prison sentence.

"I'm sorry to hear that. You have really nice things here—I'll try to come back later today, with more money and my car."

She shrugged.

"Hope you make a bundle of money."

"Too late."

I wondered if she meant too late in the season or in general, but decided not to say anything more. Maybe she wanted to be left alone more than anything. I wasn't looking forward to carrying my bag of movies all the way home (about two miles), but that's when my neighbor Suzanne drove into the alley.

"Hi." I waved at her. "Thank God. Are you going home from here?"

"Yup. Let me just look around first," she said.

She bought some of the remaining movies and several books, including a pristine copy of *Piano for Dummies*. How could I not take this as a sign? The *Dummies* book, my obsession with music, her showing up at the sale when I was there and badly needing both a car and company . . . had to be more than mere coincidence. As we drove off together, leaving the sad, Florida-bound woman behind, I told Suzanne about the arrested husband and also about the exchange between the woman and the bitter young mother.

Suzanne bit her lip. "I don't think I've ever been so depressed by a garage sale."

I nodded, erasing my smile and allowing enough respectful silence before letting her know how glad I was to see her. "How've you been?" I asked. "And how's Cheryl?"

117

"With her dad for the school year. In Michigan. Upper Penisula, where they get about a hundred feet of snow. He's going to try to straighten her out."

"Good," I said with another amiable nod, and then realized how thoughtless that sounded. Suzanne had shipped off her only child, no longer able to handle her, and what did I say? *Good?* "Hey, I'm sorry . . . ."

But she smiled. "Actually, it *is* good. I think she's going to be okay. Lawrence told me she's getting back into studying like she used to, growing her hair out, being civil to him. I guess *I* was the problem."

"No, not you personally. Sometimes mothers and daughters . . . I don't know. There's *supposed* to be friction." I managed to sound experienced in this area. "So, your ex-husband is—"

"We were never married," Suzanne corrected me. "Until a couple months ago, he'd only been an occasional summer type dad, but I called him one night, and we chatted, and I told him that I was having an awful time with *our* daughter, emphasizing how she was, after all, *ours* and I'd never asked for any help from him. And he just up and offered to take her on. So I said *fine* and he came and got her. She didn't even resist—that's how much she hates me. Last I heard, they're getting along like peas and carrots."

"Peas and carrots—Forrest Gump, right?"

"Right," she said with a chuckle. "It's so good to find another movie fanatic."

Suzanne drove slowly, spending excessive time at each stop sign, looking back and forth, back and forth. I figured we were both reminded of Tracy, just by the accident of our encounter. Her hair was longer, wavier, and more deeply auburn than I remembered, and it rustled prettily around her shoulders.

"Cheryl's dad must be a nice enough guy, huh?"

She nodded. "We grew up together but, to tell you the truth, I barely remember sleeping with him. Maybe it was only the once. All I recall is that he came too fast and I had to fake orgasm. I was young but I knew about doing that. Weird huh?"

We chuckled cozily, as though we'd been discussing sex for years.

"So," she said, "how have *you* been?"

I tested my words. "Well . . . busy." This catching-up conversation with Suzanne seemed to be a little too easy, considering all that had happened in the last few months, and that we hadn't said *boo* to each other in all that time. Another odd phrase; the idea of two people in this conversation—"Boo." "Boo yourself."—caught my interest for a split second, and then I remembered I'd actually scored a copy of *To Kill a Mockingbird* at the sale. *Hey, Boo.* Enough stalling. "I'm writing," I told Suzanne. "Quit my job and I'm writing full-time."

"You are? You did? I *thought* it seemed like you were home more during the day. I've been working mostly nights lately and I've seen you in your sunporch a lot."

So. She'd been watching through windows too, and keeping track of me. I felt that more as a comfort than an invasion of privacy. "I'm not very good yet, but I've been writing regularly, and it feels like what I was meant to do. Finally."

"God, you're lucky to have found one thing that feels just right. I've had about a thousand jobs since college. Some of them only for a day. Like this crazy singing telegram thing I tried, practically half naked. I was supposed to be Tahitian or something."

She paused long enough for me to picture her in costume.

"Are you writing a novel?" she asked.

"No, not yet. Sort of easing in with stories. Except there's nothing easy about those either. Also, I've been writing catalogue copy." I wanted to, but didn't dare, admit that our mutual friend, Mona, had inspired one of my stories with her bulimia and her lovesick note. How could I explain to her that it was more *me* than anyone else in my stories? Then I remembered Suzanne and her dead boyfriend's leather jacket, Suzanne the guilt-ridden mom of a blossoming anti-semite. And another story began to form in my head. Yes, it did occur to me what a vulture I was becoming. Perhaps I was no kind of friend to have, but I wanted to be. I especially wanted Suzanne's friendship. There was something about her and me together that seemed right. Maybe she was going to be alone on Thanksgiving too, and we could make a meal together. Maybe . . . .

"Do you have time for a cup of coffee?" I asked. "Or maybe a drink?"

Suzanne said, "Absolutely," as she pulled into her garage. "I've got a bottle of expensive French something-or-other wine I got from my boss for my birthday. Want to share it with me? We can watch one of our new movies, maybe."

"Sounds perfect."

As it turned out, she had three bottles of wine that we spent the afternoon emptying as we talked. So many blank spaces to fill in. She made me feel safe enough to tell her how I'd lost my daughter, my baby, my husband. She cried as I recounted the accident, and then I told her about meeting Jake. That launched her into her story about her deceased boyfriend, and I cried.

"I'd had boyfriends before him," she said, "and even one since. But I was never in love with any of them. Only him. He loved me too, but he didn't want to get divorced until his kids were older. Cheryl never knew about him . . . nobody did, not during our affair, and not when I lost him either. It's so horribly lonely when nobody else knows you're grieving."

"I wish we'd been friends then," I commented and sipped my wine. "Maybe I could've helped you through that."

Suzanne flashed me a grateful smile, and then after a while continued, "Cheryl and I used to be really close, tell each other stuff, but she hit puberty and pulled away, and then she sensed that I was going through something but keeping it from her, and she got totally pissed off at me. I should've just confided in her, but after awhile it seemed too late."

Again with that ominous phrase—too late. Whatever happened, I wondered, to second chances?

"I never got to know Cheryl," I said, "but it seems to me she would've gone through this phase anyway. Maybe it was unavoidable."

"Maybe." Suzanne looked at me a little shyly now. "I suppose you think I'm really awful for letting Cheryl's dad take over."

I shook my head, started to protest, "No, not in the—"

"I know him well, after all. And I trust him. He has other kids and I'd assumed he no longer thought much about Cheryl. But he told me I'd made it too hard for him to be involved and now it turns out he's really excited about getting to know his 'little girl.' I can only imagine what he thought when he saw her, though. Less than a week before she left, some so-called friend of hers had pierced Cheryl's eyebrow and it was oozing in such a charming way." Suzanne emitted a gloomy little scrap of a laugh. "How a mother loses her grip on a kid so completely—that's what you're wondering, I'll bet."

"I would never judge you," I said. "Honestly, what right would I have?" But even as I reassured her, I found myself doing just that—judging her a little. It *did* seem impossible, this letting go of a child. It occurred to me that I would've given anything to have my daughter with me, even if she was a royal pain in the ass with an oozing eyebrow. There had to be a way to reclaim a daughter, no matter what she might be thinking and doing. Of course, I resisted saying anything about this to Suzanne, who launched herself into another topic.

I continued to half-listen, but also set loose my imagination. I pictured Cheryl with her friends, assuming they were a bad influence in some interesting way. Maybe they were all pierced, both literally and figuratively. Beyond that, I saw Suzanne with that beloved leather jacket, secretive and tragically alone, but in sunlight, like she was the first day I saw her. Then I imagined being a single parent on an endless journey to reclaim—relove, in a way—a difficult teenager. A road trip somehow wove through the landscape of my busy mind, complete with trees flipping by in the car windows like the pages of a book being read too fast. In that car both characters were female—a mother, not a father, was the one trying for a second chance with the kid.

Stories and more stories—how could I ever write them all?

"Are you all right?" Suzanne broke into my thoughts and the beckoning tales, complete with images constructing themselves. But she was a warm, welcome wrecking ball.

I blinked and shook the word-debris out of my head. "It's just the wine," I said.

"Well, good."

I gazed around at Suzanne's living room. Two side-by-side reproductions of Monet paintings caught my eye.

"They're so tranquil, aren't they?" she said.

Framed photographs graced every flat surface and I ventured over to several of them, to have a closer look. There were a few old sepia family photos and two of Suzanne when she was in her twenties, all fluffy haired and grinning. But most of the pictures were of Cheryl, newborn through about sixth grade, conspicuously few after that. "These are adorable," I told Suzanne.

"Thanks," she said but avoided looking at them with me.

After an uncomfortable silence, I said, all holiday-cheery, "Say, what are you doing tomorrow? Want to make a turkey with me? Jake's going to his brother's house."

"So am I," she said. "To my parents' house. Sorry. Aren't you going with Jake?"

"I've never really fit in with his family. The 'other woman' thing, you know. They're staunch Catholics and don't believe in divorce, and his ex-wife is a doctor who has them all fooled about who she is."

"You could come with me, if you like. But Jake should stay home with you."

Her invitation seemed less than sincere, and I declined.

Suzanne slumped guiltily across from me. "I guess Cheryl will be with Lawrence's family. She called me and said Lawrence's wife is letting her make the pumpkin pie, from scratch. No canned pie filling at that house, heaven forbid. I wanted to throw up at the thought. I mean, I know it's traditional and all, but think about all those seeds and strings. A pumpkin is just a big overgrown gourd or squash or something, isn't it? And I just keep picturing a grinning face on it. Who the hell wants to eat a face? My mother always makes pecan pie or sometimes—" Suzanne continued to ramble about mincemeat and whatnot, and she didn't seem to require much response from me. Holidays were hard on everybody.

I let the mother-daughter stories unfold a bit more, wanting to begin writing immediately, but wondered how many friends I was going to use in this way. Why couldn't I leave these poor women alone? The image of a turkey carcass came to mind, with me picking the bones clean.

"More wine?" she asked while refilling my glass. "Bottoms up."

"Now *there's* an expression for you," I said with a giggle. "A slogan for spankers maybe. Did you know they have conventions? I saw a brochure once, so matter of fact it might have been for realtors or booksellers or something. A convention with speakers, equipment sales, whatever. Bring your own paddles and be ready to drop your drawers."

Wine spurted out of Suzanne's mouth and nose as she laughed. Her freckles, I noticed, were much more visible now—whether from the alcohol, the laughter or the blushing, I didn't know—and for a moment they seemed to make her rosy skin almost readable. Pigment hieroglyphics. "Maddie, you're a stitch," she finally managed to say. "Why *didn't* we get to know each other a *long* time ago, huh?"

Suzanne and I ventured gamely beyond tipsy, laughing more than was called for, getting raunchier and not in the least bit shocked. But later, melancholy invited itself back into our party and hung around like one of those shiny silver balloons that scream their greetings and never seem to deflate. It was Suzanne who brought up the topic of Mona. We were both gazing out the living room window that faced Mona's. I hadn't been aware how close together and exposed to each other these two houses were. I wanted to ask Suzanne so many things about what she may have seen or heard next door in the last year. I even toyed with the idea of casually asking her if she'd ever seen Jake over there with Mona.

"She's due soon," Suzanne whispered, as though Mona could hear, "and Jim hasn't been around since the . . . uh, funeral."

That word still had such a heavy thunk to it, even after four months, even whispered. I shuddered.

"It *is* Jim's baby, though, right?" I asked.

"Huh?"

I shook my head. "Never mind. Mona told me some stuff, that's all, but I'm sure—"

"Well, if she was having an affair, I wouldn't much blame her. Jim used to shove her around. A lot."

"He did?"

"Oh, not that he actually hit her. Just a kind of pushing away. She would get . . . I don't know, I guess you'd call it 'in his face' sometimes—you know how she was. You knew her."

I nodded, ignoring the past tense.

"Anyway, he looked like he really only wanted to be out of there, gone, alone. He's not a wife-beater. Just not a husband, you know?"

"Or father." I drained the last of my wine.

Suzanne did the same, and then said, "She *lived* for that little girl." After a moment of silence, she added, "God, I wish I'd been up that morning. I remember running after Tracy several times before that—she was always getting loose. Full of adventure, that kid. But I'd been working late . . . ."

I didn't say a word, fearful of the confession that might pour out of me if I did. Suzanne didn't seem to know that I *had* been up that morning, *was* watching, and did nothing.

We both blinked back tears. Thoughts of Tracy, on top of our long afternoon's out-of-control emotional heap, flung us into the next level of inebriation. My lips felt stuck onto my face like I was a Mr. Potatohead. I tried to recall from my childhood what color those lips were—blue? "We should've eaten something," I said.

Suzanne nodded loopily. "Goddamn, I'm drunk as a skunk. You are too. And we keep falling into a funk. Hey, I'm a poet."

It seemed natural now to invite Suzanne into my exploration of language. "I've been having fun lately playing with words," I said. "Like, since we're drunk at the moment, how about the different meanings for the word *lush*. And here's an idea—if I had lots of thick green vegetation growing on me right now, I'd be a lush lush."

Suzanne stared at me a moment. "If you had vegetation growing on you, surely alcohol would be the *least* of your problems."

"Don't call me Surely."

"Which guy in *Airplane!* said that? The doctor?"

"I don't remember." I shook my head, half expecting to hear a sloshing sound. "But here's another word. I've always loved being referred to as a broad—kind of feisty sounding. But a feisty *fat* woman could be called a broad broad."

After a few more seconds of yukking it up, we sat in silence until, as though summoned by our earlier conversation, Mona came home and turned on her lights. All of them at once, it seemed. I resisted uttering an extraordinarily wrong-headed *Ta-Dah*.

It was about 4:30 and dusk had crept up on us, so our lights were still off. We watched through Suzanne's window as though it were a big screen TV and Mona was on local access cable. She was gazing around her living room and rubbing her hands together, unaware of her audience, probably not caring if she had one. Poor Mona was hugely pregnant but more waif-like than ever. I worried that she might still be bulimic and wondered what that might be doing to the child inside her.

"She okay?" I asked.

"Yeah. I talked to her th'other day." Suzanne rubbed her lips as though she might be having the Mr. Potatohead thing happening too. "She's 'cited about the baby, has some friend, some guy she says is goin' with her to those . . . uh, those Malahz . . . Malaze . . . those whatchamacallit classes."

"Hm-m-m. Malaise?" I asked, trying and, I'm sure, failing to look serious. "She's going to classes in order to feel not-so-good?"

Suzanne scrunched up her face. "You know what I'm trying to say. Natural childbirth. No drugs."

"Oh, but what better excuse to use drugs?" I said as though I were a regular, casual user, hip beyond belief. But then something Suzanne had said several beats earlier came back to me. "A guy? She's going to Lamaze classes with some guy? Have you seen him? What nights are the classes?" I knew that Jake never seemed to be available on Tuesday nights lately. Wine and sisterhood had done nothing, apparently, to assuage my rampant paranoia.

Suzanne turned her muzzy gaze to me, and I could feel her curiosity swipe at the air like a non-smoker's hand in a bar. But before she could ask what the hell I was talking about, I pointed out the window. "Oh God." Mona had started rearranging her living room furniture, pushing heavy chairs and tables, even the sofa, this way and that, seemingly at random. She could barely bend over and her belly kept getting bumped.

Suzanne and I watched in exaggerated shock and dismay, as though that sofa had sprung to cartoonish life and was punching our friend in the gut. After a minute or so, we sprang to our feet and ran outside, through the adjoining backyards to bang on Mona's door. "Open up or we'll bust it down," I yelled at the same time that Suzanne hollered, "Stop that, you twit. You'll hurt yourself." We were both as overwrought as a country western song. And there was our friend, our sister, our child . . . in trouble. Knocked up, moving furniture, and deprived of our brilliant company.

After a few moments, there was Mona, peering out at us through the opening in her door left by the chain. "The whole neighborhood can hear you. What do you want?" she asked. "God. Are you two drunk?"

"Too drunk? NEVER." My howl came out brazen and guttural, Janis Joplin with her Southern Comfort in hand.

Suzanne and I laughed so hard we were doubled over. Concern for our pregnant sister had somehow vanished.

"We want to go to your Malaise class with you," Suzanne said.

"Yeah," I added, "since we already feel shitty, we could pretty much teach the class."

Our boisterous attempt to gather her into our oh-so-clever inside joke was lost on Mona who, after glaring at each of us, simply slammed the door in our faces.

"Oops," I said.

We meandered across the two lawns, back to Suzanne's back door. "Fuck her," she said. "We only wanted to help."

But apparently we had, in a way. By the time we reclaimed our chairs in Suzanne's living room, Mona had stopped moving furniture, leaving it in disarray. And her head could be seen in the kitchen window as she apparently started cooking herself some dinner.

Eventually, Suzanne and I fell asleep in front of the TV. We had started to watch Suzanne's new copy of *Titanic*, determined to see at least the iceberg, or Leo getting laid, whichever came first, but we didn't make it. When I woke up a few hours later, Suzanne was still out cold, so I covered her with an afghan and crept back to my own empty bed.

The next morning I woke up and groaned, ferociously hung over. Remembering all that had happened the day before, I groaned again. Then I heard another sound that wasn't coming from my own sandpapery mouth. At first it felt like I was having trouble peeling away not only the latent effects of alcohol, but also the last layer of a dream. I didn't recall what I'd been dreaming, although Suzanne was certainly in it, as well as a ghostly pair of teenage girls and two females in a speeding car. But even when I was fully awake I continued to hear sounds which seemed to be coming from my walk-in closet. The door was ajar and I couldn't remember if I'd left it that way. Damn—were the squirrels back? No. These were human sounds, sad but determined ones.

Now, in horror movies, people always manage to gather the courage to open doors onto the unknown. No flashlight, no 911 call, barely any hesitation. But I stayed safely in bed for several minutes, listening. I heard a female voice that sounded a little like Suzanne's but also parroted my own. And that's when I knew who the person in my closet was. Getting slowly out of bed and opening the closet door at last, I confronted her— my next character. She was naked except for a man's leather jacket.

"We need some light in here," she said.

I pulled the string that illuminated my mess of a closet.

"No," she said. "Sunlight. It's what heals our wounds."

"I don't think closets ever have windows, do they?"

"You're the fiction writer, dummy. You can chop a hole into any wall you want."

I left the closet door wide open and sat on my bed, staring at my new imaginary friend. Was I regressing to a lonely childhood? Delusional? Or simply creating? This new habit of giving birth to full-grown adults who immediately starting making decorating demands was unsettling, but also kind of fun.

"My daughter isn't a skinhead," she told me. "But she *is* traumatized"

I felt movement on the bed next to me, no physical body yet, only a stirring, pungent presence, waiting for me to see her. She smelled of cookies and milk, or no . . . soda pop, combined with the odors of school—chewed pencils and eraser crumbs, gym clothes, jealousy and seven-hour stretches of fear. My own bed was coming alive as well as part of my new story. And the door of my closet played an important role, separating the woman from the child taking shape and finding a voice on my bed—a female child, misguided but not lost. Crying.

"What is she crying about?" I asked.

But nobody answered. I was alone again and ready. No longer hung over. Feeling an agitated fertility. A fertile agitation.

I ended up spending Thanksgiving day, and several days after that, writing one new story, then started another. Since they were so directly inspired by my day with Suzanne, I wished I could thank her and share these pages with her. Would she be flattered? Probably not. But I didn't have much control over the process. Now I was waking up early every morning with my characters poking their insistent fingers into my back, saying *Here's what happens next. Quick, dummy, get up and write it down.*

Closet Sanctuary

Claire knew she shouldn't have eavesdropped on her daughter's conversation. She also figured that any mother who hid in a closet, naked except for a man's leather jacket, while two thirteen-year-old girls discussed Heaven and Hell was asking for trouble. But nothing could have prepared her for what she discovered: somehow, while Claire had briefly looked away, her daughter, Diane, had turned into another person.

The girls had come home early from school—a half-day that, like so many things lately, had completely slipped Claire's mind. They may have called for her but Claire didn't hear anything until they entered her room, naturally assuming they had the apartment to themselves. Caught naked in her walk-in closet like that, still shiny from the tears and sweat that always resulted from one of her "dates" with Michael's jacket, Claire panicked. And her delay was just long enough to make it impossible for her to suddenly emerge as though she'd merely been putting away laundry and hadn't heard their voices.

Her closet rituals were a secret she held carefully away from Diane and everyone else, and not just out of embarrassment. She was hiding something that was much more like pride—the kind of delicate embroidery people make of their most private and comforting memories and then keep tucked away in a safe place.

She loved her bedroom closet. It was roomy enough to dance in without holding back and daylit from the oblong window someone had found reason to poke into the outside wall. She would sit in the closet's broad wooden lap and, at precise times on clear days, an arm of sunlight would reach for her. In every place she had lived since childhood, Claire had found such a spot. The timing and intensity of sunlight depended, of course, on the season, and she liked to keep track of the sun's schedule almost as methodically as she charted her periods.

Back in the years of being a little girl whose every gesture was worth savoring and she could do no wrong, her father often followed her around with his old movie camera. If her cuteness occurred indoors, she'd find herself suddenly in a spray of artificial light so intense she couldn't look up without squinting, but the heat and focused attention of it always felt to her like love, like a blessing. Once the camera had disappeared and she had let the sun take over, that blessing became cosmic. Though never particularly religious, she believed in a God who, like her doting father, spotlighted the good in her and washed away the bad. All of it.

Not that her closet rituals were entirely religious. Some days the shaft of sunlight was so hot and bunched she felt it as a penetration. That was when the thoughts of Michael induced her to take off all her clothes and reach for his jacket. It was so heavy with rich brown leather and world-map-patterned lining and memories, it just didn't seem empty. She could bury her face in his bold, smoky scent and rub herself almost raw with one of its sleeves.

She'd given the jacket to Michael as a Christmas gift and it was so perfect on him it didn't seem new at all. He wore it everywhere, relishing the compliments he always got because the rest of his wardrobe was, well, unremarkable. Once, he greeted her at the door of his apartment wearing the jacket and a cigarette and nothing else. Only after he had peeled away every scrap of her clothing and left her body utterly naked except for the wide-roaming, invisible, but tingling imprints from his mouth, had he taken off the jacket.

A few days after Michael had suffered a fatal heart attack during his regular morning run, Claire used the key he'd given her to take back the jacket. She didn't bother with anything else—not even her own lingerie and make-up and tampons that she'd left there. Creeping into his apartment, she was afraid for some reason of getting caught. And being there filled her with more sorrow than she could contain, especially when she saw, at the side of his bed, the jeans he'd stepped out of to put on his running shorts.

No. Staying, looking around was impossible. But the thought of anyone else ever wearing his jacket enraged her. Her sorrow might have stopped her cold, but not her rage. It kept her moving.

Michael had been several years older than Claire and separated from his wife but still, technically, married. He had been Claire's friend for a long time but her lover for only eight months, and she knew that part of her rage was about all those lost years they had shared nothing more intimate than coffee or a book.

Eight months had been long enough, however, to sweep aside what was left of the dry and numbing partnership Claire's marriage had become. And long enough to leave shadowy pieces of Michael inside her like fetal tissue her body wouldn't expel. At his funeral, she assigned herself a place at the edges of his family's grief as though that's where she'd been in his life.

Now, whenever the loneliness became unbearable, she closed herself into the one room where she could still feel blessed, alternately huddling and stretching inside his jacket, trying to fill herself and to make her own hungry touch his. She hadn't anticipated being trapped in the closet.

But something else besides being "caught in the act" had kept her from quickly slipping into clothes and bursting out to face her daughter in her bedroom. As Diane and her new best friend, Stacy, settled down to share food and conversation on Claire's bed (the only real bed in the one bedroom apartment), something in their voices made her even more uneasy about *them* than about herself. How could she not listen?

It started with a prayer, and Claire might have been more amused at first (*Grace?* For granola bars and Mountain Dew?), except that it was so chillingly serious. Diane must have prematurely ripped open a wrapper. "Diane," Stacy said. Simply that—her name, and probably some kind of look. Claire shivered and quietly reached for her robe.

"God in Heaven, blessed be thy name," Stacy and Diane murmured together. "Let us put this bounty to your good use and feast forever on the strength of your word. Amen."

When, Claire wondered, had Diane started praying like that? She knew her daughter had been going to church every Sunday for several weeks with this girl. Claire had given permission without much thought. Church—why not? She herself slept in on Sundays and then read the paper. Diane would return from church, dressed up and smiling. Her cheeks were flushed pink and she sang hymns under her breath for several hours. Claire had been grateful that the inevitable gloom from divorce had finally lifted and that Diane had found some sort of peace.

Even now, sitting in the closet, Claire scolded herself for not appreciating the sweet sound of two young girls praying. But she couldn't help wondering if they recited this prayer in the school cafeteria or when someone in the hall handed them a stray chocolate chip cookie. Instead of sneaking cigarettes in the girl's bathroom, did they furtively celebrate Holy Communion or give confession? Not surprising, then, that Diane's other friends seemed to have drifted away.

Claire had naturally blamed herself for the friend situation, along with most everything else that had befallen Diane since The Divorce. Shared Custody. After all, Claire had moved to this apartment outside of the old neighborhood and Diane now had to divide her time between two distinctly different homes. A brand new friend for her daughter had seemed great at the time. Fresh start, and all that. But now . . . she wasn't even sure at the moment what Stacy looked like. Claire had been so damn distracted lately. Working three part time jobs. Digging her way out from under mounds of panic and guilt and grief.

Okay, so she hadn't been Mother of the Year lately, but she'd been doing her best, hadn't she? She bent her legs, hugged them to her chest and silenced the last nagging doubt about eavesdropping on her daughter. Please, she said in her own private version of prayer, let them start talking about boys or hair or clothes or teachers or *something* normal. Please.

To her great relief, they did. "I love that sweater, Stacy," Diane said as she chewed. "It's awesome."

"Thanks. You can borrow it if you want. Next week, okay? You must've frozen today in that T-shirt. It's almost winter, you know."

"I know," Diane said quietly.

"So why are you always dressed like that? Where are your sweaters and stuff?"

Claire didn't hear what Diane said next because the answer had already come crashing down on her where she sat in the closet. It was, in fact, October already. And winter clothes were still packed away somewhere. Diane probably didn't even know where they were, whether everything was still at her dad's house, or here, or divided, or what.

My fault. Claire thought for the thousandth time. But why hadn't Diane asked? Why had she stopped bugging her about her *things* like she'd done right after the move? Claire had heard endless complaints about never knowing where anything was, about getting ready for school and discovering that the shirt or shoes she'd planned on were at the other place. Pairs of socks, even, seemed to have divided themselves much of the time. Claire and Diane had endured more than a few tearful, angry mornings over this issue. "I feel *homeless,*" Diane had shrieked at her once.

But she didn't sound angry now. "They're just clothes, right Stacy?" she asked. "Jesus didn't worry about wearing the right clothes at the right time. He didn't feel out of it, or cold or anything."

Stacy sighed. "Forgive me, Diane. You're totally right. Sometimes I still get stupid, you know. I forget. Even me."

"Reverend Burke has helped me so much," Diane said. "Everything looks so much better now. Not at all like before. Remember when I was throwing up all the time at school? I don't know what I'd do without him . . . or you."

"Or Jesus," Stacy reminded her.

The girls were silent for several moments, eating and apparently arranging their books on the bed. Claire had closed her eyes tight, practically stopped breathing. She wished with all her heart that the girls would leave now, leave her alone. Or that she could run away. Somewhere, but where? To Michael. No. There was no Michael anymore. Where, then?

"Stacy," Diane said in a timid voice Claire barely recognized, "don't you ever feel confused though? About things that Reverend Burke tells us and reads to us from the Bible?"

"What things?" Stacy asked.

"About heaven mostly. And about what happens to all the other people—not us—when they die."

"Seems pretty clear to me."

"Well . . . it's just that . . . you know Miriam? In our English class? She was my best friend for years . . . not any more, but she's really a good person."

"So?"

"Well, she's Jewish. Won't she get to go to heaven?"

"Of course not." Stacy sighed again. "Oh, Diane . . . you really are beautiful, you know that? I love your kind heart and the way you question things, but you're only confused because you've been listening to all the wrong people your whole life. It makes me so sad I could just burst."

Tears stabbed the back of Claire's eyes as she strained to hear every word, every nuance. She just couldn't seem to get her breathing back to normal. And now her insides began to churn and twist and groan.

"I'm sure Miriam *is* a good person," Stacy was saying now. "But she does not believe in our Lord, Jesus Christ."

"So she's going to burn in hell?"

"Don't be so melodramatic," Stacy said with a breathy laugh. "She can change. Anyone can change."

"She can stop being Jewish?"

"Even Jews can see the light, yes."

A stiff silence followed. Then Claire heard a muffled sound that she gradually recognized as her daughter, crying. And a barely audible shushing from Stacy. Even though Claire's eyes were still clenched shut, the tears broke through anyway. She longed to be out there, holding her daughter and finding ways to comfort and reclaim her at the same time. Claire had almost gathered the strength to do just that when Diane's shaky voice stopped her.

"Stacy?"

"Hmmmm?"

"What about my mom? What if *she* doesn't . . . you know, *change* in time? And it's not just about Jesus either. I mean, she really sinned."

"Yes," Stacy prompted. "She committed adultery, and has she repented, Diane? Has she?"

"I don't think so. But, Stacy, she's my *mom*. I'm so scared for her. What do you think God will do? I mean, if she doesn't . . . change?"

Diane's voice was getting smaller and smaller, but somehow Claire was able to hear and feel every word. Her eyelids throbbed. Her throat ached.

"Thank you, Jesus!" Stacy said with sudden elation that made Claire jump. "Diane, you're finally facing this, aren't you? I'm so glad!" She paused as though giving Diane a chance to rejoice too and then continued, more calmly again. "Now, let's look at the facts. That man—the one she was with—he died, right?"

"Well, Mom said he was older . . . and a smoker."

"Lots of people smoke and they don't drop dead just like that. Just think about it, Diane. That's all. Think . . . and pray. Let's pray together."

The rest of the conversation was lost to Claire, but the warnings continued, in her own internal voice now. Wrath of God? Divine intervention? Retribution? She'd toppled over and the wooden floor was pressing lines and dust into her cheek. Whatever might be coming, if anything could be worse than what she'd already endured, she wished with all her strength that God would just get it over with. Now.

But that was when she felt it. The sun. It had slid into place through the window and Claire wasn't even sure it was the right time or that she was in the right spot in the closet. She was almost sure she *wasn't*. But it found her anyway. Seeped through her skin, soothed her throat and opened it so she could breathe again. Cleansed. Loved in spite of all her flaws. Maybe even because of them.

A half hour later, the girls had left. Where they'd gone and why, Claire had no idea, but she would find out. That much was clear. She rose stiffly from the floor, in shadows again now but still warm. She dug through the boxes and plastic bags in the back of her closet and, from them, pulled out all of her daughter's winter clothes.

Storm Women

Eva Storm liked to think of herself as a colorful blur. A Monet, minus the tranquility. She was rarely still and counted on whim and random encounters to determine each path she followed. Jobs lasting more than a few months got as tough to chew as yesterday's bagel. Same with men. One old boyfriend declared Eva's life a scattery mess. "You'll end up alone," he warned after she'd kissed him goodbye. "You'll have nobody to talk to." But she knew better. There was always somebody. She was rich with choice.

Not every path, however, could be so easily chosen and then un-chosen. Darcy came back into her life and said to Eva, effectively, "whatever else you may be, you're my *mother*, and don't you forget it." They didn't know each other, Eva and Darcy, the child having been raised by her father since she was only a few months old. And now after a week, Eva figured she could move on from this too. In all her meandering and self-invention, she had never imagined herself trapped in a moving car with a prickly teen-ager, battling the dreaded silent treatment. Seven solid days of hitting conversational walls, and now Eva faced several hours on the road. She was desperate.

"Well," she began again. "There's something exciting about road trips, don't you think? Anything could happen."

Darcy's response was a jaded, perfunctory snort.

"Yup," Eva continued, "on the road to the U.P. Peninsula of Michigan."

"Just U.P.—it means Upper Peninsula."

"Oh, yeah. So I was saying Upper Peninsula Peninsula, wasn't I? Am I dumb or what?"

No response, so Eva forged ahead. "I've always loved road movies. You must've seen a few, huh?"

Darcy squinted toward the windshield that was already the final resting place for a volley of juicy bugs. Eva hoped that her daughter was at least appreciating the scenery—it was autumn and they were driving through the deeply textured, multi-colored woods of northern Wisconsin.

"Did you ever see *Planes, Trains and Automobiles*? Steve Martin and John Candy? Really funny. That scene in the motel where they're in bed together, accidentally all cuddled up? I was almost in that one. Well, not in the bed, in the movie." Eva glanced sideways at Darcy. "I can see that you don't quite believe me, but I had an actual audition. Do you want to hear about that?"

Eva felt a flurry of details inside her like the flakes in a shaken snow globe; each of her stories could spin and light differently with each telling. She needed to stop now and tell this one properly, so she exited from the freeway and pulled into a Perkins. They had left Minnesota at sunrise and hadn't yet stopped for breakfast. "How about some pancakes smothered in melted butter and maple syrup? she asked Darcy, then added, "Yum," as though the girl were six, not sixteen.

Settled into a booth, Eva ordered her pancakes, but Darcy chose only an English muffin, dry. "Are you sure that's what you want? Seems more like a punishment than a breakfast. Maybe they have gruel." When Darcy didn't respond, Eva pressed on. "No strawberry jam even?"

Darcy shook her head.

Eva sighed. "So, anyway, about that movie. The part I wanted was Steve Martin's wife, but the only part they'd let me audition for was this silly little twit who buys curtain rings from John Candy, supposedly believing they're earrings."

A woman sitting by herself in the next booth showed more interest than Darcy.

Eva smiled at the stranger. "Well, I tried to go along with it and hang those ridiculous big white plastic rings on my earlobes, but then I suggested, politely, to the director that he was nuts. That no *girl* would make that mistake—maybe a guy would, or an alien. Could I play a guy dressing up in drag for the first time instead? Or like when E.T. got dolled up like a girl? Now, that I could do. Anyway, I didn't get the part."

Still no response from Darcy.

"I wonder," Eva asked their eavesdropper, "do you suppose that when a girl shaves her head and pierces her face, that English suddenly becomes her second language or something?"

Darcy blushed and scowled, but at least she offered an opinion. "I don't like comedies."

"Oh." Eva sighed. The woman looked politely away. Now what?

She had been married to Matt only briefly despite the fact that they'd grown up together. When he dropped their daughter off like an ATM bank deposit, she couldn't imagine why he hadn't at least waited for Eva to come home so he could explain himself? Darcy's answer for that was a shrug. Busy man, her daddy. But Eva knew she wasn't getting even a sliver of the story.

Since then, she had tried to talk to Darcy, woman to woman. There were a lot of blank years to fill in and it was usually what Eva did best—

recounting tales from her own life and drawing them out of others like sap from a tree. But Darcy was not exactly her typical audience. Caught off guard by Matt's sudden rejection of the father role and insistence that *she*—the wayward mother—take over, how could Eva avoid screwing up?

She knew that yesterday had been a huge mistake, for example. Taking the kid along for her singing telegram gig, the one, unfortunately, requiring the grass skirt and coconut-shell bra. And sure, Eva couldn't carry a tune but it was all in fun, this job. She'd caught this particular "birthday boy" at his office, pretty much disrupted his professional life and dignity for at least the day, maybe longer, but he'd eaten it up. Most people, Eva found, love to get attention, no matter how humiliating. On the way out of the office building, she'd been about to expound on this observation when she noticed, belatedly, that Darcy looked so horrified, she might as well have just witnessed her mother in a bloody lab coat conducting experiments on puppies.

Now today, on the road toward Matt and, hopefully, rescue, Eva recognized the problem, even though her previous experience had been limited. It had to do with mothers and daughters, the distorted way they see each other, and the way they fight. If her own mother had stayed alive long enough, Eva would've been better prepared for what was to come.

"So, Darcy . . . " Eva tapped out the William Tell Overture with her fingertips on the table. Their waitress seemed to have disappeared. "It's almost October. Aren't you missing school?"

"No," Darcy said, and took a deep breath before elaborating. "Dad said I could take a few weeks off—"

"At your age? Off from what—hanging out with the other bald girls?"

Darcy glared at her. "I needed time to think."

"Ah, so that's what you've been doing. I approve of thinking."

"*Dad* talked to the principal...you know, because of the..."

"The what?"

"I was sorta suspended."

This was news to Eva and it came at the same time as her pancakes, making them seem a lot less yummy. "Like expelled? For what?"

Darcy scowled. "My hair, and the piercings. Against the rules. Stupid private school."

"So your dad freaked? Is that why he brought you to me, two states away?"

"*Dad* doesn't freak out." Every time Darcy said *Dad* that way, Eva felt the nudge of it like a menstrual cramp. "But he's got this girlfriend now who hates me. *She* said some time with you would be good for me . . . but of course she doesn't know you."

God, this conversation was like maneuvering along a sidewalk riddled with uncovered manholes. This image caught Eva's fancy and she almost asked Darcy (or maybe the woman in the next booth) if manhole was still the politically correct term, or had it become personhole, which somehow sounded more obscene. But instead, she gazed around the packed restaurant. Everywhere she looked were normal-looking children with loving parents who cut up their pancakes and didn't look like they were planning an escape.

Eva's focus returned to Darcy. It had to. She decided it was time, once again, just to fling out some words and see how they landed. "See those three guys over there?" Eva nodded discreetly toward them. "The ones who are wearing identical suits and ties and sunglasses, gripping those suspicious looking briefcases? Probably FBI—"

Darcy glanced at the men.

"—like this guy I used to go out with. He was very intense, wore a suit and shades all the time, liked to interrogate me and force me to confess. But we broke up when I caught him stealing some of my lingerie and going all J. Edgar on me." Since Darcy appeared baffled, Eva explained, "Hoover, you know? The FBI guy who looked like a bulldog but liked to dress up in women's undies?"

Darcy turned away and muttered, "I keep forgetting not to listen to a word you say when you get that look on your face."

"Huh? What look?"

Eva took a compact out of her bag and flipped open the mirror, staring at herself, then aimed the mirror toward Darcy, who winced at her own reflection.

"Can't you just relax?" Darcy asked

"Sure, I'll relax." Eva snapped the compact shut and put it away. "When we find that fucking...uh, that father of yours. Then you'll see relaxed. I'll become rubber woman. A noodle. A goddamned Gummy Worm."

"I get the picture, Mom. And I've already told you that you can say 'fuck' in front of me."

"I never used to say that word," Eva said wistfully. "My language changed forever when I met Bob DeNiro once—hey, there's another great road movie, *Midnight Run*, with him and Charles Grodin, you know that one? Anyway, I got this major crush on DeNiro. And right after that, I sat through all, I mean ALL of his films." Eva's speech patterns and gestures, of course, became instantly DeNiro-esque; she never could stop herself. "It was fuckin' this

142

and fuckin' that for hours but, hey, comin' from that man, it sounded so fuckin' good, ya know?"

"I'm supposed to believe you met Robert DeNiro?"

"I was an extra in one of his films. He's a really sweet man. Very shy."

Darcy shook her head. "I think I'm traveling with an insane person. Certifiable. I should go into the bathroom and write *HELP ME* on the mirror in lipstick."

Eva felt stopped in her tracks, downright flummoxed. Feeling that way made her want to say the word, such an interesting word, out loud. "Well, kid, I'm flummoxed."

"I figured. I mean, look at you."

"You don't know what *flummoxed* means."

"I get the gist."

"Gists don't count. I love words, don't you? This writer I went out with for a while told me I had a real verbal flair. You could have that too, but children who get expelled from school tend to have poor vocabularies."

"I wasn't expelled. You love words? Get that one right. Suspended, not expelled. There's a simple distinction."

"Look, Sweet Pea, you need to watch your tone of voice with me." It occurred to Eva, too late, that a person can't actually *watch* a tone, but she let it go.

Darcy abruptly opened her mouth and popped in half of her muffin all at once, chewed, swallowed, licked crumbs but missed a few. Oh, that tender young face. Eva almost wanted to touch it. But those godawful silver studs—one on the side of her nose, slightly infected, and the other one off-center below her bottom lip. And the sheared-off, concentration camp hair, the boniness and pallor. When Eva first saw

Darcy, a week ago, she wondered if this wasn't yet another case of two babies switched at birth. Maybe her real daughter was out there somewhere with a couple of bikers who took better care of their Harley than their inappropriately soft, pretty teenager.

They sat in silence for a few minutes, finishing up their food. Eva chugged another cup of coffee. "Want anything else, Sweet Pea?"

Darcy scrunched her mouth and said, "I wish you'd stop calling me that."

"Calling you what?"

"I have a name, Mama."

"And I wish you'd stop calling me Mama . . . *Sweet Pea*. Let's get outta here. Onward. Eastward Ho, what do you say?"

As they walked through the restaurant toward the cashier, several people openly stared at Darcy. Eva hated herself for hoping they assumed that the kid's stubbly scalp was the result of chemotherapy. But at least she finally managed to resist telling strangers *My kid's not a skinhead, honest*.

Back in the car, Darcy said something under her breath.

Eva tried to ignore her daughter as she eased back into the traffic heading east. They'd been in Wisconsin for a long time now, but Michigan still loomed far in the distance. Michigan and Matt, and giving Darcy *back*. What if he refused? What if they couldn't find him? He could've picked up and moved God knows where.

More mumbling from Darcy from which Eva picked up only the word Mama.

"What? Speak up?"

"I *said*, you *are* my mother."

"It's possible. But I'm waiting for the maternity test results."

"Geez, you were there. Don't you remember having me even? Don't you—"

"I was kidding, Darcy. Honestly, don't you have even a smidgeon of a sense of humor? Of course I gave birth to you, but I'm new to this mother-thing. I didn't exactly apply for this job after all these years, so cut me some slack, okay? I was your age when I had you."

"You were twenty, Mama."

"Jesus, *please* stop calling me that."

"Stop changing the subject. *Mom*. You were not a kid when you had me."

"You don't know what you're talking about. I was definitely a late bloomer. The judge chose Matt, don't forget. And why don't you just call me Eva. Can you do that for me?"

"Why did you keep Dad's last name anyway? You were married about a minute."

"Because I liked it better than my own. The name Storm fits me better and it's easier to say than Schlichter. God, try saying that ten times fast."

"I'd rather not."

"It's like that old 'I slit a sheet, a sheet I slit, upon the slitted sheet I sit' tongue-twister that makes you shay sit . . . uh, say shit."

Major eye-rolling at this. But Darcy did obey, in a way. "Shit," she said. Loudly.

Now that Darcy was finally talking, silence didn't look so bad to Eva.

"Doesn't seem right," Darcy continued. "Taking his name. Our name."

"It's perfectly legal. Get over it."

"Fine."

"Fine. Anyway, call me Eva."

"I suppose we have to pretend we're sisters again, like in that store yesterday."

"You look old and I look young. The salesguy assumed, so what?"

"If I hadn't been in the way, you probably would have had sex with him."

Eva felt her stomach drop. Jesus, was there any way out of this mess?

Darcy propped her sneakered feet on the dashboard and announced, "I've had sex already." Then she added, "Twice."

Eva took another long, deep breath, thought about gulping down a nice cool fishbowl of Chablis. But Darcy was watching for her reaction. The kid was always peering at her. What was the right thing to say? Eva ended up shrugging. "Me too."

"Only twice?"

"Very funny, kid."

"Dad said you slept around."

"Well, I'll have to thank him for that, too, when we find him." She silently added, *The bastard*.

"He said it was weird that you slept around, because you had to fake orgasm."

Enough talk. It was only getting Eva deeper into trouble. She felt herself pushing too hard on the accelerator. They were going about eighty miles per hour now—maybe that was the answer. Fly off the road. Find a cliff and do a Thelma and Louise. No, too radical. But she liked the idea of being in this *together* somehow, more like two bad girls on the lam from prison, Eva busted for falsifying documents and orgasms, and Darcy for turning tricks in her Social Studies class.

"Anyway, Dad told me plenty about you. I don't know why he thought the two of us should get to know each other. He must've felt sorry for you or something."

"Hm-m-m. Sorry for *me*. You know, I have to admit it's an interesting experience being judged so harshly by a kid with a buzzcut and holes in her face. What was your dad's reaction to that?"

"He says it's *my* hair, *my* body. My friends all wish Matthew Storm was *their* dad."

That was about all Eva could take. "And yet, here you are and where is he? God, Darcy, don't you even know enough to feel abandoned?"

She shouldn't have paused, because Darcy had the chance to inject, "Of course, I feel abandoned. I always have, *Mother*."

Eva managed to dodge, but felt the sting anyway. "He didn't bother to explain, did he? Just told you he'd be right back and left you at my door?"

Darcy didn't answer. She picked at a worn spot on her shoe.

"He's home in bed with some bimbo and, meanwhile," Eva continued, "you're left to study *me* like some science project. And to cry yourself to sleep at night—I've *heard* you, kiddo. What kind of father does that?"

Darcy's face was flushing darker and darker. The tender flesh around her nose-stud throbbed. "He's a great father. He took fantastic care of me. Don't you dare . . . "

The poor kid. Eva tried to slow her heartbeat and breathing, pasted on a smile which she inspected in the rearview mirror. Then she rewound their conversation, trying to find the safest topic to return to, away from Matthew. Oddly, she chose sex. But she kept her voice low, as though others were in the car with them and she didn't want any more eavesdropping.

"Listen," she began. "Yes, I have boyfriends now and then, and we might even give each other physical pleasure—I'm not a nun or a Republican. But no, I don't sleep around. And, yes, I often fake orgasms, it's the most useful skill I have. My mantle would be covered with awards if there were such a category as best actress in bed with clueless men who can't even *find* a clitoris much less say howdy to it."

This time, bingo. A smile from Darcy.

"Okay, that's that," Eva said expecting that Darcy would probably let the conversation die a natural death now. But instead she did something Eva hadn't seen before. Darcy laughed. Who would've guessed the kid had such a great belly laugh?

"What's so funny?" Eva asked.

Darcy looked at her mother, amazed. "Howdy? Say *howdy* to it? Where do you come up with this stuff?"

Eva leaned back, felt the headrest practically cradle her aching brain, and smiled for real this time. "Never mind that. Now . . . get that map out again, will you? I want to see where the fuck we are."

Yes—where *were* they?

Eva Storm wanted . . .

No. She and Darcy started to . . .

No . . .

Dead End

I never figured out why Eva and Darcy stopped speaking to me just as they were beginning to speak to each other. They withheld the rest of their journey from me, and I set the thing aside as yet another incomplete story.

Jake came over the following week, and we shared Thanksgiving stories. Apparently, his holiday had consisted of awkward smoky silences, stomach cramps, random nostalgia riddled with accusations, football, and naps. He said he was glad Suzanne and I had become friends—she seemed like an interesting person, he told me. Naturally, my mind immediately did it's number on me and I envisioned Jake with *Suzanne* now. I was hopeless.

Meanwhile, Jake spotted a book of baby names I'd bought to help me choose character names. His face brightened pitifully until I disappointed him, again. Later that day, as though subconsciously trying to hurt Jake, I called him Michael (the boyfriend in my first new story). Jake gaped at me for a few moments, then made an excuse to go home early. For some reason this pissed me off and I tossed a wadded up page at his back in an attempt to explain; it contained a list of my characters' names. But he apparently interpreted the gesture as rebuke.

I grabbed the crumpled page and yelled out the door at him, "You wanted children, Jake. Here they are. My children."

Even if my love life was still staggering as badly as I had been after my wine/whine fest with Suzanne, my writing seemed to be going pretty well. But after finishing "Closet Sanctuary" and finally typing *Dead End* after my last paragraphs of "Storm Women," I had the Santa dream again. My mother and I at the mall to see the ho-ho-ing old fart . . . doll in red stroller . . . escalator . . . tragedy . . . police. My hand losing its grip on a tinier hand. A crib, but now me climbing into it, way too big for it, breaking it into a hundred pieces . . . . And I woke up covered in sweat, gasping, trembling.

Could this horrific nightmare stop me from writing? It could, if it recurred and even grew every time I finished (gave birth to) a story. I consoled myself that morning by paging through the preliminary galleys of "my" catalogue that had just come in the mail. I glanced almost proudly through it, forcing myself to recognize the unique contribution I'd made, even if it was barely discernible. It was my first published writing . . . sort of.

I was scheduled to meet with Nicole and the buyers soon to begin the process for the next catalogue. But then, Nicole called to tell me that there would only be two catalogues each year, winter and summer, instead of the four that had always been published in the past. The rotten economy was taking its toll on the catalogue company and I worried that they would fold altogether. But, in a way, I was relieved not to be facing that writing chore so soon (I didn't admit this to Nicole, of course). I had several months off. She said she'd talk to me when the new stock came in.

What was my first reaction to the news that my income would be cut in half? Well, I'd gotten their check for almost $7000.00, so I went shopping, of course—one of my most perverse habits, consoling myself about money by spending it irresponsibly. After supplementing my wardrobe, I bought extravagant Christmas gifts for Jake and Suzanne even though it was doubtful they were doing the same. I also glanced at but wisely passed by the baby things (I pictured myself giving Mona at least a rattle or stuffed toy, but could not hear our dialogue—not one word).

Suzanne dropped over one day unannounced, and I was glad—that's what good friends do, right? Just drop over? Even if I looked and felt like a mess? I'd been lying on my couch reading through and revising "Closet Sanctuary," staring at the no-longer neatly typed pages as they spread across my coffee table. I was trying to convince myself it was good, and also trying not to fall asleep.

Her knock and friendly voice provided a pleasant wake-up call. I invited her in, wishing I could explain to her how rarely I got company. Searching through my pantry for something to offer her, it occurred to me how hard it was to maintain friendships. I wanted to confide in her all the junk that had been passing in and out of my life lately, but as the words formed in my mouth, I realized that good friends didn't necessarily reveal how crazy they truly are.

When I returned to the living room with two glasses of wine and a bowl of semi-stale pretzels, I saw her sitting on the edge of my couch. Reading. Oh shit. The story. How could I have forgotten what I'd blithely left in plain view? "Closet Sanctuary" was filled with Suzanne, renamed but utterly undisguised and naked.

My silly attempts at being a proper hostess had given her enough time to read the first several pages. When I appeared, she dropped them and looked at me, her eyes filled equally with tears and betrayal.

"Suzanne, let me explain. My writing . . . it's a process of things that happen to me combined in some mysterious way with other things that—"

Suzanne didn't let me finish. She just left me standing there, alone, holding two glasses of wine in shaky fingers. Maybe friendship was another "normal" part of life in which I was not meant to participate.

I'm at my window . . . pausing . . .

Remembering fondly how words used to provide play for me instead of fear. How words used to feel like friends instead of ripping people away from me with their sharp teeth and claws.

Also, I'm pausing because this story takes a dramatic turn here, and I don't want to lose my place in the NOW. I don't want to keep rooting around in the past until I'm in danger of losing my resolve for the near future, for what I still see as a rescue. I'll call the next chapter **Hero** because, more than anything, that's what this story needs. The word brings to mind brave deeds but also can refer simply to the main character in a story who, after all, can have courage or a distinctive lack of it, right? My not-that-old dictionary still defines the word with gender in mind— "a man of distinguished courage . . . " forcing me to consider (but then discard) the word **Heroine** which threatens to drop its final E like a loose shoe and become a famously addictive substance. Maybe doing something admirable is just as addictive as anything else. Is it? Will it be for me?

Hero

In all our years together (and apart), Jake and I had always managed to be a couple during the Christmas season. Even when it was a bit forced, we both acknowledged that this particular holiday was unbearable alone. So Jake came over on the Saturday before Christmas, brimming with holiday cheer and mystery. "I've got a surprise for you," he announced.

I was so glad to see him, I didn't ask him what kind of surprise, or push him to reveal it. I simply basked in his warmth. But when he kept grinning and mentioning "The Surprise" with the capital T and capital S in his voice every time, I began to wonder if this was something I really wanted, or if it was one of those things Jake thought I *should* want.

And he wouldn't give it to me a week early, or even provide hints. "It's for Christmas," he said. "You have to wait."

"Fine." I tried my best not be get annoyed, only to anticipate. The evening drifted lazily into night and into morning, but we slept very little. Instead we made sweet love, cooked and devoured a pot roast, decorated a small tree, laughed, sang and, especially, talked. I showed him "Closet Sanctuary" and shed some overdue tears when I confessed how I'd inadvertently hurt Suzanne. He listened attentively and responded like the old Jake I'd known and loved for so long.

Warnings buzzed and clamored during only one conversation we had over food. I was putting together sandwiches and reaching for a jar. "Pass me the crayons."

Jake laughed at me—back then he thought my emerging verbal quirks funny. "The crayons? Do you mean the *mayonaise?*"

"What did I say?"

We joked a little about me losing my mind, and it was quickly forgotten. Until later, when I called the TV a stove, but I pretended this one was intentional, a lame attempt at making a very tired Jake laugh. He obliged.

I got up early Sunday morning to read the newspaper, letting Jake sleep in. Scanning the circular from Walgreens, I spotted several good deals on things I needed. And, since we were out of condoms, I decided to go over there as soon as they opened.

Of course, I'd conveniently forgotten that the aisles I'd be roaming would be stuffed with Christmas decorations. Averting my eyes from Santas and from other things red, I tried instead to breathe in the beautiful holiday music. Quickly filling a small basket, I presented it to the cashier with a wavery smile. There were only a few other people in the store, but I had tried to smile at each of them too, including an elderly lady I'd spotted puzzling over the various sizes and absorbencies of Depends.

When the cashier rang up my purchases and announced my total, it was considerably higher than what I'd estimated.

"Didn't you give me the sale prices?"

"You mean the *coupon* prices," said the pimply adolescent who'd been manhandling my feminine products, soaps, cosmetics, and condoms. He yawned rudely and I smelled the sourness of his breath. "If what you bought has a *coupon*, you need to give that to me."

"Coupon?"

That's when I was no longer able to ignore how the weekend was turning on me. I'd been having such a nice time with Jake, I had clung to the illusion that all was well. Good old Jake and good old Maddie, loving and talking. But words were beginning to be as much my enemies as my friends, and I repeated the word in question to myself. *Coop...on. Cou...pon.* I knew, of course, that this word should not be a problem but it insisted on sounding foreign to me. Did it have to do with mustard? Chickens? A government overthrow? I let the word slip and slide around in my head for an instant and, honestly, could not find meaning anywhere in there that had to do with buying merchandise at Walgreens. "I'm sorry," I said, trying to steady my breathing. "My mind is playing a trick on me and blanking out. I don't understand."

The kid stared at me. He was a bored little mouth-breather, who clearly wished I would just give him the damn money and disappear. "From the NEWSPAPER?" He was enunciating as though for a deaf person now. "Did you CUT OUT the COUPONS?"

Oh. The newspaper. I remembered looking at the circular. But now I was fighting tears. How little sleep had I gotten? How many orgasms?

How many weeks wrestling with language and memory and emotional pain and the rush of words, letters skittering across a screen, looping here and there, making my synapses fire and misfire, giving me hope and despair all at once?

Finally, with an exasperated sigh, the cashier took a few steps away from the desk, grabbed a circular, and painstakingly began to pull my purchases from the bag, including the condoms (which were *not* on sale). Then he took his time finding each coupon, cutting it out, and deducting the appropriate amounts from my total. "This is the wrong size of ibuprofen for the coupon," he said, still enunciating, "and the wrong kind of maxi-pads." The line behind me was growing and I cringed. "Go ahead and get the right ones," the kid said as though he were doing me such a kindness. "I can help the next customer in the meantime."

"How thoughtful of you," I mumbled, wishing instead I could point out to the little bastard that both Clearasil and Listerine were on sale and he should go grab about a barrel of each. But instead, I obediently found the correct aisles, exchanged the items, and slunk back.

Finally, I could leave, just behind the old lady who'd bought Depends. Neither of us looked at each other or at anyone else.

But the cashier called out to one of us. "Oh, ma'am? Did you forget something?" When I turned around, he was holding my bag and smirking. Jesus Christ, what next? I knew this kid was filing me away as a story to tell his friends. *This crazy lady came in today and didn't know what the fuck a coupon was, and she was buying condoms but who the hell would mess around with someone like her anyway? And then she forgot her bag, and then there was another old crone behind her who was probably wetting her pants waiting through all this so I had to help her while the other lady was getting the correct stuff . . . blah blah blah.*

I remained a few seconds between the inside door and the outside one, leaning against a wall to take a few deep breaths. It had not been a snowy December, but the Depends lady was making her way toward the bus stop very slowly, as though the sidewalk was slick with ice. Suddenly, a heavy-set guy in a green stocking cap appeared, grabbed the old lady's purse off her shoulder, and ran down the alley in back of the store. The woman stood there, stunned and silent. I yelled inside of the store, "Someone's been mugged out here—get the manager."

Of course, I knew that the cashier might simply shrug me off as a nutcase and, without giving it any more thought, I dropped my bag by the old woman's unsteady feet and ran after the mugger. My own purse was draped across my body, as was my habit ever since I read about purse-snatchers like this guy. He had a head start on me, of course, but he also had a pronounced limp, so the distance between the mugger and me began to dwindle right away. I didn't have a clue what I'd do when I caught up with him. At one point he turned his head, saw me gaining on him, and ran faster. So did I. He was wearing worn-out loafers and I was wearing running shoes. I heard him swearing. I swore back. After all the anger and powerlessness I'd been feeling that morning, this guy wasn't going to get away with mugging an old lady.

Finally, he turned, threw the purse at me, and disappeared between two garages. The purse bounced off my chest, landed in a shrub and hung there like a big ugly Christmas ornament. Did I stop then like any sensible person would do? Did I simply turn around and bring the purse back to the lady? No. My mind was still not working in a rational way, and I found myself bolting into the space between those two garages. I saw him for only an instant, saw his oversized fist, then everything went black. He'd punched me square in the jaw, after which I'd fallen backward and clunked my head on the pavement.

The next thing I knew, a stranger was leaning over me (I found out later that this was the Walgreens manager), and then everything was fuzzy for a long time. I heard a siren, very loud but also muffled, and eventually surmised that I was hearing it from the inside of an ambulance. I was stretched out and being attended to with great kindness. "Don't move," a woman at my side kept telling me. She was very pretty and I thought I might have gotten on TV somehow. One of those shows about emergency workers and ER doctors. I wished I'd taken a shower and washed my hair, even put on a little mascara. Something was packed around my neck and jaw. I tried to open my mouth and felt a searing pain inside it and along the whole right side of my face. My head throbbed.

"Ah-w m-m f-f-f—"

"Don't try to talk," she said. "You'll be fine."

Yeah, sure .

Time passed and, when I finally became relatively alert, a wonderful sight swam into view—it was Jake. He looked raw with worry. "Welcome back," he said and kissed my forehead.

Welcome back? Had I been on a trip? That was nice—I'd always wanted to travel more. I was still woozy with whatever drugs they'd been pumping into me. Jake told me later I started humming some unrecognizable song and moving an upraised hand to the beat inside my concussed head. But the more I woke up, the more aware I became that I was lying helpless in a hospital bed and in considerable pain. I also recalled making some kind of humiliating scene in a store. Had I opened up a package of adult diapers? Of condoms? And thrown my purse at someone? "Lehmedu," I started mumbling over and over. *Let me die.*

"Sh-h-h," a nurse told me gently as she worked to muffle both me and my pain.

After several more minutes, I was able to focus enough to get the whole story from Jake, who was now looking more amused than anything else. "Who'd you think you were?" he asked. "Cagney or Lacey?" We had recently watched an interview with the actresses from this old police drama, and the women had looked . . . well, old.

"Na f-f-fu . . . ." This attempt at *not funny* appeared to be the best I could do.

"Don't try to talk."

Why was everyone telling me to shut up?

"Your jaw—it's broken. Wired shut. Plus you've got some stitches in your tongue. You bit it."

Oh, Lord. Crazily, I heard my mother's voice in that room as clear as Jake's, telling me to bite my tongue. I was always sassing her.

"They caught the guy," Jake said, "and the lady got her purse back intact, thanks to you. Turns out she had some heirloom jewelry, old photos, and quite a lot of cash in there. Her son—who, by the way, appears to be filthy rich—says she loses track of all the checks she cashes, and he's incredibly grateful for your help. He usually takes her shopping himself, but she'd gotten it into her head to go to Walgreens alone . . . hates to be dependent, I guess."

I remembered that she'd been buying Depends. Maybe she'd kept it from her son that she needed them.

Jake was beaming at me by this time. "So the son is paying all your medical bills, Maddie. Plus a reward. Isn't that great? You may have to use some of the money to buy a new winter jacket—yours got ripped and bloody." He waited a millisecond for me to respond, but then rambled on. "And there was a reporter here already, thrilled to get a Good Samaritan story just in time for Christmas. You're going to be in the newspaper. "

Was there going to be a picture of me? Looking this awful? I needed to ask, but how? Feeling like I was trapped in a perverse, one-sided game of Charades, I started clicking a phantom camera in front of my face and raising my palms and eyebrows into a question.

"You bet he took a picture, honey."

I groaned.

"But dahling, you look mah-velous." Jake's amusement was now way out of proportion to his concern, it seemed to me. "Our nutty little hero," he added. "Ms. Kick-Ass."

"Mm-f."

The irony did not escape me. Because of my injured jaw and tongue, I was forced to write instead of talk most of the time. Turns out that years ago, before the purse-snatcher had wrecked his knees, he'd been a prizefighter. Lucky me.

When asked, repeatedly, what I'd been *thinking*, running after someone like that who, after all, could've been carrying a gun, I calmly printed in my little notebook, **I wasn't thinking**, without adding that lately my mind had become as mysterious an entity to me as to anyone else. Besides, the guy no more had a gun than the little old lady did—I knew that instinctively. And as for the running part, with his excess weight and his bad knees, he'd been a fool to try. But elaborating in this way involved too much writing, and may have made me look *falsely* modest. People were determined to treat me like a hero. At one point, I wrote to Jake, **Wouldn't anyone have done the same?**

He shook his head but I knew for a fact that *he* would've done the same, only better. No way would he have gotten himself clobbered.

Heroism for Dummies.

Once I was released from the hospital, I spent most of my time in my living room, ensconced on the couch. All the necessary pillows, afghans, water, and juice (with straws), books, notebooks, and remote controls were within reach. I could walk, of course, but I ached all over and moved very little. I certainly stayed away from mirrors. With one side of my face bruised and swollen, topped by flattened greasy hair, I even refused to look at my

157

newspaper photo. **No thanks. I must look like roadkill,** I wrote to Jake after he'd read me the article and offered to show it to me.

My boyfriend seemed to enjoy fussing over me. Since it was clear that I'd recover completely, he was no longer so worried and settled into enjoying all the ways he could tease me about "The Incident at Walgreens" (his made-for-TV movie title). For my nickname he stuck with the classic cop show and chose Cagney. "She was the one," he recalled, "who was single, fiercely independent, beautiful, difficult, sexy . . . and a drunk." I could never get mad at him, though. In his role as my private male nurse, he had several favorite daily inquiries, including "Do we wish to have our sponge bath?"

I was subjected to at least one Ole and Lena joke per day. After coyly peeking down the front of my nightie one morning and whistling, he said, "Did you hear about how Ole entered Lena in the Sons of Norway swim meet? He figured she'd be a natural in the hundred-yard breaststroke. But after she came in dead last, he complained to the judges, 'I tink dem udder girls ver using dere arms!'"

I stared at him blankly, having only half listened to the joke, and I was out of practice with all the missing th's and w's.

"Don't you get it?" Jake asked, jolly as Old St. Nick. "The *breast* stroke."

I gave him my best imitation of a smile and, encouraging him to do more than just peek at my chest, I stripped off my nightie altogether—sponge bath time again.

I recovered quickly in Jake's care at home. When he made me laugh too much, I slugged him because it *hurt* to laugh. He cooked for me and threw everything into a blender. Since he was such a believer in veggies, my meals looked like either green goo or orange goo, but I sucked them down without complaint. We worked out hand signals for such commonplace phrases as *I'm hungry, I'm thirsty, Help me up,* and *Thank you.* For more complex communications, I used my handy little notebook.

Eager to make more meaningful sounds, however, I decided to try playing the piano; no matter how out of tune it was, or how rusty I might be, anything was better than my speech. I was too self-conscious to practice in front of anyone, so I waited until Jake was at work or running errands and then pulled out a dusty book of Bach Two-Part Inventions. I thought of myself as "tickling the ivories," the expression my mother always used because it sounded so much less serious than *practicing*. By the time I was a teenager, we had learned a few duets, one in particular by Beethoven that always got her bouncing on the piano bench next to me. Our ticklish ivories used to cheer her up and I wished we'd played more together.

Now I practiced until my fingers ached, then remained on the bench and stared at the keys, previously dingy, now rubbed a little cleaner. I remembered the old piano tuner who used to come to our house while I was growing up. He'd let me watch while his fingers roamed through scales on the keyboard, tightening and loosening metal strings inside the piano, repeatedly playing each note until it was right with its neighbors.

I recalled one particular day when the piano tuner tapped a key with his calloused left forefinger and said, "This is F, right?" Then his middle finger played the white key a half-step lower. "And this is E?"

I nodded, already having many piano lessons under my belt.

Next he played both notes at the same time. "Dissonance," he said. "You can hear that, maybe feel it under your skin." While continuing to play the two notes, he reached inside with his tuning tool to make the sounds slide further apart, then closer together. Until, magically, they shared the same sound. "The E becomes more F," he explained, "and the F becomes more E." Then he tuned them back to where they needed to be, separate notes. "That's the secret, young lady," he said when he was done. "And I've been married almost fifty years."

His words meant more to me now, of course, but even at the time I understood that this man was teaching me about intimacy, and about what people could be with each other. And, of course, about the much more inevitable dissonance. I was giving this notion careful thought when Jake came bursting back into my house with a ridiculously huge and rich cheese cake included in his purchases (a treat he'd have to put in the *blender* for me). He leaned over the piano bench to kiss me hello and I realized that, lately, there were still times when our bodies and minds moved together—when we were an E and an F making the same sound.

One snowy morning, a week after my injury, he said, "Maybe we could keep communicating like this even after they open up your jaw. I'm kind of enjoying the peace and quiet around here."

My response was loud and clear—an upraised middle finger.

"Oh, good. Still feisty." He got up from his end of the couch and, after fluffing my pillows and refilling my juice (orange, with a shot of vodka in it), he said, "Okay. It's as good a time as any. I'll be right back."

When he returned a minute later he handed me a manila envelope and said, "Merry Christmas."

I'd nearly forgotten what day it was. I grabbed my little notebook and scribbled out,

I haven't wrapped your gift yet.

"Never mind. I can't wait another moment to give you mine."

My surprise???

"Yup. Uh-h-h, listen." He stopped my hand from opening the envelope a moment. "Your initial response will be that I'm nuts, or worse, butting in where I don't belong. But give yourself a chance to think about it, okay?"

I hesitated, then skim-read the papers inside and raised my eyebrows at Jake.

"Yes, it's a writing class. At the U. Don't give me that look, Maddie. It's a chance in a lifetime. Eugenia Crane is going to be teaching here, just for part of this one semester, eight weeks, three hours every Friday afternoon. I know you love her writing, and I hear she's an incredible teacher."

I gestured toward my face and started scribbling in my notebook, but Jake stopped my hand.

"Maddie, it doesn't start until January 4th. The doctor said you'll be healing fast now. And it's an honor to be able to attend. Only fifteen students were accepted for this workshop. Your talent got you in."

My eyebrows were going into spasm from being raised quizzically so often and so hard. "Wha d'mn?"

"I submitted 'Indigo' and 'Slow Dance' as your work sample with the application." He paused and looked nervously at me. Then he launched into the tale with exaggerated high spirits, how he'd come over one day before Thanksgiving, while I was out, taken my stories to Kinko's, sneaked them back in, filled out the application, forged my signature, and brought it all to the University the day of the deadline. "I knew you'd say you weren't ready," he said, winding down. "So I had to try, figuring if you didn't get accepted into the workshop, you'd never even know."

160

I could only lean back into my pillow and close my eyes. This should make me happy and proud, I told myself. Not angry and invaded. Eugenia Crane. Had *she* liked my story or had it been some assistant or even some university clerk? Eugenia Crane! I'd read her first book and seen the award-winning movie based on it several times. Her second novel and its movie adaptation were both considered disasters, but I liked the book anyway, flaws and all. And I'd read *about* her for years. Stories had spread throughout the literary world about writer's block, breakdowns, bad love affairs, money squandered, but incredible strength and talent. To meet this woman, learn from her . . . it *was* a great opportunity. But in my present condition? And as a beginning writer? The class description made it clear that I'd be in a workshop with much more advanced writers, people who were trying to finish and market their *novels*, for God's sake.

Jake and I argued for a few days about this class. I got writer's cramp from arguing with him. But he won. I eventually realized that it was worth a shot, this workshop, maybe just what I needed, and I finally gave Jake the big grateful kiss he deserved. "Give me another one when your mouth is back to normal, okay?" he said. "That was a little like kissing a cheese grater."

Teacher

The night before the first class, I didn't sleep even for a minute, and trying to nap in the morning turned out to be futile as well. My mind was buzzing and humming. Hemming and hawing. How would I ever be able to get through the afternoon without making a complete fool of myself? I carefully wrote down on a card that I had temporary speech limitations, together with my name, hoping Eugenia would be in the classroom early and I could show it to her. But it turned out that I was sitting at the table with the other chosen few for at least ten stagnant minutes, waiting for our teacher to arrive. As was often the case in January, our room was overheated and staticky dry.

A couple of the others knew each other and were chatting, but most of us were eerily silent, scanning our classroom but not making eye contact with anyone, jiggling our feet or rearranging our belongings. I kept glancing down at the brand new notebook I'd bought the day before, together with three new felt-tip pens, new jeans, and a slinky black sweater. Plus I got my hair cut and colored (battling back the occasional silver hair and the usual dull brown). Jake had teased me briefly about my going "back to school" but when faced with how utterly terrified I was, he'd wisely changed the subject.

Finally, the door opened and Eugenia Crane threw herself into our midst, immediately rearranging everything, it seemed, down to the molecular level. "Sorry, sorry, sorry," she called out to us. "Traffic. I didn't think Minnesota *had* traffic." She set down her battered briefcase and took a deep breath. "Plus, I'm always, always late . . . have a reputation to uphold." Another deep breath after opening her coat. "Is it hot as a Louisiana whorehouse in here or am I hot-flashing again?" She rattled on as she dug through her briefcase, pulling out papers. "Don't let anyone fool you, ladies, about menopause—it's hell and it's not exactly temporary. I suspect it's actually an alien invasion, overtaking one unsuspecting female at a time, and there's a government cover-up code-named "Gaslight" to keep us in our place by driving us mad."

Good-natured chuckles around the table. Soon her black fake-fur coat was draped over a vacant chair like a drugged panther. "Which one of you is Stephen with a *ph*?" Barely acknowledging the young man who raised his hand, she said, "First order of business for you is to change your pen name. Stephen Kink? Forget it. I realize you write strange erotic horror stories and probably hope not only to land next to but eventually push Stephen King off the book shelf, but that name will rear up and bite you on the ass instead. Such gimmickry is beneath you—you're very talented. Now, where was I?"

Then Eugenia did a swaying kind of dance as she continued to get organized, sorting through her notes that were scribbled on several different colors of paper. She was wearing pants that billowed out from her hips and licked dust from the floor, and a loose tunic on top made of the same soft, waltzing fabric, with sleeves that were also oversized and seized with movement. So, not quite standing still at the head of our table, Eugenia straightened the corners on a stack of papers (our manuscripts, as it turned out), donned a pair of horn-rimmed reading glasses and peered over them at us for several seconds. I knew from reading about her that she was in her sixties but she seemed both younger and older. Ageless. Tall and stately, with short silver hair, piercing dark eyes that seemed to dwell rather than dart around like most eyes do, and only a few more frown lines than smile lines. She was beautiful.

"God help me," she said at last. "Another new batch of writers. More greedy little faces turned up to me and following my every move like—and forgive the cliché, it's just too apt—like sunflowers to the sun. More hands ready to wave with all the same tedious questions about how to get an agent and how to become the next bestselling author to wow the critics and to pontificate on the talk shows about how writing is like *breathing* and to stop would be to die. We all know how passionate and dedicated we all are, so let's cut to the chase. Another cliché. I'm providing a useful negative example now.

"I'm Eugenia Crane and, as I'm sure you know, phenomenally successful for about a minute, fifteen years ago, and a gross disappointment to everyone except my octogenarian mother since then. But I've learned a thing or two about the craft of writing, and I'm here to move you along a bit toward your goals—that's all. Most of you have already had a few publications, and I know you want more, always more in print. You want money, literary stardom, but for all of that you need not only talent, but discipline, perseverance, and quite honestly, a huge amount of dumb luck. You do not need *me* to make you rich and famous and that's not why I'm here. Only for the work itself. Oh . . . and if you've got your heart set on getting into the movie business, write screen plays, win Oscars, or meet Brad Pitt, you've come to the wrong place. Are we clear?"

The group responded with a ripple of head bobbing and hand fidgets.

Eugenia coughed into her hand a few times, nothing tubercular sounding, just a quick throat-tuning. Her alto voice was scuffed up as though she hadn't anticipated the need to take proper care of it over the years. She started pacing now and I noticed that her stride was not as smooth as it had first appeared. She only gave an illusion of grace.

"Okay, we're clear. Now . . . if you are serious about your work, I'm here to guide you, encourage you and push you. This should be called a re-writing workshop, because that's what I'll be asking of you. You'll be reading part of your work out loud in class and getting advice from your fellow students. And you can sure expect advice from me about that work as well as the stories or novel excerpts you turn in to me. I'll help you revise, I'll get the best out of you. But please, *please* don't expect me to be some kind of guru. I despise that misused word and it's a poor fit for me." She circled behind the teacher's desk and reached for the top drawer. "My wisdom drawer," she said as she pulled it open. "Oops. Empty. Sorry."

One middle-aged, earnest-looking woman unwisely chose this moment to raise her hand with a question. Eugenia glanced at the woman and then pointed again at the empty "wisdom" drawer. The woman lowered her hand.

"One thing I want you to do at this point is to let it flow. Put a gag on your nitpicky self-censors. Yes, sometimes it can gush and other times dry up, but the ideal is a steady flow. Mozart is supposed to have claimed that writing music was, for him, like a cow pissing. Get the idea?"

We chuckled and obediently nodded our bovine heads. I wondered why cows kept coming to my attention lately. Maybe it was about grass or milk and I was about to turn vegan or freakishly begin lactating.

"So tell me . . . . How many of you are into pain?" Eugenia somehow maintained a serious expression. "Anyone blatantly masochistic? Self-mutilating? Self-flagellating? How many?"

Nobody raised their hands, of course, but it looked as though a few, especially Stephen Kink, were considering it.

Eugenia shook her head and finally sat down at our table. "Because if you're not, you shouldn't be in here. You shouldn't be writing or even *thinking* about writing. Oh, it's not just the inevitable rejection I'm talking about, the returned manuscripts, many of which you can tell haven't even been read because the paper clip hasn't been moved. And I'm not even talking about the losing of contracts and grants to people less deserving than yourself, or the agents who predict your obscurity. For any kind of artist, it's an outrageously up-and-down kind of lifestyle. More down than up, and the ups have razor wire at the top, in case you're tempted to hang on.

"No, when I say *pain* I'm talking about where you are *now*, in the *process* of writing. That's where there is, or should be, agony. Without it, you might as well be writing down recipes or instructions on how to install a faucet."

I liked this woman—don't ask me why. She seemed to be scaring some of the others in class, which I figured was her intention. Or maybe she was just, in general, pissed off and was inviting us to join her in that condition. Either way, I felt strangely welcomed by her, in spite of the fact that I was out of my league. Her mention of the fact that others in the class had been published only reinforced my fear that I was the only beginner here. I could almost hear the hiss of my leaking self-confidence; but if anyone could seal that leak, it might be Eugenia Crane.

After awhile our teacher patted the pile of papers a few times and looked at each of our faces in turn. "These are your writing samples. I read them—don't imagine that I made some underling do that. I'm a popular teacher these days. My writing career may have fallen on hard times, but as a *teacher* of writing, I'm in demand. I get the big bucks. Thousands of applications . . . well, okay, *hundreds* of applications were sent to my house between September and December, out of which I had to choose fifteen of you for this workshop. I'll be honest—there were a few other stories and novel excerpts as good as yours, some even better, or at least more polished.

But something was missing in those stories, something I saw in each of *yours*. I don't have a word for what that something is, I just have a pretty good instinct for finding *promise*."

She started scrounging around inside her briefcase as though looking for promise in there too, finally coming up with a throat lozenge which she sucked on a few times and then spat, appallingly, back into the briefcase. "So, I'm assuming you people all have the requisite open minds and open hearts, and are ready to write and rewrite until you're ready to scream at me *ENOUGH*. At which point I'll calmly tell you to go back once more into your story, to dig deeper, to make me laugh, cry, think and be glad to be alive and a writer and a reader, and a goddamned *great* teacher."

Her dark, wide-set eyes locked with mine and I felt myself blush. I'd never seen irises so black before, same color as her eyebrows, and in the starkest possible contrast to her silver-white hair.

"Kafka once wrote," she continued, "that we ought to read only what *wounds* us. He encouraged writers to affect their readers 'like a *disaster*.' A story, according to Kafka, 'must be the *ax* for the frozen sea inside us.' I love that, don't you? ' . . . the ax for the frozen sea inside us.' I've stolen that several times, paraphrasing a bit and not always bothering to attribute it to him. I give keynote speeches occasionally, and I invariably say something about axes and frozen seas. I'm considered brilliant by a lot of barely literate people. But with *you*—" again she peered at each of us in turn, as though our very souls were easily visible to her "—I'm promising to be absolutely honest. Brutally honest, sometimes."

A pony-tailed guy on the opposite side of the table raised his hand and rambled off something about the context of Kafka's quote, and I thought *shit*, why am I even here? I sat with my wired jaw and, for once, felt actually glad to have an excuse not to speak, because what the hell would I say? Glancing discreetly around the room, I counted seven men and seven other women, with an age range that I guessed to be from the early twenties to the late fifties. They all looked exceptionally bright and bold, with lots to say, lots to write. Facts from long-ago college classes bumped around in my head, and all I came up with about Kafka was that he wrote about a guy who turned into a bug.

While Pony-tail asked yet another question, I stole glances around the table once again. My eyes eventually settled on one man who had been

166

staring down at the table, rubbing it with his fingertips as though the surface—not his nerves—needed soothing. When he looked up and directly at me, there was a friendly glint in his eyes. Although not particularly handsome, there was something . . . well, noteworthy about him. He was bearded, muscular, and slouching as though trying to be inconspicuous. He wore a terrible, threadbare sweater with the sleeves pushed up past the elbows. His red-brown hair needed a trim as badly as his beard, his skin looked lived-in, and his hands calloused. On his left forearm was a swirling tattoo that did not look professionally done. Feeling like the outsider I was, it was natural for me to gravitate toward someone who *looked* like an outsider too. His table-rubbing index finger lifted a moment in miniature greeting, seemingly for me alone.

"Let's begin by introducing ourselves." Eugenia said with a practiced smile. "Go ahead," she nodded at the student closest to her. "Your name and why the hell you're sitting in here, why now, why me, why you."

The first student began to talk as though he'd been through this a dozen times and knew exactly what to say. Eugenia asked questions and made comments, stretching the process out into an actual conversation, with the rest of us as an audience. I was suddenly terrified again and began to soak the armpits of my new sweater. The introductions continued in this way for almost a half-hour, getting progressively longer and in some cases more self-assured. They didn't actually go in order, something I thought was odd. Like they were vying for attention rather than being polite. I was struck by how intense everyone looked, like we were gathered to discuss world peace and starving children, not merely the spinning of yarns. And for some reason I was the only woman present (besides Eugenia) who had applied eyeliner and lipstick which made me feel frivolous, if not vaguely slutty.

It appeared that *all* of my fellow students had been published in literary magazines, many had won grants over the years, and one had published several children's books. There were three with graduate degrees in English or creative writing. I had barely finished college. *Intellectual Pretense for Dummies: Think of life experience as the ultimate higher education. Be sure to have evidence of deep thinking etched on your face at all times and eschew the use of camouflaging makeup and mirth. Collect pithy quotes from dead guys like Kafka (and grow accustomed to using words like pithy and eschew without giggling).*

167

I decided to wait and try to take my turn last. The hirsute guy with the tattoo seemed to be thinking the same thing. When it was just he and I, we glanced at each other, I pointed to him, and he spoke up. His name was Arthur Locke. He'd recently moved back here from Chicago but had grown up in Minneapolis. "Let's see," he said. "What else should I say?" He scratched his beard and I half expected an idea to be loosened from it. "As for publications, my stories all started out in . . . uh, well, newsletters— prison newsletters. And then some of them were reprinted in journals and anthologies. Nothing you'd have heard of, though."

"What kind of stories do you like to write?" Eugenia asked him.

Arthur shrugged again. "Real stuff. Street stuff. Nothing pretty."

"I see." Eugenia flipped through the manuscripts. "You're writing the novel about the ex-con searching for his runaway sister, right?"

"That, unfortunately, is me. Yes."

"Don't apologize for God's sake. It's a worthy project."

"Is it worth the ten years it's cost me so far?" Arthur asked as though he'd been sentenced to this time by an unfair judge.

Eugenia smiled at him and nodded.

He did not look particularly uncomfortable now, but I wanted to rescue him anyway from all the attention, all the people trying to guess how autobiographical his book was and, if he'd been in prison, *why?*

"In the excerpt I read," Eugenia said, "your guy was still a juvenile and he was thrown in jail overnight for . . . what was it?"

"Drunk and disorderly."

"Ah, yes," Eugenia said. "I've always tried to be an *orderly* drunk. But, whatever the case may be, your writing is very impressive, Arthur. Amazing use of humor, considering the material. In some cases, a kind of gallows humor, right? And full of such vivid smells and sounds, it made me a little nauseous, actually."

"Thanks," Arthur said, "I think." No more table polishing, I noticed. Then he looked at me, nodded encouragement, and smiled in a way that squeezed at my stomach —a physical response that reminded me way too much of adolescence.

"Last but not least . . . ." Eugenia directed all the attention toward me. I didn't say anything at first, then mumbled, "Ah cnt tah . . . ." And held my card up so that the young woman sitting at my right could read it.

"She has a broken jaw," my fellow student told Eugenia. "Her jaw is wired shut."

Eugenia stared at me and smiled warmly. "I see."

"You're the one that was in the paper," another student said to me, then turned to Eugenia. "I saw her picture, just before Christmas. She ran after a mugger, saved an old lady's life savings or something."

My eyes flitted around the room and settled on my notebook. "Mm-f."

"Is that true?" Eugenia asked.

"I read about her too," said the pony-tailed guy who'd recognized Kafka's quote. "The mugger had been some kind of big bruiser too, an ex-boxer, and he pushed the old lady down and stole her purse, and she—" he pointed to me— "ran after him until he gave up the purse. But then he punched her in the face. If we can believe anything that's in the papers."

Eugenia was gazing at me all during this discussion. "In this case, I'm sure we can. Excellent. Your name is . . . ?" The student next to me read it off my card. "Okay. Thank you, Madelyn. Now I know how to begin. Frankly, I've taught so many of these classes, I get bored listening to myself give the same opening class over and over, so I use your introductions to launch me in whatever direction seems right at the moment."

There was a stirring all around me as the focus, finally, returned to our teacher.

"So, thanks to Madelyn's brave, some might say foolhardy act, I know where to begin."

By this time my face felt on fire, but for some reason I was beginning to like Eugenia more and more. The way she had complimented Arthur, plus something about her manner was actually making me feel more at ease.

Then her mood shifted. She looked all jaded and pissed off again, glaring at the stack of our manuscripts as though it had stuck its collective tongue out at her. After a sigh, she said, "Okay. Point. Of. View. I know you all are aware of the importance of choosing a viewpoint. But please allow me, Madelyn, to use your recent experience to illustrate."

Inwardly I groaned.

"Think about how differently this incident—we'll call it *story* now—unfolds for the three principles involved. A guy, a prizefighter who lost too many fights, who was apparently desperate for money or else just plain mean. An old lady, too generic at the moment, but never mind. And our bold female bystander, maybe packed tightly with some random rage that morning or habitually altruistic or whatever. Okay. The purse is snatched, the old lady watches as the scoundrel flees, our heroine takes off after him. For her efforts, she gets the purse back but also gets a broken jaw. Right? Not to mention a fresh dose of anger or disillusionment."

The class sat waiting for where this was taking us.

"So . . . here's your first in-class writing exercise. I don't believe in simply lecturing, as you probably know. And I don't believe in reticent students. You are here because you are writers, maybe even gifted ones, some of you. So . . . I want you to choose one of those three viewpoints—the bad guy, the hero, and the victim—and begin writing this story. I'll even make it easier for you by providing the starting point: One minute before the purse is actually snatched. Now . . . go."

I opened my notebook along with everyone else, heard the enthusiastic scratch of writing implements occurring near me, felt my fingers go numb as they tried to hold one of my new felt-tip pens. The incident that had apparently captured the imagination of both my teacher and my fellow students left me oddly uninspired. Without this assignment I probably would never have written about it. But after a few agonizing minutes during which I scribbled *I don't know what to write I don't know I don't know, Mozart's cow piss cowpies how cries.*

I felt someone looking my way. It was Arthur, smiling at me again. He gave me a thumbs-up—corny but effective. I finally started to write, from the viewpoint of the purse-snatcher. I'd been wondering about him for weeks now anyway, so what the hell? I temporarily peeled away his ratty jacket and shirt to give him some tattoos, hand-drawn while he'd been locked up somewhere, and he started to become human to me.

We had about twenty minutes to work on this exercise. Then we were given a ten-minute break. Eugenia disappeared before anyone could approach her. I never did find out where she went during our breaks.

Released from the hot room and the herd of writers—most of whom headed for rest rooms—I searched for a vending machine. Tension had drained my mouth of saliva and I'd brought a straw with me, so I plugged the machine for a Diet Coke.

"Do you have any more change?" It was Arthur, behind me, holding a dollar bill too soft and crumpled to insert into the machine for change.

I nodded and dropped quarters into his outstretched palm. When he gave me the dollar, it was only his fingers that brushed mine, and only for a split second. And yet, I felt something ignite in me. He'd found my pilot light and I hadn't even been aware of its flickering out.

He sipped on his Coke and I sucked on my straw for a few awkward moments. "I had my jaw broken once," he said amiably. "In a fight. I wish it had been over something worthy, like in your case, but it was over a song in a jukebox. The other guy kept playing Johnny Cash's "Ring of Fire" over and over. Great song, but after the tenth time or so it kinda grates on a guy's nerves. So I was delegated by my buddies to stop him. Ended up having to bust that innocent jukebox . . . with my face."

I emitted a tight-lipped chuckle and was trying to better convey how much I enjoyed his company when a pretty young thing eased in between us and asked Arthur where in Chicago he'd been living. He gave some vague answer and grinned at her with what was such a killer smile I wondered if he could've been arrested for *that*. The girl leaned in his direction, jutting out her perky breasts in a way I gave up doing years ago. I returned to the classroom feeling old and very, very tired.

After the break, we were asked to write for another twenty minutes, the exact same paragraphs we'd just written, but from one of the other viewpoints. Eventually, we were doing the same thing with the third point of view. This gave me the notion, both exhilarating and embarrassing, that everyone in class had peered inside my head, run in my shoes through that back alley, and been knocked on their asses. But writing from the so-called hero's viewpoint proved to be the most difficult for me.

We were asked, when finished, to recognize how dramatically different the event unfolded in the three versions.

Some of us nodded. I swallowed and ran my tongue over the metal in my mouth.

"Your characters *must* come to life. Let yourself forget that they are merely your creations. I've read that when Balzac was dying, he summoned a doctor who didn't exist, except in his books."

Naturally Pony-tail had something to add to this as well. I decided to dislike this show-off with all my mute strength.

When the class finally ended, I prepared to leave, but Eugenia excused herself from the questions of a few other eager students in order

171

to approach me and put her hand on my arm. "Stay a moment," she said to me. Her terse replies to the others who'd gathered around sent them scattering. I hadn't seen Arthur leave, so he must have made a quick exit, just as I'd been planning to do.

I scanned my mental notes from class for some clue as to why she wanted me to stay. Had I been cut already?

"Madelyn," she said, "I could use a drink. Will you join me? I know, I know, it's unseemly, but already you're one of my favorites. You wrote the story about the bulimic woman, right? And the one about the couple breaking up in the pizzeria? Good. I want to have a drink with you and discuss . . . oh, I don't know . . . life."

How could I say no? But when Eugenia invited me to join her, I regretted my injury more than at any other moment in the last few weeks. I would be sitting there with someone who was a bit of a hero to *me*, someone articulate and funny, full of language and full of life. And all I could do was mumble and scribble, wiggle my eyebrows and gesture with my hands. She'd get immediately bored with me.

We settled into a booth at a nearby bar, blinking to adjust our eyes in the haze. Although smoking had been kicked outside, even in most bars, this place was testing the law. A battered jukebox sat in one corner, silent at the moment (weirdly, I craved "Ring of Fire"), and behind the bar was a guy who looked asleep on his feet, even as he poured. Three men slumped separately at the bar, staring straight ahead or into their booze of choice. *Cheers* it was not.

I got my notebook out, ready to converse in writing.

"Hey, listen," she said with a much more genuine smile than I'd seen all afternoon. "I hope you didn't mind my using your mugging incident like that. It was perfect for my needs."

I smiled and shook my head no.

"It's getting hard to listen to myself in front of writing classes these days, and I can't bear to use the same old material over and over. I'm always on the lookout for something fresh."

I gave her an understanding nod.

"The fact is, Madelyn . . . as a writer, maybe even as a teacher, I'm a fraud."

"Hm-m?" I felt my smile melt.

"I don't really have much to give any more. You know the story—about my first book, how I was branded a 'phenomenon' which, believe me, is something *nobody* should have to live up to. And then the movie, which they actually let me be a consultant on, which is so rare, and it turned out, in some ways, *better* than the book and won awards . . . well, it was all pretty overwhelming. Then, the second book, the pressure to measure up and . . . ." Eugenia sipped her martini and didn't bother to finish that sentence. She knew that I knew what had happened.

"Anyway," she continued after a few moments with renewed spirit, "I've begun to look at writing classes as clusters of baby birds, all with their little beaks wide open and aimed skyward, waiting for me and my own peckish mouth to feed them. Have you ever seen regurgitated worms? Not a pretty sight."

I thought we were sunflowers was my first written response to her.

She smiled. "You got me there, overly fond of metaphors."

In my notebook I printed, **I'm a fraud too . . . not a writer yet, really. A beginner.**

She read this, glanced up at me and shrugged. "So, you're new at it. Does that make you any less passionate? I told you, what interests me is potential. Are you writing regularly?"

I nodded vigorously, ignoring how my injury had interrupted my progress.

"I thought so," Eugenia replied. "I told you I've got an instinct for this sort of thing, so don't worry—you're the real deal. With some interesting characters ready to spring forth. I enjoyed the woman you wrote about who was repulsed by the smell of her husband's shirts. And strangely interested in the other one. I've never had much patience with women like your bulimic, fretting over every tiny imperfection of her body, obsessing about every man who came her way, and every other woman who was busy having babies. God help women like that—I'm assuming you're not one of them. But good fiction can offer some insight, and you gave me that."

Fiction, yes. The bingeing and purging part was someone else, but the hunger and (I borrowed Jake's word) **longing was probably mostly me. God help women like ME.**

Eugenia laughed. "Are you married?"

I shook my head no.

"Divorced?"

I nodded.

"Me too. Five times. Maybe that's why I'm not *into* men at the moment, if you know what I mean."

I shrugged, glad for the dense smoke. My reactions could stay hazy as well.

"Any children?" she asked next.

When I swallowed hard and then shook my ahead again she said, "Me neither. By choice. Had a couple of abortions, as a matter of fact." She gave me a look that seemed to *dare* me to be offended or judgmental.

I wondered if there was something about this new writerly me that drew confessions out of people. Should I be flattered? Or was I just a blank page for other women to write on? No, I had control of the blank pages. Didn't they know I could use what they told me? Mona, Suzanne, and now Eugenia—they made it all too easy to betray their confidences.

Eager to change direction, I wrote down, **What are you working on now?**

She frowned when she read this question and I felt sorry to have disappointed her with one of those questions she's sick to death of being asked. "Not much," was her abrupt answer. Then she lit up a cigarette. "You mind?"

I shook my head and wrote down that I used to enjoy smoking too, but it had been banned in public places.

"Of course." She discreetly blew a trail of smoke off to one side, as though it could be blamed on someone else. "But I thought Minnesota was a little more behind the times."

At the risk of disappointing her again with another question, I wrote, from my heart: **I loved your books—both of them. Writing like yours is what motivates me. I think you're anything BUT a fraud.**

She read this a couple of times, puzzling over my rushed handwriting, and finally asking, "Afraid? Is it that obvious?"

I shook my head, made the letters of my last word clearer so she could see I'd been merely referring to what she'd said earlier about being a fraud. Not *afraid*, not Eugenia Crane. Then she laughed and put her hand amiably over mine. "I have to admit," she said, "that I asked you to share a drink with me initially because I knew you couldn't speak. I'm so sick of talkers. Forgive me. Because now I can't wait to hear your voice."

We had only one drink that first day after class, and I assumed that would be the end of it.

When I got home, Jake was there watching TV, eager to hear every detail of my afternoon and evening. He'd been worried when I hadn't come home at the expected time. I was too weary to write down all that had happened, so I simply let him know that the class had been interesting, Eugenia was great, and I was glad he'd forced me to go.

"I've never forced you to do anything." Jake looked tired too, and I was relieved when he gave me a quick kiss and left for his own house.

I sat and wished I'd wanted him to stay. I missed *missing* him when he was gone. And I missed the passion. My love for him no longer seemed in the present tense. It was more residual, like the rain that gets tugged from trees by wind gusts long after the actual storm has subsided. I liked that simile and wrote it down, figuring I could use it in some story . . . after extracting Jake's name from it, of course.

Then I pulled out my copy of Eugenia Crane's first book and reread it well into the night, slowly, savoring each page, each phrase, each word. Eugenia was so *in* that novel, I heard her voice, saw her, felt with her, even during the sex scenes, which were with both men and women. One of the narrator's lovers turned out to be a psychopath who liked to break bottles and threaten her with them. I knew it was fiction, of course, but reading someone's book, especially their first, and one in which she seemed so utterly naked, felt like a viable way to get to know someone better. When I finished with the first book the next day, I dove into the second one, analyzing where she went astray. Maybe it was the nakedness of the first book that led her to cover up and hide in the second one. Maybe that was the difference. Still, the writing was brilliant, seductive, uniquely Eugenia's.

I wondered if I was falling a little in love with my teacher and, when I mentioned this possibility to Jake, he surprised me by saying, "Good for you."

Class

The next Friday morning, my doctor removed the wires and stitches. My jaw and tongue had mostly healed and, although I was sore for a while after that, I found pure ecstasy in the simple opening and closing of my mouth, letting words flow outward instead of getting squashed inside. I almost looked forward to speaking up in Eugenia's workshop.

When I got to the classroom, Arthur was already there. "Hi," I said. "Are you ready to be the next Steinbeck?" I wanted my appearance and my voice (finally) to be an exclamation point for him, and the look on his face was gratifying.

"Maybe the next Nelson Algren," he replied.

"Who?"

"You know . . . Chicago knockaround guy . . . *Walk on the Wild Side.*"

"Ah, now, maybe that's why I haven't heard of him. I hardly ever *walk* on the wild side. I usually slink." My enunciation was still far from perfect and I was acutely aware of spitting out those S's.

Arthur chortled politely. "I imagined your voice to have that sexy Lauren Bacall quality, and it's close. Except younger, of course."

"And spittier," I said, wiping my mouth discreetly.

At the beginning of our second week together, Eugenia shocked us all by lifting up one pant leg and showing us what was under there, from the top of the right shoe up to her knee—a prosthetic leg. Not leg-shaped wooden but spindly metal, robotic-looking. She grinned at our reaction. "Okay, class, I'll give you your assignment up front. What happened to my leg? Write down a detailed scenario. Use your imagination, get gory if you like, or weird, science-fiction, whatever, but make it plausible and interesting. And not maudlin, please. If you *must* mention phantom limb, make it new. Work on that at home and turn it in to me next week.

"Now," she said after we'd opened our notebooks and written down her assignment, "who wants to read first today?"

And so it began. In addition to our weekly assignments, we were each asked to "workshop" one story or novel excerpt—read it aloud in class, get comments from each other and from Eugenia, rewrite, reread, and rewrite again as needed. I chose "Closet Sanctuary" for this process and during the second class, after three other students, I read my story aloud. My nervousness, however, combined with my eagerness to speak after several weeks of mumbling, caused me to speed-read.

"Whoa," a now-familiar male voice stopped me in the middle of page three. "Slow down," Arthur said. "My pea-sized brain can't work that fast."

I glanced at Eugenia who nodded.

"Sorry." I slowed down, but was aware of speeding up again, especially toward the end. The story sounded so stupid to my own ears. Trite, hopelessly amateurish. By the time I was done, my stagefright seemed to have altered my voice into someone's else's—and certainly not Lauren Bacall.

Nobody said anything at first. "I think I'd have to read it myself," one woman said, "to be able to comment."

"I know," I said quietly. "I tried to slow down but . . . ."

"Well, what I could follow, I liked," Arthur said. "A lot." But when everyone looked at him expectantly, he didn't seem to be able to add any specifics. I smiled at him gratefully anyway.

"I liked it too," Eugenia added when nobody else spoke up. "That dead lover's leather jacket—I could see it, smell it, feel it on my own skin. Very moving. I could feel that woman's heart breaking. Excellent dialogue between the girls. Strong ending, too. Madelyn, we all get nervous. It's not easy reading our work aloud, and I know this is a first for you. You'll get used to it."

I nodded, embarrassed that now *everyone* knew I was a beginner, but grateful that we were moving on. Eugenia later gave me some suggestions for revision in private, and I vowed to give a much better reading of the revised story.

Next, two students read aloud versions of the mugging story which they'd expanded from last week's in-class writing exercise. One was about the "hero" having been raped earlier in her life by a guy that looked very much like the purse-snatcher. She goes berserk, pulls out a handgun and shoots the guy in the crotch. After this student (a short round girl who seemed to be the youngest in class) finished reading and after a few scattered encouragements from others, Eugenia nodded and said that for her revision the girl might consider forgetting about how the story had started from an assignment about a purse-snatching, and instead dig more deeply into the rape victim's mind. "Write a detailed character sketch of this woman before you do anything else with the story. Who, exactly, is she and what are some more of the factors that led her to shoot someone like that. I'm grateful my assignment got you writing about something difficult, but we often have to discard our starting points. Okay?"

The girl looked on the verge of tears, and I couldn't tell if it was because of Eugenia's "criticism" or because the story itself had been too emotionally charged.

Eugenia gave her a gentle smile. "I'll give some examples of what I'm suggesting beyond the character sketch. Maybe the woman simply sees a guy on the street who looks like her rapist. He hasn't done anything at this point except have an unfortunate resemblance to someone who damaged this girl. Is it him? If he was put in jail, has he been released? Escaped? Is it his brother? Is he stalking her? Or is she imagining *all* men to be menaces and her mind is turning this poor schmuck into her attacker? After deciding who *he* is, then figure out under what circumstances your character shoots him. See what I mean?"

The girl mumbled a thank you and took a Kleenex out of her purse to blow her nose. This, I thought, is exhausting.

The other version of my Walgreens incident was by Ponytail. It was slyly bent and hilarious, so we were treated to Eugenia's hearty, snorting laugh for the first time. This story was about a gentle but dim-witted, cauliflower-eared ex-boxer named Lenny who tries to help an old lady onto the bus, but she makes an unexpected move and his oversized hand accidentally ends up under the lady's bony backside, between her legs. She screams that he's attacking her and starts to pound him with her purse, all the while clamping her legs together which makes it impossible for the guy to extricate his one hand but, with the other, he grabs her purse in self-defense. The hero of this story is the bus driver, an iron-pumping, man-hating lesbian who misreads the situation and comes to the woman's rescue. The bus driver gets her jaw broken when the boxer is finally, suddenly, able to yank his fist free of the old lady's leg-grip.

This reading finally got the class loosened up enough to speak more freely and the writer got some interesting reactions, both positive and negative. He jotted down many of the suggestions for revision, including a new starting point. Only my comment seemed to irritate him. "How does the old woman pivot enough on those stairs to pound him with the purse," I asked, "if his hand is stuck between her legs from the rear?"

"Well, maybe she's a retired acrobat," Ponytail said, but then he shrugged. "This wasn't meant to be taken seriously . . . at all." He glared at me for a moment until Eugenia spoke up. She had only a few points to add and thanked him for delighting us all.

Break time. Thank God. I grabbed my jacket and went outside for a slap of cold air. I was pleased when Arthur joined me with a cup of vending machine coffee for each of us. If he'd had cigarettes, I would've enjoyed sharing one with him.

He asked about my jaw and we chatted for a few minutes about that, and then he said, "I'm really sorry for interrupting your reading like that. I've never been much for decorum, I guess."

"No. I'm glad you spoke up. Somebody had to stop me. God, I was so nervous, and the words stopped making sense after a while. That ever happen to you?"

"Sure," he said. "I seem to have lost perspective on my own writing. That's why I'm here. I'm anxious to get suggestions for rewrites because I've hit a wall. I can handle constructive criticism, and I'm sure that's what I'll get." He seemed a lot more easy-going than I ever hoped to be. "Listen," he continued, "I wanted to tell you that I got choked up listening to your story."

"That bad, huh?"

He laughed—a deeply resonant sound that warmed the air between us. "Okay, choked up is an exaggeration, but I was moved, Madelyn. Really."

"Call me Maddie."

"Okay. That suits you better."

Oh, that smile. I began to imagine the bristle of his beard, the contrasting velvet of his lips. And there was that infuriating nudge to my stomach again.

"The thing is," he continued, "I've spent a lifetime avoiding emotions, so I'm not easily moved, but that little girl sounded so lost, and her mother even more so. I just wanted to tell you that."

"Thanks." I had to look up a few inches to meet his gaze and it was well worth the effort. We were blissfully alone out there and, seemingly, joined together in an us-against-them way even though the *them* in this case were pretty nice people. Maybe I was looking for too many complicated reasons for being just plain aroused by this man.

We were late returning to class. Everybody else was seated, waiting and silent. Eugenia gave Arthur and me meaningful glances, back and forth. Then she said a little too loudly, "Next?"

It was soon Arthur's turn. He read aloud from his novel-in-progress in which a young man is newly sprung from "the joint" and lives on the street for a few days, reluctant to go home because of his sadistic father. When he runs out of money and options (other than stealing again), he confronts his father and asks about his sixteen-year-old sister. The father says she'd been gone for months, no doubt a whore like the kids' mother. The boy stays for a few nights in a homeless shelter, where he meets a girl and tumbles into love, but after only one brief sexual encounter, she also disappears. His deep voice sounded almost actorly and continued to resonate in the classroom several seconds after he'd abruptly stopped reading.

We all sat there for a while in captivated silence. And then the comments began flying, words like "Strong" and "Amazing." Beginning that day, Arthur's main character—his alter ego—seemed to practically take a seat with us at that table, between two of the women who, by the end of his reading, were wiping tears from their eyes. But it was not Arthur's style to tug hard at our emotions. In fact, as Eugenia had mentioned the week before, he relied heavily on humor, especially in the boy's scattershot memories. In spite of the awful things that had happened, (and it's clear they would continue to happen to him), being in this young man's viewpoint was a fascinating place to be, one that was even strangely desirable.

But when I finally spoke up, I surprised myself and probably everybody else too. Unconditional raves were nice, and he'd had plenty, but Arthur had just told me he was looking for advice. He'd admitted to grinding away at this book for ten years—no wonder he'd lost perspective. So, after the person before me had praised Arthur's realistic dialogue and also his pacing,

I blurted out, "Yes, except when he meets the girl in the shelter. The romance seems too abrupt, and the dialogue virtually stops."

Everyone was looking at me. I paused for a moment, my heart pounding away. *Oh, Beginner Bitch speaks*, I could imagine them thinking. But I forged ahead. "He's just had this horrible scene with his dad and he's worried sick about his sister and about how to proceed with his life, so does it really work for him to suddenly get all moony-eyed over this homeless chick? A girl who, by the way, never says anything, and we don't quite see. They never even kiss. Then, suddenly, they're fucking like rabbits." I managed to stop myself at last but wished it could've been a few words earlier, avoiding both obscenity and cliché. Blushing, I added lamely, "But overall, really great stuff, Arthur."

I didn't quite dare look at Eugenia until she launched into *her* critique of his work. As though I'd broken the ice, her praise was overshadowed by a long list of suggestions for revision. I felt guilty, yes. And I tried to read Arthur's face as he listened and jotted down notes. Eugenia was definitely harder on him than she'd been on any of the rest of us, and she may have concentrated too much on matters of *craft*. His writing style seemed so natural, and a voice like his should probably have been allowed its idiosyncrasies. I wanted to say something about that, in part to temper what *I'd* said. But the pattern had been set—Eugenia always had the last word.

Arthur did not seem particularly troubled by her (or my) remarks, however, and he simply nodded and thanked everyone. I wanted to say something to him on our way out, but he made another quick exit and Eugenia once again stopped me from leaving.

"Same wretched bar?" she asked.

I agreed. Why not?

This time we stayed out longer and our roles as teacher and student began to dissolve. We steered clear of writing-talk and spoke instead about choices we'd made. Marriages, love affairs, thwarted crushes, mistakes, regrets, and triumphs. Even though she had more than twenty years on me, we shared some distinctly middle-aged female ground. And I couldn't help but recognize some of what she said happened to her, because so many similar events occurred to the characters in her books.

What was real and what was fiction with Eugenia? I wondered. Were the boundaries unclear even to *her*. And did I have any right to wonder such things? I reminded myself not to assume anything or judge, but she made it hard not to blend her characters' nakedness with her own.

I was trying to drink as little as possible since I was driving home. Eugenia, however, didn't seem to care about that. "I've been driving after a few drinks my whole adult life—totally accident free so far, but I know it's unwise."

I shrugged, wishing I were as good at being "bad" as she was, and as open with what others might consider secrets. I decided it was time to bum a cigarette and, what the hell, tell her about the dream. My recurring nightmare. I began obliquely. "I was wondering, do you ever write down your dreams? I mean, do you ever start a story based on a dream?"

"No," Eugenia said. "At least not intentionally. I don't usually remember my dreams. Why do you ask?"

"Just wondering—"

"And for God's sake don't even *think* about writing a nice lively, fantastical tale only to have the narrator wake up and find it was only a dream. I've been known to set fire to such tripe."

"Okay. So what you're saying, though, is that dreams can be connected in some strange ways to what we write." She started to interrupt but I forged ahead. "I've been having this nightmare, one I had as a child all the time. But now it comes only when I've just finished a story. Like I keep giving birth, over and over, to some demon. Like my writing unleashes something . . . ."

Eugenia stared at me for several seconds without responding, and I squirmed. She ordered another drink and lit another cigarette.

"I'm sorry," I said. "I didn't mean to—"

"No. It's okay. I just needed to think a bit, that's all. You threw me, and that's not easy to do." She squinted through the smoke she was blowing between us. "Maybe you *should* write the dream, in this case. Dig into the mess in your mind, get down and dirty. But . . . I'm not sure I want to see the results."

I looked down to examine my thumbnail, stung by her words.

She abruptly changed the subject, talking coolly about the class now, and I nursed my drink and grinned, desperate to regain our earlier camaraderie.

"I think Sheila is very talented, don't you?" she asked. "And incredibly sexy."

Picturing Sheila's rather somber-looking face and puffy body, I said, "Really?"

"Okay, I admit I'm mostly attracted to her writing. But I know she likes women, and I like her, so . . . who knows?"

Eugenia then admitted that one of the other female students was irritating the hell out of her. "All that domesticity," she said with exasperation. "Who wants to read about some toddler puking all over the dog? That whole young mother terrain's been explored beautifully by a lot of writers, but this woman will never be one of them. I blew it choosing her."

I too found this particular woman annoying. Her writing was as mind-numbingly ordinary as a jar of Gerber's, and her "critique" was always one of two comments: "It would make a great movie." Or, "I don't believe anyone would do *that*."

"I can imagine what she's going to write about how I lost my leg," Eugenia said, motioning for our waiter and pointing to her empty glass. "Let's see—I climbed onto my washing machine chasing after Junior's gerbil, and my leg got caught in the spin cycle."

I laughed. "So your critique should begin, 'It would make a great movie, but I don't believe anyone would do *that*.'"

Eugenia rummaged through her purse—she always seemed to be doing that, in her purse, her briefcase, her memory, and our cluttered minds. Finally pulling out a slightly used Kleenex, she blew her nose with a honk. "I'm getting a cold," she said. "Does it ever get above freezing in this godforsaken state?"

"In January? Only rarely," I replied. "By the way, what *did* really happen to your leg?"

"I can't say—you haven't written your version yet."

"I promise to use my imagination. Please tell me."

"Well, for that story, we *both* really need another drink. Trust me."

"Okay."

It took Eugenia a while to settle herself more comfortably into the booth, drain yet another martini, blot her mouth dry, finish a cigarette, and clear her throat. And I began to wonder if this was a story I really wanted to hear.

"Well, let's see. The leg. Okay, let me start with this, not to scare you but . . . . People tend to think of my first novel's success as being sudden, like I hadn't been writing for years before that. But let me assure you, I paid my fucking dues. Big time."

I was somewhat startled since I'd never before heard Eugenia use this particular obscenity.

"I started writing in college and I'm sixty-two now, so do the math. After twenty years of writing, I'd only managed to publish a few stories in tiny literary journals. But, oh boy, did I have some incredible near-misses. A story almost accepted by the New Yorker—after three sets of revisions, they finally said *no thanks*. Two other stories were accepted by major journals . . . just before they folded, so no sale. An editor who was crazy about an earlier novel of mine, worked with me for months on it, then up and died on me. His successor said *no thanks*. I was a finalist for too many grants and contests to remember, but never won. Get the picture? I'd soar for a while with some great news, then crash and burn. Soar and crash. One day, I'd finally had enough. I'd just turned forty, had practically earned a Ph.D. in failure, I was broke, and had lost my latest lover to cancer. She'd had both breasts lopped off and went through months of pain and torturous chemo, and then died anyway. So . . . I . . . well, it's humiliating, but I jumped off a bridge."

"Oh my God." I grabbed her hand and squeezed it.

"Didn't die as intended, obviously. Landed basically on one leg. Shattered it. End of story. Well, not quite. When I got out of the hospital, I found an acceptance letter from the New Yorker in my pile of mail. And a get well card from an old lover who came by and took care of me while I recovered."

"That's amazing," I said.

Eugenia shrugged. "I still get depressed, of course—who doesn't? But I've never had to battle the kind of despair I felt on that bridge. I love life, goddammit, and quite frankly, I love my prosthetic leg. It symbolizes . . . oh I don't know . . . hope, I guess. There's always that."

At the end of our second (and last) Friday night alone together, which we extended past ten o'clock, Eugenia Crane walked me to my car, paused a moment and then leaned down to kiss me squarely on the mouth. She tasted of gin, olives, cigarettes, and lipstick, with a touch of whatever moisturizer she used to battle the drawstring wrinkles around her mouth.

This was a combination I'd never before tasted in a kiss. I knew she was tasting me, testing me, and I doubted I was fooling her about my sexuality, so it was just a single kiss, not quite sisterly or just-plain-friendly. But we both knew better than to make more of it than it was.

I got into the driver's side after we'd both said good night and then was startled when Eugenia joined me in my car. What was going to happen now? I wondered. Was she going to try to convert me? I didn't feel quite prepared to actually make out with her or whatever she might want of me. Would I even know what to do with a woman? *Lesbian Sex for Dummies: Relax and relish the penis boycott. Don't worry about stained panties and ratty bras—women understand. But if you must fake orgasms, stick with men.*

I needn't have fretted about Eugenia's intentions. She motioned toward my ignition and my dashboard. "Turn it on," she said. "Heat. Please."

I obliged and we shivered together for just a moment before she spoke up again. "Next week, I was just thinking . . . maybe we should invite Sheila to join us." Then she gave me a mischievous look.

"Okay. And maybe Arthur," I added. "What do you think of him?"

"Not sure yet. I think he's incredibly talented, but . . . ." She shrugged.

"But what?"

"But nothing, really. I'm sure he's a great guy, but his writing makes me a little uneasy. There's something . . . oh, I don't know, very detached about him. Maybe damaged, pretty deeply." She chuckled. "But, of course, who isn't damaged, right?"

I nodded my agreement.

"His writing is almost pure memoir, I think," Eugenia continued. "According to his bio, he did some time in prison when he was younger."

I wondered what, exactly, Jake had ghost-written for my bio in the application he'd submitted to Eugenia, but I didn't dare ask her.

"Not that I think criminal behavior per se is a bad thing or a good thing, mind you," Eugenia said. "For most people it means trouble, but for a writer, it happens to be great material. And this guy . . . I don't know about him yet. He sure can write, though."

"Do you know how old he is?"

Eugenia nodded. "Thirty-five."

"Is that all?" I asked. "He seems a lot older. More like . . . ."

185

"Like *your* age? Sorry."

"Nothing to be sorry about," I said nervously. "It doesn't matter to *me*."

"Obviously." Eugenia was grinning at me.

"What? Why are you smiling like that?" I asked, and then we both laughed. "What is this, high school or something? Gosh, do you think he likes me?"

"Actually, yes I do," Eugenia said. "I've seen it before in classes, conferences, and writers' groups, and I'm not necessarily talking about romance or sex here. Writing is incredibly lonely work, and non-writers don't have a clue what we're going through. So, sometimes when two writers find each other, sparks fly. There's recognition or anticipation of sharing some things that are even more intimate than sex. A kinship kind of thing."

"It's hard to imagine myself forming a kinship with an ex-con six years younger than me, but maybe we both feel like outsiders or something..."

"I hope it works out," Eugenia said. "For both your sakes. But you might want to be a little careful. Don't shut the door on any current relationships in order to let this guy in."

I didn't admit to her that I may have already done just that.

After a moment I asked, "Why were you so critical of his writing?"

"Because he's good, but he's got a lot of work ahead of him. A lot of maturing to do. Maybe I wanted to see how he'd take it, to see how tough this tough guy really is. You can expect some pretty heavy criticism yourself, by the way. Because I care."

Then, before I could respond to that, she slipped out of my car with another airy "Good night."

The next week, Eugenia did ask both Sheila and Arthur to join us but he politely declined. "I have to work tonight."

"What kind of work?" she asked.

"I'm driving a cab at the moment."

"Madelyn." Eugenia turned to me, plump Sheila at her side looking, I have to admit, kind of sexy. "Didn't you just tell me that you took the bus to class tonight because your car wouldn't start?"

"Yes," I answered. "You said you'd give me a ride home."

"You know, it turns out that I can't do that." She nodded almost imperceptibly in Sheila's direction. Then she turned to Arthur again. "Maybe you and your cab could help Madelyn out. You can drive her home, right?"

"Sure, why not?" Arthur said.

"I thought so. But behave yourselves."

"Honestly, Eugenia," I said with an embarrassed laugh. "Subtlety is not exactly one of your strengths, is it?"

"Hell no."

Settled into Arthur's cab, I apologized for Eugenia putting him on the spot like that, but then boldly admitted to him that she detected a kinship between him and me.

"I agree," he said. "I felt that right away the first class. You looking so unsure of yourself and trembly, with your wired jaw and pretty black sweater." His voice veered briefly into gangsterland. "I'm a sucker for a dame in black who blushes and keeps her trap shut."

I laughed. But then it occurred to me, in retrospect, that Eugenia may not have been throwing Arthur and me together so much as dumping me so she could be alone with Sheila. I didn't share this troubling thought with Arthur, but what should I say instead? When in doubt, confession always seems the right choice. "I'm so new at this whole writing thing," I told him. "I really don't belong in that class."

"Eugenia obviously would disagree with that."

"I didn't even apply for her workshop myself. A friend did it for me, as a surprise."

"Boyfriend?"

Uh oh. Why I had brought Jake into this conversation? "I guess you could call him that," I said. "But not every day."

"I'm not sure what that means," Arthur said.

"Me neither. But sometimes, lately, we're like a badly healed fracture, you know? Not aligned right, threatening to break again." I thought of, but did not talk about the day Jake had spotted the book of baby names I'd bought, and so predictably misunderstood.

When I pointed out my house, Arthur parked in front and stared at it a long time. The streetlamps, freshly coated with light snow, gave the scene a beguiling glow. But, inside the car, I felt the next few moments charged with awkward, unasked questions. His fingers drummed the steering wheel. "Nice neighborhood," he said.

"I grew up here," I told him. "Inherited the house and everything in it. I've barely moved an inch my whole life." Not even while I was married,

I could've added, but for some reason I didn't want to talk about that with Arthur just yet.

"You're lucky," he told me.

Lucky? There were so many ways to refute that statement, I didn't know where to begin. Did he sense my holding back? Probably. Did he mind? Not at all. I wanted to simply get out of the cab at that point, let the man go to work and ponder what little I *had* said. What kind of woman claims to have a boyfriend but "not every day?" Real classy. But instead of leaving, I asked about Arthur's novel-in-progress.

He looked relieved, reanimated. "Well, I've been working on the damn thing so long, I'm sick of it, but even at 500 pages, it's not done. It doesn't hold together as a novel yet but I'm still plugging away at it, in between, you know . . . other things."

I said I'd love to read it and he nodded, saying thanks and, if I meant it, he'd bring the whole "opus delicti" to class at some point.

"Nice wordplay," I told him. How could I *not* be falling for this guy?

He wouldn't take my money for the fare so I said I'd make him dinner sometime. When I ran into my house, I felt a bit discouraged, again, about a new friendship. And incredibly disloyal to Jake. In case he might be able to detect what I'd been doing and thinking that night, I decided not to call him for my weekly post-class pep talk. And the only message on my phone was from some slick-talker offering to consolidate debt from too many credit cards. "We all let things spin out of control at times," the guy said.

"Ain't that the truth," I said as I erased his toll free number and his easy fixes.

Despite her attraction to Sheila, and to some extent *me*, Eugenia managed to be very fair and impartial in class. She was also an excellent facilitator, making sure nobody got too badly bruised. "No piling on," she would say when one criticism led to another and another. She had a gift for finding positive things to say . . . then she turned things around back toward revision—what each of us might try next. I don't know how many times I heard her say, "Dig deeper." And she was always right.

I valued Eugenia on so many levels, but I kept reminding myself that our friendship was a fleeting thing, that she lived in Boston and would be gone after the eight-week class was over. I didn't delude myself into thinking we'd keep in touch or see each other again.

188

The exercises we were given to write were interesting and I worked hard on them, not wanting to let Eugenia down. This writing did not feel authentic to me, however, until we were told to write a recurring dream. When Eugenia gave us this assignment, she nodded discreetly at me. I had once again inspired an exercise, and I found myself, again, resisting it. But eventually I found the strength to jot down my recurring nightmare, surrendering it now to a fictional character named Esther who was happily married with two perfect kids . . . until tragedy struck. Since the dream was no longer mine, I was able to flesh it out, so to speak, making the doll all too real, a baby girl, kidnapped, and ultimately dead.

I handed in the assignment and felt that maybe I had thus exorcised some kind of demon. But I was wrong.

This time when I had the nightmare, it took an unexpected, nasty turn. It still started in a mall, Santa was there all fake-fat and fake-cheery, beckoning, and I was holding but then letting go of someone's hand, presumably my mother's. Down the escalator I went, except then it turned into an elevator, enclosing me, alone and descending too fast. When it finally stopped, the doors wouldn't open and fluid began seeping onto the floor around my red boots, rising fast, and the fluid was the same color as my boots. I woke up certain that my feet would be soaked in blood.

Lying in my bed, shuddering, I recalled an image that I hadn't thought of in years. It was from the theatrical trailer for the Kubrick film "The Shining." One of the simplest and scariest movie previews I've seen—nothing more than a pair of old, ornate elevator doors, closed but clearly ready, maybe even straining to open. The music rumbles and gradually swells, the kind that so effectively expresses *oh shit, something awful is about to happen.* We can only wonder what is hiding or building behind those doors and be ready to avert our eyes. Until finally the doors swoosh open to a tidal wave of blood, rising fast to lap against even the camera lens and, therefore, in a way, the viewers eyes. If I'm remembering it correctly, that was all there was to it, aside from the title, and the words "Coming Soon." Yikes.

When it was a halfway reasonable hour, I dialed Eugenia's phone number. She had given it to me that first night we got together for a drink and told me to call her anytime. I hoped she'd meant it.

Her *hello* sounded half-asleep and I almost hung up, but my nightmare was still resonating so strongly, rattling not only my nerves but deeper, into my bones. I needed to talk to someone, and she seemed the best choice.

"Eugenia? This is Maddie. I'm sorry to call you at this hour. Do you want to call me back?"

"No, I'm fine." I heard a yawn and a smacking of lips. "What's up?"

That's when I realized I didn't have a clue what to say. Should I tell her the details of my dream? No, I hated when people did that to me, as though the intensity and importance could possibly be transmitted to someone outside your own stifling consciousness. "Do you believe in ghosts?" I blurted out. "I mean, can a person be haunted? Can death or any kind of horrible loss, leave a mark or glitch in the brain or something?"

"Maddie, what's wrong? The nightmare again?"

"Yes . . . and no. I don't know."

"Well, good. Now that we've cleared *that* up."

"I shouldn't have called you. I'm so sorry."

"But you did, so . . . what is it you *really* want to ask me?"

I took a deep breath, pressed my hand against my heart. I needed to stay away from that dream. "Do you think I'm trying too hard to write outside my*self* somehow?" I asked her. "Am I using other people too much instead of myself? Am I holding back?"

"Yes, you are. You're playing it a bit safe for now, but you won't always do that."

"What's so bad about being safe?" I asked, trying not to whine.

"You are full of questions this morning, aren't you? I'm not sure I'm up to this, not without some coffee in me. Do you want to get together today?"

I did, but I didn't want to bother her any more than I already had. "No, that's okay," I said. "I know you're busy. See you Friday."

By the time we'd hung up, my dream had started to disperse. I decided, or maybe *vowed* that it couldn't hurt me.

Strokes

Jake asked several times how the class was going and I gave him plenty of details about Eugenia. "I'd love to meet this woman," he said.

"I'll see if I can arrange that." One of many lies during this time.

Needless to say, I studiously avoided mentioning Arthur whenever Jake and I discussed my class. When I got Arthur's manuscript and brought it home, I found myself hiding it and reading it on the sly. Jake walked in on me once, however. He saw the two stacks of paper—the already-read and the yet-to-be-read—and what must've been an unreadable expression on my face. Dropping the bag he'd carried in, he asked, "Maddie, what's the matter?" He came over to glance at the manuscript. "Did you write all of *that?*"

"No," I said, crumpling the page I'd been reading against my stomach. "It's a friend's book, a really good writer, from my class." Tears began to spill down my cheeks and, when I actually started to sob, I added a barely intelligible, "It's so sad." But as I fled my sunroom and ran upstairs, I knew that my crying had nothing to do with Arthur's book. It was about Jake, and the fact that I was already being unfaithful to him—not sexually, but in just about every other way. I wished I could've set Arthur aside as easily as his manuscript pages, but this didn't feel like a mere crush. In my most vivid fantasies about him, I wasn't *me;* I seemed to be the person I'd always meant to become.

Of course, I wanted to return wholeheartedly to Jake. *He* deserved a better version of me, too. But I didn't have the strength to breach the growing chasm between us. It was all I could do just to keep from unraveling in more and more peculiar ways. Between the verbiage I was struggling with in my writing and the endlessly embroidered imaginary conversations I had in my head with both Eugenia and Arthur, it's not surprising how badly communication with Jake had broken down.

One particular night sent our relationship into the worst downward spiral yet. I'd been working on Eugenia's assignments, revising parts of

"Closet Sanctuary" for her, just beginning to wade into Arthur's manuscript, and also trying to prepare a steak dinner with all the trimmings I'd promised Jake. Disaster was inevitable. I tried fussing over the dinner and attending to him, to *us*, as he wanted. We sat at a cleaned, polished and place-matted dining room table that was usually heaped with books and bags. Jake did most of the talking. As it turned out, I probably shouldn't have even tried to respond.

"I was you today," I said, "driving past the . . . uh, the place . . . where I was buying the steaks."

He frowned at me. "What?"

"I was you when you were driving past the . . . the . . . ."

"The store? Store is the word, I believe. But what do you mean, you were me?"

"I *was* . . . I mean, *saw* you."

"What the fuck . . . you're flipping letters now? Latent dyslexia?"

I jammed a piece of steak into my mouth to avoid answering him, but then I couldn't seem to swallow. The meat sat in my mouth like that misplaced W had gristled there.

We avoided each other's eyes for a while. Then he said, "I think you should see a doctor. Maybe you've had a small stroke or something?"

I gaped at him. "A what?"

"A stroke," he repeated but with little conviction. "Or something."

I gnarled up my hands in pretend-paralysis—my lame attempt (no pun intended) at humor.

"Maddie, cut it out. You know what I mean. You've been acting odd for months and it's getting worse. Seems like since last summer, really. Since that little girl—"

"Jake, shut up. Please. No more." I got up from the table with as much dignity as I could muster and headed for my kitchen sink. I focused on the broiler pan I would eventually have to scrub or throw away—it never seemed to get totally clean. Black crust, grease, it was disgusting. "We should stop eating meat," I muttered to myself, and then realized I'd said such a natural "we." Jake would've approved of that. Leaving the pan to soak, I filled the sink with clean soapy water and started washing dishes.

"It's hereditary," I called out to Jake, and he came into the kitchen to ask me what I meant. "My mother used to do that. She'd get distracted

192

and mix up words. I remember her saying things like 'Go do the crib' when she meant 'Go do the dishes.' And switching around the letters of my name, sometimes calling me 'Dammie' instead of Maddie."

"Hmmm." Jake looked even more baffled than before. "Are you sure she was saying your name at all?" he asked. "Sounds more like she was saying a different name, or maybe 'damn me.'"

I shrugged. "She was a depressed woman. At least I'm trying to do something with this mixed-up head of mine, but she just sat and brooded." I paused, pretending to be calmly washing dishes, the picture of mental health. "You know, they were always telling me how great it was to have me as an only child, how they 'treasured' me. But I know for a fact that she was trying her whole life to have more babies." That last word echoed in my head and in the room—*babies*. It was so clear, I was afraid Jake could hear it too. When the phone rang, I jumped and my heart banged on the walls of my chest. *Knock knock . . . who's there?*

"Want me to answer the phone?" Jake asked.

I told him to leave it. Probably just a telemarketer. He answered it anyway and then quickly hung up. Oh no, I thought. Was it Arthur? Had he hung up when Jake answered as though . . . Jesus, didn't he have a right to call me?

Jake rejoined me in the kitchen and leaned against the counter. "It was a telemarketer."

"So, why did you answer it?"

He shrugged.

"You wanted to know who might be calling me, didn't you?"

"Don't be silly," Jake said.

"Yeah, silly me. Dyslexic, bonkers, dried-up stroke victim, and now 'silly' on top of everything, like a cherry." *Cherry?* Now *there* was an odd simile. And where had dried-up come from? I felt myself blush, remembering snippets of other strange conversations I'd had with my mother, aware that questions about sexual health had come straight from her somehow. "Anyway," I muttered, "I'll answer my own phone."

"Fine. I hate phones anyway." Jake stuffed his hands into his pockets and glanced at me sideways. "Hey, that reminds me . . . . Let's see. Oh yeah. So, Ole showed up for work one day with both his ears bandaged—"

"You don't say." I grinned, relieved.

"Yup. And when a friend asked what happened, Ole said, 'Vell, last night I vas ironing my shirt when da phone rang and I picked up da iron by mistake.' The friend asked what happened to the other ear and Ole answered, 'Oh . . . dat. Vell, I had to call da doctor.'"

I laughed and threw a dishtowel at Jake. "Cute. Now dry the wineglasses, okay?"

He obliged and then carefully aligned them next to their companions in my cupboard. After a minute, he said, "It was just a suggestion, Maddie. I know you're basically fine, but what harm could a routine checkup do? You seem pretty hormonal and, honestly, when was the last time you saw a doctor? Do you even have an ob-gyn these days? You must be due for at least a pap smear. Maybe even a . . . you know, a pregnancy test?"

I shook my head emphatically. "No, Jake. Sorry. Had my period just last week." I didn't really blame him for wondering whether I might be pregnant—that was simply Jake being hopeful. But the rest of his inquiry made me feel incredibly invaded. Hormones? A pap smear? An ob-gyn, like his ex-wife? How could he drag *her* of all people into the kitchen with us? What next? I wanted to draw up a picket sign, like in the old days of feminism, reclaiming my body as mine—hands off.

But I also knew that Jake meant well, and that pushing him away was a treacherous game. Not a game at all, really. "Tell me, Jake," I said with what might pass for another sincere grin. "What happened to Lena? I thought all your jokes were Ole and Lena jokes."

"No. Sometimes Ole's on his own. A dumb Norwegian bachelor, like me."

"Not exactly." I skittered around his reference to being on his own. "You're anything but dumb." I finished the dishes and returned to the stubborn broiler pan.

Jake became unusually quiet.

"I'm sorry if I've been acting odd," I said. "Really and truly. But I don't think I need to see a doctor. I've been doing some difficult work, that's all. Writing, reading, re-writing, agonizing over every word, every syllable, every transition, every move my characters make, every word that comes out of their mouths. I'm surprised I can converse with you *this* well."

He nodded but didn't say anything.

"You're the one that signed me up for the damn workshop," I reminded him.

"I might as well have sent you to Siberia," he replied. "No, on second thought, maybe *I'm* the one in exile." He finished drying and gently frisbeed a dinner plate into the cupboard.

"Take it easy on the dishes—they were my mom's."

"Sorry."

After another moment of silence—a rather "pregnant" one—he asked, "Are you having an affair?"

"Good Lord . . . " I grabbed onto the broiler in the dark greasy water like a life raft but felt myself about to go under anyway.

"Are you?" When I still didn't give him a definite *no*, Jake's voice started gaining some muscle. "Are you fucking Eugenia Crane?"

Rising to the surface with a gasp of relief, I glanced over at Jake. He looked like he was about to start sparring but, at the same time, protecting his stomach from a knockout punch. I smiled gently and shook my head. "No, Jake. Absolutely not."

He didn't look reassured, maybe because he could tell I was stifling a giggle. A part of me wanted to shout, *Yes. I'm finally having my one lesbian fling, and it's a blast, but she'll be leaving soon and then I'll be back in your arms, more hot and loving for the experience. We can talk dirty about threesomes.*

"What, then?" he asked.

"I told you. It's the work, it's seductive. It takes me to strange places."

"It takes you away from me."

"Again, I'm sorry. I'll try to do better. But let me just finish what I'm doing, okay? Can I have some time? I don't want to break up for the fiftieth time, Jake. And I don't want to go see a doctor *or* a shrink which will be your next suggestion, I know. Or a couples counselor either. Forgive me for wanting to work through things myself, in my own way, without being forced to *disclose* every little thing in my head. As I've told you a million times before, inside my head is *not* such a great place to be."

"I'm sorry, too. We're both always so *sorry.*" Jake wiped down the counter, rinsed and hung up the dishrag. "You're lucky to have this talent, Maddie," he said with the edge in his voice carefully smoothed away. "And to be so passionate about *something*. Most of us ordinary, unartistic types get excited about really dumb shit, like a steak dinner or snuggling with their sweethearts on a cold winter night."

The word *sweetheart* demanded my attention. What would be the opposite? A bitterheart? A sourheart? Either one seemed to fit better in *my* chest than sweetheart.

"Okay, I'll let you be *you*," Jake said with renewed gusto—from where did he always get it? Could I have some? Gusto sounded so good to me.

"Thanks," was all I could manage.

"No problem, Maddie. And . . . You want Lena? Here's a quickie for you: Ole was so dumb he ran downtown to get wheels for Lena's menstrual cycle."

I groaned.

"No? Okay, how about this one: Ole bought Lena a wig because he heard she was 'getting bald' at work." Jake leaned over, apparently to give me a peck on the cheek, but I turned at the wrong moment and our foreheads collided instead.

"Ouch," I blurted. "Dammit,"

This sent him slouching into my living room. A soundless bell had rung and we were retreating to our separate corners.

I heard TV voices, raucous music, singing. He'd put in the movie we'd rented, *Chicago*, which we'd first seen in the theater together years ago and both loved. This time we watched it with less toe-tapping glee, probably because of all those female killers in the movie with mates as disposable as Bic lighters. Two hours later Jake left, humming one of the gloomier songs from the musical. When I went to bed I noticed a note on my pillow. He must've scribbled it and left it there after a visit to the bathroom.

I'll leave you alone. Hope you'll call . . . Mr. Cellophane

That's what he'd been humming—John C. Reilly's song "Mr. Cellophane." The heart-wrenching lyrics include: *You can look right through me, walk right by me, and never know I'm there.*

So, of course, I did call him, left a message promising to make a doctor's appointment soon. What was one more lie tossed onto the heap? "See you soon," I said to his voicemail. "Love you."

I'm at the window now because . . .

A tsunami of guilt has hit, flooding my house and pushing me with a cold thwack up against the glass. This will be a tricky section to write, this one about me and Arthur. Because this is where I betrayed Jake, a good man, a friend who did nothing to deserve the way I treated him. My feelings alternate, however, between shame and delight. Is it selfish to want the kind of happiness I thought Arthur offered? Eugenia predicted (maybe it was more of a warning) that he would become important to me, and I sometimes wonder how she knew. Beyond the obvious factors—the physical attraction, the shared passion for writing, and books, maybe she guessed about our shared obsession with lost children. So there could've been a kinship, especially once he stopped working long enough to be seduced by me . . . until I scared him off. Some tough guy—scared by the likes of me. Thanks, once again, to Mona. We've pushed her so far off stage in the last several pages, she almost vanished, right? If only she had.

Now I recall sitting here, Arthur standing behind me, bending to kiss the top of my head, maybe trying to wander amiably into my thoughts. And Mona coming out of the house with her baby, on good behavior that day—the picture-perfect version of attentive, doting mommy. And I made a mistake, a laughably common one (especially post-coital). I opened my mouth, my heart, and the true deepness of my mind . . . all to my new lover.

Touched

Arthur's book was both flawed and brilliant. I had heard parts of it in class, and Eugenia had read a few more sections on her own, but she did not have time to give his work the attention it deserved. He had handed it to me a bit shyly, warning me of the structural problems and asking me if I might write down my major criticisms as I read his 500 plus pages. I agreed and said I would also make note of what I particularly liked, because I knew he needed encouragement as well. But it was not easy to keep extracting myself from the web of his words to jot down my own in response. Reading the book only made me feel more hopelessly drawn to Arthur because the attraction now included his young alter-ego Sam.

This was February, toward the end of my class. I did little writing of my own during the time I was reading Arthur's. I resorted to sharing discarded catalogue copy with the class one day, not the dull edited version that ended up in print, of course. When faced with one item to describe— a framed and autographed photo of a youngish Laurel and Hardy, derbies and all—I had let myself write a whole page about my childhood. My father, my mother, and me, watching Laurel and Hardy movies over and over and actually laughing out loud. So rare for us. And certain lines became in-jokes for us ("Is there gonna be a fight?" "Why don't you do something to help me?" "Horns! Horns!" etc.). Such a cozy little threesome. This was before their divorce, long before I started dating and occasionally hating them, before the word cozy morphed into crazy. And, of course, before my dad up and died on me.

I'd been in semi-catalogue-mode while writing this simple piece about my family, so I was shocked to find that I couldn't quite read it out loud without choking up. The class responded warmly and with compassion. Eugenia said it was some of my best prose and I should consider expanding it into a personal essay. I said I *might* do that . . . eventually. She understood.

After class, she pulled me aside and asked if I'd lost a sibling at some point during my childhood.

"What? No," I answered. "I was an only child."

"Oh." She peered into my face for several unnerving seconds. "It's just that I thought I detected something in the piece you read today. You wrote about the three of you as though there were some . . . I don't know . . . missing piece in your family. Some missing person."

"Maybe I've always wished for a sister or something," I answered, finding myself choking up once again. It was very strange.

Eugenia asked me to join her and Sheila at the bar that night, but I was in a dismally quiet mood and said I had other plans. I drove home avoiding any more thoughts about my writing, thinking instead about everyone else's, especially Arthur's. Being in Eugenia's class had given me a lot, but I was feeling most grateful for finding my way into the world of Arthur Locke, as provided by his troubled narrator, Sam.

Starting out as a twenty-two-year-old who has just been sprung from jail, Sam's tale revolves primarily around his long, desperate search for his sister, Serena. Their mother had died when Sam was seven and Serena was less than a year old, and their father was such a drunken tyrant, he verged (as I noted to Arthur) on a stereotype. In flashbacks, we get hints of the physical abuse that had been heaped on Sam, and the possible sexual abuse of Serena, but the father really isn't in the story much—it's just Sam and his sister all those childhood years, exceptionally close, struggling to survive.

But Sam starts getting into trouble when he hits his teens and is sent away the first time to a correctional facility when he's fifteen. After that first incarceration, Sam vows to stay out of trouble. He knows Serena depends on him, even though she's now in a foster home. But at eighteen, the young man decides it's time for him to make a move, and to take Serena with him. Borrowing a handgun from a friend, he attempts to rob an electronics store and is caught. This time he will have to do hard time. By the time he finally returns home, his now sixteen-year-old sister has run away.

He follows her from Minneapolis to Chicago and from there to the west coast and back. Most of Sam's narrative moves forward at a leisurely pace, depicting the young man's various jobs, friends, a junkie girlfriend, and a brief but disastrous marriage. He occasionally falls into bed with women, but love is a fleeting thing for this young man. And always, throughout the story, he is searching for Serena. When he finds girls who knew her, they tell him Serena stayed in shelters for a while but ultimately became a prostitute. His search has him hitchhiking for months that turn into years. The one constant as the story unfolds is the humor—sometimes dark, always surprising and much-needed. But sadness keeps its hold on the reader nonetheless.

Within the last few pages that Arthur gave me, Sam does, in fact, find his sister. They are *both* survivors. But the ending felt tacked on to me, anti-climactic, and it needed much more work than the rest of the book.

When I finished reading and sorting through my reactions to his book, I called Arthur and we agreed to get together for lunch the next day. It was a Wednesday, two days before our last class with Eugenia and the party she'd be hosting for us afterwards. Eugenia had been staying all that time with a friend whose apartment building (only a few blocks from where we had our class) had a community room. We were all invited to bring spouses, significant others, even children if we wished. I had not told Jake about this party, choosing instead to let him think I was simply going out for a drink Friday evening with Eugenia and the rest of the class. He had stopped asking to meet my teacher or anyone else by then, and was probably still baffled about why.

Arthur and I met in a restaurant, where he said he'd pick up the tab in return for my attention to his manuscript. He was also very excited about some news he'd just gotten. "I'm a finalist for this major grant. It's just me and two others. And I know one of the judges, had her as a teacher once so I know she likes my work. Seems like a good possibility, but we'll see...I mean, it's a life-changing kind of grant. $30,000."

I nearly choked on the water I'd just sipped. "Arthur, that's fantastic. My God! Congratulations."

"Hey, I haven't won yet."

"Well, for being a finalist then. What did Eugenia say?"

"I haven't told anyone else about this yet. If I win, then I'll tell everyone."

So he'd taken me into his confidence. Not a bad sign. I ordered wine with my meal, he drank cup after cup of black coffee.

"It couldn't come at a better time," he said. "I've been driving my cousin's cab just until his busted leg is healed, and that'll be next week already, so I'll have to find some other job. And I'm about to be evicted from this really nice furnished room I've been renting. The landlady who's about 120 but sweet as can be said she wants a female tenant instead, more of a live-in companion, which I suppose means she's starting to need help in the bathroom. So now I have to either find another furnished place or an unfurnished place and get furniture. Can't afford either one of those options at the moment."

"Sorry to hear that," I said. "I suppose it's tough when you have a rapper sheet and—"

"*Rap* sheet, actually." He grinned at me.

"Right. I mean, I assume you do, from what I've read here, and from what Eugenia . . . I mean, shit. Sorry, it's none of my business."

"You're cute when you get rattled, you know that?"

"Well, then I've been cute an awful lot lately, because I've been nothing *but* rattled."

"I know what you mean. But as far as my finding work, in spite of my rap sheet, I've never had that much trouble. I've had lots of jobs, mostly in construction. But since the economy tanked . . . I don't know . . . maybe next month when it starts to warm up outside . . . ."

I pictured him with a very large hammer, in a hard hat, stripped to the waist and sunburned, then played with the idea of employing him as my personal assistant, emphasis on the *personal*. Or if he got the grant, he could employ *me*. We could employ each other . . . a couple times a day.

"That's a very enigmatic smile," he said, pulling my attention back to our table. "Are you working on something in your head, and am I in it?"

"How did you guess?"

"Maybe I've been doing the same." He had a habit of stroking his beard and smoothing stray hairs away from his lips.

"Have you always had that beard?" I asked, trying to picture him without it.

"It dates back to my hitchhiking days. Seemed easier than shaving."

"And now? I mean, I like it, but . . . ."

"I know, it's not exactly fashionable. And I don't exactly care." His eyes took a little stroll downward from my face. "You wore my favorite black sweater today. The one you wore the first day of Eugenia's class. It looks very soft." Then he reached across the table to touch my sleeve with two of his fingers. My forearm instantly acquired new nerve-endings.

"Black makes me feel thinner," I mumbled. His hand had returned to his side of the table but I could still feel the imprint of his fingers.

"You women and your body image issues," he said, shaking his head. "I *love* a woman's curves. Well, maybe I just love women."

"Nothing wrong with that," I said. But Eugenia's comments about Arthur pecked away at me. How, exactly, did she see him as high risk for me? He seemed neither detached nor damaged to me at the moment. But, in part to obey my invisible mentor, I veered back to business. "So . . . about your manuscript—" I handed him my notes.

"Oh, do we have to spoil a nice lunch?" He tensed up and I almost said *Nah*.

But when I told him how much I'd loved his book, he relaxed and became more focused at the same time. We were suddenly all business. I could tell he took writing more seriously than I did. Flirtation and wherever it might lead could wait.

After reading through my notes and nodding, he said, "Thanks. You're very kind and helpful. But are there any other more serious problems you had, that you didn't write down? Or questions?"

"Mostly about the ending," I replied. "It needs work."

"Yeah. I know." He'd pushed up the sleeves of his sweater as was his habit and I stared at the tattoo on his forearm. Now that I could examine it more closely, I could see that what he had inscribed were ornate, entwined capital A's.

Arthur followed my gaze and grinned a little sheepishly. "Most people think it's my tribute to AA. I've never been to a meeting, but some of my best friends are drunks and junkies, so . . . I let people read what they want into my tattoo—never hurts to add more color to my checkered past."

To me the two A's seemed to be in motion, hand-in-hand. "What is your sister's name, Arthur?"

He sipped his coffee, nodded, and let sadness pull up a chair to join us at the small table. "Ashley," he said. "A and A. I'm busted. You have to remember I was a kid at the time that I pricked this—if you'll pardon the expression—into my skin."

The obvious question about Ashley tried to barge into the conversation. "I was just wondering: How is—?"

"You use India ink," he interrupted. "You know, and a needle wrapped with thread. Hundreds of little needle pricks. I watched older guys in St. Cloud do it. I guess I thought it was cool at the time."

"Must've hurt like hell."

"Yeah, I guess. Sometimes you seek out the merely physical pain, though."

I decided to try again. "How is Ashley now?"

He shrugged. "The thing about the ending of my book is, I got to that point, on page 500 or whatever, and just wanted to . . . I don't know . . . get it over with, I guess. Sometimes I wish I could put it all aside and write about someone totally different."

"You will, when you finish this book. You'll move on." I sincerely hoped he *could* move on. "In a way, I'm actually the opposite."

"What do you mean?" he asked.

"I wish I could write more about me, more straight-forward and true. But, of course, my life has been a supreme bore compared to yours."

"Believe me, your life is probably foreign and exotic and fascinating to me. Other side of the fence, you know. I'll bet you even had piano lessons. I've always wished I'd had a few."

I wanted, all of a sudden, to unleash my past for him, to see if he was right about finding it fascinating. Or to confirm that he'd never want to spend time with me again. At least *his* prison had walls and doors, in and out, and he hadn't been back inside for many years. What about *mine*?

"But the whole truth thing," he continued, "you can't be sure about. I mean, this *is* a novel. I lied on every single fuckin' page. I'm not sure even I know what's true and what's not anymore."

"Well, that's good. That's what good fiction-writing is all about, I think."

"My old man? He didn't beat me. And I'm pretty sure he never touched my sister in the ways I have this asshole touch Serena. It just seemed too hard to describe what really happened. He was not a good man, my dad. A terrible father. But in such subtle ways. Warm one minute and ice-cold the next, charming and funny with everyone else, but with us? The words don't seem to come to mind, even now, talking about him with you, after all these years of trying."

"I guess you have to keep trying to find the words." I meant in the book but something had been loosened in him.

"He had these ways," Arthur continued, "of bad-mouthing us, putting us down, making us feel worthless. He tried—and failed miserably, by the way—to make me view the world and everyone in it as rotten. I didn't know how to write my real dad, so I made him evil in ways everyone could recognize without going into details, you know?"

"And Ashley? Did she—?"

"Ashley was never put in a foster home," Arthur interrupted, effectively changing my question. "Nobody we talked to about our father understood why that should be necessary. He was a good provider, drank only in moderation, never brought women home except a few nice ladies who made us dinner. When I had to write about this guy's dad in my novel, I didn't want to have to explain too much. I didn't want *my* old man to infect my story, you know? He poisoned so much else in my life just by *being*. I wanted my book to be free of him."

"So you used a stereotype instead."

Arthur nodded. "Busted again," he said with a disarming smile. "I knew I couldn't get away with it. That's why I put myself in your hands."

I resisted taking that last comment sexually. "You saw the note I made somewhere in the manuscript about the father. In your next rewrite, you might want to try to make the father more complex, the way your father was. I know that's hard but . . . ."

He nodded. "I'll try."

"But back to the ending . . . the way you have Sam just suddenly find Serena like that, after all those years. I don't know, it just felt . . . less real than the rest. A fairy tale ending. Not that Sam shouldn't find her, or that, heaven forbid, he finds out she died, or whatever. I'm just saying, the *way* you—"

"Listen, I hear you. I'll see what I can do. But the other thing I wanted feedback from you is . . . well, this is actually kind of embarrassing. How should I say this? Okay, what about the love scenes? In class you nailed me for that one in the homeless shelter and you were right on. I have a terrible time with love and . . . well, in bed."

"I'm sorry to hear that," I joked.

He laughed. "In my *writing*, smart ass. In real life beds . . . well . . . let's not go there."

"Oh, let's." Back to flirting shamelessly. He seemed to be ready to enjoy it again.

"You know, you *look* like such a *lady*, kind of cautious and maybe even straight-laced. But that day, when you said my characters had started fucking like rabbits, I knew I'd had you pegged all wrong."

"Yes, you did," I said with a suggestive chuckle. "Anyway, what I see happening in your love scenes is not enough build up. And I'm not necessarily talking foreplay here."

"What, then?"

"Emotional build up. Anticipation. So much about Sam's life is brutal and cold and hard. It'd be great if the way he is with a lover could be a complete surprise to us, and maybe to him, a real contrast with the rest of his life. Make a lot more out of kissing especially. Think about how it feels the first time you kiss someone . . . ." I could feel my face and neck flush, and now I was also feeling the unmistakable moisture between my legs. "And how it feels when you've been kissing for hours and begin to feel a more profound penetration of her long before the *other* kind. Hopefully. Sam reminds me too much of guys who kiss too hard and long right away and think that makes a woman swoon because it's so intense. But instead it can be downright painful, not to mention hard to breathe. Not that much fun."

"Seems to me I've been told that," he admitted, averting his eyes from mine. "Jesus, here I am sitting with this beautiful, smart, sexy woman I've been trying to impress, a woman who even the great Eugenia Crane somehow sees me connected with, and did I just admit to being a bad kisser, possibly a lousy lay? Could I be that stupid?"

I laughed and felt the warmth spread from his calling me beautiful and smart and sexy. Oh my. "That's not what I'm suggesting," I said. "And sometimes two lovers are both *playing* rough, so then it's different. And fun. But probably should come later, when there's trust. God, I sound like Dr. Ruth. Remember her? That tiny old lady with the accent. Was it German? Am I *that* much older than you? Am I babbling? Save me, please."

"Okay, okay. More rattled, more cute, but I'll stop you anyway. You're saying that I should, as the old song says, try a little tenderness."

"Exactly. The old romantic build-up of meaningful looks, skin accidentally brushing against skin, a warm hand on the small of her back . . . ." Then shifting in my seat uncomfortably, I added, "In your *writing*, I mean. Of course."

"Yeah, of course. Thanks."

We stared at each other for several ticks of the clock and of my heart, until the waiter broke the spell by stacking our plates and setting down the check. I tossed a twenty towards him, and when Arthur started to protest, I said, "I'm the one who had two ridiculously overpriced glasses of wine. And when you get the grant, I'll gladly let you pick up the tab. We can go out to dinner. Maybe dancing too. We'll do research into romance."

"For my writing."

"Right. For *both* of us struggling authors. Oh, and by the way. You might want to sift through what I say about this and not take it all too seriously. Because, to tell you the truth, I haven't actually written any good sex scenes yet myself. There were two that I tried and failed to complete— one involving an old harp, and the other about meatloaf, you know, the cold raw mixture, squishing it together. So, clearly, I'm no expert."

"Hm-m-m, intriguing. I happen to love meatloaf. But, listen, I have to go. This has been great, and I can't thank you enough." He gathered together all my notes and slipped them into the box along with his manuscript.

"Yeah. I've gotta go too," I lied. Then I got brave. Or foolish, hard to tell which. "Next time I'll make you lunch at my house, okay? Maybe even meatloaf."

He stood up, dropped his forgotten napkin, snagged his jacket on the chair, and hit his elbow on the table as he retrieved the napkin. God, it was great to have such an effect on someone. As he fumbled to leave, all attempts at coolness now set aside, I noticed that he was neither as tall nor as square-shouldered as he'd been in my elaborate fantasies, but it didn't matter. How, I wondered, was he envisioning me when I wasn't around? Did he give me a better body than I had? Prettier eyes? A sexier voice? Oh well.

"Hey, good luck with the grant," I said as I stood and put my coat on, thankful that women don't have to worry about visible erections. "When do you find out if you won?"

"This week," he replied. "Probably tomorrow."

"Let me know," I told him as he disappeared out the door.

Passion

Friday morning. Last day of class and I was getting ready several hours early, taking all the extra care that a dating woman takes, just in case. The phone rang but I didn't answer it, afraid it might be Jake. But then it occurred to me that it might be Arthur and I sprang for the receiver. Too late. Caller ID simply said Out of Area as it often did, as though relishing secrets. Whoever it was didn't leave a message. There was really no reason for me to expect a call from either of these men but, in a way, I wanted them both at my door, offering me choice. I felt incredibly foolish, and selfish. Selfoolish. I wanted to call the dictionary people and add my new word, together with my picture, complete with newly shaved legs and goofball grin.

By the time I got to class, wearing a new jade green, slinky sweater that I hoped would be Arthur's new favorite, I was a nervous wreck. But I looked good.

He snuck up behind me and tugged at my arm, pulling me into the hall.

"Hi, Arthur," I said.

"Hi. Listen, Maddie. I didn't get it. The grant. So please don't mention it to anybody, not even Eugenia, okay?"

"Oh no. You . . . okay . . . but who . . . I'm sorry." My stammering seemed to cheer him up. But he didn't really seem to be all that upset. I gazed at him, more impressed than ever.

He said he was fine, it was nice being a finalist, and gave me the name of the winner, a professor who had already published many books, who clearly needed neither the money nor affirmation as much as Arthur did.

"But that's so unfair," I said.

"The grant was based on talent, not need. It's okay, Maddie. Don't look so stricken! I haven't been diagnosed with Lou Gehrig's Disease. I haven't been arrested—not recently anyway. I'll keep trying. Sooner or later . . . ."

As we sat in class for the next hour I watched him for signs that he was, in fact, devastated. But he seemed fine. He was like an inflatable raft that can be punctured but not sunk, that simply repairs itself by reversing the hiss of escaping air. Since the water I was flailing around in was cold and lonely, I wanted to climb on. He absolutely deserved this grant, had worked hard, needed a real break, perhaps more than anyone I knew. But no, the world was a swollen, putrid mass of unfairness. Was that an overstatement? Didn't seem like it. He'd called it a life-changing grant, and clearly his life needed at least a tweaking. As I watched him bluff his way through class—letting my eyes settle on his scruffy, not-quite-handsome visage—I decided to be the tweaker.

Another big surprise: Eugenia was not at her best that last day. In fact, she looked awful. Her hair appeared slept on, her outfit may have been retrieved from the laundry basket. And she was, for the first time *during* class, slightly drunk. Sheila, I noticed, was missing. So they probably had a fight. What else could they do, with Eugenia leaving for Boston soon? Maybe even tomorrow. How dim-witted of me not to know that lesbians break each other's hearts just like everyone else.

The last few readings in class, however, were great. Other students had worked hard, revised hard, obsessed over every turn of phrase, and every twist of plot. I was in awe and embarrassed that I'd spent the day primping instead of sweating away at my computer. I didn't read, nor did Arthur. We continued to play footsy with our eyes, but it felt like a very literary thing to do. We would both undoubtedly write about our relationship, if that's what we were headed into. We might both, after tonight, write about our first kiss. And he would try, both for real and in his fiction, to apply my suggestions about kissing, the build-up, the tenderness, the passion that is quiet rather than explosive. Love as stealth rather than terrorist attack. We could always explode later.

"I'm glad to have met all of you," Eugenia said as she closed the class. By this time she was fully sober and more in command as usual. "You have been a memorable bunch and I promise not to simply toss you into the mix of all the classes I've taught, and all the writers I've worked with. Maybe it's the climate here—everything feels more preservable."

She gave us directions to the party that was to commence immediately, and we tried not to appear too eager to get there, taking our time getting our coats on, making stray comments to each other.

"I'll give you a ride," Arthur said. We left the room paired up as naturally as peanut butter and jelly. Nobody seemed scandalized, or even to notice.

"See, now that's what it means to have a kinship," I said with what I hoped was a vixenish smile. "You *knew* I took the bus here today."

"No. Actually, I saw you get off the bus."

"Same thing. You *knew* to be looking at the bus stop at the exact right time."

He chuckled. Something in his face signaled to me that we were not going to talk about the grant, the near-miss, the back-to-square-one of his life any more that evening.

Once we got to the party, it was clear we wouldn't be staying long. Eugenia and her hostess had invited several other university friends as well. They'd all started drinking before we got there. The music was too loud, the talking and laughing cacophonous. Arthur and I had to shout into each other's ears and this odd kind of tickly intimacy gave me gooseflesh. Nobody would be able to overhear what we said to each other. Nobody cared.

Eugenia was skulking around from one group of people to the other, getting more intoxicated but not in a happy way. At one point she plopped herself down in a beanbag chair, one of a pair. They were cream-colored vinyl and I decided to occupy the other one, next to her. It was less a chair than a habitat, engulfing, enfolding me, on the verge of obscene the way it cupped my entire backside. Shockingly comfortable. But from across the room Eugenia and I probably looked like a couple of huge hatchlings, not quite ready to shrug off our shells.

"Nice party," I told her.

"Yeah, right."

"Where's Sheila?" I asked.

"With her husband." Eugenia repositioned her bottom and I heard the chair's innards rustling.

"Are you all right?"

"I was a pit stop," she said. "And she's back on the track with that prick as the driver. I'm in shock. Did I just make her a race car? Is that the worst metaphor ever?"

"Not the absolute worst, no. And I liked all those *ck* sounds bunched together. Back, track, prick, shock . . . ."

"Do you feel like a 'real' writer now?" Eugenia asked. "You were so insecure when I met you."

I shrugged. She didn't want to hear my answer.

"Don't get diverted, Maddie. Keep writing, keep *feeling*, even if it scares the crap out of you. Better yet, though, keep the crap in, use it for your stories."

"Okay. So, you want me to keep writing but in a constipated sort of way. Good advice, Teach."

"I have no advice," Eugenia moaned. "I told you that the very first day."

"I remember."

"Are you screwing Arthur yet?"

In spite of all my fantasies and my apparently naked desire for this man, Eugenia's question startled me. "No," I told her. "We're friends."

"Right." She smirked and tried to stand up, but then chose to sink back down into the beanbag again with an audible *whoosh*. "He's probably not going to be much good at relationships, you know."

"Well, neither am I. So, we're alike."

"One of you should be good at it."

A clumsy bean-baggy silence followed during which I tried *not* to look ahead twenty years. Then I decided to tell Eugenia about the grant Arthur almost won.

She gave me an odd look. "I don't think so."

"What do you mean?"

"I don't think he'd qualify for that particular grant. He doesn't have enough major publications to even apply."

"Well, he did qualify, almost won," I said. I felt blood rush into my face and it felt more like anger than anything else, so I extricated myself from the beanbag and brusquely said my goodbye and thanks to Eugenia, leaving her behind, possibly for good.

She'd basically accused Arthur of lying to me but it wasn't hard to brush that aside. I appreciated her mother-hennish concern, but she didn't much like or trust men, after all, and she was quite possibly an alcoholic. Besides, she knew Arthur only through his writing.

I found him at the snack table, loading up one of the tiny plates so that it had at least four layers of food. Looking sheepish, he admitted he hadn't eaten much that day. I loaded up a similar plate and we left the party room to sit on the floor of the coat room. It was not the most comfortable place to eat, and the air was filled with the wintry wet smell of all the coats and scarves and hats stuffed into a small indoor space, but at least we were alone.

Questions about the damn grant—how he'd qualified to apply, why he was so calm about losing, had he fabricated the whole thing and, if so, *why*—all were burning inside me, but I managed to snuff them. Thoughts of kissing him helped a lot. I dipped a broccoli sprig into dill dip and wondered what kind of breath this would leave me with—couldn't be good, so I ate fast as though that would help and then washed it all down with the white wine that had come out of a big box on the bar, discreetly swishing the liquid around my teeth. It seemed to have remarkably little alcohol in it, but that could've been rationalization on my part. I noticed that Arthur was drinking beer and I automatically wondered how much he'd had. Enough to lose any leftover inhibitions with me? Enough to stop lying to me (if he was)? Enough to feel aroused and make the first move? Too much to *act* on that arousal? I was overanalyzing again and vowed to shut off my infuriating mind, if only for one night.

We chatted about the class, awarding with make-believe statuettes the best story (besides our own, of course), the best dialogue, best setting, funniest writer, saddest, angriest, most hopelessly inept, hardest worker with minimal talent, laziest one with the most talent (he insisted that was me), sexiest (also me), and the all around best and the brightest (I said it was him, and he agreed because he'd had enough beer to eradicate any modesty). He stood to accept the award—a stale breadstick—and thanked all the little people. "I knew a few in the joint," he said. "There are a surprising number of midgets behind bars."

"I didn't know that. Is there one behind the bar here? Get me a decent glass of wine."

"The penitentiary type of bars, I meant."

"I knew that. Trying to be witty."

He slung an arm across my shoulders. "Let's get the hell outta here."

"Let's."

He still had the borrowed cab and we climbed in. The heater rattled like a maraca. "My cousin goes back to work tomorrow," Arthur said.

211

"Then I'm without wheels again. Wheel-less. In the eyes of some women, that's about the same as dickless."

"Hm-m-m. Don't see the connection." I tried to keep my gaze well above his crotch.

"You know what I mean," he said. "Women expect a 'real man' to have certain things—at *least* a car."

"Not this woman. I hate cars. I have one that hates me back. Maybe because you're a man—a real man's man, no less—it would like you better."

I wondered what had happened to all my difficulties speaking, mixing up some words, swallowing down others? Was that only with Jake? Now I couldn't seem to shut up. "If wheels and dicks amount to the same thing," I continued without stopping to think or edit myself, "take my car as a gift. But just make sure to give me a ride whenever I need one. Was that as crude as it sounded?"

"Maybe," he said with a laugh, "but I'm not easily shocked."

He remembered the way to my house, but when we were only a few blocks away, I told him about my favorite parking spot, in a small lot overlooking the Mississippi River. It was a beautiful night, not too cold, gently snowing. He kept the car running and the barely functioning heater on high. The rattle gave way to a sound like someone sighing near our laps. Sitting next to him, not quite but almost touching, it felt like the idling car engine was housed in his body. The vibrations, the warmth, the promise of power . . . all from him, not some rusted hulk of a taxi.

The bare trees afforded us a view of the river, water that never completely freezes because of its deep currents, movement that is rarely as visible as it is powerful. Impossibly intricate snowflakes were swirling and turning to lace on our windshield, slowly taking away our outward view. We looked at each other instead and I leaned over to kiss him. I was surprised, at first, by the feel of his beard—much softer than I'd expected, and it was not blocking access to his lips. His tongue seemed bashful, probably because I'd made him self-conscious about bad kisses, but my tongue sought his out and reassured it. Our faces knew what to do together. Our breath was visible in the cold and when I opened my eyes momentarily, I watched it mingle, happy to stay where we were. Until his fingers slipped between my thighs as though merely for the pocket of warmth there.

"Let's go to my house," I said.

"Is it . . . you know, empty?" he asked.

I nodded. "Completely." When I said it, I realized how true it was. My house always seemed to be completely empty, even when I was in it. So many people had left.

Within a few minutes we were inside my living room and shedding our coats, but there, much to my dismay, the disrobing stopped. Arthur started looking around instead of at me. If I'd had Eugenia's distrust of him, I'd have thought he was casing the joint. But I decided he was suddenly, disarmingly shy. And maybe trying not to appear overeager.

I had not turned the furnace down before leaving, hoping to need the extra heat, hoping to be naked. On the coffee table was a pack of Tic Tacs, set their as naturally as the TV remote, and I'd tucked condoms discreetly into drawers throughout the house. *Seduction for Dummies: Be ready for anything, any time, anywhere. Any.*

"Now, where were we?" I looped my arms around Arthur's neck and started kissing him again. But then the phone rang and I felt him freeze in my arms. I didn't answer it, but he sat down on the other side of the room from me, still fully clothed, now seemingly sober in every sense of the word. Damn, I really needed to learn how to turn off that ringer.

"Let me guess," he said. "Your boyfriend?"

"You know, there really should be another word for it once we get to a certain age. Forty or whatever. 'Boyfriend' sounds so—"

"You're evading my question."

"No. Actually what I'm doing is revealing my age. I'm over forty. Practically an old crone."

"Maddie, stop. I'm asking whether you are still involved with this other guy. Does he live here or what?"

"He's got his own house and, no, we're not as involved as we used to be," I answered. "He doesn't like me lately."

"He's a boyfriend of convenience only? And tonight he's out of the picture?"

"Not just tonight. It's hard to explain. I'm pretty much free to explore a relationship with you." Shoot—I should've left off the "pretty much" part.

"I never used to have many scruples," Arthur said, "and maybe I still don't. But about this one thing, I do."

"Is it possible to have one scruple?"

"I'm serious. I've been in his shoes. I've been two-timed."

"Haven't we all?" Actually, I hadn't. At least not to my knowledge. Dumped, yes. Two-timed, no.

"Listen, Maddie," Arthur continued. "We can talk about this some more tomorrow but—"

"If you're not attracted to me, just say so. I mean, I know your usual female companion is much younger than I am, with . . . " I stopped myself before referring to youthful skin and muscle tone, or bringing attention to any of the other ways my body had aged.

"That's not it," he said with almost no hesitation. "Of course I'm attracted to you. That should be obvious. But, frankly, I've had a rough day and I'm in no shape to resolve this or anything else tonight."

"I'm sorry. I didn't know I was something needing resolution. But, hey, you're right. What's my rush, huh? It's not like we'll be dead tomorrow."

When I reached for his coat to hand him, however, he shook his head. "Listen, Maddie. I hate to put you in this position, especially now."

"What position is that?" I asked, automatically adding a flip remark about preferring to be on top.

He gave me at least a half-hearted grin. "I'll keep that in mind. But what I'm trying to get at, if you could put a leash on your libido for a minute, is that . . . well, I could use a place to sleep tonight."

My insides did little back flips at this news. Maybe after a good night's sleep . . . together . . . .

"If you have a guest room."

Shit, I thought. "Sure," I said. "Upstairs. First door on the right. But . . . just for tonight? I mean, have you been evicted for good?"

"For good, for bad. We'll see how it plays out. My stuff's in the cab."

I watched him go outside, admiring his rather lopsided walk, the way he shoved his hands in his pockets, knowing I'd be trying to sleep with the female equivalent of blue balls. Blue clit? Throbbing with desire. But also grateful that at least one of us had "scruples." There was nothing wrong with taking our time, Arthur and I. Or maybe it would be better if we stayed merely friends. Did I really need a younger man as a lover? Wouldn't that consign me to a lifetime of diet and exercise, possibly even plastic surgery? And did I really want to be with someone who was such a strange combo

214

of optimism and tragedy, of come-hither and shove-off? He kept me guessing at every turn. But maybe that's what I liked.

Arthur brought a large beat-up sports bag in from the cab, said an exhausted—though early—good night and trudged upstairs. He was at least pretending to regret his decision about going to bed alone.

The next morning, I was scrambling some eggs while Arthur was in the shower. The sound of my front door opening and Jake's hearty *hello* sent me scurrying into my pantry. As though I could *hide*, with the sound of the shower upstairs, the table set for two, fresh-squeezed orange juice, and a pan-full of steaming eggs blended with gooey cheddar and whatever veggies my fridge offered—my traditional couplish breakfast. How had I convinced myself this couldn't happen, that Jake was completely out of the picture? That day I gave my condition of chronic stupidity a name: *Arthuritis*.

"Maddie?" Jake's voice sounded muted. He was heading upstairs, naturally assuming it was me in the shower.

I emerged from my pantry with a bogus excuse for being in there—a bag of chips clutched in my hand, like a quick cover for my privates. "Hi, Jake," I called out to him. "I'm in here."

Jake came into the kitchen with a tentative smile, but not for long. When the shower stopped, he glanced upward to the ceiling as though looking for leaking ghost-water, or a message. This whole scene was just too much—the only thing that would've been more predictable and unseemly would be for Jake to have walked in on Arthur and me in bed.

"A friend stayed over," I told Jake, trying but I'm sure failing to look innocent. I had, after all, applied make up for breakfast—he hadn't seen that phenomenon for years. And I was speaking in a hushed voice. "This friend's from my workshop, the one whose book I read, you know? The ex-con? He lost this major grant, you see, even though he's so talented. But now he got evicted and his cousin needs his cab back and . . . and, actually nothing *happened* between Arthur and me. Not really. I mean, he's—" I stopped my frenzied explanation because the pain I was inflicting on Jake took hold of *me* as well. A dull ache I knew I deserved.

My old friend was waiting for more from me. He'd always thought I was better than I was. Now he knew the truth.

"I'm sorry, Jake," I finally said in a hushed voice. "I thought you were gone for good. The house felt . . . so empty."

215

Jake nodded and didn't wait around to meet my unfortunate but now clean and possibly naked friend. He fled, first dropping his copy of my house key onto one of the plates I'd set for breakfast. He closed the front door quietly, never one to slam anything.

"Jake, *wait*," I called after him.

But he knew I didn't mean it.

I hoped he at least *half*-believed that nothing much had happened. Because the fact seemed glaring to me that I had slept very much alone and badly, with Arthur snug-as-a-bug in the guest bedroom. I had sneaked downstairs to avoid waking him up, although in my best robe and with my hair combed and teeth brushed in case he *should* hear me and change his mind about sleeping with me. And I headed for my computer. No, I was not going to write about Arthur, or about our kissing or fantasy sex or any of that. A new character had introduced herself to me. She'd come uninvited, eased in from some dream that I no longer remembered, pregnant, broke, hooked on the wrong man, locked out of her warm house. And it was not-so-gently snowing.

As I wrote, warily, I recognized the man she needed to ditch. No wonder I'd been especially shaken by Jake's appearance—I'd written a "wrong man" who looked like him but was probably Arthur inside.

The real Arthur came downstairs after his shower, a few minutes after Jake's hasty departure. He looked uncomfortable, almost as though he wasn't dressed, but he was wearing his faded, frayed jeans—the only pair I'd ever seen on him, so worn that they looked like their next washing could be the last—and the same threadbare sweater I'd seen on him the first night of class, the sleeves pushed up above the elbows as usual. His hair was wet and slicked back, curling at his neck.

"It smells great in here. I'm starved."

We sat down and I served him the food, coffee, juice, and my biggest smile, scoured clean of my confrontation with Jake.

"Did you say something to me?" he asked.

"When?"

He tilted his chin toward upstairs. "Right when I got out of the shower. I thought I heard you say something like 'Shake. Wake.'"

I filled my mouth with cheesy eggs until I figured out what Arthur had heard. *Jake, wait.* "Well, actually, I was talking to myself," I told Arthur.

"Something I say to myself every morning. You know, *shake awake*." I punctuated this outrageous statement with the vigorous shaking of my hands and muddled head. "It's a stupid ritual. Meaningless, really. My mom used to do it." Poor Mom was acquiring a lot of quirks—some fictional, but who knew which ones?

Arthur merely stared at me, looking puzzled, as though I'd just burst into song. In French. An oafish Piaf.

"Did you sleep okay?" I asked.

"Great." He returned to his food, shoveling it in so eagerly I gave him half of my eggs when he'd finished his own. Then he pushed himself back from the table, sighed, and gave me a bashful grin that made him seem more handsome than he was. "Maddie, I'm sorry about last night."

I shrugged, a bit shy myself now. I wondered what he was sorry for— that we'd parked and kissed, or that he'd refused to sleep with me. He seemed altered from the night before, more distant. His smile seemed less than sincere. Eugenia's occasional words of warning about him came creeping back to sit in my lap, nudge me in the gut.

"If you and your boyfriend have split up," he said, "of course, it's tempting for me to . . . well, you know what I mean. But I don't think it's a good idea right now. I'm not—"

"You're *not* attracted to me," I said, folding my arms across my belly, trying to tamp the pain into that sturdy space.

"I *am*. But I value your friendship so much. Maybe that's all I can handle right at this moment. Maybe down the line, but . . . . Falling for someone . . . what I'm trying to say is that a new relationship needs so much attention. And I need to focus on my book."

"I understand, Arthur," I said, even though I did *not*. "Don't worry about it."

He watched me clear the table of our dishes and busy myself. I must have looked more fine than I felt because he said, "I really admire you. You're so . . . oh, I don't know . . . comfortable with yourself. So stable."

I snorted. *Stable? Comfortable with myself?* He had to be kidding. This man did not know me at *all*. Why did I even want him around?

"You have no idea," he continued "how rare this seems to me—your living in this house, the one you grew up in. And happily single, independent. And a writer, so you understand what I'm doing, or trying to do."

He apparently assumed I'd never been married. I hadn't told him much of anything yet about my past. The urge presented itself now, but the time wasn't right. Instead I focused on his other illusions about me. "Arthur, I'm not much of a writer. Okay, I started what could be a story last night, but mostly I've been thinking about catalogue items and pretend *Dummies* books."

"Pretend what?"

"Never mind. Can I get you anything else?" I asked. This little independent-yet-charmingly domestic act of mine was obviously working on Arthur. "More coffee? Juice? Anything?" In my mind, the list couldn't stop itself: *A kiss? Hug? Blowjob? Haircut? New clothes?*

But he cleared his throat. "Maddie, I hope we *are* friends . . . "

Uh oh . I thought.

" . . . because I need to ask you for a favor." He took a contemplative sip of coffee, cleared his throat again. "It's difficult."

Now I was both uneasy and curious. But then, sitting down across from him again to get a good look at his eyes, I knew what was happening. "You need a place to stay."

"It's not so much that I *need* a place. I can sleep most anywhere. But I'm not working at the moment anyway, so what I'd really love to do is write. All day, every day. I'm ready to rewrite this book, thanks to you, and thanks to Eugenia's class. It feels like a powerful itch and I refuse to let losing that grant do anything but push me forward, harder than ever. I'm ready to rewrite, especially the father, some of the sex scenes, even the ending."

"Sounds good." I waited, wanted him to ask for his favor more directly. I was beginning to feel used by this guy, of course, but I didn't really mind. Maybe I'd been using him, too.

"You've got this great house, with lots of room, and . . . *you*. My work would go so much better here than if I found some awful little hole of a room somewhere, alone except for noisy transients and couples fucking and fighting, whatever. Anyway, if I could just have a month or two . . . I've got some money saved and can pay for my food, plus a *little* rent . . . . The environment here would help me along, the stability, the—"

"Arthur, stop. Stability is definitely in the eye of the beholder. But you're welcome to stay here. Of course. Will that old desk in the spare room be big enough?"

"It's perfect." With that, he sprang from the table and, without bothering to put his jacket on, rushed out to the cab parked in front of my house. It took him only two trips to empty the trunk and haul in his meager belongings. Meanwhile, I went up to the guest bedroom to make sure there was nothing of mine in there that would get in his way.

The desk seemed sturdy enough but so small, so unable to sustain a whole life's work being rewritten on it. I was wrong. Arthur stacked two reams of paper on the floor and set up his typewriter on the desk. I gawked, suppressing a smirk. I'd known, of course, from reading his manuscript, that he used a typewriter, but I hadn't pictured this one. Portable, manual, practically pre-historic. "How do you even get ribbons for this thing?" I asked.

He laughed. "I stocked up years ago, when there was still such a thing as a typewriter store. Don't you dare insult her . . . yes, it's a her. A great old pal that I rescued from a thrift shop almost fifteen years ago. She's traveled all over the country with me. I can't afford a laptop, and a regular computer doesn't exactly fit with my lifestyle."

"I suppose not. Did you learn to type in the slam?"

He chuckled. "In the slammer, yes. I did learn, but not very well."

"Geez, rap sheet, slammer. I thought I knew the lingo from movies, but at least I'm good for laughs, right? You can just *tell* that words are my life, huh?"

"Hey, it's all a matter of where we come from. You can throw some Beethoven on the stereo and I'll call it a string quintuplet."

We laughed together for a few seconds and then things got awkward again. "Okay," I said, swinging my arms as though they'd propel me out the door, or maybe the window. "So . . . make yourself at home."

And he did.

After Arthur and I returned his cousin's cab and I drove him back home, he said *thanks* for the umpteenth time and bounded upstairs, to get to work. And I went into the kitchen to finally clean up after breakfast. I tried not to be disappointed by how easily he left me behind, his work being worthy and artistic, mine being household chores, plus I was good for laughs. Had I gotten married to F. Scott Fitzgerald when I wasn't looking, and turned into Zelda?

219

I listened to his typing—slow but steady, oh so steady, like he was typing from dictation. Remembering vaguely what it was like on a manual machine, I imagined I could hear not only the space bar separating his words, but also which letters he was typing, especially those using his weaker little fingers. At the end of each line, I could hear the satisfying *ding* and manual carriage return, a handy flourish. I hadn't realized what an integral part of the process that might still be.

Arthur's loud, steady typing provided a strange accompaniment while I did the dishes and then some mopping and dusting. Compared to computer keyboards with their tense little tap-tapping sounds barely audible, the boldly torturous clackety clack was like listening to an old telegraph machine or, at its best, an oldies radio station. Buddy Holly, maybe. Or one of the other guys who died in the plane with him. *The Big Bopper*, I thought, as I bopped through my pseudo-wifely duties. *A-whop-bop-a-lu-op-a-whop-bam* . . . fuck. That wasn't Big Bopper, it was Little Richard who only seemed Big. I was a *Tutti* fruitcake indeed.

I didn't think I'd ever be able to endure these new companions—Arthur and his aggressively *female* typewriter. And yet, over time and with more bopping in my addled brain, I managed to adapt to Arthur's closed door, his clackety racket and creative surge. I even felt a part of it, proud in a way.

I finally sat down in my sunroom, at my computer. If he was going to be such a (pardon the expression) great Scott it was time for me to be a better Zelda. I recalled reading that her one novel/memoir—virtually her only writing that Scott did not absorb into his own—had been entitled *Save Me The Waltz* and I tap-tapped into my computer the title "Save Me The Tango." But I erased it immediately. Why had tango come to mind? Jake, of course. I wondered where he went after he left my kitchen, what he was doing now. My longing for him was automatic and yet so powerful, how was it that I'd managed to keep it a secret from him?

I surveyed my street, hoping for inspiration. The pregnant waif I'd started writing the night before had gotten herself buried in my imaginary snow that was more like bad TV reception than a blizzard. I knew, and feared, she'd have Mona's face and be bulging with one of Mona's babies. She could go knocking on someone else's door for now.

The only other thing I'd written lately was the piece about my parents, the one that had me choked up in class as I read it. The one that Eugenia had perceived what she called "a missing piece, a missing person." The about-to-sob feeling returned and I swatted it away. Writing that piece was apparently too dangerous as well. But why, I had no idea.

Standing up and leaning into my sunroom window, I suddenly felt weak and empty. I exhaled on the glass until there was a foggy space big enough for me to write my name on it. The next time I wrote my name backwards so that people outside, if they cared to, would be able to read it. This is a gift—to be able to write backwards, a useless gift I've always had. If I wrote a story in longhand, backwards, people would have to stand in front of mirrors to read it. That might start a whole new trend in literature, forcing readers to face themselves, even if it makes them shudder with recognition.

Movement across the street caught my eye and I automatically pulled back from the window, into a corner. It was Mona and her bundled-up baby, coming out for a snowy walk to the park or the store. Mona looked pale and frazzled, at least ten years older than when I knew her and, at the same time, like a child herself—awkward, scowling, ready to pitch a fit. The baby started to wail and I saw Mona shake her, not hard, but hard enough. The baby stopped her crying, and I started mine.

That was the day I began not just to watch but to really study Mona and her baby as they lived their lives across the street. That was the day I began to fear that this new baby, this latest on the list, was not safe.

I'm at the window, leaning on it now, and . . .

I realize I've come close to the end . . . the end of what? My rope? The road? The line? Nothing quite so final as that—simply the end of this account, story, novel, memoir, confession, whatever it is. I started writing it a few months ago, in that July middle-of-the-night, a year after Tracy's funeral. Many pages have piled up, many thoughts, words, deeds from this past year. In these pages, last winter is winding down, I'm longing for a man to an embarrassing degree, and I'm just beginning to notice Mona's treatment of her second child. Noticing and seething about it. Also getting ready to begin my last short story entitled "Foundling." Jake has escaped the trap our relationship had become. Eugenia has flown away for good. Arthur is upstairs typing and, although moved into my house and, to some extent, my heart, he has done no more than kiss me. But I sit here now, knowing what comes next, and it's obvious I'm stalling. The End sits smugly on the other side of the next section, one that is the most painful to write down. I'd rather forget, but I won't.

I had hoped to finish writing all of this down by the end of summer but the weeks got away from me. It's chilly before it should be, windy, sepia-colored. A few dry leaves are already scritch-scratching along the sidewalk. I am beginning to tire of this effort, but I will keep going. Because as soon as I'm done writing, and as soon as I reread, revise, and include my last story, isn't it time to act instead? To be real—a person , a mother, a hero—instead of a writer? Words are easy. Make-believe can be powerful but also easy. Reality? Ah, there's the rub.

Now, it's interesting how that odd and infamous phrase popped into my head, seemingly appropriate, but maybe not. Looking it up gives me one more stall tactic. Shakespeare, of course. Hamlet. But interestingly the whole sentence in which this rubbing old phrase is buried goes like this (weird punctuation and all):

To sleep: perchance to dream: ay, there's the rub;

For in that sleep of death what dreams may come,

When we have shuffled off this mortal coil,

Must give us pause.

My God. I'm pausing again all right. Considering my history with dreams and with death, I am thunderstruck by this quote, especially when my eyes wander up to the sentence before, containing these wondrous words: . . . the heartache and the thousand natural shocks that flesh is heir to . . .

Indeed.

222

Family

We marched briskly through March and into April. Jake stayed away and the one time I called him, he told me he was too busy to talk. "No, I'm not mad," he lied. Then he wished me luck and said goodbye. It felt like an amputation.

Arthur labored on, and I barely saw him. He got up early, worked all day, went to bed early and slept long hours. He gave me money for food but didn't ask for anything specific; a few times I coaxed him out to shop with me but that was only when he needed another ream of paper. Sometimes we ate our meals together downstairs, but other times he ate up in "his" room. He kept it tidy except for the wadded up sheets of paper amassing on the floor like irregular unmeltable snowballs. Periodically, I collected them into a large black garbage bag all their own, counting them and sometimes touching them with the tip of my tongue. Even though they were exclusively his, these tossed-aside efforts seemed also to be a materialization of all the words and paragraphs I had deleted from my computer.

After typing a chapter, Arthur would sit with it and a fresh cup of coffee (or sometimes across the kitchen table from me as we ate), calmly crossing things out, adding things, scribbling away, then retyping the new version, and I was dumfounded at how many times he must have to type the same pages to get them right, when it's so easy to revise on the computer. He said it was the only way he'd ever worked and he didn't want to change anything now, mid-stream. Arthur's work was really flowing, and his superstitious nature helped explain his refusal to shave or cut his hair or change clothes (I had to launder his jeans and sweater while he slept)...and, of course, this also explained his resistance to me. If he was mid-stream, that put me somewhere on the dry riverbank running clumsily along, cheerleading, and waiting patiently for his journey's end.

Still devising metaphors, this stream-one comforted me somewhat, until I eventually began to think of Arthur not so much as *in* water but the water itself. He was one of the most *placid* individuals I'd ever met. At first this had been part of his appeal to me, an attractive opposite to my raging torrent. But there's a significant and heartbreaking difference between an inviting sun-drenched pool of water and an icy, languid creek full of hidden rocks.

Arthur apologized nearly every day for being so consumed and unsociable, assuring me that he would make it up to me. But I always said, "No need." When I muttered other, less gracious, more greedy replies to myself, he never heard.

God, how I envied him. And yet I knew the situation was precisely as it should be. There was not enough creative energy in the house to sustain us both, so I let him have it all. I had an April deadline for my catalogue anyway, and this time around I didn't bother dipping into my imagination for the words, knowing they'd only be trimmed anyway.

One of the benefits for me of not writing, of only listening to Arthur slave away, was that I was having fewer communication problems. No more mixing up words or inverting letters. Of course, I had very few people to speak *to*, and I don't mean to suggest that I was, as they say, of sound mind. Being in a state of limbo is never healthy, and that's where I was—between something and something else. But it was appallingly unclear what either of those somethings were.

Every day I watched Mona and her baby come and go, play and fuss, walk and sit. Mona was a single mom and it was taking a toll on her. The baby seemed . . . different somehow. Maybe not entirely there, mentally. She often seemed way too compliant, not feisty enough. Like a puppy who'd been given only scraps to eat and kicked too many times. Or was I imagining too much, writing a story again, even though it had been awhile since I'd had that urge? I wanted to live instead. But how?

Sleep became more and more of a problem. And I suddenly remembered something about my childhood, something my mother had often mentioned: that I'd been an incredibly *sound* sleeper. She used to have to practically roll me off my bed to wake me up for school. Now, if I slept at all, I could be awakened by the most minute disturbance—by dust gathering, by Arthur bending his legs, by a tree's buds unfolding.

Along with my writing, the usual post-writing nightmare about the doll and the stroller had dropped away, together with the new one about the horror-movie elevator doors. But I felt these images lurking, waiting for the most effective moments to pop back up like funhouse spooks. And, of course, I recognized that the movie from which those elevator doors originated—*The Shining*—had been about a writer who had gone stark mad. (Does *raving* always have to sit between these two words to sound right? Will I soon begin to rave? Why doesn't that word sound right without the *–ing*? Will I soon stop wondering or caring about words altogether and just spew them?)

I made an effort to seem okay on the surface. Just tired. I led Arthur to believe that I'd been working hard too, and that's why I looked like hell, just as he did. We managed to exchange daily smiles and pleasantries, seemed to fit nicely together in my house. He had no idea what was happening with me because I was afraid that, if he knew, it would interrupt his work. His work had become mine, in a way. It was certainly more important. Scott and Zelda again. Zelda also went mad, or so everyone said.

Insanity for Dummies.

I played a lot of music, putting rock 'n roll aside and going through all my classical CD's alphabetically from Albinoni to Zelenka. This was in part to soothe me, but also to drown out Arthur's typing and proclaim this *my* house, after all, so I could do anything I like. Even my love of music, however, had a downside. Every day some tune would get caught in the loop of my mind, playing over and over.

This is, of course, a common experience, but I have always had a tendency to overplay it. During this dizzying time with Arthur, while he pounded away at his novel/memoir/barricade against me, I felt like I had a tiny pianist in my head pounding away too, practicing endlessly to get a musical passage just right but always failing, until finally he seemed about to smash the keys with a sledgehammer or kick the instrument's body. If the piece playing over and over was something lovely like "Für Elise" or "Jesu Joy of Man's Desiring" it was tolerable. But often it was some annoying little ditty from a TV commercial or a sitcom theme song. Keeping the TV off didn't seem to help. Music, both good and bad, can burble up to the surface at any time. Especially to a chronic insomniac.

Meanwhile, functions I'd had on automatic pilot all my life now required step-by-step instructions. At night, I kept jerking awake every couple of hours, jaw clenched, eyes sandy and raw. When even a few nights go by with only this kind of spotty, tension-filled sleep, a person really starts to lose her grip, believe me. I was actually becoming afraid to go to bed, to face failure, knowing the next day would be even worse than the last. The fact that I was *alone* in bed and hearing Arthur nearby made the situation more difficult. And pitiful.

Yes, of course I wanted to throw the bastard out, take back my life, such as it was. But I couldn't seem to find the right time, or the words . . . or the backbone. My spirit had developed such a limp, I even pondered seeking out the crutch of religion. But the haunting hymn from Tracy's long-ago funeral waylaid me, repunctuated with question marks: *Jesus Loves? Me? This I Know?*

So we continued, Arthur and I, on our separate journeys.

One evening I discovered that we'd run out of food. There wasn't so much as a smidgeon of peanut butter or a cornflake to be found. I forced myself to drive, bleary-eyed, to the grocery store. But when I parked in the lot and tried to get out of my car, my limbs each seemed to weigh 100 pounds. My heartbeat started to feel like a frantic fist at a dead-bolted door, my breathing became impossibly shallow, and blood rushed up the back of my head. My first true panic attack. I was accompanied on my inner piano by, of all things, a bruising rendition of "Chop Sticks."

I almost left, but then took several deep breaths and thought of Arthur. I owed it to him as much as to myself to restock my empty cupboards and fridge. I tried imagining him standing behind me, encircling me with his arms as I fried pork chops and boiled potatoes and tossed salad—such lovely mundane activities. And soon my panic subsided enough to go inside. But the grocery store assaulted me with its shrieking bright lights. I closed my eyes—gritty with fatigue—and plunged ahead. Food. Had to have it. Grabbing a cart, I wandered up the first aisle with no urge to grab anything. The fruit looked like too much work to eat, and the vegetables looked hard and cold. Even my teeth were tired. I was having trouble swallowing and reached up to massage my throat.

When I found myself standing in front of a huge display of bottled fruit juices, I blinked a few times and surveyed the contents of my cart: six cans of soup and carton of milk. Canned chicken soup with stars? I hated that watery stuff—it was nothing like the chicken soup my mother used to make when I was sick. Had I put those cans in there? Couldn't recall.

Maybe I'd been mostly asleep at the time, a zombie roaming up one grocery aisle and down the next. God, what must I look like to the other customers? Or maybe I'd grabbed one of their carts by mistake.

Glancing up again, I stepped back from the rows of glistening glass and plastic bottles before me. So many labels. So many of the juices *red*. They all seemed to be mixtures—cranberry raspberry, strawberry banana, and guava-papaya-mango. The labels began to blur, and I simply could not choose. My hand reached for one bottle at random, then hesitated and veered toward another. What *was* a guava anyway? A papaya? A mango? I used to know these things, now I could barely picture a cranberry. I grew more and more frightened facing those bottles whose contents seemed to be spilling from my memory, drop by drop. It seemed like the most important thing in the world to remember exactly what a papaya or a mango looked like, even tasted like.

People stared at me, at my mumbling mouth, as I created a few bizarre blends of my own—sweet potato hunk sweat ink juice, dried shrunken female squeezed brain juice. Then, after abandoning my quest and cart, I slipped out of the store to drive through haze. Home.

To my amazement, what I came home *to* was Arthur, emptying several grocery bags into my cupboards. A frozen something was baking in the oven and a bottle of wine was waiting to be opened. "My cousin stopped by with his cab," he said, "and I figured it was a perfect time to help out. Finally. You look. . . stressed."

My extreme gratitude and affection for him at that moment— undoubtedly my neediest (so far)—left me unable to speak. I simply sat down and let *him* serve *me* for a change. He talked gently to me about some meditation and relaxation practices he'd learned along the way. So he *knew* I wasn't sleeping? How much else did he know?

"Let me do more," he said. "I know I get obsessed sitting at that typewriter, but just come upstairs once in a while and give me a punch in the head."

I was still tongue-tied, but I nodded. Smiled a little shyly. And that night I slept . . . for twelve hours straight.

Who would've guessed the affect of a few groceries, an undercooked meal, cheap wine, and sage-sounding advice from someone who wasn't much more functional than I? Had he really tuned in to my needs? Or was

227

he simply trying to avoid being tossed into the street, him and his precious girl-typewriter?

It didn't matter. For a while I felt much better.

When I finally convinced Arthur to let me read some of the revisions, he dumped a pile of pages into my lap, looking grimly resigned to my criticism. Even if I'd had problems with what he wrote, I doubt I could've told him. But I needn't have worried. When Arthur revised, he didn't mess around. He'd been able to ruthlessly toss out whole scenes (some of which had probably been with him for years), and replace them with better ones. The father had sprung cruelly to life, not so much evil as fatally flawed. Not sympathetic, but real. The new sex scenes made me almost cry out with arousal and longing for Sam/Arthur, and I fought tears knowing he was capable of the love now bestowed on these various girls. They didn't deserve him, none of them.

On a day after reading his best love scene, I knocked on his door and crept in behind him, slipped my arms around his neck and whispered in his ear that he'd done it. He'd pulled the reader into bed with his characters in a way that was not embarrassing, gratuitous, or pornographic, but was incredibly exciting. He'd provided Sam with emotional depth and tenderness that was a complete surprise without being implausible. "I'd love to kiss that boy, right here, right now," I said, directly into Arthur's ear.

And so I did. He kissed me back exactly the way I'd craved, expressing deep, reckless need. Neatly typed pages scattered across the floor and neither of us gave them a glance. His typewriter edged away, nearly falling off the desk. His arms around me felt able to overpower any crippling condition—physical or mental—I could come up with. We necked for what seemed hours and I gave only momentary thought to the term *necked* and why it included such a small part of the human anatomy. We took our time removing clothes, smiling into each other's mouths, and I could hear Etta James cry out in song, *At Last* . . . .

When we finally had sex, however, I had to admit it was brief and by-the-numbers. We reached out to each other, achieved some kind of satisfaction, then returned to our previous arrangement. The odd thing was, I didn't mind. I knew *why* the intimacy was missing. I wasn't *real* to him. I wasn't in his book, so I didn't really count. For the first time I realized what life had been like for Jake the last few months with me, as he engaged in the same futile tug-a-war. *I'm here,* he kept letting me know. *Come back.*

Later, when I'd set dinner on the table and went up to fetch Arthur, I found him sprawled on his bed, sound asleep. I ate a few bites of lasagna alone and put the rest away for him to eat the next day. After taking a sleeping pill, I made it through that night as though feverish, with dreams and delirium and reality blending together into a baffling mix, not unlike those bottled juices.

May in Minnesota is uncommonly beautiful, plump with promise. Although true warmth is slow in coming, the landscape rushes toward greening and unfurling as though in time-lapse photography. This past spring, nearby bushes and trees offered me white, pink and impossibly purple blossoms, sending out fragrances thick enough to chew. And since winter seemed to be lingering inside my house, I stayed outside more and more. Before the first of June I pulled myself together enough to plant marigolds and petunias in the front of my house, along with tomatoes, carrots, and zucchini in the back. I fertilized my lawn and primped my shrubs as though at least *they* were dating and having fun with other shrubs. I ate mostly greens to match the view outside my window and I walked for hours every day, so I was thinner than I'd been in years.

Taking advantage of the privacy fence in back, I began to lie outside in a black underwire bra and bikini panties. I got tanner and tanner each day, hoping Arthur might get up to stretch and look out the window, spotting me out there. I listened to my Bach cello CD's through a headset and let my spirit sing along with those plaintive strings.

Then one day in mid-June I got the mail, and my life took another unexpected turn, the most treacherous one of all. A large manila envelope was stuck in there, the kind in which writers (real writers) get their returned, rejected manuscripts. On the outside was the warning: *Photographs-do not bend.* I knew the name on the return address—the daughter of my mother's cousin, Beatrice—so the photos were likely to be of the family variety. But I hadn't spoken to this woman or her mother in years—why was she contacting me now?

Inside the big envelope was a smaller one, sealed and marked "photos." But I turned my attention first to a paper-clipped sheaf of papers, opened flat but creased from previously being folded into letter size. My heart began hammering away when I recognized my mother's spidery

229

handwriting. She had put dates in the upper right corners and, flipping through them, I could see that they were in chronological order, all from the 1960's. On top of this pile of letters was a brief note from my cousin, or more accurately, my mother's cousin's daughter—I'm not sure what that made her to me. I had one of those pitifully small, scattered families with no relatives I saw regularly.

In her note, this particular relative informed me that her mother, Beatrice, had recently died, well into her eighties. And in going through her belongings, the daughter had found the letters and photos she was enclosing, figuring that I'd want them. She also assured me that she had not read them herself and was sending them exactly as she'd found them, except for one thing: her mother's attached note instructing Do Not Throw Away.

I set aside the letters for a moment to open the envelope containing three black and white photos. Each one pictured two fair-haired children— a little girl and a baby. The older child I recognized to be me, somewhere between my second and third birthdays, although I'd never seen these particular images. Gazing at the baby's face, the name Betty came to mind and hung there inside a red heat like a long-forgotten valentine. Then I remembered that I'd named my baby doll Betty—the one I'd lost. Flipping the pictures over I saw dates on the back, confirming that I was about two-and-a-half. Also on the backs I saw two names—"Maddie and Tammy." The baby appeared to be newborn in the earliest photo, and then a couple of weeks and a month old in the others. In all three, she was held snugly in my arms.

These images knocked the support right out of my legs and I crumpled to my living room floor, with the envelope's contents landing at my side. I waited a moment for my heartbeat and breathing to slow to a more normal rate. Tears stung the backs of my eyes as I picked up the letters. The first one was dated at about the time of my birth and there was nothing surprising in it except for how in awe both my parents were at finally conceiving, both of them over forty and assumed to be sterile.

I paged through the next several, vowing to read them later—I needed to rush ahead to the time of the *other* birth. I knew even before I read the letters who this baby was. Tammy, of course. Even without recalling her name and existence, something buried deep inside me had always known about her. And that she was gone. If discovering the details of her birth was difficult, reading about "little Maddie's" gleeful reaction to having a baby sister was torture. Tears were blurring my vision now and I kept wiping at my eyes and nose with the hem of my shirt.

Finally I skipped ahead to the final letter, dated January 10th, took several deep breaths and forced myself to read.

Dear Beatrice,

My heart is breaking. I don't know where to begin and I don't even think I could write this letter to you if I didn't feel it was absolutely essential. I'm sending it to let you know not only what has befallen us, but also to request that you keep all my letters and the photos I sent you the last few months safely locked away, and a secret. I do not want Madelyn to ever know about what has happened— what would be the point of burdening her poor little shoulders with this knowledge?

I paused in my reading to grab a box of Kleenex and then sank back onto the same spot on my floor, surrounded by paper, knowing this might take more strength than I possessed. But I read on . . . .

A few days before Christmas, we put baby Tammy in her bassinet to sleep, and shortly after that we put Maddie in her crib (we'd bought her a junior bed but hadn't set it up yet). It was late and Tammy had not been feeling well that day, spitting up constantly, crying more than usual. Well, Tammy woke up screaming and no matter what we did, we couldn't seem to quiet her. We paced with her, rocked her, fed her, changed her, tried everything. I think I mentioned in earlier letters what a lovely surprise Maddie was, after all those years not conceiving. And then, another baby so soon after! It was wonderful, of course, but not easy, especially at night.

Anyway, Maddie usually slept through everything, but this time she'd awakened and was standing in her crib with her big solemn eyes, watching us. She said "Beh-Teh"

231

over and over again, her shorthand way of saying Baby Tammy, and that gave us the idea that maybe she could help. For weeks, whenever we had put Tammy in Maddie's eager little arms, or even at her side so she could jabber at her, the baby was quieter, smiling at her big sister, reaching for her.

So, we put Tammy into Maddie's crib. Just as we expected, as soon as Maddie sat down and started in with her gibberish and "singing" in her way to Tammy and grabbing at her hands and feet, Tammy was happy and drifted off to sleep. We left the room, exhausted, and went to bed.

Oh, Beatrice . . . how do I finish telling this? I can't see for all the tears in my eyes. I can't swallow for the terrible throbbing in my throat. Were we so wrong to try this? Were we negligent? Stupid? Are we being punished? Don't children sleep together all the time, especially in other cultures?

When we got up the next morning and it was still so quiet, we went to look into the crib. There was Maddie sound asleep on her stomach, and Tammy's sweet little face was underneath her. She wasn't breathing.

The letter ended a few paragraphs later but I could not read any more. My spine buckled. I curled up on the floor in a fetal position and sobbed. The sounds that were coming from me didn't even sound human, but rather more like some animal who has been fatally wounded and slowly bleeding to death. The room around me had faded into shadow and I was not aware of any sounds other than the ones I was making. When I felt arms around me, lifting me back into a sitting position, I had no idea to whom they belonged. They could have been my mother's trembling arms as she lifted me from my baby sister's still body. I wanted them to be hers, I wanted her to be hugging me and saying she forgave me, that it was an accident, that it wasn't really my fault. And I tried to understand why she had turned my sister into a secret. Why my parents had fictionalized my early childhood the way they had. Who had they been protecting—me or themselves?

It had been futile anyway. I recognized the sadness now, the slips of the tongue, the shadows. There was no way to really keep my baby sister hidden from me. Hadn't I known all along? I just hadn't gotten the details, or I'd absorbed the *wrong* details, remembering vividly being at a mall that same Christmas, on an escalator, rushing toward a Santa, a lost doll in a red stroller named Betty (Beh-Teh?), and mistaking this incident for the real loss and the real role I'd played in it. Until now.

When I finally opened my eyes, I saw that it was Arthur who was trying to comfort me. He was kneeling on the floor, enclosing me in his arms and rocking me. "What is it? What is it?" he kept asking.

I showed him the pictures as though that would explain everything about me. But the best way I could answer was to surrender, wordlessly, into his embrace. To receive his worry and panic and give him my despair and emptiness, and reassemble all of this into love. After what I had just learned about myself and my family, the deceptions and (Laurel and Hardy movie-watching aside) cozy cheer as fake as Santa, the implicit *choice* of my being their only child, treasured, and the terrible denial (or at least the storing away in a distant cousin's closet) of a human being's whole life, however short it had been, as though she had never existed . . . after all of that, it is only with mild shame that I confess making love with Arthur right then and there on the floor on top of my mother's letters, in view of the photographs which I could no longer look at.

Was there something darker at work than the usual kind of passion between us that day? Yes. And it wasn't only my demons at work; Arthur had been writing the end of his book, and dealing at last with what had happened to *his* little sister. We were two incomplete, guilt-drenched, mournful figures reaching out for completion from each other. And, of course, that is nothing at all like love. This kind of sex only adds extra weight to the sorrow.

When we were finished and exhausted and so utterly naked together, Arthur grabbed an afghan from the couch in which to wrap us. He listened as I haltingly told him what was in the letters. And after he was sure I had nothing else I wanted to add about my family, *he* began to talk. Oh my, did he talk. I had never heard so many words from him, and never seen his pain so clearly.

He told me he'd finished the new ending and that he had still made it a happy one, with the sister being found safe, because he *had* to. It was the only

233

way to make things better, to fix things. Because he had never found his sister. He had found a body at one point, a "Jane Doe" that *could* have been her, but there was no way to be sure. No fingerprints, no dental records (their father hadn't believed in dentists), nothing except an instinct, a pull toward the body, a sickening desire to kiss the decomposed forehead, to hold the skeletal hand. These feelings, combined with the circumstances and location, the estimated age and size of the girl, and what was left of her attire, had convinced him. It was almost certainly Ashley. And his search had to end.

I'm not sure what it is about good sex and its immediate aftermath that sometimes results in a verbal deluge, especially when too many secrets have been dammed up. But, as I listened to Arthur tell me, finally, about his sister, I felt more of my own private stories build up and swell inside my throat. And I probably already knew that I wouldn't be able to stop once I started. Questionable timing or not, there was so much more to tell him. If he was ever going to know me, to love me for real, he had to know it all. Didn't he?

The image I'd been dreaming—elevator doors straining to open and gush blood—flickered briefly in my mind's eye as a warning. But it was too late. The flood of words started and the doors wouldn't close again. I told Arthur about my marriage, my child who died, my miscarriage, my divorce, Jake's ex-wife and our affair, the little boy I'd seen drown, the little neighbor girl I'd seen killed by a car on my street. On and on. Arthur was silent throughout this spillage, but I could see the growing dismay on his face, see the panic come back in his eyes. I was making his life harder, I knew, rather than giving him the help *he* needed after finishing his book. I was Zelda all right, the aging, fading flapper who ran off to take those maniacal ballet lessons, Zelda heading toward that insane asylum she died in, leaving Scott to his booze and literary success.

Then, at one point, Arthur managed to interject with, "Wait . . . what?" And I was finally able to stop talking. I had stopped just shy of confessing all I knew and felt about Mona and her new baby—the things I'd seen that made me certain that the baby needed to be rescued. I didn't tell him that finally there was a child I could save. I didn't quite get there.

"Nothing," was the way I concluded. "Nonsense stuff. Sex makes me loony."

We dove into kisses that seemed bottomless. No way to speak or spoil things too badly when you're kissing in this way. And then we fell asleep, exhausted and emptied out, as though I'd shaken that big black garbage bag stuffed full of discarded manuscript and, *poof*, all gone.

The next few weeks were filled with reading Arthur's revised book and making love. It was a bittersweet time; even as I was lying in Arthur's arms, I realized that it was not exactly *him* I was having such strong feelings for. It was his alter-ego, Sam. Arthur was becoming too real to me—his vanishing acts in all but the physical sense, his disregard for basic grooming habits, the day-to-day sounds of him echoing in my house now that he was no longer typing, and, last but not least, the unpredictability of his erections. All too real.

We slept together in a shallow pool of words and phrases, scratched out and scribbled in, polishing and nurturing something that was outside of our bodies, something more important. Because I knew that his book would be published to critical acclaim. He would win awards, appear on talk shows and give readings, flashing his killer smile. He'd land solidly on his author-feet and move on. I might be remembered as more landlady or patron than lover.

But how could I *not* imagine my name on a dedication or acknowledgements page? Beyond that, it seemed entirely possible that I'd be immortalized in his future writing—barely recognizable, of course, but still . . . He'd sift through his months with me and pick out a few choice bits of my history, verbiage, idiosyncrasies, maybe even various body parts, mixed with those of others he's run across in his erratic life, to create a whole new set of characters. While large sections of his first book were nakedly autobiographical, in his second book Arthur would—like Eugenia—reveal much less of himself. It would be the rest of us who would be spread-eagled across his next heap of pages.

The Fourth of July opened up as a resplendent morning that should have drawn me outside, but I was sitting in my sunroom staring at my computer, wishing it would explode or something so I wouldn't have to face how impossible it had become to write anything. Mona's front door opened and out they came—mommy and baby all sunny and dressed sparingly for the heat. No matter what had happened between Arthur and me (or, in another life, with Jake, Suzanne, Eugenia, whoever), I was still more obsessed with these two virtual strangers than with any lover or friend.

Arthur approached me from behind and kissed the top of my head, dwelling in that area as though to help pull electrifying prose from beneath my stubborn scalp.

I pointed at my neighbors. "Watch them now," I told him, done with self-editing, done with straining to keep all the doors closed and my life tidy.

"Who is that? Cute baby—do you know them?"

"Yes, Arthur. Of course I do." I tried not to sound infuriated that he was so clueless about Mona, after all I'd shared with him. "She's the one I told you about, the one whose child was run over last year. And any minute now you're bound to see her shake that baby or walk off and leave her on the lawn by herself or something. Just watch."

We watched. But that particular day, Mona was the perfect little mommy. Of course. Arthur got bored spying and started heavy-breathing on my neck and groping my breasts instead. I felt his touch as bruising pressure and steeled myself against it. His beard rasped against my skin and made me want to sneeze from every pore. Pulling away, I stood by the window, certain good Mona would turn bad any moment.

Arthur gave me one of his baffled looks and lumbered toward the kitchen. I hated his crooked walk—when had that started? "Did you hurt your leg?"

"Yeah," he called back to me. "About twenty years ago."

"Oh," I said. Deluded little me, ex-writer, ex-girlfriend, ex-everything. My powers of perception came and went like the roar of an airplane.

Joining him in the kitchen for breakfast I asked him, feigning a casual interest, who a person should call to report a negligent or abusive parent.

"Why? You're talking about your neighbor? What did you see her do?"

I busied myself with a bowl of Cheerios. No more fancy post-coital egg concoctions. "You just can't see it today," I told him. "But she's going to end up losing that little girl too. I feel it."

Arthur sat down and studied my face from across the table, sipping his coffee. His face said *Oh God—another confessional deluge?* But he calmly asked, "Are you all right, Maddie?"

"Fine. Really. But you of all people should understand an impulse to rescue a child, right? I mean, maybe I should just take that baby away from her myself."

236

Oops. There it was, spilled onto the kitchen table like my Cheerios milk. My hand, along with the cereal spoon in it, seemed to be convulsing.

He didn't say anything, this man of many *written* words, but few spoken (except that one explosive time together). We finished breakfast in silence and, within the hour, I could hear him packing his things upstairs. After setting his belongings by my front door, he came back to give me a hug. "Maddie, I think it's time for me to move on."

"Sure," I said. "Your book's done—your contribution to the gazillion Great American Novel wannabes. Sam is cleverly typed into his proper place, and so is his poor doomed sister . . . except she's miraculously saved."

Not surprisingly, Arthur didn't react well to my denigrating his life's work. "Well, I suppose that's one way of looking at it, hopefully wrong. And I thought we could stay friends, but . . . "

He was halfway out the door before I stopped him with an apology. Also by grabbing hold of his bagful of typed manuscript, fat as a multiple-birth belly. "Your book is great," I reassured him. "I'm just jealous. Ignore what I said, but . . . I hope you won't forget . . . maybe let me know how to reach you, in case . . . " I considered hinting that I might be pregnant from one of our careless times together. My last period had been late, in fact, but then it came like a cat-burglar one night. I'd sobbed for an hour, not because I'd wanted a baby with Arthur. I knew better than that. And I certainly hadn't forgotten my years of avoiding babies. But shedding another squandered, unfertilized egg seemed to be a tragedy at that moment, something more for me to mourn. I swallowed the teary begging and fibbing that would only have chased him away faster and with more justification.

"Hey, when I get resettled, I'll give you a call," Arthur said now, as unconvincing as his loose-limbed hug. "Thanks for everything. I couldn't have done it without you."

"Glad to be of service." My voice probably sounded icy enough to give him frostbite. I was ridiculously hurt by his abrupt and yet completely expected departure. I was a bit fearful of my re-emptied house and sad that things didn't work out. But I was also relieved . . . yes, intensely *relieved*.

He appeared to be pretending that this goodbye was routine. Maybe it was. "Take care," were his last words to me. And he was gone.

But I wondered if he didn't have more to say. Not about love or friendship or connections or erections, or anything like that. More about our last, ugly little breakfast scene, my admission to having criminal thoughts. Maybe he would've liked to warn me about obsessions, or suggest I see a psychiatrist, or have me committed. The kind-hearted part of him that I saw when we first met might have wanted to assure me that my baby sister's death was *not at all* my fault and that I should simply mourn, if mourning is *ever* simple. No. Most likely, what the real Arthur would've wanted to add was this: Leave your neighbors alone and mind your own fucking business.

Good job, I told myself, *You've run another male intruder off the property*. But here's the most interesting thing about his departure: he left only the best kind of vacuum, the kind I was forced to fill on my own. With my own writing.

I sat down to my dusty keyboard, shut off my regrets, my guilt, my fears, and my unfathomable grief. There was my window world and, like the persistent muse she was, Mona gave me the next chapter of her life. A man had driven up, not Jim, not Jake—a stranger. Handsome, young. She greeted him with an enthusiastic kiss, and they went into the house together. The baby was left in a playpen, on the lawn, in the sun. In my spotlight.

Foundling

The child was dead-center in the yard across my street, in the kind of searing July sun that could, if called upon by some over-zealous weatherman, fry an egg on the sidewalk. I wondered what it might do to an already damaged baby. She was caught in a safety net (for now) of umbrella shade and playpen mesh, but the sun was ticking toward her, the widening stripe of it bleaching inch-by-inch a toy dinosaur that lay near her bare feet. My view of her began to zoom in and out, and I saw those ten pale pink-pearl toes as an invitation for my mouth, my nibble, mine.

I called her Cammy. She was unsettlingly docile, swaying like a lone sunflower, but there was no whiff of movement in the air. That umbrella should be moved, I decided, or better yet, the child brought inside. But as I watched and Cammy continued to sway and not cry, and the swath of sun widened, no mother, no rescue appeared.

I told myself much later, that this vision of Cammy in a pocket of safety so shallow, so precarious, had been presented to me by some higher power. After all, I rarely looked out my porch windows like that, rarely looked anywhere except inward toward my womb, which had just emptied itself again.

I'd just that morning, the same day of seeing and rescuing Cammy for the first time, flushed down the toilet what could have been another fetus. Could have been. Blood clots the size and shape and scrape of metal shavings. My boyfriend had left months ago, it was true, but I still had some of his semen in my freezer—left there by him before his getaway, without a word of how deranged or desperate he judged my demand for sperm to be.

I had felt my ovary ache six weeks earlier, felt its hopeful little egg-toss, had been particularly deft in my use of the turkey baster. The little swimmers had to be thrilled to be thawed and sent on their mission. But my eggs seldom went beyond that stage. The hope, the throb, the fragile union, maybe. Then gone. Only once had I made it all the way to six months.

Meanwhile, there sat Cammy, left to fry in the sun. Some women don't *deserve* to have babies, it seemed to me that day, as though for the first time. And I ran outside to move that inadequate, drooping patio umbrella so she would be safe a little longer. Then, I sat down at my window and continued to watch. She didn't glance my way, but why should she? Minutes slithered muggily by. Outside, the heat soared and glazed every surface. Inside, my womb made a fist, my head pinballed her name.

Cammy never did cry that day. She sat in her filled-to-overflowing diaper, no shirt, no bonnet. No water. A bottle of milk lay there on the playpen floor, probably curdling. She just swayed. Blond curls, flushed cheeks, slender arms and legs. Not a sound out of her. Not even when I ran out to her the second time. But I approached cautiously from an angle, peering into the windows of her house, listening for a voice. When I reached the playpen and moved the umbrella again, she halted in her metronome movement, but not to acknowledge me. It was a large black ant, journeying up her leg, which snagged her attention, and I watched as she squashed the thing with one finger and tucked it into her mouth. I tasted it, peppery, on my own tongue.

After she resumed swaying, I called out a half-hearted *hello* to whoever might be, *must* be home or at least nearby. Then, finally, I bent down to pick her up and hold her tight. The halt in her movement felt like the metronome was switched off too suddenly, maybe in frustration over whatever music might be trying to play inside her. But the rhythm still resonated through us both, and I took up the sway as a slow dance with her. I kissed her cheeks and forehead, buried my face in her neck. She smelled terrible—shit and sweat and spit-up. At least six months old, this child, and her eyes revealed no recognition of my hug, or maybe of any hug. She hadn't started living yet, I decided. Another fetus, only much bigger, allowed to grow and be born, and *then* flushed away.

With Cammy limp in my arms, I pounded on the door, expecting it to crack open and reveal a bloodshot eye, ragged fingernails, a junkie perhaps? Or a woman who'd emptied out her bottle of Prozac, or her soul. Nobody answered at first, but then, finally, the door swung open wide and not only a woman greeted me but also the man in whose arms she was entangled. They were not morons or miscreants. I can still see them as they were that day, framed to photographic perfection by the doorway, so complete, the two of them minus the child. Young, disheveled, laughing, flushed with heat, sex, each other. I was shocked, as though I'd happened upon them fucking in the street while leaving Cammy to play in traffic. And, yes, I admit to feeling jealous of the way they were woven around and into each other, but that feeling was easily overtaken by my rage.

241

"Your daughter needs some attention here," I said, shooting my voice directly into their thick, smug joy. "She was in the hot sun, and she's almost certain to be dehydrated."

Now, I know I shouldn't have done this, made myself known to these neighbors, especially to the woman whose body happened to expel Cammy (notice I resist calling her Cammy's mother). And later I did regret revealing myself to them in this way. But my appeal to their conscience worked that day in July. They let go of each other, grew serious and embarrassed, thanked me, and grasped the little girl to pull her inside. And I returned to my silent house and imprinted arms, tears and terror washing away what was left of the child's taste in my mouth.

I had seen autistic children before. In another one of God's cruel jokes, they always seemed to be exceptionally beautiful, as Cammy was. She should have been getting special care, I knew. Some flowers need constant tending in order to bloom, but then when they do, the explosion of color is the most vibrant of all. Of course, I wasn't sure she really was autistic. If she had been severely neglected or abused since birth, could she not behave and look much the same?

I began to spend all of my spare time huddled in my porch, watching whatever happened across the street. They were smart enough not to leave her in the playpen again, at least not in the *front* yard. Several times, I saw the woman depart with Cammy strapped into a stroller, out for a walk. She had a jauntiness about her, this well-loved, well-fucked woman. Aside from the continued absence of a bonnet on Cammy's blonde head, I saw no other sign of neglect for weeks. A truly cynical conclusion might be that I was eagerly watching for more signs that Cammy needed to be rescued. By me. And I have to admit that my relief at seeing her unharmed alternated with a dark, hazy kind of disappointment. Or disbelief, maybe. Even if I'd seen her in actual peril, I vowed immediately not to call an agency. No, I'd read about how children can get chewed up in the flawed child welfare system. And, besides, she had *me*, didn't she? She didn't need more.

I wasn't expecting or watching for anything in particular. I simply saw myself, at first, as a kind of engaged witness. A fly on a not-too-distant wall, on alert, ready to buzz into the scene. And of course the day finally came. Luckily (or fatefully), the moment came a safe distance from my home. It was at the mall, early one morning before it got busy. In the lingerie department, there she was, in the same stroller—it was Cammy all right, alone except for a scantily clad mannequin who posed nearby. I scanned the immediate area, and nearby aisles for that so-called mother. I finally found her way over in the men's department, chatting with a very pretty man, apparently about neckties. An unpardonable distance from her baby. Of course, Cammy was not crying out or even moving; she and the mannequin seemed to be kin. Except for her open eyes, she might have been napping.

I pondered what to do next. The woman was no doubt accustomed to exactly this kind of placid acceptance by the child, of whatever distance there was between them. Crouching behind a rack of men's suits, I made sure she was still deeply involved with the necktie debate, oblivious. Then I crept back to lingerie, to the stroller. The store was not busy, and those few scattered shoppers who were there appeared entirely self-absorbed.

One last look around before pushing the stroller away from the mannequin's dead eyes. And we were out the door, Cammy and I. My car was parked at the far end of the lot and I tried not to run or appear agitated—here we were, just me and my baby, heading for our car.

As soon as I unstrapped her from the stroller I confirmed how neglected she was. She reeked of urine. There were scratches on her legs and a bruise inside her right arm. The stroller was second-hand, shit-stained and probably hazardous, and I tossed it into an out-of-the-way dumpster. I didn't have my car seat with me—the one I'd bought long ago when I'd stupidly thought six months along meant I'd have a live, healthy infant in my car. What to do with Cammie stopped me only momentarily. I ended up laying her down on the backseat floor. She stared up at the overhead light, so I made sure it stayed on even after I'd closed my car door and started driving home.

We were inside my house before I really thought about what I was doing beyond it being the *right* thing. Meant to be. Out of breath, crying, laughing a little hysterically, I clasped my sweet girl against my chest, felt her arms—I swear—almost begin to encircle my neck.

I held her all the while I hastily packed my things, whatever I could manage in the next few minutes. After a quick stop at the bank, and the much longer stop at a discount store twenty miles from my neighborhood—careful to pay cash for the diapers, bottles, clothing, toys, and baby food—we were on the road, probably before the police had even finished interviewing people in the store and its vicinity, and certainly long before the woman thought of me and my appearance at their door several weeks earlier.

As I drove, I scanned the possible traps waiting for me. Unbelievably, my escape seemed almost foolproof. My ex-boyfriend was now working overseas and the car was still in his name (another parting gift). We'd only been together a year, both intensely private, and there was no way for anybody in my neighborhood to know his name or where he was. So the license plate on my car was no problem (unless, for some reason, a nosy neighbor had memorized it as I drove in and out of my garage). No employer awaited me, since I was between jobs, and I owned the house—it had belonged to my parents, so there were no mortgage or rent payments to be missed and to bring attention to my sudden absence. Property tax and other records would take awhile.

Things seemed lined up perfectly. I didn't even need a map or, for that matter, a definite destination. It was simply a matter of following the freeway straight south. I started singing in a goofy lofty voice, aimed at Cammy in the backseat, *Up up and away-ay-ay, in my beautiful, my beautiful bal . . . looooon!* Did I see her smile at me in the rearview mirror? Did I hear a burbling sound from her as though she could sing too? Someday?

Anything seemed possible.

Until I heard the scream, so startling I nearly lost control of the car. Pulling off the next exit, I stopped to look at Cammie, waited for what was to come next. But she was asleep. Sound asleep, soundless as usual. This time when I looked in the rearview mirror, it was not at her. I saw a view that was close-up but far away, here but left behind. I saw a mother. As I stared, her mouth stretched wide open in horror and unspeakable loss. This time I did not hear the scream.

I'm no longer at my window . . .

Because, while inserting my last story into this narrative, I forced myself to really read it for the first time since July. It is now October and I've written myself up to the midsummer day I started this account, the day I watched a middle-of-the-night film noir and wished I could write in that vein. The darkness I'd entered by the creation of "Foundling" had seemed to demand such an effort. Setting aside the story last July, I pushed away enough of the lurking shadows to embrace Technicolor for awhile. I thought I was merely postponing the inevitable: story turning into life instead of the opposite. And the act I contemplated—a kidnapping dressed up as rescue—required some explanation.

I think I understood the consequences, and it was not an impulse, obviously, since I wrote for months leading up to it. Fortunately, I had tried it first in story form; I'd tested the results of such a crime by ratcheting up the crazy in my "character" and seeing what happened next. But writing this account of the past year not only made me pause, it made me stop. And move away from the window at last.

The first thing I did after rereading "Foundling" was add a paragraph at the end, to give it a new, truer ending. In the original last paragraph, the last words are: Anything seemed possible. There is the implication that, not only was the kidnapping successful, but it even ended with a new mother-daughter bond and a more-or-less clean getaway. An old boyfriend's car, a barren but singing woman, an only slightly damaged baby, all headed for the horizon and happily-ever-after. In other words, it was pure delusional bullshit.

And then, since I remembered so clearly the day I'd finished writing my last tale, I thought about my old recurring dreams—the terrible price I'd paid each time I finished a story. It occurred to me that, even after I wrote "Foundling" with its original ending, no nightmare followed. Now I realize why: the story was my nightmare, and I have finally awakened to see Mona, Tracy, her baby, mine, Jake, Suzanne, Eugenia, Arthur, and me—the ways we are interconnected—in a different, brighter light. We don't exist merely as a string of letters forming sentences, clumped together in paragraphs; the pulsating cursor on this monitor does not represent a heartbeat. I can lift my right hand off the keyboard to place *it on my chest and feel the actual beat, and a quickening as I work toward* The End *of this book. Does Jake return? Is there another presence as well, a new heartbeat that is louder than all the rest combined?*

These are not idle questions. Their answers comprise my final chapter, based on the events of yesterday. Events that are grounded in reality but, like everything else that gets written down, they're open to embellishment. Truth is always subjective, it seems. What follows is my truth, with the story-teller's natural hope to satisfy, and with the belief that a good ending is really just a good beginning that appears at the end. I'm both writer and, in a way, reader here; I can savor being alive amidst a messy crowd of similarly ordinary and extraordinary characters. And I'm hoping, by following along on this word-journey, to smuggle a little light and color and song and joy into the final black-on-white words.

Help

I heard the crying first, the sound of a baby who needs food or a diaper change or maybe just attention. And it was coming from outside my front door. I nearly fled in panic at this sound, so close, so aimed at me. But when I opened the door, it was Jake out there, smiling nervously, holding a little girl in his arms. Even crying, she was a beauty, with light brown skin and coppery curls. Her amber eyes were immense, liquid, long-lashed, the kind of eyes that somehow both draw you in and coolly reflect.

"Maddie, hello," Jake said. His voice sounded different from what I remembered. "How are you?"

"I'm fine," I said in a voice that was similarly altered. I liked our new voices together. "God, it's good to see you. Come in."

"No more houseguests?"

"Arthur left months ago. He finished his book here."

Jake still held back. "Oh yes, Arthur. The ex-con. Did he rob you blind?"

I chuckled. "Something like that. Please . . . come in." I wanted so badly to hug him, but his arms were fully occupied by the little girl. My gaze shifted back and forth between their faces.

Jake entered my home as though he'd never been there before, looking around, nodding. The child's cries had subsided as though this house, my house, had simply been what she'd been demanding and finally Jake had given in. He set her down and I was surprised to see this tiny creature walk around my living room—she couldn't be quite a year old yet.

"She took her first real steps today," Jake whispered, maybe afraid his voice would knock her over. "Seems symbolic to me."

I nodded and watched. She was wearing a mint green dress with matching tights and white patent leather shoes that were impossibly small. Her legs were set widely apart, straight down from the hem of her skirt, wobbly but determined, her arms outstretched like the classic pose of a sleepwalker. I noticed the diaper bag slung over Jake's shoulder only when he eased it off and onto the floor. He rescued the vase on my coffee table a split second before she could grab it.

"Sophie," he said, as though her name was all the explanation I needed. I knew that sooner or later he'd tell me about her, but I waited patiently as we watched her together.

"Would you like some coffee?" I asked. "Or maybe some milk or juice?" I gestured toward Sophie.

"No thanks. I suppose you're wondering . . . ."

"Well, I assume you neither gave birth to her or stole her. Babysitting maybe?"

He shook his head. "She's mine."

For this news, I needed to sit down.

He continued to follow her around, snatching danger or breakage out of her reach. "I found her through my parents. A distant relative of mine has a sixteen-year-old who's become a holy terror. Drugs, sex, running away, the whole shebang. She hooked up with a drug dealer, a black man more than twice her age, and Sophie was the result."

"Oh," I said, relieved. "You adopted her." I couldn't keep my eyes off the child.

"Yup." Jake did not sit down—he couldn't. Sophie had not stopped moving since her arrival. Her lovely forehead was creased a bit into a scowl. She appeared set on discovery and my domain had effortlessly become hers.

"After quite a bit of soul-searching," he continued to explain, "well... not that much, actually... yes, I adopted her. When I heard that the birth-mother had decided to leave rehab and give Sophie up, presumably to strangers, I stepped in. The father also signed away his rights, so neither one of them will come charging back into her life down the road. We got social workers, drug counselors, and lawyers involved, and the paperwork was completed as of today."

"Is she okay? I mean, she looks like she is, but did her mother stop using drugs during her pregnancy."

"Unfortunately, no. Sophie was born addicted. But HIV negative, thank God. And she's doing remarkably well—a bit hyper, as you can see. But the doctors who have examined her all marvel at what a little fighter she is. She'll be fine, as long as she gets plenty of love. And, well . . . I've got a lot to give. So . . . she's mine now." He paused, then added, "I wanted you two to meet."

My eyes filled with tears as I watched her toddle around my house, with Jake, tall and husky and completely smitten with her, following close behind. "You rescued her," I said.

But he didn't hear me. Sophie had tumbled and scraped her forehead against a bookcase. Renewed, more vigorous crying resulted, but Jake took it in stride. No panic, no overreaction, no rush to the hospital. She leaned into his shoulder and sniffled, clinging to his shirt.

He grinned at me over her head. "You probably think I'm nuts, huh? But look at her. What else could I do?"

"You're not nuts," I said.

"Here's the thing," he said with more shyness than I'd ever heard in his voice, "I could use some help sometimes. I mean, I've got excellent daycare lined up and all. But I thought . . . oh, I don't know . . . I thought . . . ."

"Jake, let me hold her," I said.

She came to me willingly and we studied each other's tear-stained faces. When she touched my mouth, I opened it so she could slip her fingers inside. They felt like cool beans on my tongue. I pretended to gobble them up, making a silly slobbery sound, and she withdrew her fingers but didn't look scared. Sophie's first smile in my house sent rays of sun into all the shadowy corners. She then poked her fingers back into my mouth for more gobbling, pulled them back, giggled, pushed them in further. Our first game together. It had been a favorite of my baby daughter's.

Jake watched us and blinked a few times, then handed us a book he'd pulled from the diaper bag. It was a small board book, simply designed and illustrated, with a different domestic animal on each page staring out at the reader. "Her favorite," Jake said and then went into the kitchen to help himself to coffee and a sandwich. I heard him humming and recognized the theme song from *Sesame Street*—was that still on? Impossible. I pictured them watching TV together, Jake adopting the voice of Cookie Monster or Grover as he handed her a snack or put on her socks and shoes. I wondered if he'd told his baby any Ole and Lena jokes yet. Maybe Ole and Lena *had* a baby together and got smarter because of her, fell in love all over again.

Sophie's oversized eyes, which had probably seen way too much for her age, followed her daddy's departure from the room, but she did not cry or strain to get back to him. We "read" the wordless book together, with me pointing to each animal, naming it and providing the sound each one makes: cow, dog, horse, duck, cat, and sheep. And she was finally still, as though the rooms and objects she'd been dashing around to explore had all folded tidily, along with our book, into my lap, my face, my voice.

Then I heard *her* voice for the first time. "Da," she said. Could've been dog or duck, I suppose, but she said it loudly and repeatedly, toward the kitchen. Jake answered, "What, honey?" Then she closed the book and pressed her lips together. The m-sound emerged, sustained, bold, expectant. She could've been speaking for the animals—as in *moo* or *meow*. Smart little cookie. But I chose to answer on cue. "Yes, Sophie. Mama's here."

ACKNOWLEDGEMENTS

My deepest gratitude to the McKnight Foundation for generous support when this book was first coming together. Thank you to Seal and Corinne Dwyer at North Star Press for believing in me and helping to make this the book I'd dreamed it could be. Thank you also to my earliest, most helpful and patient readers: Andy Hjelmeland, Marion Dane Bauer, Ethna McKiernan, Georgia Greeley, Barb and Roger Bren, and Jessica Guernsey. To my daughters, Meghan and Jessica, as well as the rest of my wonderful family, thank you for supporting and loving me no matter how crazy I become while writing (and *not* writing). Finally, to my beloved parents—Mildred and Alvin Bren—thank you for being my first fans and my inspiration each and every day. I miss you.